PHILOSOPHY AND SCIENCE FICTION

PHILOSOPHY AND SCIENCE FICTION

EDITED BY MICHAEL PHILIPS

Prometheus Books
BUFFALO, NY 14215

Published 1984 by Prometheus Books
700 East Amherst Street, Buffalo, NY 14215

Library of Congress Catalog Number: 83-62874
ISBN: 0-87975-248-3

Printed in the United States of America

Acknowledgments

"Who Can Replace a Man?" by Brain Aldiss is reprinted by permission of the author and the author's agents, Scott Meredith Literary Agency, Inc., 845 Third Avenue, New York, NY 10022.

"Bicentennial Man," by Isaac Asimov, Copyright © 1976 by Random House, Inc., is reprinted by permission of the author.

"Library of Babel," translated by Anthony Kerrigan, is from *Ficciones* by Jorge Luis Borges. Reprinted by permission of Grove Press, Inc. Copyright © 1962 by Grove Press, Inc. Translated from the Spanish © 1956 by Emece Editores, S.A., Buenos Aires.

"Balaam," by Anthony Boucher, is from *Far and Away,* Copyright © 1954 by Anthony Boucher, and is reprinted by permission of Curtis Brown Associates, Ltd.

"The Show Must Go On," by James Causey, appeared in *The Pseudo-People: Androids in Science Fiction,* published by Sherbourne Press in Nashville, Tennessee.

"Impostor," by Philip K. Dick, is reprinted by permission of the author and the author's agents, Scott Meredith Literary Agency, Inc., 845 Third Avenue, New York, NY 10022.

"The Machine Stops," by E. M. Forster, is reprinted by permission of Sidgwick & Jackson, Ltd., Publishers, London.

"All You Zombies—" by Robert Heinlein is reprinted by permission of the author and the author's agents, Spectrum Literary Agency, 432 Park Ave., S., New York, NY 10016.

"They," by Robert Heinlein, is reprinted by permission of the author and the author's agents, Spectrum Literary Agency, 432 Park Ave., S., New York, NY 10016.

"Catch That Zeppelin," by Fritz Leiber, Copyright © 1975 by Mercury Press, Inc., is reprinted from *The Magazine of Fantasy and Science Fiction* by permission of the author.

Selections from Stanislaw Lem's *Solaris* are reprinted by permission of the publishers, Walker and Company, 720 Fifth Avenue, NY 10019.

"Breath's a Ware That Will Not Keep," by Thomas F. Monteleone, is reprinted by permission of the author and the author's agent, Howard Morhaim Literary Agency, 501 Fifth Ave., New York, NY 10017.

"A Word to Space," by Winston Sanders, is reprinted by permission of the author and the author's agents, Scott Meredith Literary Agency, Inc., 845 Third Avenue, New York, NY 10022.

"Seventh Victim," by Robert Sheckley, Copyright © 1953, 1954 by Robert Sheckley, is reprinted by permission of the author.

"The Weed of Time," by Norman Spinrad, is reprinted by permission of the author and the author's agents, Scott Meredith Literary Agency, Inc., 845 Third Avenue, New York, NY 10022.

Contents

Introduction

Were philosophy like any number of other disciplines, it would be fitting to begin this book with an account of the nature of the discipline. The problem is that the proper methods and uses of philosophy are themselves philosophical questions and have been almost since its beginning. Rather than attempting to settle these issues by outlining and defending some ideal of philosophical practice, it seems wiser in this introduction to provide a brief account of the sorts of intellectual activities that have been characteristic of philosophers historically and that have served largely, though imperfectly, to distinguish philosophical thinking from thinking of other kinds. I shall describe five such activities and very briefly discuss how science fiction (and philosophical literature in general) may be relevant to each.

Philosophers since Plato have asked questions like "What is justice?" "What is knowledge?" "What is art?" and so forth. In the mid-twentieth century, at least, these questions came to be understood as questions about the meanings of words. Thus, the question "What is art?" was construed to mean "What does *art* mean?"; or, roughly, "On the basis of what criteria are we entitled to call something a work of art?" According to some practitioners, the purpose of this enterprise is to equip us with explicit, articulate knowledge of our basic categories of thought.

This activity, sometimes referred to as "meaning analysis," assumes as data a set of clear cases. In the case of art, the clear cases are those objects that everyone would accept as works of art, e.g., the Mona Lisa, *Richard III, War and Peace,* etc. According to some practitioners, the point of meaning analysis is to say what it is that all of the clear cases have in common that makes them members of the relevant class. Other practitioners, however, deny that there is any set of characteristics of this kind for "art" and other philosophically interesting words. Rather than sharing some clear set of defining characteristics, these philosophers claim that works of art are members of the same class by virtue of "family resemblances" they bear to one another. Accordingly, meaning analysis became a matter of describing what these "family resemblances" are, i.e., of describing the significant ways in which various kinds of art resemble each other by virtue of which they are properly said to be art.

As a number of meaning analysts have acknowledged, science fiction can be a valuable resource in discussions of meanings. Science fiction sometimes describes beings and cultures that are so exotic or alien to us that it is not clear that our ordinary concepts apply. Stanislaw Lem's *Solaris,* for example, describes a planet that "behaves" in ways that tempt some to maintain that it thinks, perceives, and experiences emotions such as curiosity and anger. By considering the reasons for and against attributing these characteristics to the planet, we may learn something about the meaning of *think, perceive,* and so forth, that we might overlook were we to restrict ourselves to the more standard cases.

This respect for ordinary language that blossomed in the mid-fifties was rather unusual in the history of philosophy. The more standard tendency has been to regard the categories of ordinary speech as unfit for philosophical purposes. Indeed, many philosophers have maintained that certain categories of ordinary speech (and science) rest on assumptions about the world that are false and/or paradoxical or that they strongly suggest misleading and/or incoherent pictures of the world. For most philosophers who have held this view, a major task of philosophy is to expose these inadequate concepts and to replace them with more adequate ones. We might call these activities conceptual criticism and conceptual reform, respectively.

The history of philosophy abounds with conceptual criticism. Among the more dramatic examples are Berkeley's attack on the notion of matter, Hume's attacks on the idea of the substantial self and on the idea of a cause (as something more than a certain kind of correlation), Leibniz's attack on the idea of absolute space and time, and Kant's criticism of the traditional concept of God. The question of whether these are critiques of the *meanings* of terms in ordinary language or critiques of misleading pictures suggested by these meanings need not concern us here. In either case the point of this philosophical activity is to expose the inadequacies of certain deeply rooted habits of thought with the purpose of reforming them.

Few, if any, science fiction stories can be read as literary arguments for conceptual reform. Some stories, however, illustrate the need for a reform. Perhaps the best examples of this are time-travel stories. The obvious assumption of time-travel stories is that time is a sort of medium in (or through) which one can move. But as those familiar with this genre recognize, this assumption is rich in paradoxical possibilities. Perhaps the most obvious of these is the case of the time traveler who kills her father before her father impregnates her mother. This clearly renders her own future existence impossible, and therefore makes it impossible that she had traveled back in time to begin with. And this suggests that there may be something deeply wrong with thinking of time as a sort of medium. This way of thinking, then, stands in need of reform. (On the other hand, we can all easily imagine experiences that would count as compelling evidence for such claims as "The Connecticut Yankee found himself in Camelot during the reign of King Arthur." And this at least apparent conflict between what reason tells us—namely, that time travel is paradoxical—and what experience tells us—namely, that we are in another time—raises interesting philosophical questions.)

Historically, philosophers have attempted not only to reform concepts but to develop whole systems of concepts to help us know the world or some part of it. Indeed, this is perhaps the most important and interesting activity of traditional metaphysicians. Thus Leibniz offers an account of the world in terms of the language of monads, Hegel provides an account in terms of the activities of the Absolute Spirit, and Whitehead in terms of actual occasions (and related notions). Such accounts are "global" in the sense that they aim to describe the most basic and fundamental "facts" about the universe. But philosophers have introduced less global "vocabularies" for the purpose of illuminating more restricted aspects of the world. Twentieth-century English-language philosophy has been especially fecund in its production of concepts meant to illuminate the nature of knowledge in general, and scientific knowledge in particular. In addition philosophers have made contributions to the languages of psychology, linguistics, history, and other disciplines. Indeed, at the higher levels of theory—in relation to the introduction of new concepts—psychologists, linguists, historians, and so forth, philosophize.

Science fiction writers do not, of course, introduce sets of concepts that are likely to be incorporated by the sciences and/or to form the basis of a new metaphysics. But some science fiction reminds us vividly of various influences on concept formation and conceptual change that raise important philosophical questions about the nature of knowledge; and, more specifically, about the relationship between the knower and the known. It does this by describing alien cultures that organize the world in thought differently from the way we do. In some cases these differences result from differences in physiology; an alien may be blind, deaf, and without the senses of smell and touch, but nonetheless be sensitive to all matter of fields, waves, and vibrations to which we are "blind." His concepts will reflect this. In other cases the differences may result from differences in social organization (e.g., in the tendency of a ruling class to elaborate a way of looking at the world that justifies its position). In either case, the differences may influence science as well. Given that there are influences of these kinds on the concepts of science (and on thought in general), some philosophers have asked to what degree our theories may be said to describe "the world as it is in itself" and to what degree they reflect our own nature.

Philosophers have also devoted considerable energy to the development, defense, and critique of ideals. Thus the history of philosophy contains numerous attempts to describe the ideal life, the ideal person, the ideal state or society, the ideal morality, and even the ideal knower. The function of an ideal is to provide us with a standpoint for evaluating the actual. If we do not know what an ideal society is, the argument goes, we cannot be in a position to say what is wrong with our own. Philosophers of different times and places, of course, have presented important different social and human ideals. And the question of whether ideals can be rationally justified is a matter of some philosophical controversy.

Some very interesting science fiction has been written from the standpoint of social ideals. Where this is done well, such stories provide us with a detailed picture of what life in a society designed to satisfy the relevant ideal would be like. In this way they sometimes help us to understand and to evaluate the ideal better than an abstract philosophical description of it. An excellent recent example of this is Ursula Le Guin's sensitive portrait of an anarchist society in *The Dispossessed.* Science fiction may also provide us with reason to reflect on our current social and moral ideals by examining our current practices and principles from the standpoint of some other tradition, real or imagined (recently, for example, Robert Heinlein's *Stranger in a Strange Land).* Other works may give us reason to reflect on certain contemporary practices and principles by describing a future society in which these practices and principles predominate. Two fine examples in this collection are E. M. Forster's "The Machine Stops" and Thomas Monteleone's "Breath's a Ware That Will Not Keep."

Another important philosophical activity practiced mainly by non-English-language philosophers may be called cultural hermaneutics. Hermaneutics is the science of interpretation. The goal of cultural hermaneutics, then, is to provide an interpretation of the meaning of some set of social or cultural practices (e.g., punishment, contemporary art, or psychoanalysis) or, indeed, of a culture in its entirety. Practitioners of hermaneutics differ in their accounts of the proper methods of this enterprise and differ even on any very specific description of its goals. But the sort of understanding they are after is neither scientific (in the strict sense), conceptual, or "subjective." That is, a hermaneutical understanding of a domain does not simply consist in having a set of statistical correlations (or causal laws), or of having analyses of the central concepts of that domain, or of having an account of how that domain is experienced by the participants. And yet any particular hermaneutical understanding may integrate scientific, conceptual, and subjectivist findings. The idea is to provide the sort of deep understanding that certain historians and philosophers aim at when they attempt to characterize, e.g., the culture of the Enlightenment or the world of classical Greece.

Although I can present only the briefest and most simple-minded sketch of an example of this sort of understanding here, perhaps I should do so. Imagine a culture in which painting and the plastic arts are religious activities. Their point is to represent divine creation for certain holy persons who are thought to enter into a special relationship with God when they paint or sculpt. Moreover, though originality in style is permitted and admired, this originality is thought to owe its origin to the many-sided nature of the deity (as opposed to the creativity of a private individual). Suppose, further, that paintings and sculptures produced by these people closely resembled paintings and statues that have a prominent position in the history of Western painting and sculpture. For this reason, on some analyses of the meaning of the word *art,* they would count as works of art, i.e., they would fit our definition. Nonetheless, the meaning of art in that culture—*hermaneutically* speaking—would differ significantly from its meaning in our own. Any account of the meaning of art in our culture—hermaneutically speaking—would need to take into account the facts that art is supposed to express the individuality and uniqueness of the artist; that appreciation of art works is supposed to be a sign of cultivation and sensitivity; that art is displayed in museums rather than churches; that there are movements in art that justify themselves by issuing theories about the meaning of art; that art is a commodity; that the culture rewards most practicing "creative" artists badly;

that most people with training in the arts who are employed as artists design packaging, billboards, company logos, etc. It would also take into account the various analyses of the concept of art developed by philosophers and artists, and various descriptions of esthetic experience and of the experience of creativity.

Some hermaneuticists may attempt to get beyond cultural barriers and provide interpretations of what it is to live a human life. Such theories attempt to discern basic structural features common to human life in all of its forms, or to describe a certain limited range of possibilities (or types) in relation to which historical cultures could be understood. In either case, a hermaneutical understanding of any particular culture would be a specification or an application of this more general sort of understanding.

Of course science fiction writers do not engage in hermaneutical analyses. But they do sometimes provide us with detailed and highly imaginative accounts of alien cultures that contrast interestingly with our own culture and with human cultures in general. And they describe human futures in which the meanings of certain important human practices and activities have changed dramatically. By reflecting on these contrasts we may come to a better understanding of the meaning of certain of our contemporary practices and activities and, indeed, of what it is to be human.

Part 1

Knowledge and the Meaning of Life

Introduction to Part 1

Epistemology—the theory of knowledge—has been the core discipline of twentieth-century English-language philosophy. Not only have most of the major figures in this century focused on epistemological questions, but to an important degree most of the traditional questions of philosophy have been discussed from an epistemological standpoint. Questions about the justification of knowledge claims, for example, have been central to ethical theory, esthetics, metaphysics, the philosophy of religion, the philosophy of mind, and so forth. In fact, epistemology has so thoroughly permeated other areas of philosophy that it is not always easy to say where epistemology stops and they begin.

The purpose of epistemology is to give us a coherent account of the nature of knowledge. Some philosophers have attempted to contribute to this by offering definitions of the term *knowledge.* For a time, many philosophers seemed to agree that a person **P** knows a proposition *r* to be true if and only if (1) **P** believes *r* is true; (2) *r* is true; and (3) **P** has sufficiently good reason for believing that *r* is true. But it was pointed out by Gettier that each of these conditions may be satisfied, but that **P**'s reasons for believing that *r* is true may not *explain r*'s truth. For example, **P** may believe truly that someone in the room owns a Ford because person **A** is in the room, and **P** has very good reason to believe that **A** owns a Ford. Yet, although **A** does not own a Ford, **P**'s belief may be true since **B** is in the room and **B** does own a Ford. In this case we will be reluctant to say that **P** knows that *r* is true despite the fact that *r* is true, and **P** has excellent reasons for believing this. Most attempts by philosophers to define *knowledge* in recent years have been attempts to come to terms with this criticism of the previously accepted view.

Many philosophers—myself included—are doubtful that these attempts have contributed significantly to a deep understanding of the nature of knowledge. More illuminating are questions concerning the justification of knowledge claims and questions concerning the relation between the knower and the known. Questions about justification may arise in a number of ways. They arise most naturally in relation to conflicting beliefs or theories. Suppose that one is interested in explaining the level of violence in the world. The Fundamentalist Christian explains this in relation to our sinful nature; the psychoanalyst in relation to our destructive instinct and/or the repression of our erotic impulses; the behaviorist in relation to our conditioning, and the Marxist in relation to our form of economic and social life. We need to decide which of these theories are inconsistent with one another and which are best supported by the evidence. But this task is more complex than it may first appear to be. To decide these questions we may need to decide what should count as evidence for a theory to begin with and what kinds of evidence deserve what kind of weight. Thus, for example, the Fundamentalist may claim that he knows his explanation is correct because that is the explanation presented in the Bible and the Bible represents the Holy Word of God. When asked how he knows that there is a God, and that the Bible in fact reflects His beliefs, he may reply that he has had direct personal experience of God, and that God has assured him that the Bible is accurate. How are we to evaluate this experience as evidence? Is it conclusive evidence for the Fundamentalist's theory? How is it like or unlike the sorts of evidence chemists, for example, offer for their theories? To what extent are we justified in extending the standards of scientific inquiry to religion?

Or consider the psychoanalyst. Perhaps she will argue that she knows Freud's theory of the instincts to be true on the basis of certain clinical (therapeutic) successes. But how much weight ought we to give these successes? The theory of the instincts, after all, does not by itself dictate any *particular* therapeutic practice. Moreover, assuming that we know how to measure success to begin with, suppose it can be shown that other methods (say, religious conversion) enjoy comparable success in treating neurotic symptoms. To what degree would *that* weaken the evidence for the Freudian theory? To answer any of these questions we need to raise deeper questions about the nature of evidence.

The claim that what counts as evidence for a religious proposition may not count as evidence for a scientific proposition suggests another reason for interest in questions about justification. For knowledge is claimed in many different areas, and it is clear that justificatory procedures may differ from area to area. Consider geometry. There the method of justification is deductive. We begin with a set of axioms, definitions, and postulates and we prove theorems. But obviously this is not how we proceed in science. There, our method of confirmation requires experimentation. Nor is it the way we proceed in interpretation. We justify claims about what a text means by presenting a coherent reading of that text. Finally, on the surface at least, none of these methods appears appropriate for justification in ethics or esthetics or, indeed, to philosophical inquiry in general. There we proceed by argument.

One strong tendency in the history of philosophy has been to deny the importance of these apparent differences and to take justification in one area to be the model of justification in at least some others. Thus Descartes, and the rationalist tradition in general, takes mathematics (or his understanding of mathematics) as the model. Descartes held that we can *deduce* fundamental laws of physics from the principles of metaphysics (which are themselves either self-evidently true or derived from self-evident truths). Empiricists, on the other hand, take the sciences (or their understanding of the sciences) as a model. Very roughly, they hold that any statement that cannot be verified by sense perception either has no meaning at all or is merely true by definition. Since it is difficult to understand how moral judgments can be verified in this way (we can't see or taste the rightness of an action), there is a tendency among empiricists to deny that moral judgments have any meaning at all. Hermaneuticists, moreover, argue that most justification must be understood on the model of interpretation. To understand any domain we must approach it as a text.

More recently however, some philosophers influenced by Wittgenstein have argued against any attempt to reduce justification to a single model. These philosophers maintain that the forms of justification characteristic of various domains of knowledge are adequate to those domains. To the extent to which this sort of pluralism can be defended, of course, all the various attempts by philosophers to reduce justification to a single model are mistaken. One of the major issues in twentieth-century epistemology—and philosophy—is the extent to which this sort of reduction is defensible.

Importantly related to the question of reduction is the question of foundations. One advantage of both the empiricist and the rationalist attempts to reduce justification to the models they propose is that they enable us to think of human knowledge as an ordered system that rests on a foundation of certain and indisputable truths. According to the rationalists, these truths are said to be self-evident (for example, every event has a cause). Every important proposition of physics, philosophy, and mathematics is thought to be deducible from such truths in the way in which we deduce theorems from axioms in geometry. According to the empiricists these truths are, roughly, descriptions of what we observe by the senses. In either case, it is thought that there are bedrock touchstones for evaluating knowledge claims.

Pluralistic accounts of justification do not accept that there is one sort of foundation or touchstone for knowledge in general, although they may allow that certain *types* of knowledge rest on foundations (for example, that descriptions of what we observe are the foundations of science). Some philosophers, however, deny that there are touchstones or foundations in *any* significant area of investigation. According to this view, knowledge is less like a building that rests on foundations than it is like a web whose various strands and fibers reinforce each other in various ways. No proposition stands alone or may be evaluated "on its own merits." Some propositions are far more central and important than others in the sense that if we revise those we will be forced to revise more of whatever else we believe. But we are entitled to believe them, in the last analysis, only because they are part of the most coherent systematic pattern of belief we can arrive at at the time. In the future we may come to have reasons for giving up anything we might happen to believe now.

A more traditional challenge to the foundationalist account of knowledge is posed by certain forms of skepticism. Philosophical skeptics challenge our ability to justify certain of our most fundamental beliefs about the world, e.g., our beliefs that other people are conscious. There are as many forms of skepticism as there are fundamental beliefs that philosophers have been skeptical about. When we speak of someone as a skeptic, then, we must specify in relation to what he or she is skeptical.

Some forms of skepticism pose a serious challenge to a great many of our ordinary beliefs. Among the best known of these is David Hume's argument to the effect that we have no rational ground for supposing that past experience is a reliable guide to the future, i.e., that correlations that have held in the past will continue to hold. If Hume's argument is correct, we have no rational ground for believing that any of our predictions will turn out to be true. Let's look briefly at Hume's argument.

To begin with, Hume observes that some propositions are true in virtue of the meaning of their terms (roughly, true by definition), e.g., "Dogs are mammals." But any proposition that is not true for this reason must be justified by appeal to experience. Thus, since the proposition "The future will resemble the past" is not true in virtue of what it means, that proposition must be justified by appeal to experience. The problem is, however, that we cannot justify this proposition by appeal to experience without involving ourselves in a vicious circle, i.e., without assuming the very thing we are trying to prove. For in order to prove anything *at all* on the basis of *past* experience we must assume that the future will resemble the past in the sense described (and this is the very thing that we are trying to prove). Accordingly, Hume argues, we have no rational justification for believing that correlations that have held in the past will continue to hold. As I suggested, this is a very serious conclusion.

Philosophers have responded to skepticism in a variety of ways. Some have tried to refute it in the straightforward common-sensical way that might occur to anyone. Thus, G. E. Moore claimed to refute skepticism concerning the existence of the "external world"—the world that exists independent of experience—by holding up his hands and saying "Here is one hand, there is another" (hands being examples of things external). The skeptic's reply, obviously, is that this begs the question. Other philosophers have argued that since there is *in principle* no way to determine whether *certain* forms of skepticism are true—e.g., whether there is an external world—the questions the skeptic asks are *meaningless*. The assumption behind this approach is that if nothing *could* count as evidence for what appears to be a statement about the world, that apparent statement in fact asserts nothing. Still other philosophers have attempted to refute skeptical arguments in more traditional ways, namely, by the argument that there are logical flaws in the skeptic's arguments. Finally, some philosophers maintain that at least some important skeptical arguments are correct and conclude from this that, at the deepest level, knowledge—or some of it—rests on unprovable assumptions. This conclusion, of course, strikes at the very heart of foundationalism.

Let us turn now to the question of the relation between the knower and the known. To begin with, let us consider the common sense position that a knowing subject stands to the world (object) to be known as a mapmaker stands to a terrain. On this view, just as the lay of the land is in no way dependent upon the nature of the cartographer, so the world-to-be-known is in no way dependent upon the nature of the knowing subject. And just as the goal of the cartographer is to represent the terrain as it is in itself, the goal of the knower is to understand the world as it is in itself.

This view sounds so obviously true it is hard to imagine why someone might deny it. There are, however, a number of reasons. To begin with, it seems clear that the world, as we experience it, owes something to our own construction. Were our eyes physiologically different we might see colors different from those we now see. Were we blind we would see no colors at all. That we live in a world of colors, textures, sounds, odors, etc., is a consequence of how we are made. Other creatures—made differently—may have no such experience at all but may have types of experiences that we cannot even begin to imagine (i.e., they may stand in relation to us as the congenitally blind stand to the sighted). To the extent that the world we come to know is the world we perceive by our senses, then, there is a point to the claim that the world we know owes something important to the way we are structured.

What I have just said of the "raw matter" of experience—visual sensations, auditory sensations, and so forth—has also been said of the way we organize that "raw matter" in thought, i.e., by concepts. Thus many philosophers have argued that our concepts are intimately related to sensations; some have even argued that to define a word *e* (roughly, to describe the concept of an 'e') is to describe that set of sights, sounds, etc., sufficient for the true application of 'e' to something in the world. On this view one describes the concept 'chair' by saying what sorts of sensations we must have, to say truthfully of something that it is a chair. Most philosophers now reject this account. But it is difficult to resist the conclusion that in the case of expressions like *chair,* there is an important relationship between meanings (or concepts), on the one hand, and sensations on the other. If this is so, at least some of our concepts are as they are because we are structured in certain ways.

Moreover, at least one very important philosophical tradition, originating with Kant, maintains that the structures by which we organize experiences conceptually are at the most fundamental levels "built in." As the reference to "the most fundamental level" suggests, this view does not assert that concepts like 'table' and 'chair' are simply reflections of how we are constructed. But it does assert that all such mundane concepts are in some sense instances of some basic concepts, and that these are built in. Kant's examples of basic concepts (his categories of the understanding) included cause and effect, unity and plurality, and substance and accident. To the extent that they are instances of these, then, all of our concepts owe something to how we are structured.

Kant believed that the structures by means of which we organize "the given" of experience are built in to individuals and do not change historically. Some neo-Kantian philosophers deny this. They hold, rather, that the fundamental categories in relation to which we organize "the given" may vary from culture to culture and from historical epoch to historical epoch. These categories are transmitted to individuals by their cultures. Nonetheless, we have no reason to believe that these categories are reflections of the world as it is in itself; they are, rather, reflections of a certain way of life, a certain form of collective existence.

As this suggests, Kant and the neo-Kantians believed that there is such a thing as the-world-as-it-is-in-itself, but that that world is essentially unknowable. All knowledge is knowledge from a human standpoint. We cannot get beyond that standpoint or outside of it to compare it to the world as it is itself. Indeed, we can say virtually nothing significant about *that* world at all. Disturbed by the idea of a something about which nothing can be said, but convinced by the general direction of Kant's argument, some idealistic philosophers surrendered the notion of the thing-in-itself and attempted to explain the entire world as we understand it in relation to a kind of generalized subject (Hegel's Spirit).

As outrageous as these lines of thought may seem to common sense, recent developments in epistemology and the philosophy of science have inclined some philosophers to greater sympathy with these traditions. The issues here are difficult and subtle and cannot briefly be summarized without considerable distortion. But it is worth noting that the work of Thomas Kuhn and his followers has led many philosophers to question the common-sense interpretation of scientific theory. Roughly, this is the view that science describes the-world-as-it-is-in-itself. According to the Kuhnian view scientists come to the world equipped with concepts, theories, and methods of inquiry that determine what they will investigate and how they will investigate it. And these concepts, theories, and methods of inquiry reflect at least as much about the scientific community as they reflect about the world itself. It is tempting to conclude from this that scientists do not describe the world-as-it-is-in-itself, but rather describe the world in a manner that in some important ways reflects their standpoint within it. But this conclusion is hotly disputed by a good many philosophers.

Finally, common sense tells us that some bits of knowledge are trivial or insignificant while others are momentous and sublime. In fact, many people suppose that were we to know certain kinds of things about the universe we would know the meaning of Being, and hence the meaning of our own lives, and that without that knowledge we do not know the meaning of our own lives. This *sine qua non* of salvation is sometimes called The Truth.

Most contemporary philosophers do not take the idea of The Truth seriously. Although the relationship between factual assertions and value assertions is a matter of concern and discussion, few philosophers hold that knowledge of some privileged set of facts about the universe will provide insight into the cosmic order of the kind necessary to tell us the meaning of our lives. With the exception of philosophers committed to some religious traditions, there is general agreement that any quest for The Truth is bound to end in failure.

The works included in this section illustrate and/or raise some of the questions about knowing that I have described. This section begins with excerpts from Stanislaw Lem's brilliant novel *Solaris:* among other things, it is a sort of parable about the relation between the knower and the known. The scientists of Lem's novel confront a planet whose orbit defies known physical laws, and whose colloidal surface regularly fashions itself into enormous and ornate structures of no apparent function, including structures that imitate human artifacts. For well over a century scientists have theorized about the planet, scientific models succeeding scientific models like so many fashions. Most recently, apparently as a result of x-ray bombardment, the planet has fashioned sentient "visitors" for the scientists at the research station on its surface; visitors modeled on memories and fantasies of the scientists themselves and deeply disturbing to them. What is going on? Is the planet angry? Does it think, feel, and have values, motives, and purposes? Are these questions even meaningful in relation to something as alien as Solaris? When we attribute consciousness, thought, motives, and so forth to something so utterly alien to us as the planet, are we merely projecting a structure onto something whose true nature we can never be in a position to know? As Lem's history of Solaristic studies reveals, the tendency to personalize the planet in this way is just the last of a long series of theoretical attempts to understand it. Each attempt (each theory) goes well beyond what can be established by observation and reflects something important about the needs, personalities, allegiances, and so forth, of the scientists who support it. The suggestion is that science (and knowledge) inevitably is this way.

Robert Heinlein's story "They" raises the skeptical question concerning the existence of others whose thoughts and feelings are like our own. Strictly speaking, the protagonist of Heinlein's story is not a skeptic: he does not insist merely that he has no justification for believing that others have such thoughts and feelings, but maintains the stronger claim that he has convincing reasons for asserting the contrary. His evidence, however, is not very strong. Still, he has some evidence, and the interest of Heinlein's story is that it challenges us to produce evidence to the contrary, i.e., to answer the skeptic with respect to other minds.

Jorge Luis Borges's story "The Library of Babel" raises a number of interesting questions. Perhaps most important however, it is a story about the search for The Truth. The Library of Babel contains every possible book of a certain length (two hundred pages, thirty-six lines per page, etc.) that can be written in a twenty-six character alphabet. Assuming that The Truth must be somewhere in the library, some of Borges's characters wander through the stacks in search of it. But among all that has been said (and believed), how will they know if they happen to stumble across it? (And how will you?)

Solaris

Stanislaw Lem

[*Kris Kelvin arrives at the experimental station on the planet Solaris. There is no one to meet him at the shuttle dock. Making his way to the interior he finds the place in chaos.*]

. . . Another green arrow directed me to the central door. Behind this stretched a narrow corridor, hardly wide enough for two men to walk side by side, lit by slabs of glass set into the ceiling. Then another door, painted in green and white squares, which was ajar; I went in.

The cabin had concave walls and a big panoramic window, which a glowing mist had tinged with purple. Outside the murky waves slid silently past. Open cupboards lined the walls, filled with instruments, books, dirty glasses, vacuum flasks—all covered with dust. Five or six small trolleys and some collapsible chairs cluttered up the stained floor. One chair alone was inflated, its back raised. In this armchair there was a little thin man, his face burnt by the sun, the skin on his nose and cheeks coming away in large flakes. I recognized him as Snow, a cybernetics expert and Gibarian's deputy. In his time he had published articles of great originality in the Solarist Annual. It so happened that I had never had the opportunity of meeting him. He was wearing a mesh shirt which allowed the grey hairs of his sunken chest to poke through here and there, and canvas trousers with a great many pockets, mechanic's trousers, which had once been white but now were stained at the knees and covered with holes from chemical burns. He was holding one of those pear-shaped plastic flasks which are used in spaceships not equipped with internal gravitational systems. Snow's eyes widened in amazement as he looked up and saw me. The flask dropped from his fingers and bounced several times, spilling a few drops of transparent liquid. Blood drained from his face. I was too astonished to speak, and this dumbshow continued for so long that Snow's terror gradually communicated itself to me. I took a step forward. He cringed in his chair.

"Snow?"

He quivered as though I had struck him. Gazing at me in indescribable horror, he gasped out:

"I don't know . . ." His voice croaked. "I don't know you . . . What do you want?"

The spilt liquid was quickly evaporating; I caught a whiff of alcohol. Had he been drinking? Was he drunk? What was he so terrified of? I stood in the middle of the room; my legs were trembling; my ears roared, as though they were stuffed with cotton wool. I had the impression that the ground was giving way beneath my feet. Beyond the curved window, the ocean rose and fell with regularity. Snow's blood-shot eyes never left me. His terror seemed to have abated, but his expression of invincible disgust remained.

"What's the matter? Are you ill?" I whispered.

"You seem worried," he said, his voice hollow. "You actually seem worried . . . So it's like that now, is it? But why concern yourself about me? I don't know you."

"Where's Gibarian?" I asked.

He gave a gasp and his glassy eyes lit up for an instant.

"Gi . . . Giba . . . No! No!"

His whole frame shook with stifled, hysterical laughter; then he seemed to calm down a little.

"So it's Gibarian you've come for, is it? Poor old Gibarian. What do you want with him?"

His words, or rather his tone of voice, expressed hatred and defiance; it was as though I had suddenly ceased to represent a threat to him.

Bewildered, I mumbled:

"What . . . Where is he?"

"Don't you know?"

Obviously he was drunk and raving. My anger rose. I should have controlled myself and left the room, but I had lost patience. I shouted:

"That's enough! How could I know where he is since I've only just arrived? Snow! What's going on here?"

His jaw dropped. Once again he caught his breath and his eyes gleamed with a different light. He seized the arms of his chair with both hands and stood up with difficulty. His knees were trembling.

"What? You've just arrived . . . Where have you come from?" he asked, almost sober.

"From Earth!" I retorted angrily. "Maybe you've heard of it? Not that anyone would ever guess it."

"From Earth? Good God! Then you must be Kelvin."

"Of course. Why are you looking at me like that? What's so startling about me?"

He blinked rapidly.

"Nothing," he said, wiping his forehead, "nothing. Forgive me, Kelvin, it's nothing, I assure you. I was simply surprised. I didn't expect to see you."

"What do you mean, you didn't expect to see me? You were notified months ago, and Moddard radioed only today from the *Prometheus.*"

"Yes; yes, indeed. Only, you see, we're a bit disorganized at the moment."

"So I see," I answered dryly.

Snow walked around me, inspecting my atmosphere suit, which was standard issue with the usual harness of wires and cables attached to the chest. He coughed, and rubbed his bony nose:

"Perhaps you would like a bath? It would do you good. It's the blue door, on the other side."

"Thanks—I know the Station lay-out."

"You must be hungry."

"No. Where's Gibarian?"

Without answering, he went over to the window. From behind he looked considerably older. His close-cropped hair was grey, and deep wrinkles creased his sunburnt neck.

The wave-crests glinted through the window, the colossal rollers rising and falling in slow-motion. Watching the ocean like this one had the illusion—it was surely an illusion—that the Station was moving imperceptibly, as though teetering on an invisible base; then it would seem to recover its equilibrium, only to lean the opposite way with the same lazy movement. Thick foam, the color of blood, gathered in the troughs of the waves. For a fraction of a second, my throat tightened and I thought longingly of the *Prometheus* and its strict discipline; the memory of an existence which suddenly seemed a happy one, now gone forever.

Snow turned around, nervously rubbing his hands together.

"Listen," he said abruptly, "except for me there's no one around for the moment. You'll have to make do with my company for today. Call me Ratface; don't argue. You know me by my photograph, just imagine we're old friends. Everyone calls me Ratface, there's nothing I can do about it."

Obstinately, I repeated my question:

"Where is Gibarian?"

He blinked again.

"I'm sorry to have received you like that. It's . . . it's not exactly my fault. I had completely forgotten . . . A lot has been happening here, you see . . ."

"It's all right. But what about Gibarian? Isn't he on the Station? Is he on an observation flight?"

Snow was gazing at a tangled mass of cables.

"No, he hasn't left the Station. And he won't be flying. The fact is . . ."

My ears were still blocked, and I was finding it more and more difficult to hear.

"What? What do you mean? Where is he then?"

"I should think you might guess," he answered in a changed voice, looking at me coldly in the eyes. I shivered. He was drunk, but he knew what he was saying.

"There's been an accident?"

He nodded vigorously, watching my reactions closely.

"When?"

"This morning, at dawn."

By now, my sensations were less violent; this succinct exchange of questions and answers had calmed me. I was beginning to understand Snow's strange behavior.

"What kind of accident?"

"Why not go to your cabin and take off your spacesuit? Come back in, say, an hour's time."

[*Kelvin goes to Gibarian's quarters to investigate. He encounters a number of strange phenomena. For example, the bathroom cabinet was filled with strange objects: "misshapen forms in a dark metal, grotesque replicas of the instruments in the racks. Not one of the tools was usable. They were blunted, distorted, melted as though they had been in a furnace. Strangest of all, even the porcelain handles, virtually incombustible, were twisted out of shape. Even at maximum temperature, no laboratory furnace could have melted them; only, perhaps, an atomic pile."*]

. . . I sat down on a tubular stool in the middle of the clear space, glad to be alone, and seeing with satisfaction that I had over half an hour to myself. (By nature, I have always been scrupulous about keeping engagements, whether important or trivial.) The hands of the clock, its face divided into twenty-four hours, pointed to seven o'clock. The sun was setting. 07.00 hours here was 20.00 hours on board the *Prometheus*. On Moddard's screens, Solaris would be nothing but an indistinct dust-cloud, mingled with the stars. But what did the *Prometheus* matter to me now? I closed my eyes. I could hear no sound except the moaning of the ventilation pipes and a faint trickling of water from the bathroom.

If I had understood correctly, it was only a short time since Gibarian had died. What had they done with his body? Had they buried it? No, that was impossible on this planet. I puzzled over the question for a long time, concentrating on the fate of the corpse; then, realizing the absurdity of my thoughts, I began to pace up and down. My toe knocked against a canvas bag half-buried under a pile of books; I bent down and picked it up. It contained a small bottle made of colored glass, so light that it might have been blown out of paper. I held it up to the window in the purplish glow of the somber twilight, now overhung by a sooty fog. What was I doing, allowing myself to be distracted by irrelevancies, by the first trifle which came to hand?

I gave a start: the lights had gone on, activated by a photo-electric relay; the sun had set. What would happen next? I was so tense that the sensation of an empty space behind me became unbearable. In an attempt to pull myself together, I took a chair over to the bookshelves and chose a book familiar to me: the second volume of the early monograph by Hughes and Eugel, *Historia Solaris*. I rested the thick, solidly bound volume on my knees and began leafing through the pages.

The discovery of Solaris dated from about 100 years before I was born.

The planet orbits two suns: a red sun and a blue sun. For 45 years after its discovery, no spacecraft had visited Solaris. At that time, the Gamow-Shapley theory—that life was impossible on planets which are satellites of two solar bodies—was firmly believed. The orbit is constantly being modified by variations in the gravitational pull in the course of its revolutions around the two suns.

Due to these fluctuations in gravity, the orbit is either flattened or distended and the elements of life, if they appear, are inevitably destroyed, either by intense heat or an extreme drop in temperature. These changes take place at intervals estimated in millions of years—very short intervals, that is, according to the laws of astronomy and biology (evolution takes hundreds of millions of years if not a billion).

According to the earliest calculations, in 500,000 years' time Solaris would be drawn one half of an astronomic unit nearer to its red sun, and a million years after that would be engulfed by the incandescent star.

A few decades later, however, observations seemed to suggest that the planet's orbit was in no way subject to the expected variations: it was stable, as stable as the orbit of the planets in our own solar system.

The observations and calculations were reworked with great precision; they simply confirmed the original conclusions: Solaris's orbit was stable.

A modest item among the hundreds of planets discovered annually—to which official statistics devoted only a few lines defining the characteristics of their orbits—Solaris eventually began to attract special attention and attain a high rank.

Four years after this promotion, overflying the planet with the *Laakon* and two auxiliary craft, the Ottenskjöld expedition undertook a study of Solaris. This expedition being in the nature of a preliminary, not to say improvised, reconnaissance, the scientists were not equipped for a landing. Ottenskjöld placed a quantity of automatic observation satellites into equatorial and polar orbit, their principal function being to measure the gravitational pull. In addition, a study was made of the planet's surface, which is covered by an ocean dotted with innumerable flat, low-lying islands whose combined area is less than that of Europe, although the diameter of Solaris is a fifth greater than Earth's. These expanses of barren, rocky territory, irregularly distributed, are largely concentrated in the southern hemisphere. At the same time the composition of the atmosphere—devoid of oxygen—was analyzed, and precise measurements made of the planet's density, from which its albedo and other astronomical characteristics were determined. As was foreseeable, no trace of life was discovered, either on the islands or in the ocean.

During the following ten years, Solaris became the center of attraction for all observatories concerned with the study of this region of space, for the planet had in the meantime shown the astonishing faculty of maintaining an orbit which ought, without any shadow of doubt, to have been unstable. The problem almost developed into a scandal: since the results of the observations could only be inaccurate, attempts were made (in the interests of science) to denounce and discredit various scientists or else the computers they used.

Lack of funds delayed the departure of a proper Solaris expedition for three years. Finally Shannahan assembled his team and obtained three C-tonnage vessels from the Institute, the largest starships of the period. A year and a half before the arrival of the expedition, which left from the region of Alpha in Aquarius, a second exploration fleet, acting in the name of the Institute, placed an automatic satellite—Luna 247—into orbit around Solaris. This satellite, after three successive reconstructions at roughly ten-year intervals, is still functioning today. The data it supplied confirmed beyond doubt the findings of the Ottenskjöld expedition concerning the active character of the ocean's movements.

One of Shannahan's ships remained in orbit, while the two others, after some preliminary attempts, landed in the southern hemisphere, in a rocky area about 600 miles square. The work of the expedition lasted eighteen months and was carried out under favorable conditions, apart from an unfortunate accident brought about by the malfunction of some apparatus. In the meantime, the scientists had split into two opposing camps; the bone of contention was the ocean. On the basis of the analyses, it had been accepted that the ocean was an organic formation (at that time, no one had yet dared to call it living). But, while the biologists considered it as a primitive formation—a sort of gigantic entity, a fluid cell, unique and monstrous (which they called "prebiological"), surrounding the globe with a colloidal envelope several miles thick in places—the astronomers and physicists asserted that it must be an organic structure, extraordinarily evolved. According to them, the ocean possibly exceeded terrestrial organic structures in complexity, since it was capable of exerting an active influence on the planet's orbital path. Certainly, no other factor could be found that might explain the behavior of Solaris; moreover, the planeto-physicists had established a relationship between certain processes of the plasmic ocean and the local measurements of gravitational pull, which altered according to the "matter transformations" of the ocean.

Consequently it was the physicists, rather than the biologists, who put forward the paradoxical formulation of a "plasmic mechanism," implying by this a structure, possibly without life as we conceive it, but capable of performing functional activities—on an astronomic scale, it should be emphasized.

It was during this quarrel, whose reverberations soon reached the ears of the most eminent authorities, that the Gamow-Shapley doctrine, unchallenged for eighty years, was shaken for the first time.

There were some who continued to support the Gamow-Shapley contentions, to the effect that the ocean had nothing to do with life, that it was neither "parabiological" nor "prebiological" but a geological formation—of extreme rarity, it is true—with the unique ability to stabilize the orbit of Solaris, despite the variations in the forces of attraction. Le Chatelier's law was enlisted in support of this argument.

To challenge this conservative attitude, new hypotheses were advanced—of which Civito-Vitta's was one of the most elaborate—proclaiming that the ocean was the product of a dialectical development: on the basis of its earliest pre-oceanic form, a solution of slow-reacting chemical elements, and by the force of circumstances (the threat to its existence from the changes of orbit), it had reached in a single bound the stage of "homeostatic ocean," without passing through all the stages of terrestrial evolution, by-passing the unicellular and multicellular phases, the vegetable and the animal, the development of a nervous and cerebral system. In other words, unlike terrestrial organisms, it had not taken hundreds of millions of years to adapt itself to its environment—culminating in the first representatives of a species endowed with reason—but dominated its environment immediately.

This was an original point of view. Nevertheless, the means whereby this colloidal envelope was able to stabilize the planet's orbit remained unknown. For almost a century, devices had existed capable of creating artificial magnetic and gravitational fields; they were called gravitors. But no one could even guess how this formless glue could produce an effect which the gravitors achieved by the use of complicated nuclear reactions and enormously high temperatures. The newspapers of the day, exciting the curiosity of the layman and the anger of the scientist, were full of the most improbable embroideries on the theme of the "Solaris Mystery," one reporter going so far as to suggest that the ocean was, no less, a distant relation to our electric eels!

Just when a measure of success had been achieved in unravelling this problem, it turned out, as often happened subsequently in the field of Solarist studies, that the explanation replaced one enigma by another, perhaps even more baffling.

Observations showed, at least, that the ocean did not react according to the same principles as our gravitors (which, in any case, would have been impossible), but succeeded in controlling the orbital periodicity directly. One result, among others, was the discovery of discrepancies in the measurement of time along one and the same meridian on Solaris. Thus the ocean was not only in a sense "aware" of the Einstein-Boevia theory; it was also capable of exploiting the implications of the latter (which was more than we could say of ourselves).

With the publication of this hypothesis, the scientific world was torn by one of the most violent controversies of the century. Revered and universally accepted theories foundered; the specialist literature was swamped by outrageous and heretical treatises; "sentient ocean" or "gravity-controlling colloid"—the debate became a burning issue.

All this happened several years before I was born. When I was a student—new data having accumulated in the meantime—it was already generally agreed that there was life on Solaris, even if it was limited to a single inhabitant.

The second volume of Hughes and Eugel, which I was still leafing through mechanically, began with a systematization that was as ingenious as it was amusing. The table of classification comprised three definitions: Type: Polythera; Class: Syncytialia; Category: Metamorph.

It might have been thought that we knew of an infinite number of examples of the species, whereas in reality there was only the one—weighing, it is true, some seven hundred billion tons.

Multicolored illustrations, picturesque graphs, analytical summaries and spectral diagrams flickered through my fingers, explaining the type and rhythm of the fundamental transformations as well as chemical reactions. Rapidly, infallibly, the thick tome led the reader on to the solid ground of mathematical certitude. One might have assumed that we knew everything there was to be known about this representative of the category Metamorph, which lay some hundreds of metres below the metal hull of the Station, obscured at the moment by the shadows of the four-hour night.

In fact, by no means everybody was yet convinced that the ocean was actually a living "creature," and still less, it goes without saying, a rational one. I put the heavy volume back on the shelf and took up the one next to it, which was in two parts. The first part was devoted to a resumé of the countless attempts to establish contact with the ocean. I could well remember how, when I was a student, these attempts were the subject of endless anecdotes, jokes and witticisms. Compared with the proliferation of speculative ideas which were triggered off by this problem, medieval scholasticism seemed a model of scientific enlightenment. The second part, nearly 1500 pages long, was devoted exclusively to the bibliography of the subject. There would not have been enough room for the books themselves in the cabin in which I was sitting.

The first attempts at contact were by means of specially designed electronic apparatus. The ocean itself took an active part in these operations by remodelling the instruments. All this, however, remained somewhat obscure. What exactly did the ocean's "participation" consist of? It modified certain elements in the submerged instruments, as a result of which the normal discharge frequency was completely disrupted and the recording instruments registered a profusion of signals—fragmentary indications of some outlandish activity, which in fact defeated all attempts at analysis. Did these data point to a momentary condition of stimulation, or to regular impulses correlated with the gigantic structures which the ocean was in the process of creating elsewhere, at the antipodes of the region under investigation? Had the electronic apparatus recorded the cryptic manifestation of the ocean's ancient secrets? Had it revealed its innermost workings to us? Who could tell? No two reactions to the stimuli were the same. Sometimes the instruments almost exploded under the violence of the impulses, sometimes there was total silence; it was impossible to obtain a repetition of any previously observed phenomenon. Constantly, it seemed, the experts were on the brink of deciphering the ever-growing mass of information. Was it not, after all, with this object in mind that computers had been built of virtually limitless capacity, such as no previous problem had ever demanded?

And, indeed, some results *were* obtained. The ocean as a source of electric and magnetic impulses and of gravitation expressed itself in a more or less mathematical language. Also, by calling on the most abstruse branches of statistical analysis, it was possible to classify certain frequencies in the discharges of current. Structural homologues were discovered, not unlike those already observed by physicists in that sector of science which deals with the reciprocal interaction of energy and matter, elements and compounds, the finite and the infinite. This correspondence convinced the scientists that they were confronted with a monstrous entity endowed with reason, a protoplasmic ocean-brain enveloping the entire planet and idling its time away in extravagant theoretical cognitation about the nature of the universe. Our instruments had intercepted minute random fragments of a prodigious and everlasting monologue unfolding in the depths of this colossal brain, which was inevitably beyond our understanding.

So much for the mathematicians. These hypotheses, according to some people, underestimated the resources of the human mind; they bowed to the unknown, proclaiming the ancient doctrine, arrogantly resurrected, of *ignoramus et ignorabimus.* Others regarded the mathematicians' hypotheses as sterile and dangerous nonsense, contributing towards the creation of a modern mythology based on the notion of this giant brain—whether plasmic or electronic was immaterial—as the ultimate objective of existence, the very synthesis of life.

Yet others . . . but the would-be experts were legion and each had his own theory. A comparison of the "contract" school of thought with other branches of Solarist studies, in which specialization had rapidly developed, especially during the last quarter of a century, made it clear that a Solarist-cybernetician had difficulty in making himself understood to a Solarist-symmetriadologist. Veubeke, director of the Institute when I was studying there, had asked jokingly one day: "How do you expect to communicate with the ocean, when you can't even understand one another?" The jest contained more than a grain of truth.

The decision to categorize the ocean as a metamorph was not an arbitrary one. Its undulating surface was capable of generating extremely diverse formations which resembled nothing ever seen on Earth, and the function of these sudden eruptions of plasmic "creativity," whether adaptive, explorative or what, remained an enigma.

Lifting the heavy volume with both hands, I replaced it on the shelf, and thought to myself that our scholarship, all the information accumulated in the libraries, amounted to a useless jumble of words, a sludge of statements and suppositions, and that we had not progressed an inch in the 78 years since researches had begun. The situation seemed much worse now than in the time of the pioneers, since the assiduous efforts of so many years had not resulted in a single indisputable conclusion.

The sum total of known facts was strictly negative. The ocean did not use machines, even though in certain circumstances it seemed capable of creating them. During the first two years of exploratory work, it had reproduced elements of some of the submerged instruments. Thereafter, it simply ignored the experiments we went on pursuing, as though it had lost all interest in our instruments and our activities—as though, indeed, it was no longer interested in *us*. It did not possess a nervous system (to go on with the inventory of "negative knowledge") or cells, and its structure was not proteiform. It did not always react even to the most powerful stimuli (it ignored completely, for example, the catastrophic accident which occurred during the second Giese expedition: an auxiliary rocket, falling from a height of 300,000 metres, crashed on the planet's surface and the radioactive explosion of its nuclear reserves destroyed the plasma within a radius of 2500 metres).

Gradually, in scientific circles, the "Solaris Affair" came to be regarded as a lost cause, notably among the administrators of the Institute, where voices had recently been raised suggesting that financial support should be withdrawn and research suspended. No one, until then, had dared to suggest the final liquidation of the Station; such a decision would have smacked too obviously of defeat. But in the course of semi-official discussions a number of scientists recommended an "honorable" withdrawal from Solaris.

Many people in the world of science, however, especially among the young, had unconsciously come to regard the "affair" as a touchstone of individual values. All things considered, they claimed, it was not simply a question of penetrating Solarist civilization, it was essentially a test of ourselves, of the limitations of human knowledge. For some time, there was a widely held notion (zealously fostered by the daily press) to the effect that the "thinking ocean" of Solaris was a gigantic brain, prodigiously well-developed and several million years in advance of our own civilization, a sort of "cosmic yogi," a sage, a symbol of omniscience, which had long ago understood the vanity of all action and for this reason had retreated into an unbreakable silence. The notion was incorrect, for the living ocean was active. Not, it is true, according to human ideas—it did not build cities or bridges, nor did it manufacture flying machines. It did not try to reduce distances, nor was it concerned with the conquest of Space (the ultimate criterion, some people thought, of man's superiority). But it was engaged in a never-ending process of transformation, an "ontological autometamorphosis." (There were any amount of scientific neologisms in accounts of Solarist activities.) Moreover, any scientist who devotes himself to the study of Solariana has the indelible impression that he can discern fragments of an intelligent structure, perhaps endowed with genius, haphazardly mingled with outlandish phenomena, apparently the product of an unhinged mind. Thus was born the conception of the "autistic ocean" as opposed to the "ocean-yogi."

These hypotheses resurrected one of the most ancient of philosophical problems: the relation between matter and mind, and between mind and consciousness. Du Haart was the first to have the audacity to maintain that the ocean possessed a consciousness. The problem, which the methodologists hastened to dub metaphysical, provoked all kinds of arguments and discussions. Was it possible for thought to exist without consciousness? Could one, in any case, apply the word *thought* to the processes observed in the ocean? Is a mountain only a huge stone? Is a planet an enormous mountain? Whatever the terminology, the new scale of size introduced new norms and new phenomena.

The question appeared as a contemporary version of the problem of squaring the circle. Every independent thinker endeavored to register his personal contribution to the board of Solarist studies. New theories proliferated: the ocean was evidence of a state of degeneration, of regression, following a phase of "intellectual repletion"; it was a deviant neoplasm, the product of the bodies of former inhabitants of the planet, whom it had devoured, swallowed up, dissolving and blending the residue into this unchanging, self-propagating form, supracellular in structure.

By the white light of the fluorescent tubes—a pale imitation of terrestrial daylight—I cleared the table of its clutter of apparatus and books. Arms outstretched and my hands gripping the chromium edging, I unrolled a map of Solaris on the plastic surface and studied it at length. The living ocean had its peaks and its canyons. Its islands, which were covered with a decomposing mineral deposit, were certainly related to the nature of the ocean bed. But did it control the eruption and subsidence of the rocky formations buried in its depths? No one knew. Gazing at the big flat projection of the two hemispheres, colored in various tones of blue and purple, I experienced once again that thrill of wonder which had so often gripped me, and which I had felt as a schoolboy on learning of the existence of Solaris for the first time.

[*Kelvin leaves Gibarian's room.*]

. . . As I was passing the foot of the stairway, I noticed that the aluminum treads were streaked with light falling from above. Sartorius was still at work. I decided to go up and see him.

It was hotter on the upper deck, but the paper strips still fluttered frenziedly at the air-vents. The corridor was wide and low-ceilinged. The main laboratory was enclosed by a thick panel of opaque glass in a chrome embrasure. A dark curtain screened the door on the inside, and the light was coming from windows let in above the lintel. I pressed down the handle, but, as I expected, the door refused to budge. The only sound from the laboratory was an intermittent whine like that of a defective gas jet. I knocked. No reply. I called:

"Sartorius! Dr. Sartorius! I'm the new man, Kelvin. I must see you, it's very important. Please let me in!"

There was a rustling of papers.

"It's me, Kelvin. You must have heard of me. I arrived off the *Prometheus* a few years ago."

I was shouting, my lips glued to the angle where the door joined the metal frame.

"Dr. Sartorius, I'm alone. Please open the door!"

Not a word. Then the same rustling as before, followed by the clink of metal instruments on a tray. Then . . . I could scarcely believe my ears . . . there came a succession of little short footsteps, like the rapid drumming of a pair of tiny feet, or remarkably agile fingers tapping out the rhythm of steps on the lid of an empty tin box.

I yelled:

"Dr. Sartorius, are you going to open this door, yes or no?"

No answer. Nothing but the pattering, and, simultaneously, the sound of a man walking on tiptoe. But, if the man was moving about, he could not at the same time be tapping out an imitation of a child's footsteps.

No longer able to control my growing fury, I burst out:

"Dr. Sartorius, I have not made a sixteen-month journey just to come here and play games! I'll count up to ten. If you don't let me in, I shall break down the door!"

In fact, I was doubtful whether it would be easy to force this particular door, and the discharge of a gas pistol is not very powerful. Nevertheless, I was determined somehow or other to carry out my threat, even if it meant resorting to explosives, which I could probably find in the munition store. I could not draw back now; I could not go on playing an insane game with all the cards stacked against me.

There was the sound of a struggle—or was it simply objects being thrust aside? The curtain was pulled back, and an elongated shadow was projected onto the glass.

A hoarse, high-pitched voice spoke:

"If I open the door, you must give me your word not to come in."

"In that case, why open it?"

"I'll come out."

"Very well, I promise."

The silhouette vanished and the curtain was carefully replaced.

Obscure noises came from inside the laboratory. I heard a scraping—a table being dragged across the floor? At last, the lock clicked back, and the glass panel opened just enough to allow Sartorius to slip through into the corridor.

He stood with his back against the door, very tall and thin, all bones under his white sweater. He had a black scarf knotted around his neck, and over his arm he was carrying a laboratory smock, covered with chemical burns. His head, which was unusually narrow, was cocked to one side. I could not see his eyes: he wore curved dark glasses, which covered up half his face. His lower jaw was elongated; he had bluish lips and enormous, blue-tinged ears. He was unshaven. Red anti-radiation gloves hung by their laces from his wrists.

For a moment we looked at one another with undisguised aversion. His shaggy hair (he had obviously cut it himself) was the color of lead, his beard grizzled. Like Snow, his forehead was burnt, but the lower half only; above it was pallid. He must have worn some kind of cap when exposed to the sun.

"Well, I'm listening," he said.

I had the impression that he did not care what I had to say to him. Standing there, tense, still pressed against the door panel, his attention was mainly directed to what was going on behind him.

Disconcerted, I hardly knew how to begin.

"My name is Kelvin," I said, "You must have heard about me. I am, or rather I was, a colleague of Gibarian's."

His thin face, entirely composed of vertical planes, exactly as I had always imagined Don Quixote's, was quite expressionless. This blank mask did not help me to find the right words.

"I heard that Gibarian was dead..." I broke off.

"Yes. Go on, I'm listening." His voice betrayed his impatience.

"Did he commit suicide? Who found the body, you or Snow?"

"Why ask me? Didn't Dr. Snow tell you what happened?"

"I wanted to hear your own account."

"You've studied psychology, haven't you, Dr. Kelvin?"

"Yes. What of it?"

"You think of yourself as a servant of science?"

"Yes, of course. What has that to do with..."

"You are not an officer of the law. At this hour of the day, you should be at work, but instead of doing the job you were sent here for, you not only threaten to force the door of my laboratory, you question me as though I were a criminal suspect."

His forehead was dripping with sweat. I controlled myself with an effort. I was determined to get through to him. I gritted my teeth and said:

"You *are* suspect, Dr. Sartorius. What is more, you're well aware of it!"

"Kelvin, unless you either retract or apologize, I shall lodge a complaint against you."

"Why should I apologize? You're the one who barricaded himself in this laboratory instead of coming out to meet me, instead of telling me the truth about what is going on here. Have you gone completely mad? What are you—a scientist, or a miserable coward?"

I don't know what other insults I hurled at him. He did not even flinch. Globules of sweat trickled down over the enlarged pores of his cheeks. Suddenly I realized that he had not heard a word I was saying. Both hands behind his back, he was holding the door in position with all his strength; it was rattling as though someone inside were firing bursts from a machine-gun at the panel.

In a strange, high-pitched voice, he moaned:

"Go away. For God's sake, leave me. Go downstairs, I'll join you later. I'll do whatever you want, only please go away now."

His voice betrayed such exhaustion that instinctively I put out my arms to help him control the door. At this, he uttered a cry of horror, as though I had pointed a knife at him. As I retreated, he was shouting in his falsetto voice: "Go away! Go away! I'm coming, I'm coming, I'm coming! No! No!" He opened the door and shot inside. I thought I saw a shining yellow disc flash across his chest.

Now a muffled clamor rose from the laboratory; a huge shadow appeared, as the curtain was brushed momentarily aside; then it fell back into place and I could see nothing more. What was happening inside that room? I heard running footsteps, as though a mad chase were in progress, followed by a terrifying crash of broken glass and the sound of a child's laugh.

My legs were trembling, and I stared at the door, appalled. The din had subsided, giving way to an uneasy silence. I sat down on a window ledge, too stunned to move; my head was splitting.

From where I was, I could see only a part of the corridor encircling the laboratory. I was at the summit of the Station, beneath the actual shell of the superstructure; the walls were concave and sloping, with oblong windows a few yards apart. The blue day was ending, and, as the shutters grated upwards, a blinding light shone through the thick glass. Every metal fitting, every latch and joint, blazed, and the great glass panel of the laboratory door glittered with pale coruscations. My hands looked grey in the spectral light. I noticed that I was holding the gas pistol; I had not realized that I had taken it out of its holster, and replaced it. What use could I have made of it—or even of a gamma pistol, had I one? I could hardly have taken the laboratory by force.

I got up. The disc of the sun, reminiscent of a hydrogen explosion, was sinking into the ocean, and as I descended the stairway I was pierced by a jet of horizontal rays which was almost tangible. Halfway downstairs I paused to think, then went back up the steps and followed the corridor round the laboratory. Soon, I came across a second glass door, exactly like the first; I made no attempt to open it, knowing that it would be locked.

I was looking for an opening or vent of some sort. The idea of spying on Sartorius had come to me quite naturally, without the least sense of shame. I was determined to have done with conjecture and discover the truth, even if, as I imagined it would, the truth proved imcomprehensible. It struck me that the laboratory must be lit from above by windows let into the dome. It should be possible, therefore, to spy on Sartorius from the outside. But first I should have to equip myself with an atmosphere-suit and oxygen gear.

When I reached the deck below, I found the door of the radio-cabin ajar. Snow sunk in hned sourly.

"Oh, really? Well, that's something. Has he got visitors?"

"I can't understand why you won't tell me what's going on," I retorted impulsively. "Since I have to remain here, I'm bound to find oufore, to

spy on Sartorius from the outside. But first I should have to equip myself with an atmosphere-suit and oxygen gear.

When I reached the deck below, I found the door of the radio-cabin ajar. Snow, sunk in ht the truth sooner or later. Why the mystery?"

"When you've received some visitors yourself, you'll understand."

I had the impression that my presence annoyed him and he had no desire to prolong the conversation.

I turned to go.

"Where are you off to?"

I did not answer.

The hangar-deck was just as I had left it. My burnt-out capsule still stood there, gaping open, on its platform. On my way to select an atmosphere-suit, I suddenly realized that the skylights through which I hoped to observe Sartorius would probably be made of slabs of opaque glass, and I lost interest in my venture onto the outer hull.

[*After conducting an elaborate experiment on a computer to test his sanity and to determine that he is not dreaming, Kelvin returns to his own room.*]

. . . Desperation and a sort of dumb rage had sustained me while working with the computer. Now, overcome with exhaustion, I could not even remember how to let down a mechanical bed. Forgetting to push back the clamps, I hung on the handle with all my weight and the mattress tumbled down on top of me.

I tore off my clothes and flung them away from me, then collapsed onto the pillow, without even taking the trouble to inflate it properly. I fell asleep with the lights on.

I reopened my eyes with the impression of having dozed off for only a few minutes. The room was bathed in a dim red light. It was cooler, and I felt refreshed.

I lay there, the bedclothes pushed back, completely naked. The curtains were half drawn, and there, opposite me, beside the window-pane lit by the red sun, someone was sitting. It was Rheya. She was wearing a white beach dress, the material stretched tightly over her breasts. She sat with her legs crossed; her feet were bare. Motionless, leaning on her sun-tanned arms, she gazed at me from beneath her black lashes: Rheya, with her dark hair brushed back. For a long time, I lay there peacefully gazing back at her. My first thought was reassuring: I was dreaming and I was aware that I was dreaming. Nevertheless, I would have preferred her not to be there. I closed my eyes and tried to shake off the dream. When I opened them again, Rheya was still sitting opposite me. Her lips were pouting slightly—a habit of hers—as though she were about to whistle; but her expression was serious. I thought of my recent speculations on the subject of dreams.

She had not changed since the day I had seen her for the last time; she was then a girl of nineteen. Today, she would be twenty-nine. But, evidently, the dead do not change; they remain eternally young. She went on gazing at me, an expression of surprise on her face. I thought of throwing something at her, but, even in a dream, I could not bring myself to harm a dead person.

I murmured: "Poor little thing, have you come to visit me?"

The sound of my voice frightened me; the room, Rheya, everything seemed extraordinarily real. A three-dimensional dream, colored in half-tones. . . . I saw several objects on the floor which I had not noticed when I went to bed. When I wake up, I told myself, I shall check whether these things are still there or whether, like Rheya, I only saw them in a dream.

"Do you mean to stay for long?" I asked. I realized that I was speaking very softly, like someone afraid of being overheard. Why worry about eavesdroppers in a dream?

The sun was rising over the horizon. A good sign. I had gone to bed during a red day, which should have been succeeded by a blue day, followed by another red day. I had not slept for fifteen hours at a stretch. So it *was* a dream!

Reassured, I looked closely at Rheya. She was silhouetted against the sun. The scarlet rays cast a glow over the smooth skin of her left cheek and the shadows of her eyelashes fell across her face. How pretty she was! Even in my sleep my memory of her was uncannily precise. I watched the movements of the sun, waiting to see the dimple appear in that unusual place slightly below the corner of the lips. All the same, I would have preferred to wake up. It was time I did some work. I closed my eyelids tightly.

I heard a metallic noise, and opened my eyes again. Rheya was sitting beside me on the bed, still looking at me gravely. I smiled at her. She smiled back at me and leant forward. We kissed. First a timid, childish kiss, then more prolonged ones. I held her for a long time. Was it possible to feel so much in a dream, I wondered. I was not betraying her memory, for it was of her that I was dreaming, only her.

It had never happened to me before. . . .

Was it then that I began to have doubts? I went on telling myself that it was a dream, but my heart tightened.

I tensed my muscles, ready to leap out of bed. I was half-expecting to fail, for often, in dreams, your sluggish body refuses to respond. I hoped that the effort would drag me out of sleep. But I did not wake; I sat on the edge of the bed, my legs dangling. There was nothing for it, I should have to endure this dream right to the bitter end. My feeling of well-being had vanished. I was afraid.

"What . . ." I asked. I cleared my throat. "What do you want?"

I felt around the floor with my bare feet, searching for a pair of slippers. I stubbed my toe against a sharp edge, and stifled a cry of pain. That'll wake me up, I thought with satisfaction, at the same time remembering that I had no slippers.

But still it went on. Rheya had drawn back and was leaning against the end of the bed. Her dress rose and fell lightly with her breathing. She watched me with quiet interest.

Quick, I thought, a shower! But then I realized that in a dream a shower would not interrupt my sleep.

"Where have you come from?"

She seized my hand and, with a gesture I knew well, threw it up and caught it again, then played with my fingers.

"I don't know," she replied. "Are you angry?"

It was her voice, that familiar, low-pitched, slightly faraway voice, that air of not caring much about what she was saying, of already being preoccupied with something else. People used to think her offhand, even rude, because the expression on her face rarely changed from one of vague astonishment.

"Did . . . did anyone see you?"

"I don't know. I got here without any trouble. Why, Kris, is it important?"

She was still playing with my fingers, but her face now wore a slight frown.

"Rheya."

"What, my darling?"

"How did you know where I was?"

She pondered. A broad smile revealed her teeth.

"I haven't the faintest idea. Isn't it funny? When I came in you were asleep. I didn't wake you up because you get cross so easily. You have a very bad temper."

She squeezed my hand.

"Did you go down below?"

"Yes. It was all frozen. I ran away."

She let go of my hand and lay back. With her hair falling to one side, she looked at me with the half-smile that had irritated me before it had captivated me.

"But, Rheya..." I stammered.

I leaned over her and turned back the short sleeve of her dress. There, just above her vaccination scar, was a red dot, the mark of a hypodermic needle. I was not really surprised, but my heart gave a lurch.

I touched the red spot with my finger. For years now I had dreamt of it, over and over again, always waking with a shudder to find myself in the same position, doubled up between the crumpled sheets—just as I had found *her,* already growing cold. It was as though, in my sleep, I tried to relive what she had gone through; as though I hoped to turn back the clock and ask her forgiveness, or keep her company during those final minutes when she was feeling the effects of the injection and was overcome by terror. She, who dreaded the least scratch, who hated pain or the sight of blood, had deliberately done this horrible thing, leaving nothing but a few scribbled words addressed to me. I had kept her note in my wallet. By now it was soiled and creased, but I had never had the heart to throw it away.

Time and time again I had imagined her tracing those words and making her final preparations. I persuaded myself that she had only been play-acting, that she had wanted to frighten me and had taken an overdose by mistake. Everyone told me that it must have happened like that, or else it had been a spontaneous decision, the result of a sudden depression. But people knew nothing of what I had said to her five days earlier; they did not know that, in order to twist the knife more cruelly, I had taken away my belongings and that she, as I was closing my suitcases, had said, very calmly: "I suppose you know what this means?" And I had pretended not to understand, even though I knew quite well what she meant; I thought her too much of a coward, and had even told her as much.... And now she was lying across the bed, looking at me attentively, as though she did not know that it was I who had killed her.

"Well?" she asked. Her eyes reflected the red sun. The entire room was red. Rheya looked at her arm with interest, because I had been examining it for so long, and when I drew back she laid her smooth, cool cheek in the palm of my hand.

"Rheya," I stammered, "it's not possible..."

"Hush!"

I could sense the movement of her eyes beneath their closed lids.

"Where are we, Rheya?"

"At home."

"Where's that?"

One eye opened and shut again instantly. The long lashes tickled my palm.

"Kris."

"What?"

"I'm happy."

Raising my head, I could see part of the bed in the washbasin mirror: a cascade of soft hair—Rheya's hair—and my bare knees. I pulled towards me with my foot one of the misshapen objects I had found in the box and picked it up with my free hand. It was a spindle, one end of which had melted to a needle-point. I held the point to my skin and dug it in, just beside a small pink scar. The pain shot through my whole body. I watched the blood run down the inside of my thigh and drip noiselessly onto the floor.

What was the use? Terrifying thoughts assailed me, thoughts which were taking a definite shape. I no longer told myself: "It's a dream." I had ceased to believe that. Now I was thinking: "I must be ready to defend myself."

I examined her shoulders, her hip under the close-fitting white dress, and her dangling naked feet. Leaning forward, I took hold of one of her ankles and ran my fingers over the sole of her foot.

The skin was soft, like that of a newborn child.

I knew then that it was not Rheya, and I was almost certain that she herself did not know it.

The bare foot wriggled and Rheya's lips parted in silent laughter.

"Stop it," she murmured.

Cautiously I withdrew my hand from under the cheek and stood up. Then I dressed quickly. She sat up and watched me.

"Where are your things?" I asked her. Immediately, I regretted my question.

"My things?"

"Don't you have anything except that dress?"

From now on, I would pursue the game with my eyes open. I tried to appear unconcerned, indifferent, as though we had parted only yesterday, as though we had never parted.

She stood up. With a familiar gesture, she tugged at her skirt to smooth out the creases. My words had worried her, but she said nothing. For the first time, she examined the room with an enquiring, scrutinizing gaze. Then, puzzled, she replied:

"I don't know." She opened the locker door. "In here, perhaps?"

"No, there's nothing but work-suits in there."

I found an electric point by the basin and began to shave, careful not to take my eyes off her.

She went to and fro, rummaging everywhere. Eventually, she came up to me and said:

"Kris, I have the feeling that something's happened. . . ."

She broke off. I unplugged the razor, and waited.

"I have the feeling that I've forgotten something," she went on, "that I've forgotten a lot of things. I can only remember you. I . . . I can't remember anything else."

I listened to her, forcing myself to look unconcerned.

"Have I... Have I been ill?" she asked.

"Yes... in a way. Yes, you've been slightly ill."

"There you are then. That explains my lapses of memory."

She had brightened up again. Never shall I be able to describe how I felt then. As I watched her moving about the room, now smiling, now serious, talkative one moment, silent the next, sitting down and then getting up again, my terror was gradually overcome by the conviction that it was the real Rheya there in the room with me, even though my reason told me that she seemed somehow stylized, reduced to certain characteristic expressions, gestures and movements.

Suddenly, she clung to me.

"What's happening to us, Kris?" She pressed her fists against my chest. "Is everything all right? Is there something wrong?"

"Things couldn't be better."

She smiled wanly.

"When you answer me like that, it means things could hardly be worse."

"What nonsense!" I said hurriedly. "Rheya, my darling, I must leave you. Wait here for me." And, because I was becoming extremely hungry, I added: "Would you like something to eat?"

"To eat?" She shook her head. "No. Will I have to wait long for you?"

"Only an hour."

"I'm coming with you."

"You can't come with me. I've got work to do."

"I'm coming with you."

She had changed. This was not Rheya at all; the real Rheya never imposed herself, would never have forced her presence on me.

"It's impossible, my sweet."

She looked me up and down. Then suddenly she seized my hand. And my hand lingered, moved up her warm, rounded arm. In spite of myself I was caressing her. My body recognized her body; my body desired her, my body was attracted towards hers beyond reason, beyond thought, beyond fear.

Desperately trying to remain calm, I repeated:

"Rheya, it's out of the question. You must stay here."

A single word echoed round the room:

"No."

"Why?"

"I . . . I don't know." She looked around her, then, once more, raised her eyes to mine. "I can't," she whispered.

"But why?"

"I don't know. I can't. It's as though... as though..."

She searched for the answer which, as she uttered it, seemed to come to her like a revelation. "It's as though I mustn't let you out of my sight."

The resolute tone of her voice scarcely suggested an avowal of affection; it implied something quite different. With this realization, the manner in which I was embracing Rheya underwent an abrupt, though not immediately noticeable, change.

I was holding her in my arms and gazing into her eyes.

Imperceptibly, almost instinctively, I began to pull her hands together behind her back at the same time searching the room with my eyes: I needed something with which to tie her hands.

Suddenly she jerked her elbows together, and there followed a powerful recoil. I resisted for barely a second. Thrown backwards and almost lifted off my feet, even had I been an athlete I could not have freed myself. Rheya straightened up and dropped her arms to her sides. Her face, lit by an uncertain smile, had played no part in the struggle.

She was gazing at me with the same calm interest as when I had first awakened—as though she was utterly unmoved by my desperate ploy, as though she was quite unaware that anything had happened, and had not noticed my sudden panic. She stood before me, waiting—grave, passive, mildly surprised.

Leaving Rheya in the middle of the room, I went over to the washbasin. I was a prisoner, caught in an absurd trap from which at all costs I was determined to escape. I would have been incapable of putting into words the meaning of what had happened or what was going through my mind; but now I realized that my situation was identical with that of the other inhabitants of the Station, that everything I had experienced, discovered or guessed at was part of a single whole, terrifying and incomprehensible. Meanwhile, I was racking my brain to think up some ruse, to work out some means of escape. Without turning round, I could feel Rheya's eyes following me. There was a medicine chest above the basin. Quickly I went through its contents, and found a bottle of sleeping pills. I shook out four tablets—the maximum dose—into a glass, and filled it with hot water. I made little effort to conceal my actions from Rheya. Why? I did not even bother to ask myself.

When the tablets had dissolved, I returned to Rheya, who was still standing in the same place.

"Are you angry with me?" she asked, in a low voice.

"No. Drink this."

Unconsciously, I had known all along that she would obey me. She took the glass without a word and drank the scalding mixture in one gulp. Putting down the empty glass on a stool, I went and sat in a chair in the corner of the room.

Rheya joined me, squatting on the floor in her accustomed manner with her legs folded under her, and tossing back her hair. I was no longer under any illusion: this was not Rheya—and yet I recognized her every habitual gesture. Horror gripped me by the throat; and what was most horrible was that I must go on tricking her, pretending to take her for Rheya, while she herself sincerely believed that she *was* Rheya—of that I was certain, if one could be certain of anything any longer.

She was leaning against my knees, her hair brushing my hand. We remained thus for some while. From time to time, I glanced at my watch. Half an hour went by; the sleeping tablets should have started to work. Rheya murmured something.

"What did you say?"

There was no reply.

Although I attributed her silence to the onset of sleep, secretly I doubted the effectiveness of the pills. Once again, I did not ask myself why. Perhaps it was because my subterfuge seemed too simple.

Slowly her head slid across my knees, her dark hair falling over her face. Her breathing grew deeper and more regular; she was asleep. I stooped in order to lift her onto the bed. As I did so, her eyes opened; she put her arms round my neck and burst into shrill laughter.

I was dumbfounded. Rheya could hardly contain her mirth. With an expression that was at once ingenuous and sly, she observed me through half-closed eyelids. I sat down again, tense, stupefied, at a loss. With a final burst of laughter, she snuggled against my legs.

In an expressionless voice, I asked:

"Why are you laughing?"

Once again, a look of anxiety and surprise came over her face. It was clear that she wanted to give me an honest explanation. She sighed, and rubbed her nose like a child.

"I don't know," she said at last, with genuine puzzlement. "I'm behaving like an idiot, aren't I? But so are you . . . you look idiotic, all stiff and pompous like . . . like Pelvis."

I could hardly believe my ears.

"Like who?"

"Like Pelvis. You know who I mean, that fat man. . . ."

Rheya could not possibly have known Pelvis, or even heard me mention him, for the simple reason that he had returned from an expedition three years after her death. I had not known him previously and was therefore unaware of his inveterate habit, when presiding over meetings at the Institute, of letting sessions drag on indefinitely. Moreover, his name was Pelle Villis and until his return I did not know that he had been nicknamed Pelvis.

Rheya leaned her elbows on my knees and looked me in the eyes.

I put out my hand and stroked her arms, her shoulders and the base of her bare neck, which pulsed beneath my fingers. While it looked as though I was caressing her (and indeed, judging by her expression, that was how she interpreted the touch of my hands) in reality I was verifying once again that her body was warm to the touch, an ordinary human body, with muscles, bones, joints. Gazing calmly into her eyes, I felt a hideous desire to tighten my grip.

Suddenly I remembered Snow's bloodstained hands, and let go.

"How you stare at me," Rheya said, placidly.

[*Kelvin tricks Rheya into entering a shuttle craft, which he sends into indefinite orbit around Solaris. Returning to his room he encounters Snow. Snow informs him that he and Sartorius also have "visitors" and that Gibrarian had one as well. Kelvin tells Snow of Rheya's suicide.*]

... Seeing that I was upset, he added, hastily: "No, no, you still don't understand. Of course it's a terrible burden to carry around, and you must feel like a murderer, but... there are worse things."

"Oh, really?"

"Yes, really. And I'm almost glad that you refuse to believe me. Certain events, which have actually happened, are horrible, but what is more horrible still is what hasn't happened, what has never existed."

"What are you saying?" I asked, my voice faltering.

He shook his head from side to side.

"A normal man," he said. "What is a normal man? A man who has never commited a disgraceful act? Maybe, but has he never had uncontrollable thoughts? Perhaps he hasn't. But perhaps something, a phantasm, rose up from somewhere within him, ten or thirty years ago, something which he suppressed and then forgot about, which he doesn't fear since he knows he will never allow it to develop and so lead to any action on his part. And now, suddenly, in broad daylight, he comes across this thing ... this thought, embodied, riveted to him, indestructible. He wonders where he is ... Do you know where he is?"

"Where?"

"Here," whispered Snow, "on Solaris."

"But what does it mean? After all, you and Sartorius aren't criminals. ..."

"And you call yourself a psychologist, Kelvin! Who hasn't had, at some moment in his life, a crazy daydream, an obsession? Imagine... imagine a fetishist who becomes infatuated with, let's say, a grubby piece of cloth, and who threatens and entreats and defies every risk in order to acquire this beloved bit of rag. A peculiar idea, isn't it? A man who at one and the same time is ashamed of the object of his desire and cherishes it above everything else, a man who is ready to sacrifice his life for his love, since the feeling he has for it is perhaps as overwhelming as Romeo's feeling for Juliet. Such cases exist, as you know. So, in the same way, there are things, situations, that no one has dared to externalize, but which the mind has produced by accident in a moment of aberration, of madness—call it what you will. At the next stage, the idea becomes flesh and blood. That's all."

Stupefied, my mouth dry, I repeated:

"That's all?" My head was spinning. "And what about the Station? What has it got to do with the Station?"

"It's almost as if you're purposely refusing to understand," he groaned. "I've been talking about Solaris the whole time, solely about Solaris. If the truth is hard to swallow, it's not my fault. Anyhow, after what you've already been through, you ought to be able to hear me out! We take off into the cosmos, ready for anything: for solitude, for hardship, for exhaustion, death. Modesty forbids us to say so, but there are times when we think pretty well of ourselves. And yet, if we examine it more closely, our enthusiasm turns out to be all sham. We don't want to conquer the cosmos, we simply want to extend the boundaries of Earth to the frontiers of the cosmos. For us, such and such a planet is as arid as the Sahara, another as frozen as the North Pole, yet another as lush as the Amazon basin. We are humanitarian and chivalrous; we don't want to enslave other races, we simply want to bequeath them our values and take over their heritage in exchange. We think of ourselves as the Knights of the Holy Contact. This is another lie. We are only seeking Man. We have no need of other worlds. We need mirrors. We don't know what to do with other worlds. A single world, our own, suffices us; but we can't accept it for what it is. We are searching for an ideal image of our own world: we go in quest of a planet, of a civilization superior to our own but developed on the basis of a prototype of our primeval past. At the same time, there is something inside us which we don't like to face up to, from which we try to protect ourselves, but which nevertheless remains, since we don't leave Earth in a state of primal innocence. We arrive here as we are in reality, and when the page is turned and that reality is revealed to us—that part of our reality which we would prefer to pass over in silence—then we don't like it any more."

[*An hour or so later, without explanation and apparently without memory of being sent into orbit in the shuttle craft, Rheya (or her duplicate) returns. Kelvin acts as though he never tried to get rid of her.*]

. . . I was lying on my back, with Rheya's head resting on my shoulder.

The darkness was peopled now. I could hear footsteps. Something was piling up above me, higher and higher, infinitely high. The night transfixed me; the night took possession of me, enveloped and penetrated me, impalpable, insubstantial. Turned to stone, I had ceased breathing, there was no air to breathe. As though from a distance, I heard the beating of my heart. I summoned up all my remaining strength, straining every nerve, and waited for death. I went on waiting . . . I seemed to be growing smaller, and the invisible sky, horizonless, the formless immensity of space, without clouds, without stars, receded, extended and grew bigger all round me. I tried to crawl out of bed, but there was no bed; beneath the cover of darkness there was a void. I pressed my hands to my face. I no longer had any fingers or any hands. I wanted to scream...

The room floated in a blue penumbra, which outlined the furniture and the laden bookshelves, and drained everything of color. A pearly whiteness flooded the window.

I was drenched with sweat. I glanced to one side. Rheya was gazing at me.

She raised her head.

"Has your arm gone to sleep?"

Her eyes too had been drained of color; they were grey, but luminous, beneath the black lashes.

"What?" Her murmured words had seemed like a caress even before I understood their meaning. "No. Ah, yes!" I said, at last.

I put my hand on her shoulder; I had pins and needles in my fingers.

"Did you have a bad dream?" she asked.

I drew her to me with my other hand.

"A dream? Yes, I was dreaming. And you, didn't you sleep?"

"I don't know. I don't think so. I'm sleepy. But that mustn't stop you from sleeping... Why are you looking at me like that?"

I closed my eyes. Her heart was beating against mine. Her heart? A mere appendage, I told myself. But nothing surprised me any longer, not even my own indifference. I had crossed the frontiers of fear and despair. I had come a long way—further than anyone had ever come before.

I raised myself on my elbow. Daybreak . . . and the peace that comes with dawn? A silent storm had set the cloudless horizon ablaze. A streak of light, the first ray of the blue sun, penetrated the room and broke up into sharp-edged reflections; there was a crossfire of sparks, which coruscated off the mirror, the door handles, the nickel pipes. The light scattered, falling onto every smooth surface as though it wanted to conquer ever more space, to set the room alight. I looked at Rheya; the pupils of her grey eyes had contracted.

She asked in an expressionless voice, "Is the night over already?"

"Night never lasts long here."

"And us?"

"What about us?"

"Are we going to stay here long?"

Coming from her, the question had its comic side; but when I spoke, my voice held no trace of gaiety.

"Quite a long time, probably. Why, don't you want to stay here?"

Her eyes did not blink. She was looking at me inquiringly. Did I see her blink? I was not sure. She drew back the blanket and I saw the little pink scar on her arm.

"Why are you looking at me like that?"

"Because you're very beautiful."

She smiled, without a trace of mischief, modestly acknowledging my compliment.

"Really? It's as though . . . as though . . ."

"What?"

"As though you were doubtful of something."

"What nonsense!"

"As though you didn't trust me and I were hiding something from you . . ."

"Rubbish!"

"By the way you're denying it, I can tell I'm right."

The light became blinding. Shading my eyes with my hand, I looked for my dark glasses. They were on the table. When I was back by her side, Rheya smiled.

"What about me?"

It took a minute to understand what she meant.

"Dark glasses?"

I got up and began to hunt through drawers and shelves, pushing aside books and instruments. I found two pairs of glasses, which I gave to Rheya. They were too big; they fell halfway down her nose.

The shutters slid over the window; it was dark once more. Groping, I helped Rheya remove her glasses and put both pairs down under the bed.

"What shall we do now?" she asked.

"At night-time, one sleeps!"

"Kris . . ."

"Yes?"

"Do you want a compress for your forehead?"

"No, thanks. Thank you . . . my darling."

I don't know why I had added those two words. In the darkness, I took her by her graceful shoulders. I felt them tremble, and I knew, without the least shadow of doubt, that I held Rheya in my arms. Or rather, I understood in that moment that she was not trying to deceive me; it was I who was deceiving her, since she sincerely believed herself to be Rheya.

I dropped off several times after that, and each time an anguished start jolted me awake. Panting, exhausted, I pressed myself closer to her; my heart gradually growing calmer. She touched me cautiously on the cheeks and forehead with the tips of her fingers, to see whether or not I was feverish. It was Rheya, the real Rheya, the one and only Rheya.

A change came over me; I ceased to struggle and almost at once I fell asleep.

I was awakened by an agreeable sensation of coolness. My face was covered by a damp cloth. I pulled it off and found Rheya leaning over me. She was smiling and squeezing out a second cloth over a bowl.

"What a sleep!" she said, laying another compress on my forehead. "Are you ill?"

"No."

I wrinkled my forehead; the skin was supple once again. Rheya sat on the edge of my bed, her black hair brushed back over the collar of a bathrobe—a man's bathrobe, with orange and black stripes, the sleeves turned back to the elbow.

I was terribly hungry; it was at least twenty hours since my last meal. When Rheya had finished her ministrations I got up. Two dresses, draped over the back of a chair caught my eye—two absolutely identical white dresses, each decorated with a row of red buttons. I myself had helped Rheya out of one of them, and she had reappeared, yesterday evening, dressed in the second.

She followed my glance.

"I had to cut the seam open with scissors," she said. "I think the zip fastener must have got stuck."

The sight of the two identical dresses filled me with a horror which exceeded anything I had felt hitherto. Rheya was busy tidying up the medicine chest. I turned my back and bit my knuckles. Unable to take my eyes off the two dresses—or rather the original dress and its double—I backed towards the door. The basin tap was running noisily. I opened the door and, slipping out of the room, cautiously closed it behind me. I heard the sound of running water, the clinking of bottles; then, suddenly, all sound ceased. I waited, my jaw clenched, my hands gripping the door handle, but with little hope of holding it shut. It was nearly torn from my grasp by a savage jerk. But the door did not open; it shook and vibrated from top to bottom. Dazed, I let go of the handle and stepped back. The panel, made of some plastic material, caved in as though an invisible person at my side had tried to break into the room. The steel frame bent further and further inwards and the paint was cracking. Suddenly I understood: instead of pushing the door, which opened outwards, Rheya was trying to open it by pulling it towards her. The reflection of the lighting strip in the ceiling was distorted in the white-painted door-panel; there was a resounding crack and the panel, forced beyond its limits, gave way. Simultaneously the handle vanished, torn from its mounting. Two bloodstained hands appeared, thrusting through the opening and smearing the white paint with blood. The door split in two, the broken halves hanging askew on their hinges. First a face appeared, deathly pale, then a wild-looking apparition, dressed in an orange and black bathrobe, flung itself sobbing upon my chest.

I wanted to escape, but it was too late, and I was rooted to the spot. Rheya was breathing convulsively, her dishevelled head drumming against my chest. Before I could put my arms round to hold her up, Rheya collapsed.

Avoiding the ragged edges of the broken panel, I carried her into the room and laid her on the bed. Her fintertips were grazed and the nails torn. When her hands turned upwards, I saw that the palms were cut to the bone. I examined her face; her glazed eyes showed no sign of recognition.

"Rheya."

The only answer was an inarticulate groan.

I went over to the medicine chest. The bed creaked; I turned round; Rheya was sitting up, looking at her bleeding hands with astonishment.

"Kris," she sobbed, "I... I... what happened to me?"

"You hurt yourself trying to break down the door," I answered curtly.

My lips were twitching convulsively, and I had to bite the lower one to keep it under control.

Rheya's glance took in the pieces of door-panel hanging from the steel frame, then she turned her eyes back towards me. She was doing her best to hide her terror, but I could see her chin trembling.

I cut off some squares of gauze, picked up a pot of antiseptic powder and returned to the bedside. The glass jar slipped through my hands and shattered—but I no longer needed it.

I lifted one of Rheya's hands. The nails, still surrounded by traces of clotted blood, had regrown. There was a pink scar in the hollow of her palm, but even this scar was healing, disappearing in front of my eyes.

I sat beside her and stroked her face, trying to smile without much success.

"What did you do that for, Rheya?"

"I did... that?"

With her eyes, she indicated the door.

"Yes... Don't you remember?"

"No . . . that is, I saw you weren't there, I was very frightened, and ..."

"And what?"

"I looked for you. I thought perhaps you were in the bathroom . . ."

Only then did I notice that the sliding door covering the entrance to the bathroom had been pushed back.

"And then?"

"I ran to the door."

"And after that?"

"I can't remember . . . Something must have happened . . ."

"What?"

"I don't know."

"What do you remember?"

"I was sitting here, on the bed."

She swung her legs over the edge of the bed, got up and went over to the shattered door.

"Kris!"

Walking up behind her, I took her by the shoulders; she was shaking. She suddenly turned and whispered:

"Kris, Kris . . ."

"Calm yourself!"

"Kris, if it's me . . . Kris, am I an epileptic?"

"What an extraordinary idea, my sweet! The doors in this place are rather special . . ."

[*Kelvin examines Rheya's blood in the laboratory.*]

. . . I pulled the big black hood round the eye-piece of the microscope towards me, and leaned my forehead against the resilient foam-rubber viewer. I could hear Rheya's voice, but without taking in what she was saying. Beneath my gaze, sharply foreshortened, was a vast desert flooded with silvery light, and strewn with rounded boulders—red corpuscles—which trembled and wriggled behind a veil of mist. I focused the eye-piece and penetrated further into the depths of the silvery landscape. Without taking my eyes away from the viewer, I turned the view-finder; when a boulder, a single corpuscle, detached itself and appeared at the junction of the cross-hairs, I enlarged the image. The lens had apparently picked up a deformed erythrocyte, sunken in the center, whose uneven edges projected sharp shadows over the depths of a circular crater. The crater, bristling with silver ion deposits, extended beyond the microscope's field of vision. The nebulous outlines of threads of albumen, distorted and atrophied, appeared in the midst of an opalescent liquid. A worm of albumen twisted and turned beneath the cross-hairs of the lens. Gradually I increased the enlargement. At any moment, I should reach the limit of this exploration of the depths; the shadow of a molecule occupied the whole of the space; then the image became fuzzy.

There was nothing to be seen. There should have been the ferment of a quivering cloud of atoms, but I saw nothing. A dazzling light filled the screen, which was flawlessly clear. I pushed the lever to its utmost. The angry, whirring noise grew louder, but the screen remained a blank. An alarm signal sounded once, then was repeated; the circuit was overloaded. I took a final look at the silvery desert, then I cut the current.

I looked at Rheya. She was in the middle of a yawn which she changed adroitly into a smile.

"Am I in good health?" she asked.

"Excellent. Couldn't be better."

I continued to look at her and once more I felt as though something was crawling along my lower lip. What had happened exactly? What was the meaning of it? Was this body, frail and weak in appearance but indestructible in reality, actually made of nothing? I gave the microscope cylinder a blow with my fist. Was the instrument out of order? No, I knew that it was working perfectly. I had followed the procedure faithfully: first the cells, then the albumen, then the molecules; and everything was just as I was accustomed to seeing it in the course of examining thousands of slides. But the final step, into the heart of the matter, had taken me nowhere.

I put a ligature on Rheya, took some blood from a median vein and transferred it to a graduated glass, then divided it between several test-tubes and began the analyses. These took longer than usual; I was rather out of practice. The reactions were normal, every one of them.

I dropped some congealed acid onto a coral-tinted pearl. Smoke. The blood turned grey and a dirty foam rose to the surface. Disintegration, decomposition, faster and faster! I turned my back to get another test-tube; when I looked again at the experiment, I nearly dropped the slim glass phial.

Beneath the skin of dirty foam, a dark coral was rising. The blood, destroyed by the acid, was re-creating itself. It was crazy, impossible!

[*Kelvin shares his findings by video with Snow and Sartorius and theorizes that the "visitors" are made up of neutrinos. Snow and Sartorius agree that this is plausible. The three also agree to meet together before long to discuss possible solutions to their predicament.*]

. . . I woke up in the middle of the night to find the light on and Rheya crouched at the end of the bed, wrapped in a sheet, her shoulders shaking with silent tears. I called her name and asked her what was wrong, but she only curled up tighter.

Still half asleep, and barely emerged from the nightmare which had been tormenting me only a moment before, I pulled myself up to a sitting position and shielded my eyes against the glare to look at her. The trembling continued, and I stretched out my arms, but Rheya pushed me away and hid her face.

"Rheya . . ."

"Don't talk to me!"

"Rheya, what's the matter?"

I caught a glimpse of her tear-stained face, contorted with emotion. The big childish tears streamed down her face, glistened in the dimple above her chin and fell onto the sheets.

"You don't want me."

"What are you talking about?"

"I heard . . ."

My jaw tightened: "Heard what? You don't understand . . ."

"Yes I do. You said I wasn't Rheya. You wanted me to go, and I would, I really would . . . but I can't. I don't know why. I've tried to go, but I couldn't do it. I'm such a coward."

"Come on now. . . ." I put my arms round her and held her with all my strength. Nothing mattered to me except her: everything else was meaningless. I kissed her hands, talked, begged, excused myself and made promise after promise, saying that she had been having some silly, terrible dream. Gradually she grew calmer, and at last she stopped crying and her eyes glazed, like a woman walking in her sleep. She turned her face away from me.

"No," she said at last, "be quiet, don't talk like that. It's no good, you're not the same person any more." I started to protest, but she went on: "No, you don't want me. I knew it before, but I pretended not to notice. I thought perhaps I was imagining everything, but it was true . . . you've changed. You're not being honest with me. You talk about dreams, but it was you who were dreaming, and it was to do with me. You spoke my name as if it repelled you. Why? Just tell me why."

"Rheya, my little. . . ."

"I won't have you talking to me like that, do you hear? I won't let you. I'm not your little anything, I'm not a child. I'm. . . ."

She burst into tears and buried her face in the pillow. I got up. The ventilation hummed quietly. It was cold, and I pulled a dressing-gown over my shoulders before sitting next to her and taking her arm: "Listen to me, I'm going to tell you something. I'm going to tell you the truth."

She pushed herself upright again. I could see the veins throbbing beneath the delicate skin of her neck. My jaw tightened once more. The air seemed to be colder still, and my head was completely empty.

"The truth?" she said. "Word of honor?"

I opened my mouth to speak, but no sound came. "Word of honor" . . . it was our special catch-phrase, our old way of making an unconditional promise. Once these words had been spoken, neither of us was permitted to lie, or even to take refuge behind a half-truth. I remembered the period when we used to torture each other in an exaggerated striving for sincerity, convinced that this ingenuous honesty was the precondition of our relationship.

"Word of honor, Rheya," I answered gravely, and she waited for me to continue. "You have changed too—we all change. But that is not what I wanted to say. For some reason that neither of us understands, it seems that... you are forced to stay near me. And that's fine with me, because I can't leave you either..."

"No, Kris. The change is not in you," Rheya whispered. "It's me. Something is wrong. Perhaps it has to do with the accident?"

She looked at the dark, empty rectangle of the door. The previous evening, I had removed the shattered remains—a new one would have to be fitted. Another thought struck me:

"Have you been managing to sleep?"

"I don't know."

"What do you mean?"

"I have dreams . . . I don't know whether they really are dreams. Perhaps I'm ill. I lie there and think, and..."

"What?"

"I have strange thoughts. I don't know where they come from."

It took all my self-control to steady my voice and tell her to go on, and I found myself tensing for her answer as if for a blow in the face.

"They are thoughts . . ." She shook her head helplessly. ". . . all around me."

"I don't understand."

"I get a feeling as if they were not from inside myself, but somewhere further away. I can't explain it, can't put words to it..."

I broke in almost involuntarily: "It must be some kind of dream." Then, back in control again: "And now, we put the light out and we forget our problems until morning. Tomorrow we can invent some new ones if you like. Ok?"

She pressed the switch, and darkness fell between us. Stretched out on the bed, I felt her warm breathing beside me, and put my arms round her.

"Harder!" she whispered, and then, after a long pause:

"Kris!"

"What?"

"I love you."

I almost screamed.

In the red morning, the sun's swollen disc was rising over the horizon.

An envelope lay in the doorway, and I tore it open. I could hear

Rheya humming to herself in the bath, and from time to time she looked into the room and I would see her face, half hidden by her wet hair.

I went to the window, and read:

"Kelvin, things are looking up. Sartorius had decided that it may be possible to use some form of energy to destabilize the neutrino structure. He wants to examine some Phi plasma in orbit. He suggests that you make a reconnaissance flight and take a certain quantity of plasma in the capsule. It's up to you, but let me know what you decide. I have no opinion. I feel as if I no longer have anything. If I am more in favor of your going, it's because we would at least be making some show of progress. Otherwise, we can only envy G.

Snow

P.S. All I ask is for you to stay outside the cabin. You can call me on the videophone."

I felt a stir of apprehension as I read the letter, and went over it again carefully before tearing it up and throwing the pieces into the disposal unit.

I went through the same terrible charade that I had begun the previous day, and made up a story for Rheya's benefit. She did not notice the deception, and when I told her that I had to make an inspection and suggested that she come with me she was delighted. We stopped at the kitchen for breakfast—Rheya ate very little—and then made for the library.

Before venturing on the mission suggested by Sartorius, I wanted to glance through the literature dealing with magnetic fields and neutrino structures. I did not yet have any clear idea of how I would set about it, but I had made up my mind to make an independent check on Sartorius's activities. Not that I would prevent Snow and Sartorius from "liberating" themselves when the annihilator was completed: I meant to take Rheya out of the Station and wait for the conclusion of the operation in the cabin of an aircraft. I set to work with the automatic librarian. Sometimes it answered my queries by ejecting a card with the laconic inscription "Not on file," sometimes it practically submerged me under such a spate of specialist physics textbooks that I hesitated to use its advice. Yet I had no desire to leave the big circular chamber. I felt at ease in my egg, among the rows of cabinets crammed with tape and microfilm. Situated right at the center of the Station, the library had no windows: It was the most isolated area in the great steel shell, and made me feel relaxed in spite of finding my researches held up.

Wandering across the vast room, I stopped at a set of shelves as high as the ceiling, and holding about six hundred volumes—all classics on the history of Solaris, starting with the nine volumes of Giese's monumental and already relatively obsolescent monograph. Display for its own sake was improbable in these surroundings. The collection was a respectful tribute to the memory of the pioneers. I took down the massive volumes of Giese and sat leafing through them. Rheya had also located some reading matter. Looking over her shoulder, I saw that she had picked one of the many books brought out by the first expedition, the *Interplanetary Cookery Book,* which could have been the personal property of Giese himself. She was poring over the recipes adapted to the arduous conditions of interstellar flight. I said nothing, and returned to the book resting on my knees. *Solaris—Ten Years of Exploration* had appeared as volumes 4-12 of the Solariana collection, whose most recent additions were numbered in the thousands.

Giese was an unemotional man, but then in the study of Solaris emotion is a hindrance to the explorer. Imagination and premature theorizing are positive disadvantages in approaching a planet where—as has become clear—anything is possible. It is almost certain that the unlikely descriptions of the "plasmatic" metamorphoses of the ocean are faithful accounts of the phenomena observed, although these descriptions are unverifiable, since the ocean seldom repeats itself. The freakish character and gigantic scale of these phenomena go too far outside the experience of man to be grasped by anybody observing them for the first time, and who would consider analogous occurrences as "sports of nature," accidental manifestations of blind forces, if he saw them on a reduced scale, say in a mud-volcano on Earth?

Genius and mediocrity alike are dumbfounded by the teeming diversity of the oceanic formations of Solaris; no man has ever become genuinely conversant with them. Giese was by no means a mediocrity, nor was he a genius. He was a scholarly classifier, the type whose compulsive application to their work utterly divorces them from the pressures of everyday life. Giese devised a plain descriptive terminology, supplemented by terms of his own invention, and although these were inadequate, and sometimes clumsy, it has to be admitted that no semantic system is as yet available to illustrate the behavior of the ocean. The *tree-mountains, extensors, fungoids, mimoids, symmetriads* and *asymmetriads, vertebrids* and *agilus* are artificial, linguistically awkward terms, but they do give some impression of Solaris to anyone who has only seen the planet in blurred photographs and incomplete films. The fact is that in spite of his cautious nature the scrupulous Giese more than once jumped to premature conclusions. Even when on their guard, human beings inevitably theorize. Giese, who thought himself immune to temptation, decided that the "extensors" came into the category of basic forms. He compared them to accumulations of gigantic waves, similar to the tidal movements of our Terran oceans. In the first edition of his work, we find them originally named as "tides." This geocentrism might be considered amusing if it did not underline the dilemma in which he found himself.

As soon as the question of comparisons with Earth arises, it must be understood that the "extensors" are formations that dwarf the Grand Canyon, that they are produced in a substance which externally resembles a yeasty colloid (during this fantastic "fermentation," the yeast sets into festoons of starched open-work lace; some experts refer to "ossified tumors"), and that deeper down the substance becomes increasingly resistant, like a tensed muscle which fifty feet below the surface is as hard as rock but retains its flexibility. The extensor appears to be an independent creation, stretching for miles between membranous walls swollen with "ossified growths," like some colossal python which after swallowing a mountain is sluggishly digesting the meal, while a slow shudder occasionally ripples along its creeping body. The extensor only looks like a lethargic reptile from overhead. At close quarters, when the two "canyon walls" loom hundreds of yards above the exploring aircraft, it can be seen that this inflated cylinder, reaching from one side of the horizon to the other, is bewilderingly alive with movement. First you notice the continual rotating motion of a greyish-green, oily sludge which reflects blinding sunlight, but skimming just above the "back of the python" (the "ravine" sheltering the extensor now resembles the sides of a geological fault), you realize that the motion is in fact far more complex, and consists of concentric fluctuations traversed by darker currents. Occasionally this mantle turns into a shining crust that reflects sky and clouds and then is riddled by explosive eruptions of the internal gases and fluids. The observer slowly realizes that he is looking at the guiding forces that are thrusting outward and upward the two gradually crystallizing gelatinous walls. Science does not accept the obvious without further proof, however, and virulent controversies have reverberated down the years on the key question of the exact sequence of events in the interior of the extensors that furrow the vast living ocean in their millions.

Various organic functions have been ascribed to the extensors. Some experts have argued that their purpose is the transformation of matter; others suggested respiratory processes; still others claimed that they conveyed alimentary materials. An infinite variety of hypotheses now moulder in library basements, eliminated by ingenious, sometimes dangerous experiments. Today, the scientists will go no further than to refer to the extensors as relatively simple, stable formations whose duration is measurable in weeks—an exceptional characteristic among the recorded phenomena of the planet.

The "mimoid" formations are considerably more complex and bizarre, and elicit a more vehement response from the observer—an instinctive response, I mean. It can be stated without exaggeration that Giese fell in love with the mimoids and was soon devoting all his time to them. For the rest of his life, he studied and described them and brought all his ingenuity to bear on defining their nature. The name he gave them indicates their most astonishing characteristic, the imitation of objects, near or far, external to the ocean itself.

Concealed at first beneath the ocean surface, a large flattened disc appears, ragged, with a tar-like coating. After a few hours, it begins to separate into flat sheets which rise slowly. The observer now becomes a spectator at what looks like a fight to the death, as massed ranks of waves converge from all directions like contorted, fleshy mouths which snap greedily around the tattered, fluttering leaf, then plunge into the depths. As each ring of waves breaks and sinks, the fall of this mass of hundreds of thousands of tons is accompanied for an instant by a viscous rumbling, an immense thunderclap. The tarry leaf is overwhelmed, battered and torn apart; with every fresh assault, circular fragments scatter and drift like feebly fluttering wings below the ocean surface. They bunch into pear-shaped clusters or long strings, merge and rise again, and drag with them an undertow of coagulated shreds of the base of the primal disc. The encircling waves continue to break around the steadily expanding crater. This phenomenon may persist for a day or linger on for a month, and sometimes there are no further developments. The conscientious Giese dubbed his first variation a "stillbirth," convinced that each of these upheavals aspired towards an ultimate condition, the "major mimoid," like a polyp colony (only covering an area greater than a town) of pale outcroppings with the faculty of imitating foreign bodies. Uyvens, on the other hand, saw this final stage as constituting a degeneration or necrosis: according to him, the appearance of the "copies" corresponded to a localized dissipation of the life energies of the ocean, which was no longer in control of the original forms it created.

Giese would not abandon his account of the various phases of the process as a sustained progression towards perfection, with a conviction which is particularly surprising coming from a man of such a moderate, cautious turn of mind in advancing the most trivial hypothesis on the other creations of the ocean. Normally he had all the boldness of an ant crawling up a glacier.

Viewed from above, the mimoid resembles a town, an illusion produced by our compulsion to superimpose analogies with what we know. When the sky is clear, a shimmering heat-haze covers the pliant structures of the clustered polyps surmounted by membranous palisades. The first cloud passing overhead wakens the mimoid. All the outcrops suddenly sprout new shoots, then the mass of polyps ejects a thick tegument which dilates, puffs out, changes color and in the space of a few minutes has produced an astonishing imitation of the volutes of a cloud. The enormous "object" casts a reddish shadow over the mimoid, whose peaks ripple and bend together, always in the opposite direction to the movement of the real cloud. I imagine that Giese would have been ready to give his right hand to discover what made the mimoids behave in this way, but these "isolated" productions are nothing in comparison to the frantic activity the mimoid displays when "stimulated" by objects of human origin.

The reproduction process embraces every object inside a radius of eight or nine miles. Usually the facsimile is an enlargement of the original, whose forms are sometimes only roughly copied. The reproduction of machines, in particular, elicits simplifications that might be considered grotesque—practically caricatures. The copy is always modelled in the same colorless tegument, which hovers above the outcrops, linked to its base by flimsy umbilical cords; it slides, creeps, curls back on itself, shrinks or swells and finally assumes the most complicated forms. An aircraft, a net or a pole are all reproduced at the same speed. The mimoid is not stimulated by human beings themselves, and in fact it does not react to any living matter, and has never copied, for example, the plants imported for experimental purposes. On the other hand, it will readily reproduce a puppet or a doll, a carving of a dog, or a tree sculptured in any material.

The observer must bear in mind that the "obedience" of the mimoid does not constitute evidence of cooperation, since it is not consistent. The most highly evolved mimoid has its off-days, when it "lives" in slow-motion, or its pulsation weakens. (This pulsation is invisible to the naked eye, and was only discovered after close examination of rapid-motion film of the mimoid, which revealed that each "beat" took two hours.)

During these "off-days," it is easy to explore the mimoid, especially if it is old, for the base anchored in the ocean, like the protuberances growing out of it, is relatively solid, and provides a firm footing for a man. It is equally possible to remain inside the mimoid during periods of activity, except that visibility is close to nil because of the whitish colloidal dust continually emitted through tears in the tegument above. In any case, at close range it is impossible to distinguish what forms the tegument is assuming, on account of their vast size—the smallest "copy" is the size of a mountain. In addition, a thick layer of colloidal snow quickly covers the base of the mimoid: this spongy carpet takes several hours to solidify (the "frozen" crust will take the weight of a man, though its composition is much lighter than pumice stone). The problem is that without special equipment there is a risk of being lost in the maze of tangled structures and crevasses, sometimes reminiscent of jumbled colonnades, sometimes of petrified geysers. Even in daylight it is easy to lose one's direction, for the sun's rays cannot pierce the white ceiling ejected into the atmosphere by the "imitative explosions."

On gala days (for the scientist as well as for the mimoid), an unforgettable spectacle develops as the mimoid goes into hyperproduction and performs wild flights of fancy. It plays variations on the theme of a given object and embroiders "formal extensions" that amuse it for hours on end, to the delight of the non-figurative artist and the despair of the scientist, who is at a loss to grasp any common theme in the performance. The mimoid can produce "primitive" simplifications, but is just as likely to indulge in "baroque" deviations, paroxysms of extravagant brilliance. Old mimoids tend to manufacture extremely comic forms. Looking at the photographs, I have never been moved to laughter; the riddle they set is too disquieting to be funny.

During the early years of exploration, the scientists literally threw themselves upon the mimoids, which were spoken of as open windows on the ocean and the best opportunity to establish the hoped-for contact between the two civilizations. They were soon forced to admit that there was not the slightest prospect of communication, and that the entire process began and ended with the reproduction of forms. The mimoids were a dead end.

Giving way to the temptations of a latent anthropomorphism or zoomorphism, there were many schools of thought which saw various other oceanic formations as "sensory organs," even as "limbs," which was how expert like Maartens and Ekkonai classified Giese's "vertebrids" and "agilus" for a time. Anyone who is rash enough to see protuberances that reach as far as two miles into the atmosphere as limbs, might just as well claim that earthquakes are the gymnastics of the Earth's crust!

Three hundred chapters of Giese catalogue the standard formations which occur on the surface of the living ocean and which can be seen in dozens, even hundreds, in the course of any day. The symmetriads—to continue using the terminology and definitions of the Giese school—are the least "human" formations, which is to say that they bear no resemblance whatsoever to anything on Earth. By the time the symmetriads were being investigated, it was already clear that the ocean was not aggressive, and that its plasmatic eddies would not swallow any but the most foolhardy explorer (of course I am not including accidents resulting from mechanical failures). It is possible to fly in complete safety from one part to another of the cylindrical body of an extensor or of the vertebrids, Jacob's ladders oscillating among the clouds: the plasma retreats at the speed of sound in the planet's atmosphere to make way for any foreign body. Deep funnels will open even beneath the surface of the ocean (at a prodigious expenditure of energy, calculated by Scriabin at around 10^{10} ergs). Nevertheless the first venture into the interior of a symmetriad was undertaken with the utmost caution and discipline, and involved a host of what turned out to be unnecessary safety measures. Every schoolboy on Earth knows of these pioneers.

It is not their nightmare appearance that makes the gigantic symmetriad formations dangerous, but the total instability and capriciousness of their structure, in which even the laws of physics do not hold. The theory that the living ocean is endowed with intelligence has found its firmest adherents among those scientists who have ventured into their unpredictable depths.

The birth of a symmetriad comes like a sudden eruption. About an hour beforehand, an area of tens of square miles of ocean vitrifies and begins to shine. It remains fluid, and there is no alteration in the rhythm of the waves. Occasionally the phenomena of vitrification occurs in the neighbourhood of the funnel left by an agilus. The gleaming sheath of the ocean heaves upwards to form a vast ball that reflects sky, sun, clouds and the entire horizon in a medley of changing, variegated images. Diffracted light creates a kaleidoscopic play of color.

The effects of light on a symmetriad are especially striking during the blue day and the red sunset. The planet appears to be giving birth to a twin that increases in volume from one moment to the next. The immense flaming globe has scarcely reached its maximum expansion above the ocean when it bursts at the summit and cracks vertically. It is not breaking up; this is the second phase, which goes under the clumsy name of the "floral calyx phase" and lasts only a few seconds. The membranous arches soaring into the sky now fold inwards and merge to produce a thick-set trunk enclosing a scene of teeming activity. At the center of the trunk, which was explored for the first time by the seventy-man Hamalei expedition, a process of polycrystallization on a giant scale erects an axis commonly referred to as the "backbone," a term which I consider ill-chosen. The mind-bending architecture of this central pillar is held in place by vertical shafts of a gelatinous, almost liquid consistency, constantly gushing upwards out of wide crevasses. Meanwhile, the entire trunk is surrounded by a belt of snow foam, seething with great bubbles of gas, and the whole process is accompanied by a perpetual dull roar of sound. From the center towards the periphery, powerful buttresses spin out and are coated with streams of ductile matter rising out of the ocean depths. Simultaneously the gelatinous geysers are converted into mobile columns that proceed to extrude tendrils that reach out in clusters towards points rigorously predetermined by the over-all dynamics of the entire structure: they call to mind the gills of an embryo, except that they are revolving at fantastic speed and ooze trickles of pinkish "blood" and a dark green secretion.

The symmetriad now begins to display its most exotic characteristic—the property of "illustrating," sometimes contradicting, various laws of physics. (Bear in mind that no two symmetriads are alike, and that the geometry of each one is a unique "invention" of the living ocean.) The interior of the symmetriad becomes a factory for the production of "monumental machines," as these constructs are sometimes called, although they resemble no machine which it is within the power of mankind to build: the designation is applied because all this activity has finite ends, and is therefore in some sense "mechanical."

When the geysers of oceanic matter have solidified into pillars or into three-dimensional networks of galleries and passages, and the "membranes" are set into an inextricable pattern of storeys, panels and vaults, the symmetriad justifies its name, for the entire structure is divided into two segments, each mirroring the other to the most infinitesimal detail.

After twenty or thirty minutes, when the axis may have tilted as much as eight to ten degrees from the horizontal, the giant begins slowly to subside. (Symmetriads vary in size, but as the base begins to submerge even the smallest reach a height of half a mile, and are visible from miles away.) At last, the structure stabilizes itself, and the partly submerged symmetriad ceases its activity. It is now possible to explore it in complete safety by making an entry near the summit, through one of the many syphons which emerge from the dome. The completed symmetriad represents a spatial analogue of some transcendental equation.

It is a commonplace that any equation can be expressed in the figurative language of non-Euclidean geometry and represented in three dimensions. This interpretation relates the symmetriad to Lobachevsky's cones and Riemann's negative curves, although its unimaginable complexity makes the relationship highly tenuous. The eventual form occupies an area of several cubic miles and extends far beyond our whole system of mathematics. In addition, this extension is four-dimensional, for the fundamental terms of the equations use a temporal symbolism expressed in the internal changes over a given period.

It would be only natural, clearly, to suppose that the symmetriad is a "computer" of the living ocean, performing calculations for a purpose that we are not able to grasp. This was Fremont's theory, now generally discounted. The hypothesis was a tempting one, but it proved impossible to sustain the concept that the living ocean examined problems of matter, the cosmos and existence through the medium of titanic eruptions, in which every particle had an indispensable function as a controlled element in an analytical system of infinite purity. In fact, numerous phenomena contradict this oversimplified (some say childishly naive) concept.

Any number of attempts have been made to transpose and "illustrate" the symmetriad, and Averian's demonstration was particularly well received. Let us imagine, he said, an edifice dating from the great days of Babylon, but built of some living, sensitive substance with the capacity to evolve: the architectonics of this edifice pass through a series of phases, and we see it adopt the forms of a Greek, then of a Roman building. The columns sprout like branches and become narrower; the roof grows lighter, rises, curves; the arch describes an abrupt parabola then breaks down into an arrow shape: the Gothic is born, comes to maturity and gives way in time to new forms. Austerity of line gives way to a riot of exploding lines and shapes, and the Baroque runs wild. If the progression continues—and the successive mutations are to be seen as stages in the life of an evolving organism—we finally arrive at the architecture of the space age, and perhaps too at some understanding of the symmetriad.

Unfortunately, no matter how this demonstration may be expanded and improved (there have been attempts to visualize it with the aid of models and films), the comparison remains superficial. It is evasive and illusory, and sidesteps the central fact that the symmetriad is quite unlike anything Earth has ever produced.

The human mind is only capable of absorbing a few things at a time. We see what is taking place in front of us in the here and now, and cannot envisage simultaneously a succession of processes, no matter how integrated and complementary. Our faculties of perception are consequently limited even as regards fairly simple phenomena. The fate of a single man can be rich with significance, that of a few hundred less so, but the history of thousands and millions of men does not mean anything at all, in any adequate sense of the word. The symmetriad is a million—a billion, rather—raised to the power of *N*: it is incomprehensible. We pass through vast halls, each with a capacity of ten Kronecker units, and creep like so many ants clinging to the folds of breathing vaults and craning to watch the flight of soaring girders, opalescent in the glare of searchlights, and elastic domes which criss-cross and balance each other unerringly, the perfection of a moment, since everything here passes and fades. The essence of this architecture is movement synchronized towards a precise objective. We observe a fraction of the process, like hearing the vibration of a single string in an orchestra of supergiants. We know, but cannot grasp, that above and below, beyond the limits of perception or imagination, thousands and millions of simultaneous transformations are at work, interlinked like a musical score by mathematical counterpoint. It has been described as a symphony in geometry, but we lack the ears to hear it.

Only a long-distance view would reveal the entire process, but the outer covering of the symmetriad conceals the colossal inner matrix where creation is unceasing, the created becomes the creator, and absolutely identical "twins" are born at opposite poles, separated by towering structures and miles of distance. The symphony creates itself, and writes its own conclusion, which is terrible to watch. Every observer feels like a spectator at a tragedy or a public massacre, when after two or three hours—never longer—the living ocean stages its assault. The polished surface of the ocean swirls and crumples, the desiccated foam liquifies again, begins to seeth, and legions of waves pour inwards from every point of the horizon, their gaping mouths far more massive than the greedy lips that surround the embryonic mimoid. The submerged base of the symmetriad is compressed, and the colossus rises as if on the point of being shot out of the planet's gravitational pull. The upper layers of the ocean redouble their activity, and the waves surge higher and higher to lick against the sides of the symmetriad. They envelop it, harden and plug the orifices, but their attack is nothing compared to the scene in the interior. First the process of creation freezes momentarily; then there is "panic." The smooth interpenetration of moving forms and the harmonious play of planes and lines accelerates, and the impression is inescapable that the symmetriad is hurrying to complete some task in the face of danger. The awe inspired by the metamorphosis and dynamics of the symmetriad intensifies as the proud sweep of the domes falters, vaults sag and droop, and "wrong notes"—incomplete, mangled forms—make their appearance. A powerful moaning roar issues from the invisible depths like a sigh of agony, reverberates through the narrow funnels and booms through the collapsing domes. In spite of the growing destructive violence of these convulsions, the spectator is rooted to the spot. Only the force of the hurricane streaming out of the depths and howling through the thousands of galleries keeps the great structure erect. Soon it subsides and starts to disintegrate. There are final flutterings, contortions, and blind, random spasms. Gnawed and undermined, the giant sinks slowly and disappears, and the space where it stood is covered with whirlpools of foam.

So what does all this mean?

I remembered an incident dating from my spell as assistant to Gibarian. A group of schoolchildren visiting the Solarist Institute in Aden were making their way through the main hall of the library and looking at the racks of microfilm that occupied the entire left-hand side of the hall. The guide explained that among other phenomena immortalized by the image, these contained fragmentary glimpses of symmetriads long since vanished—not single shots, but whole reels, more than ninety thousand of them!

One plump schoolgirl (she looked about fifteen, peering inquisitively over her spectacles) abruptly asked: "And what is it for?"

In the ensuing embarrassed silence, the schoolmistress was content to dart a reproving look at her wayward pupil. Among the Solarists whose job was to act as guides (I was one of them), no one would produce an answer. Each symmetriad is unique, and the developments in its heart are, generally speaking, unpredictable. Sometimes there is no sound. Sometimes the index of refraction increases or diminishes. Sometimes, the rhythmic pulsations are accompanied by local changes in gravitation, as if the heart of the symmetriad were beating by gravitating. Sometimes the compasses of the observers spin wildly, and ionized layers spring up and disappear. The catalogue could go on indefinitely. In any case, even if we did ever succeed in solving the riddle of the symmetriads, we would still have to contend with the asymmetriads!

The asymmetriads are born in the same manner as the symmetriads but finish differently, and nothing can be seen of their internal processes except tremors, vibrations and flickering. We do know, however, that the interior houses bewildering operations performed at a speed that defies the laws of physics and which are dubbed "giant quantic phenomena." The mathematical analogy with certain three-dimensional models of the atom is so unstable and transitory that some commentators dismiss the resemblance as of secondary importance, if not purely accidental. The asymmetriads have a very short life-span of fifteen to twenty minutes, and their death is even more appalling than that of the symmetriads: with the howling gale that screams through its fabric, a thick fluid gushes out, gurgles hideously, and submerges everything beneath a foul, bubbling foam. Then an explosion, coinciding with a muddy eruption, hurls up a spout of debris, which rains slowly down into the seething ocean. This debris is sometimes found scores of miles from the focus of the explosion, dried up, yellow and flattened, like flakes of cartilage.

Some other creations of the ocean, which are much more rare and of very variable duration, part company with the parent body entirely. The first traces of these "independents" were identified—wrongly, it was later proved—as the remains of creatures inhabiting the ocean deeps. The free-ranging forms are often reminiscent of many-winged birds, darting away from the moving trunks of the agilus, but the preconceptions of Earth offer no assistance in unravelling the mysteries of Solaris. Strange, seal-like bodies appear now and then on the rocky outcrop of an island, sprawling in the sun or dragging themselves lazily back to merge with the ocean.

There was no escaping the impressions that grew out of man's experience on Earth. The prospects of Contact receded.

Explorers travelled hundreds of miles in the depths of symmetriads, and installed measuring instruments and remote-control cameras. Artificial satellites captured the birth of mimoids and extensors, and faithfully reproduced their images of growth and destruction. The libraries overflowed, the archives grew, and the price paid for all this documentation was often very heavy. One notorious disaster cost one hundred and six people their lives, among them Giese himself: while studying what was undoubtedly a symmetriad, the expedition was suddenly destroyed by a process peculiar to the asymmetriads. In two seconds, an eruption of glutinous mud swallowed up seventy-nine men and all their equipment. Another twenty-seven observers surveying the area from aircraft and helicopters were also caught in the eruption.

Following the Eruption of the Hundred and Six, and for the first time in Solarist studies, there were petitions demanding a thermonuclear attack on the ocean. Such a response would have been more cruelty than revenge, since it would have meant destroying what we did not understand. Tsanken's ultimatum, which was never officially acknowledged, probably influenced the negative outcome of the vote. He was in command of Giese's reserve team, and had survived owing to a transmission error that took him off his course, to arrive in the disaster area a few minutes after the explosion, when the black mushroom cloud was still visible. Informed of the proposal for a nuclear strike, he threatened to blow up the Station, together with the nineteen survivors sheltering inside it.

Today, there are only three of us in the Station.

[*Snow enters Kelvin's cabin to discuss strategies for dealing with the visitors. Sartorius has proposed two plans. One is to send electroencephalogram readings of scientists to the ocean by means of high-powered X-rays. If the ocean is using the visitors to gather information about the scientists, this direct transmission of brainwaves might eliminate that need. The second strategy is to construct a "disruptor"—a device that will generate a negative neutrino field around the station, destroying any neutrino structures. Kelvin opposes the second idea, challenging the physics on which it is based. He claims—though he does not believe this—that a "disruptor" could produce an explosion of the force of a small atomic bomb.*]

... I have no idea how long I had been lying in the dark, staring at the luminous dial of my wristwatch. Hearing myself breathing, I felt a vague surprise, but my underlying feeling was one of profound indifference both to this ring of phosphorescent figures and to my own surprise. I told myself that the feeling was caused by fatigue. When I turned over, the bed seemed wider than usual. I held my breath; no sound broke the silence. Rheya's breathing should have been audible. I reached out, but felt nothing. I was alone.

I was about to call her name, when I heard the tread of heavy footsteps coming towards me. A numb calm descended:

"Gibarian?"

"Yes, it's me. Don't switch the light on."

"No?"

"There's no need, and it's better for us to stay in the dark."

"But you are dead..."

"Don't let that worry you. You recognize my voice, don't you?"

"Yes. Why did you kill yourself?"

"I had no choice. You arrived four days late. If you had come earlier, I would not have been forced to kill myself. Don't worry about it, though, I don't regret anything."

"You really are there? I'm not asleep?"

"Oh, you think you're dreaming about me? As you did with Rheya?"

"Where is she?"

"How should I know?"

"I have a feeling that you do."

"Keep your feelings for yourself. Let's say I'm deputizing for her."

"I want her here too!"

"Not possible."

"Why not? You know very well that it isn't the real you, just my..."

"No, I am the real Gibarian—just a new incarnation. But let's not waste time on useless chatter."

"You'll be leaving again?"

"Yes."

"And then she'll come back?"

"Why should you care about that?"

"She belongs to me."

"You are afraid of her."

"No."

"She disgusts you."

"What do you want with me?"

"Save your pity for yourself—you have a right to it—but not for her. She will always be twenty years old. You must know that."

I felt suddenly at ease again, for no apparent reason, and ready to hear him out. He seemed to have come closer, though I could not see him in the dark.

"What do you want?"

"Sartorius has convinced Snow that you have been deceiving him. Right now they are trying to give you the same treatment. Building the X-ray beamer is a cover for constructing the magnetic field disruptor."

"Where is she?"

"Didn't you hear me? I came to warn you."

"Where is she?"

"I don't know. Be careful. You must find some kind of weapon.

You can't trust anyone."

"I can trust Rheya."

He stifled a laugh: "Of course, you can trust Rheya—to some extent. And you can always follow my example, if all else fails."

"You are not Gibarian."

"No? Then who am I? A dream?"

"No, you are only a puppet. But you don't realize that you are."

"And how do you know what *you* are?"

I tried to stand up, but could not stir. Although Gibarian was still speaking, I could not understand his words; there was only the drone of his voice. I struggled to regain control of my body, felt a sudden wrench and . . . I woke up, and drew down great gulps of air. It was dark, and I had been having a nightmare. And now I heard a distant, monotonous voice: ". . . a dilemma that we are not equipped to solve. We are the cause of our own sufferings. The Polytheres behave strictly as a kind of amplifier of our own thoughts. Any attempt to understand the motivation of these occurrences is blocked by our own anthropomorphism. Where there are no men, there cannot be motives accessible to men. Before we can proceed with our research, either our own thoughts or their materialized forms must be destroyed. It is not within our power to destroy our thoughts. As for destroying their material forms, that could be like committing murder."

I had recognized Gibarian's voice at once. When I stretched out my arm, I found myself alone. I had fallen asleep again. This was another dream. I called Gibarian's name, and the voice stopped in mid-sentence. There was the sound of a faint gasp, then a gust of air.

"Well, Gibarian," I yawned, "You seem to be following me out of one dream and into the next..."

There was a rustling sound from somewhere close, and I called his name again. The bedsprings creaked, and a voice whispered in my ear:

"Kris...it's me..."

"Rheya? Is it you? What about Gibarian?"

"But...you said he was dead, Kris."

"He can be alive in a dream," I told her dejectedly, although I was not completely sure that it had been a dream. "He spoke to me... He was here..."

My head sank back onto the pillow. Rheya said something, but I was already drifting into sleep.

In the red light of morning, the events of the previous night returned. I had dreamt that I was talking to Gibarian. But afterwards, I could swear that I had heard his voice, although I had no clear recall of what he had said, and it had not been a conversation—more like a speech.

Rheya was splashing about in the bathroom. I looked under the bed, where I had hidden the tape-recorder a few days earlier. It was no longer there.

"Rheya!" She put her face round the door. "Did you see a tape-recorder under the bed, a little pocket one?"

"There was a pile of stuff under the bed. I put it all over there." She pointed to a shelf by the medicine cabinet, and disappeared back into the bathroom.

There was no tape-recorder on the shelf, and when Rheya emerged from the bathroom I asked her to think again. She sat combing her hair, and did not answer. It was not until now that I noticed how pale she was, and how closely she was watching me in the mirror. I returned to the attack:

"The tape-recorder is missing, Rheya."

"Is that all you have to tell me?"

"I'm sorry. You're right, it's silly to get so worked up about a tape-recorder."

Anything to avoid a quarrel.

Later, over breakfast, the change in Rheya's behavior was obvious, yet I could not define it. She did not meet my eyes, and was frequently so lost in thought that she did not hear me. Once, when she looked up, her cheeks were damp.

"Is anything the matter? You're crying."

"Leave me alone," Rheya blurted. "They aren't real tears."

Perhaps I ought not to have let her answer go, but straight talking was the last thing I wanted. In any case, I had other problems on my mind; I had dreamt that Snow and Sartorius were plotting against me, and although I was certain that it had been nothing more than a dream, I was wondering if there was anything on the Station that I might be able to use to defend myself. My thinking had not progressed to the point of deciding what to do with a weapon once I had it. I told Rheya that I had to make an inspection of the storerooms, and she trailed behind me silently.

I ransacked packing-cases and capsules, and when we reached the lower deck I was unable to resist looking into the cold store. Not wanting Rheya to go in, I put my head inside the door and looked around. The recumbent figure was still covered by its dark shroud, but from my position in the doorway I could not make out whether the black woman was still sleeping by Gibarian's body. I had the impression that she was no longer there.

I wandered from one storeroom to another, unable to locate anything that might serve as a weapon, and with a rising feeling of depression. All at once I noticed that Rheya was not with me. Then she reappeared; she had been hanging back in the corridor. In spite of the pain she suffered when she could not see me, she had been trying to keep away. I should have been astonished: instead, I went on acting as if I had been offended—but then, who had offended me?—and sulking like a child.

My head was throbbing, and I rifled the entire contents of the medicine cabinet without finding so much as an aspirin. I did not want to go back to the sick bay. I did not want to do anything. I had never been in a blacker temper. Rheya tiptoed about the cabin like a shadow. Now and then she went off somewhere. I don't know where, I was paying her no attention; then she would creep back inside.

That afternoon, in the kitchen (we had just eaten, but in fact Rheya had not touched her food, and I had not attempted to persuade her), Rheya got up and came to sit next to me. I felt her hand on my sleeve, and grunted: "What's the matter?"

I had been meaning to go up to the deck above, as the pipes were carrying the sharp crackling sound of high-voltage apparatus in use, but Rheya would have had to come with me. It had been hard enough to justify her presence in the library; among the machinery, there was a chance that Snow might drop some clumsy remark. I gave up the idea of going to investigate.

"Kris," she whispered, "what's happening to us?"

I gave an involuntary sigh of frustration with everything that had been happening since the previous night: "Everything is fine. Why?"

"I want to talk."

"All right, I'm listening."

"Not like this."

"What? You know I have a headache, and that's not the least of my worries..."

"You're not being fair."

I forced myself to smile; it must have been a poor imitation: "Go ahead and talk, darling, please."

"Will you tell me the truth?"

"Why should I lie?" This was an ominous beginning.

"You might have your reasons... it might be necessary... But if you want... Look, I am going to tell you something, and then it will be your turn—only no half-truths. Promise!" I could not meet her gaze. "I've already told you that I don't know how I came to be here. Perhaps you do. Wait!—perhaps you don't. But if you do know, and you can't tell me now, will you tell me one day, later on? I couldn't be any the worse for it, and you would at least be giving me a chance."

"What are you talking about, child," I stammered. "What chance?"

"Kris, whatever I may be, I'm certainly not a child. You promised me an answer."

Whatever I may be... my throat tightened, and I stared at Rheya shaking my head like an imbecile, as if forbidding myself to hear any more.

"I'm not asking for explanations. You only need to tell me that you are not allowed to say."

"I'm not hiding anything," I croaked.

"All right."

She stood up. I wanted to say something. We could not leave it at that. But no words would come.

"Rheya..."

She was standing at the window, with her back turned. The blue-black ocean stretched out under a cloudless sky.

"Rheya, if you believe... You know very well I love you..."

"Me?"

I went to put my arms round her, but she pulled away.

"You're too kind," she said. "You say you love me? I'd rather you beat me."

"Rheya, darling!"

"No, no, don't say any more."

She went back to the table and began to clear away the plates. I gazed out at the ocean. The sun was setting, and the Station cast a lengthening shadow that danced on the waves. Rheya dropped a plate on the floor. Water splashed in the sink. A tarnished golden halo ringed the horizon. If I only knew what to do . . . if only . . . Suddenly there was silence. Rheya was standing behind me.

"No, don't turn round," she murmured. "It isn't your fault, I know. Don't torment yourself."

I reached out, but she slipped away to the far side of the room and picked up a stack of plates: "It's a shame they're unbreakable. I'd like to smash them, all of them."

I thought for a moment that she really was going to dash them to the floor, but she looked across at me and smiled: "Don't worry, I'm not going to make scenes."

In the middle of the night, I was suddenly wide awake. The room was in darkness and the door was ajar, with a faint light shining from the corridor. There was a shrill hissing noise, interspersed with heavy, muffled thudding, as if some heavy object was pounding against a wall. A meteor had pierced the shell of the Station! No, not a meteor, a shuttle, for I could hear a dreadful labored whining....

I shook myself. It was not a meteor, nor was it a shuttle. The sound was coming from somebody at the end of the corridor. I ran down to where light was pouring from the door of the little workroom, and rushed inside. A freezing vapor filled the room, my breath fell like snow, and white flakes swirled over a body covered by a dressing-gown, stirring feebly then striking the floor again. I could hardly see through the freezing mist. I snatched her up and folded her in my arms, and the dressing-gown burnt my skin. Rheya kept on making the same harsh gasping sound as I stumbled along the corridor, no longer feeling the cold, only her breath on my neck, burning like fire.

I lowered Rheya onto the operating table and pulled the dressing gown open. Her face was contorted with pain, the lips covered by a thick, black layer of frozen blood, the tongue a mass of sparkling ice crystals.

Liquid oxygen . . . The Dewar bottles in the workroom contained liquid oxygen. Splinters of glass had crunched underfoot as I carried Rheya out. How much of it had she swallowed? It didn't matter. Her trachea, throat and lungs must be burnt away—liquid oxygen corrodes flesh more effectively than strong acids. Her breathing was more and more labored, with a dry sound like tearing paper. Her eyes were closed. She was dying.

I looked across at the big, glass-fronted cabinets, crammed with instruments and drugs. Tracheotomy? Intubation? She had no lungs! I stared at shelves full of colored bottles and cartons. She went on, gasping hoarsely, and a wisp of vapor drifted out of her open mouth.

Thermophores . . .

I started looking for them, then changed my mind, ran to another cupboard and turned out boxes of ampoules. Now a hypodermic—where are they?—here—needs sterilizing. I fumbled with the lid of the sterilizer, but my numb fingers had lost all sensation and would not bend.

The harsh rattle grew louder, and Rheya's eyes were open when I reached the table. I opened my mouth to say her name but my voice had gone and my lips would not obey me. My face did not belong to me; it was a plaster mask.

Rheya's ribs were heaving under the white skin. The ice-crystals had melted and her wet hair was entangled in the headrest. And she was looking at me.

"Rheya!" It was all I could say. I stood paralyzed, my hands dangling uselessly, until a burning sensation mounted from my legs and attacked my lips and eyelids.

A drop of blood melted and slanted down her cheek. Her tongue quivered and receded. The labored panting went on.

I could feel no pulse in her wrist, and put my ear against her frozen breast. Faintly, behind the raging blizzard, her heart was beating so fast that I could not count the beats, and I remained crouched over her, with my eyes closed. Something brushed my head—Rheya's hand in my hair. I stood up.

"Kris!" A harsh gasp.

I took her hand, and the answering pressure made my bones creak. Then her face screwed up with agony, and she lost consciousness again. Her eyes turned up, a guttural rattle tore at her throat, and her body arched with convulsions. It was all I could do to keep her on the operating table; she broke free and her head cracked against a porcelain basin. I dragged her back, and struggled to hold her down, but violent spasms kept jerking her out of my grasp. I was pouring with sweat, and my legs were like jelly. When the convulsions abated, I tried to make her lie flat, but her chest thrust out to gulp at the air. Suddenly her eyes were staring out at me from behind the frightful blood-stained mask of her face.

"Kris... how long... how long?"

She choked. Pink foam appeared at her mouth, and the convulsions racked her again. With my last reserves of strength I bore down on her shoulders, and she fell back. Her teeth chattered loudly.

"No, no, no," she whimpered suddenly, and I thought that death was near.

But the spasms resumed, and again I had to hold her down. Now and then she swallowed drily, and her ribs heaved. Then the eyelids half closed over the unseeing eyes, and she stiffened. This must be the end. I did not even try to wipe the foam from her mouth. A distant ringing throbbed in my head. I was waiting for her final breath before my strength failed and I collapsed to the ground.

She went on breathing, and the rasp was now only a light sigh. Her chest, which had stopped heaving, moved again to the rapid rhythm of her heartbeat. Color was returning to her cheeks. Still I did not realize what was happening. My hands were clammy, and I heard as if through layers of cotton wool, yet the ringing sound continued.

Rheya's eyelids moved, and our eyes met.

I could not speak her name from behind the mask of my face. All I could do was look at her.

She turned her head and looked round the room. Somewhere behind me, in another world, a tap dripped. Rheya levered herself up on her elbow. I recoiled, and again our eyes met.

"It... it didn't work," she stammered. "Why are you looking at me like that?" Then she screamed out loud: "Why are you looking at me like that?"

Still I could say nothing. She examined her hands, moved her fingers...

"Is this me?"

My lips found her name, and she repeated it as a question—"Rheya?"

She let herself slide off the operating table, staggered, regained her balance and took a few steps. She was moving in a daze, and looking at me without appearing to see me.

"Rheya? But... I am not Rheya. Who am I then? And you, what about you?" Her eyes widened and sparkled, and an astonished smile lit up her face. "And you, Kris. Perhaps you too..."

I had backed away until I came up against the wall. The smile vanished.

"No. You are afraid. I can't take any more of this. I can't . . . I didn't know, I still don't understand. It's not possible." Her clenched fists struck her chest. "What else could I think, except that I was Rheya! Maybe you believe this is all an act? It isn't, I swear it isn't."

Something snapped in my mind, and I went to put my arms round her, but she fought free:

"Don't touch me! Leave me alone! I disgust you, I know I do. Keep away! I'm not Rheya..."

We screamed at each other and Rheya tried to keep me at arms' length. I would not let her go, and at last she let her head fall to my shoulder. We were on our knees, breathless and exhausted.

"Kris... what do I have to do to put a stop to this?"

"Be quiet!"

"You don't know!" She lifted her head and stared at me. "It can't be done, can it?"

"Please . . ."

"I really tried... No, go away. I disgust you—and myself. I disgust myself. If I only knew how..."

"You would kill yourself."

"Yes."

"But I want you to stay alive. I want you here, more than anything."

"You're lying."

"Tell me what I have to do to convince you. You are here. You exist. I can't see any further than that."

"It can't possibly be true, because I am not Rheya."

"Then who are you?"

There was a long silence. Then she bowed her head and murmured:

"Rheya... But I know that I am not the woman you once loved."

"Yes. But that was long time ago. That past does not exist, but you do, here and now: Don't you see?"

She shook her head:

"I know that it was kindness that made you behave as you did, but there is nothing to be done. That first morning when I found myself waiting by your bed for you to wake up, I knew nothing. I can hardly believe it was only three days ago. I behaved like a lunatic. Everything was misty. I didn't remember anything, wasn't surprised by anything. It was like recovering from a drugged sleep, or a long illness. It even occurred to me that I might have been ill and you didn't want to tell me. Then a few things happened to set me thinking—you know what I mean. So after you met that man in the library and you refused to tell me anything, I made up my mind to listen to that tape. That was the only time I have lied to you, Kris. When you were looking for the tape-recorder, I knew where it was. I'd hidden it. The man who recorded the tape—what was his name?"

"Gibarian."

"Yes. Gibarian—he explained everything. Although I still don't understand. The only thing missing was that I can't . . . that there is no end. He didn't mention that, or if he did it was after you woke up and I had to switch off. But I heard enough to realize that I am not a human being, only an instrument."

"What are you talking about?"

"That's what I am. To study your reactions—something of that sort. Each one of you has a . . . an instrument like me. We emerge from your memory or your imagination, I can't say exactly—anyway you know better than I. He talks about such terrible things . . . so far-fetched . . . if it did not fit in with everything else I would certainly have refused to believe him."

"The rest?"

"Oh, things like not needing sleep, and being compelled to go wherever you go. When I think that only yesterday I was miserable because I thought you detested me. How stupid! But how could I have imagined the truth? He—Gibarian—didn't hate that woman, the one who came to him, but he refers to her in such a dreadful way. It wasn't until then that I realized that I was helpless whatever I did, and that I couldn't avoid torturing you. More than that though, an instrument of torture is passive, like the stone that falls on somebody and kills them. But an instrument of torture which loves you and wishes you nothing but good—it was too much for me. I wanted to tell you the little that I *had* understood. I told myself that it might be useful to you. I even tried to make notes. . . ."

"That time when you had the light switched on?"

"Yes. But I couldn't write anything. I searched myself for . . . you know, some sign of 'influence' . . . I was going mad. I felt as if there was no body underneath my skin and there was something else instead: as if I was just an illusion meant to mislead you. You see?"

"I see."

"When you can't sleep at night and your mind keeps spinning for hours on end, it can take you far away; you find yourself moving in strange directions . . ."

"I know what you mean."

"But I could feel my heart beating. And then I remembered that you had made an analysis of my blood. What did you find? You can tell me the truth now."

"Your blood is like my own."

"Truly?"

"I give you my word."

"What does that indicate? I had been telling myself that the . . .

unknown force might be concealed somewhere inside me, and that it might not occupy very much space. But I did not know whereabouts it was. I think now that I was evading the real issue because I didn't have the nerve to make a decision. I was afraid, and I looked for a way out. But Kris, if my blood is like yours . . . if I really . . . no, it's impossible. I would already be dead, wouldn't I? That means there really is something different—but where? In the mind? Yet it seems to me that I think as any human being does . . . and I know nothing! If that alien thing was thinking in my head, I would know everything. And I would not love you. I would be pretending, and aware that I was pretending. Kris, you've got to tell me everything you know. Perhaps we could work out a solution between us."

"What kind of solution?" She fell silent. "Is it death you want?"

"Yes, I think it is."

Again silence. Rheya sat on the floor, her knees drawn up under her chin. I looked around at the white-enamelled fittings and gleaming instruments, perhaps looking for some unsuspected clue to suddenly materialize.

"Rheya, I have something to say, too." She waited quietly. "It is true that we are not exactly alike. But there is nothing wrong with that. In any case, whatever else we might think about it, that . . . difference . . . saved your life."

A painful smile flickered over her face: "Does that mean that I am . . . immortal?"

"I don't know. At any rate, you're far less vulnerable than I am."

"It's horrible . . ."

"Perhaps not as horrible as you think."

"But you don't envy me."

"Rheya, I don't know what your fate will be. It cannot be predicted, any more than my own or any other member's of the Station's personnel. The experiment will go on, and anything can happen . . ."

"Or nothing."

"Or nothing. And I have to confess that nothing is what I would prefer. Not because I'm frightened—though fear is undeniably an element of this business—but because there can't be any final outcome. I'm quite sure of that."

"Outcome? You mean the ocean?"

"Yes, contact with the ocean. As I see it, the problem is basically very simple. Contact means the exchange of specific knowledge, ideas, or at least of findings, definite facts. But what if no exchange is possible? If an elephant is not a giant microbe, the ocean is not a giant brain. Obviously there can be various approaches, and the consequence of one of them is that you are here, now, with me. And I am trying my hardest to make you realize that I love you. Just your being here cancels out the twelve years of my life that went into the study of

Solaris, and I want to keep you.

"You may have been sent to torment me, or to make my life happier, or as an instrument ignorant of its function, used like a microscope with me on the slide. Possibly you are here as a token of friendship, or a subtle punishment, or even as a joke. It could be all of those at once, or—which is more probable—something else completely. If you say that our future depends on the ocean's intentions, I can't deny it. I can't tell the future any more than you can. I can't even swear that I shall always love you. After what has happened already, we can expect anything. Suppose tomorrow it turns me into a green jellyfish! It's out of our hands. But the decision we make today is in our hands. Let's decide to stay together. What do you say?"

"Listen Kris, there's something else I must ask you . . . Am I . . . do I look very like her?"

"You did at first. Now I don't know."

"I don't understand."

"Now all I see is you."

"You're sure?"

"Yes. If you really were her, I might not be able to love you."

"Why?"

"Because of what I did."

"Did you treat her badly?"

"Yes, when we . . ."

"Don't say any more."

"Why not?"

"So that you won't forget that I am the one who is here, not her."

. . . The following morning, I received another note from Snow: Sartorius had left off working on the disruptor and was getting ready for a final experiment with high-power X-rays.

"Rheya, darling, I have to pay a visit to Snow."

The red dawn blazing through the window divided the room in two. We were in an area of blue shadow. Everything outside this shadow-zone was burnished copper: if a book had fallen from a shelf, my ear would have listened instinctively for a metallic clang.

"It's to do with the experiment. Only I don't know what to do about it. Please understand, I'd rather . . ."

"You needn't justify yourself, Kris. If only it doesn't go on too long."

"It's bound to take a while. Look, do you think you could wait in the corridor?"

"I can try. But what if I lose control?"

"What does it feel like? I'm not asking just out of curiosity, believe me, but if we can discuss how it works you might find some way of keeping it in check."

Rheya had turned pale, but she tried to explain:

"I feel afraid, not of some thing or some person—there's no focus, only a sense of being lost. And I am terribly ashamed of myself. Then, when you come back, it stops. That's what made me think I might have been ill."

"Perhaps it's only inside this damned Station that it works. I'll make arrangements for us to get out as soon as possible."

"Do you think you can?"

"Why not? I'm not a prisoner here. I'll have to talk it over with Snow. Have you any idea how long you could manage to remain by yourself?"

"That depends . . . If I could hear your voice, I think I might be able to hold out."

"I'd rather you weren't listening. Not that I have anything to hide, but there's no telling what Snow might say."

"You needn't go on. I understand. I'll just stand close enough to hear the sound of your voice."

"I'm going to the operating room to phone him. The doors will be open."

Rheya nodded agreement.

I crossed the red zone. The corridor seemed dark by contrast, in spite of the lighting. Inside the open door of the operating room, fragments of the Dewar bottle, the last traces of the previous night's events, gleamed from under a row of liquid oxygen containers. When I took the phone off the hook, the little screen lit up, and I tapped out the number of the radio-cabin. Behind the dull glass, a spot of bluish light grew, burst, and Snow was looking at me, perched on the edge of his chair.

"I got your note and I want to talk to you. Can I come over?"

"Yes. Right away?"

"Yes."

"Excuse me, but are you coming alone or . . . accompanied?"

"Alone."

His creased forehead and thin, tanned face filled the screen as he leant forward to scrutinize me through the convex glass. Then he appeared to reach an abrupt decision:

"Fine, fine, I'll be expecting you."

I went back to the cabin, where I could barely make out the shape of Rheya behind the curtain of red sunlight. She was sitting in an armchair, with her hands clutching the armrests. She must have failed to hear my footsteps, and I saw her for a moment fighting the inexplicable compulsion that possessed her and wrestling with the fierce contractions of her entire body which stopped immediately when she saw me. I choked back a feeling of blind rage and pity.

We walked in silence down the long corridor with its polychromed walls; the designers had intended the variations in color to make life more tolerable inside the armored shell of the Station. A shaft of red light ahead of us meant that the door of the radio-cabin was ajar, and I looked at Rheya. She made no attempt to return my smile, totally absorbed in her preparations for the coming battle with herself. Now that the ordeal was about to begin, her face was pinched and white. Fifteen paces from the door, she stopped, pushing me forward gently with her fingertips as I started to turn around. Suddenly I felt that Snow, the experiment, even the Station itself were not worth the agonizing price that Rheya was ready to pay, with myself as assistant torturer. I would have retraced my steps, but a shadow fell across the cabin doorway, and I hurried inside.

Snow stood facing me with the red sun behind him making a halo of purple light out of his grey hair. We confronted one another without speaking, and he was able to examine me at his leisure in the sunlight that dazzled me so that I could hardly see him.

I walked past him and leaned against a tall desk bristling with microphones on their flexible stalks. Snow pivoted slowly and went on staring at me with his habitual cheerless smile, in which there was no amusement, only overpowering fatigue. Still with his eyes on mine, he picked his way through the piles of objects, littered about the cabin—thermic cells, instruments, spare parts for the electronic equipment—pulled a stool up against the door of a steel cabinet, and sat down.

I listened anxiously, but no sound came from the corridor. Why did Snow not speak? The prolonged silence was becoming exasperating.

I cleared my throat:

"When will you and Sartorius be ready?"

"We can start today, but the recording will take some time."

"Recording? You mean the encephalogram?"

"Yes, you agreed. Is anything wrong?"

"No, nothing."

Another lengthening silence. Snow broke it:

"Did you have something to tell me?"

"She knows," I whispered.

He frowned, but I had the impression that he was not really surprised. Then why pretend? I lost all desire to confide in him. All the same, I had to be honest:

"She started to suspect after our meeting in the library. My behavior, various other indications. Then she found Gibarian's tape-recorder and played back the tape."

Snow sat intent and unmoving. Standing by the desk, my view of the corridor was blocked by the half-open door. I lowered my voice again:

"Last night, while I was asleep, she tried to kill herself. She drank liquid oxygen . . ." There was a sound of rustling, like papers stirred by the wind. I stopped and listened for something in the corridor, but the noise did not come from there. A mouse in the cabin? Out of the question, this was Solaris. I stole a glance at Snow.

"Go on," he said calmly.

"It didn't work, of course. Anyway, she knows who she is."

"Why tell me?"

I was taken aback for an instant, then I stammered out:

"So as to inform you, to keep you up to date on the situation . . ."

"I warned you."

"You mean you knew?" My voice rose involuntarily.

"What you have just told me? Of course not. But I explained the position. When it arrives, the visitor is almost blank—only a ghost made up of memories and vague images dredged out of its . . . source. The longer it stays with you, the more human it becomes. It also becomes more independent, up to a certain point. And the longer that goes on, the more difficult it gets . . ." Snow broke off, looked me up and down, and went on reluctantly: "Does she know everything?"

"Yes, I've just told you."

"Everything? Does she know that she came once before, and that you . . ."

"No!"

"Listen Kelvin," he smiled ruefully, "if that's how it is, what do you want to do—leave the Station?"

"Yes."

"With her?"

The silence while he considered his reply also revealed something else. Again, from somewhere close, and without being able to pin it down, I heard the same faint rustling in the cabin, as if through a thin partition.

Snow shifted on his stool.

"All right. Why look at me like that? Do you think I would stand in your way? You can do as you like, Kelvin. We're in enough trouble already without putting pressure on each other. I know it will be a hopeless job to convince you, but there's something I have to say: you are doing all you can to stay human in an inhuman situation. Noble it may be, but it isn't going to get you anywhere. And I'm not so sure about it being noble—not if it's idiotic at the same time. But that's your affair. Let's get back to the point. You renege on the experiment and take her away with you. Has it struck you that you'll only be embarking on a different kind of experiment?"

"What do you mean? If you want to know whether she can manage it, as long as I'm with her, I don't see . . ." I trailed to a halt.

Snow sighed:

"All of us have our heads in the sand, Kelvin, and we know it.

There's no need to put on airs."

"I'm not putting anything on."

"I'm sorry, I didn't want to offend you. I take back the airs, but I still think that you are playing the ostrich game—and a particularly dangerous version. You deceive yourself, you deceive her, and you chase your own tail. Do you know the necessary conditions for stabilizing a neutrino field?"

"No, nor do you. Nor does anyone."

"Exactly. All we know is that the structure is inherently unstable and can only be maintained by means of a continuous energy input. Sartorius told me that. This energy creates a rotating stabilization field. Now, does that energy come from outside the 'visitor,' or is it generated internally? You see the difference?"

"Yes. If it is external, she..."

Snow finished the sentence for me:

"Away from Solaris, the structure disintegrates. It's only a theory, of course, but one that you can verify, since you have already set up an experiment. The vehicle you launched is still in orbit. In my spare moments, I've even calculated its trajectory. You can take off, intercept, and find out what happened to the passenger..."

"You're out of your mind," I yelled.

"You think so? And what if we brought the shuttle down again? No problem—it's on remote control. We'll bring it out of orbit, and..."

"Shut up!"

"That won't do either? There's another method, a very simple one. It doesn't involve bringing the shuttle down, only establishing radio contact. If she's alive, she'll reply, and..."

"The oxygen would have run out days ago."

"She may not need it. Shall we try?"

"Snow... Snow..."

He mimicked my intonation angrily:

"Kelvin... Kelvin... Think, just a little. Are you a man or not? Who are you trying to please? Who do you want to save? Yourself? Her? And which version of her? This one or that one? Haven't you got the guts to face them both? Surely you realize that you haven't thought it through. Let me tell you one last time, we are in a situation that is beyond morality."

The rustling noise returned, and this time it sounded like nails scraping on a wall. All at once I was filled with a dull indifference. I saw myself, I saw both of us, from a long way off, as if through the wrong end of a telescope, and everything looked meaningless, trivial, and slightly ridiculous.

"So what do you suggest? Send up another shuttle? She would be back tomorrow. And the day after, and the day after that. How long do you want it to go on? What's the good of disposing of her if she keeps returning? How would it help me, or you, or Sartorius, or the Station?"

"No, here's my suggestion: leave with her. You'll witness the transformation. After a few minutes, you'll see..."

"What? A monster, a demon?"

"No, you'll see her die, that's all. Don't think that they are immortal—I promise you that they die. And then what will you do? Come back . . . for a fresh sample?" He stared at me with bantering condescension.

"That's enough!" I burst out, clenching my fists.

"Oh, I'm the one who has to be quiet? Look, I didn't start this conversation, and as far as I'm concerned it has gone on long enough. Let me just suggest some ways for you to amuse yourself. You could scourge the ocean with rods, for instance. You've got it into your head that you're a traitor if you . . ." He waved his hand in farewell, and raised his head as if to watch an imaginary ship in flight. ". . . and a good man if you keep her. Smiling when you feel like screaming, and shamming cheerful when you want to beat your head against a wall, isn't that being a traitor? What if it is not possible, here, to be anything but a traitor? What will you do? Take it out on that bastard Snow, who is the cause of it all? In that case, Kelvin, you just put the lid on the rest of your troubles by acting like a complete idiot!"

"You are talking from your own point of view. I love this girl."

"Her memory, you mean?"

"No, herself. I told you what she tried to do. How many 'real' human beings could have that much courage?"

"So you admit..."

"Don't quibble."

"Right. So she loves you. And you want to love her. It isn't the same thing."

"You're wrong."

"I'm sorry, Kelvin, but it was your idea to spill all this. You don't love her. You do love her. She is willing to give her life. So are you. It's touching, it's magnificent, anything you like, but it's out of place here—it's the wrong setting. Don't you see? No, you don't want to. You are going around in circles to satisfy the curiosity of a power we don't understand and can't control, and she is an aspect, a periodic manifestation of that power. If she was . . . if you were being pestered by some infatuated hag, you wouldn't think twice about packing her off, right?"

"I suppose so."

"Well then, that probably explains why she is not a hag! You feel as if your hands are tied? That's just it, they are!"

"All you are doing is adding one more theory to the millions of theories in the library. Leave me alone, Snow, she is... No, I won't say any more."

"It's up to you. But remember that she is a mirror that reflects a part of your mind. If she is beautiful, it's because your memories are. You provide the formula. You can only finish where you started, don't forget that."

"What do you expect me to do? Send her away? I've already asked you why, and you don't answer."

"I'll give you an answer. It was you who wanted this conversation, not me. I haven't meddled with your affairs, and I'm not telling you what to do or what not to do. Even if I had the right, I would not. You come here of your own free will, and you dump it all on me. You know why? To take the weight off your own back. Well, I've experienced that weight—don't try to shut me up—and I leave you free to find your own solution. But you *want* opposition. If I got in your way, you could fight me, something tangible, a man just like you, with the same flesh and blood. Fight me, and you could feel that you too were a man. When I don't give you the excuse to fight, you quarrel with me, or rather with yourself. The one thing you've left out is telling me you'd die of grief if *she* suddenly disappeared... No, please, I've heard enough!"

I countered clumsily:

"I came to tell you, because I thought you ought to know that I intend leaving the Station with her."

"Still on the same track," Snow shrugged. "I only offered my opinion because I realized that you were losing touch with reality. And the further you go, the harder you fall. Can you come and see Sartorius around nine tomorrow morning?"

"Sartorius? I thought he wasn't letting anybody in. You told me you couldn't even phone him."

"He seems to have reached some kind of settlement. We never discuss our domestic troubles. With you, it's another matter. Will you come tomorrow morning?"

"All right," I grunted.

I noticed that Snow had slipped his left hand inside the cabinet. How long had the door been ajar? Probably for some time, but in the heat of the encounter I had not registered that the position of his hand was not natural. It was as if he was concealing something—or holding somebody's hand.

I licked my lips:

"Snow, what have you..."

"You'd better leave now," he said evenly.

I closed the door in the final glow of the red twilight. Rheya was huddled against the wall a few paces down the corridor. She sprang to her feet at once:

"You see? I did it, Kris. I feel so much better... Perhaps it will be easier and easier..."

"Yes, of course..." I answered absently.

We went back to my quarters. I was still speculating about that cabinet, and what had been hiding there, perhaps overhearing our entire conversation. My cheeks started to burn so hard that I involuntarily passed the back of my hand over them. What an idiotic meeting! And where did it get us? Nowhere. But there was tomorrow morning...

An abrupt thrill of fear ran through me. My encephalogram, a complete record of the workings of my brain, was to be beamed into the ocean in the form of radiation. What was it Snow had said—would I suffer terribly if Rheya departed? An encephalogram records every mental process, conscious and unconscious. If I want her to disappear, will it happen? But if I wanted to get rid of her would I also be appalled at the thought of her imminent destruction? Am I responsible for my unconscious? No one else is, if not myself. How stupid to agree to let them do it. Obviously I can examine the recording before it is used, but I won't be able to decode it. Nobody could. The experts can only identify general mental tendencies. For instance, they will say that the subject is thinking about some mathematical problem, but they are unable to specify its precise terms. They claim that they have to stick to generalizations because the encephalogram cannot discriminate among the stream of simultaneous impulses, only some of which have any psychological "counterpart," and they refuse point-blank to hazard any comment on the unconscious processes. So how could they be expected to decipher memories which have been more or less repressed?

Then why was I so afraid? I had told Rheya only that morning that the experiment could not work. If Terran neurophysiologists were incapable of decoding the recording, what chance was there for that great alien creature...?

Yet it had infiltrated my mind without my knowledge, surveyed my memory, and laid bare my most vulnerable point. That was undeniable. Without any assistance or radiation transmissions, it had found its way through the armored shell of the Station, located me, and come away with its spoils...

"Kris?" Rheya whispered.

Standing at the window with unseeing eyes, I had not noticed the coming of darkness. A thin veiling of high cloud glowed a dim silver in the light of the vanished sun, and obscured the stars.

If she disappears after the experiment, that will mean that I wanted her to disappear—that I killed her. No, I will not see Sartorius. They can't force me to cooperate. But I can't tell them the truth, I'll have to dissemble and lie, and keep on doing it... Because there may be thoughts, intentions and cruel hopes in my mind of which I know nothing, because I am a murderer unawares. Man has gone out to explore other worlds and other civilizations without having explored his own labyrinth of dark passages and secret chambers, and without finding what lies behind doorways that he himself has sealed. Was I to abandon Rheya there out of false shame, or because I lacked the courage?

"Kris," said Rheya, more softly still.

She was standing quite close to me now. I pretended not to hear. At that moment, I wanted to isolate myself. I had not yet resolved anything, or reached any decision. I stood motionless, looking at the dark sky and the cold stars, pale ghosts of the stars that shone on Earth. My mind was a blank. All I had was the grim certainty of having crossed some point of no return. I refused to admit that I was travelling towards what I could not reach. Apathy robbed me of the strength even to despise myself.

. . . Another three weeks. The shutters rose and fell on time. I was still a prisoner in my nightmares, and every morning the play began again. But was it a play? I put on a feigned composure, and Rheya played the same game. The deception was mutual and deliberate, and our agreement only contributed to our ultimate evasion. We talked about the future, and our life on Earth on the outskirts of some great city. We would spend the rest of our lives among green trees and under a blue sky, and never leave Earth again. Together we planned the layout of our house and garden and argued over details like the location of a hedge or a bench.

I do not believe that I was sincere for a single instant. Our plans were impossible, and I knew it, for even if Rheya could leave the Station and survive the voyage, how could I have got through the immigration checks with my clandestine passenger? Earth admits only human beings, and even then only when they carry the necessary papers. Rheya would be detained for an identity check at the first barrier, we would be separated, and she would give herself away at once. The Station was the one place where we could live together. Rheya must have known that, or found it out.

One night I heard Rheya get out of bed silently. I wanted to stop her; in the darkness and silence we occasionally managed to throw off our despair for a while by making each other forget. Rheya did not notice that I had woken up. When I stretched my hand out, she was already out of bed, and walking barefoot towards the door. Without daring to raise my voice, I whispered her name, but she was outside, and a narrow shaft of light shone through the doorway from the corridor.

There was a sound of whispering. Rheya was talking to somebody . . . but whom? Panic overtook me when I tried to stand up, and my legs would not move. I listened, but heard nothing. The blood hammered through my temples. I started counting, and was approaching a thousand when there was a movement in the doorway and Rheya returned. She stood there for a second without moving, and I made myself breathe evenly.

"Kris?" she whispered.

I did not answer.

She slid quickly into bed and lay down, taking care not to disturb me. Questions buzzed in my mind, but I would not let myself be the first to speak, and made no move. The silent questioning went on for an hour, maybe more. Then I fell asleep.

The morning was like any other. I watched Rheya furtively, but could not see any change in her behavior. After breakfast, we sat at the big panoramic window. The Station was hovering among purple clouds. Rheya was reading, and as I stared out I suddenly noticed that by holding my head at a certain angle I could see us both reflected in the window. I took my hand off the rail. Rheya had no idea that I was watching her. She glanced at me, obviously decided from my posture that I was looking at the ocean, then bent to kiss the place where my hand had rested. In a moment she was reading her book again.

"Rheya," I asked gently, "where did you go last night?"

"Last night?"

"Yes."

"You . . . you must have been dreaming, Kris. I didn't go anywhere."

"You didn't leave the cabin?"

"No. It must have been a dream."

"Perhaps . . . yes, perhaps I dreamt it."

The same evening, I started talking about our return to Earth again, but Rheya stopped me:

"Don't talk to me about the journey again, Kris. I don't want to hear any more about it, you know very well . . ."

"What?"

"No, nothing."

After we went to bed, she said that she was thirsty:

"There's a glass of fruit juice on the table over there. Could you give it to me?" She drank half of it then handed it to me.

"I'm not thirsty."

"Drink to my health then," she smiled.

It tasted slightly bitter, but my mind was on other things. She switched the light off.

"Rheya . . . If you won't talk about the voyage, let's talk about something else."

"If I did not exist, would you marry?"

"No."

"Never?"

"Never."

"Why not?"

"I don't know. I was by myself for ten years and I didn't marry again. Let's not talk about that..." My head was spinning as if I had been drinking too much.

"No, let's talk about it. What if I begged you to?"

"To marry again? Don't be silly, Rheya. I don't need anybody except you."

I felt her breath on my face and her arms holding me:

"Say it another way."

"I love you."

Her head fell to my shoulder, and I felt tears.

"Rheya, what's the matter?"

"Nothing... nothing... nothing..." Her voice echoed into silence, and my eyes closed.

The red dawn woke me with a splitting head and a neck so stiff that I felt as if the bones were welded together. My tongue was swollen, and my mouth felt foul. Then I reached out for Rheya, and my hand touched a cold sheet.

I sat up with a start.

I was alone—alone in bed and in the cabin. The concave window reflected a row of red suns. I dragged myself out of bed and staggered over to the bathroom, reeling like a drunkard and propping myself up on the furniture. It was empty. So was the workshop.

"Rheya."

Calling, running up and down the corridor.

"Rheya!" I screamed, one last time, then my voice gave out. I already knew the truth...

I do not remember the exact sequence of events after that, as I stumbled half naked through all the length and breadth of the Station. It seems to me that I even went into the refrigeration section, searched through the storage rooms, hammered with my fists on bolted doors, then came back again to throw myself against doors which had already resisted me. I half fell down flights of steps, picked myself up and hurried onwards. When I reached the double armoured doors which opened onto the ocean I was still calling, still hoping that it was a dream. Somebody was standing by me. Hands took hold of me and pulled me away.

I came to my senses again lying on a metal table in the little workshop and gasping for breath. My throat and nostrils were burning with some alcoholic vapor, my shirt was soaked in water, and my hair plastered over my skull.

Snow was busy at a medicine cupboard, shifting instruments and glass vessels which clattered with an unbearable din. Then his face appeared, looking gravely down into my eyes.

"Where is she?"

"She is not here."

"But... Rheya..."

He bent over me, brought his face closer, and spoke very slowly and clearly:

"Rheya is dead."

"She will come back," I whispered.

Instead of dreading her return, I wanted it. I did not attempt to remind myself why I myself had once tried to drive her away, and why I had been so afraid of her return.

"Drink this."

Snow held out a glass, and I threw it in his face. He staggered back, rubbing his eyes, and by the time he opened them again I was on my feet and standing over him. How small he was...

"It was you."

"What do you mean?"

"Come on, Snow, you know what I mean. It was you who met her the other night. You told her to give me a sleeping pill . . . What has happened to her? Tell me!"

He felt in his shirt pocket and took out an envelope. I snatched it out of his hand. It was sealed, and there was no inscription. Inside was a sheet of paper folded twice, and I recognized the sprawling, rather childish handwriting:

"My darling, I was the one who asked him. He is a good man. I am sorry I had to lie to you. I beg you to give me this one wish—hear him out, and do nothing to harm yourself. You have been marvellous."

There was one more word, which she had crossed out, but I could see that she had signed "Rheya."

My mind was now absolutely clear. Even if I had wanted to scream hysterically, my voice had gone, and I did not even have the strength to groan.

"How...?"

"Later, Kelvin. You've got to calm down."

"I'm calm now. Tell me how."

"Disintegration."

"But... what did you use?"

"The Roche apparatus was unsuitable. Sartorius built something else, a new destabilizer. A miniature instrument, with a range of a few yards."

"And she..."

"She disappeared. A pop, and a puff of air. That's all."

"A short-range instrument..."

"Yes, we didn't have the resources for anything bigger."

The walls loomed over me, and I shut my eyes.

"She will come back."

"No."

"What do you know about it?"

"You remember the wings of foam? Since that day, they do not come back."

"You killed her," I whispered.

"Yes . . . In my place, what else would you have done?"

I turned away from him and began pacing up and down the room. Nine steps to the corner. About turn. Nine more rapid steps, and I was facing Snow again.

"Listen, we'll write a report. We'll ask for an immediate link with the Council. It's feasible, and they'll accept—they must. The planet will no longer be subject to the four-power convention. We'll be authorized to use any means at our disposal. We can send for anti-matter generators. Nothing can stand up against them, nothing . . ." I was shouting now, and blinded with tears.

"You want to destroy it? Why?"

"Get out, leave me alone!"

"No, I won't get out."

"Snow!" I glared at him, and he shook his head. "What do you want? What am I supposed to do?"

He walked back to the table.

"Fine, we'll draw up a report."

I started pacing again.

"Sit down!"

"I'll do what I like!"

"There are two distinct questions. One, the facts. Two, our recommendations."

"Do we have to talk about it now?"

"Yes, now."

"I won't listen, you hear? I'm not interested in your distinctions."

"We sent our last message about two months ago, before Gibarian's death. We'll have to establish exactly how the 'visitor' phenomena function . . ."

I grabbed his arm:

"Will you shut up!"

"Hit me if you like, but I will not shut up."

"Oh, talk away, if it gives you pleasure . . ." I let him go.

"Good, listen. Sartorius will want to conceal certain facts. I'm almost certain of it."

"And what about you? Won't you conceal anything?"

"No. Not now. This business goes further than individual responsibilities. You know that as well as I do."

[*Before leaving the Station, Kelvin visits the surface of the planet.*]

. . . I flew past the island; and slowly, yard by yard, I descended to the level of the eroded peaks. The mimoid was not large. It measured about three quarters of a mile from end to end, and was a few hundred yards wide. In some places, it was close to splitting apart. This mimoid was obviously a fragment of a far larger formation. On the scale of Solaris it was only a tiny splinter, weeks or perhaps months old.

Among the mottled crags overhanging the ocean, I found a kind of beach, a sloping, fairly even surface a few yards square, and steered towards it. The rotors almost hit a cliff that reared up suddenly in my path, but I landed safely, cut the motor and slid back the canopy. Standing on the fuselage I made sure that there was no chance of the flitter sliding into the ocean. Waves were licking at the jagged bank about fifteen paces away, but the machine rested solidly on its legs, and I jumped to the "ground."

The cliff I had almost hit was a huge bony membrane pierced with holes, and full of knotty swellings. A crack several yards wide split this wall diagonally and enabled me to examine the interior of the island, already glimpsed through the apertures in the membrane. I edged warily onto the nearest ledge, but my boots showed no tendency to slide and the suit did not impede my movements, and I went on climbing until I had reached a height of about four storeys above the ocean, and could see a broad stretch of petrified landscape stretching back until it was lost from sight in the depths of the mimoid.

It was like looking at the ruins of an ancient town, a Moroccan city tens of centuries old, convulsed by an earthquake or some other disaster. I made out a tangled web of winding sidestreets choked with debris, and alleyways which fell abruptly towards the oily foam that floated close to the shore. In the middle distance, great battlements stood intact, sustained by ossified buttresses. There were dark openings in the swollen, sunken walls—traces of windows or loop-holes. The whole of this floating town canted to one side or another like a foundering ship, pitched and turned slowly, and the sun cast continually moving shadows, which crept among the ruined alleys. Now and again a polished surface caught and reflected the light. I took the risk of climbing higher, then stopped; rivulets of fine sand were beginning to trickle down the rocks above my head, cascading into ravines and alleyways and rebounding in swirling clouds of dust. The mimoid is not made of stone, and to dispel the illusion one only has to pick up a piece of it: it is lighter than pumice, and composed of small, very porous cells.

Now I was high enough to feel the swaying of the mimoid. It was moving forward, propelled by the dark muscles of the ocean towards an unknown destination, but its inclination varied. It rolled from side to side, and the languid oscillation was accompanied by the gentle rustling sound of the yellow and grey foam which streamed off the emerging shore. The mimoid had acquired its swinging motion long before, probably at its birth, and even while it grew and broke up it had retained its initial pattern.

Only now did I realize that I was not in the least concerned with the mimoid, and that I had flown here not to explore the formation but to acquaint myself with the ocean.

With the flitter a few paces behind me, I sat on the rough, fissured beach. A heavy black wave broke over the edge of the bank and spread out, not black, but a dirty green. The ebbing wave left viscous streamlets behind which flowed back quivering towards the ocean. I went closer, and when the next wave came I held out my hand. What followed was a faithful reproduction of a phenomenon which had been analyzed a century before: the wave hesitated, recoiled, and then enveloped my hand without touching it, so that a thin covering of "air" separated my glove inside a cavity which had been fluid a moment previously, and now had a fleshy consistency. I raised my hand slowly, and the wave, or rather an outcrop of the wave, rose at the same time, enfolding my hand in a translucent cyst with greenish reflections. I stood up, so as to raise my hand still higher, and the gelatinous substance stretched like a rope, but did not break. The main body of the wave remained motionless on the shore, surrounding my feet without touching them, like some strange beast patiently waiting for the experiment to finish. A flower had grown out of the ocean, and its calyx was moulded to my fingers. I stepped back. The stem trembled, stirred uncertainly and fell back into the wave, which gathered it and receded.

I repeated the game several times, until—as the first experimenter had observed—a wave arrived which avoided me indifferently, as if bored with a too familiar sensation. I knew that to revive the "curiosity" of the ocean I would have to wait several hours. Disturbed by the phenomenon I had stimulated, I sat down again. Although I had read numerous accounts of it, none of them had prepared me for the experience as I had lived it, and I felt somehow changed.

In all their movements, taken together or singly, each of these branches reaching out of the ocean seemed to display a kind of cautious but not feral alertness, a curiosity avid for quick apprehension of a new, unexpected form, and regretful at having to retreat, unable to exceed the limits set by a mysterious law. The contrast was inexpressible between that lively curiosity and the shimmering immensity of the ocean that stretched away out of sight . . . I had never felt its gigantic presence so strongly, or its powerful changeless silence, or the secret forces that gave the waves their regular rise and fall. I sat unseeing, and sank into a universe of inertia, glided down an irresistible slope and identifed myself with the dumb, fluid colossus; it was as if I had forgiven it everything, without the slightest effort of word or thought.

During that last week, I had been behaving so normally that Snow had stopped keeping a watchful eye on me. On the surface, I was calm: in secret, without really admitting it, I was waiting for something. Her return? How could I have been waiting for that? We all know that we are material creatures, subject to the laws of physiology and physics, and not even the power of all our feelings combined can defeat those laws. All we can do is detest them. The age-old faith of lovers and poets in the power of love, stronger than death, that *finis vitae sed non amoris,* is a lie, useless and not even funny. So must one be resigned to being a clock that measures the passage of time, now out of order, now repaired, and whose mechanism generates despair and love as soon as its maker sets it going? Are we to grow used to the idea that every man relives ancient torments, which are all the more profound because they grow comic with repetition? That human existence should repeat itself, well and good, but that it should repeat itself like a hackneyed tune, or a record a drunkard keeps playing as he feeds coins into the jukebox...

That liquid giant had been the death of hundreds of men. The entire human race had tried in vain to establish even the most tenuous link with it, and it bore my weight without noticing me any more than it would notice a speck of dust. I did not believe that it could respond to the tragedy of two human beings. Yet its activities did have a purpose... True, I was not absolutely certain, but leaving would mean giving up a chance, perhaps an infinitesimal one, perhaps only imaginary . . . Must I go on living here then, among the objects we both had touched, in the air she had breathed? In the name of what? In the hope of her return? I hoped for nothing. And yet I lived in expectation. Since she had gone, that was all that remained. I did not know what achievements, what mockery, even what tortures still awaited me. I knew nothing, and I persisted in the faith that the time of cruel miracles was not past.

They

Robert Heinlein

They would not let him alone.

They would never let him alone. He realized that that was part of the plot against him—never to leave him in peace, never to give him a chance to mull over the lies they had told him, time enough to pick out the flaws, and to figure out the truth for himself.

That damned attendant this morning! He had come busting in with his breakfast tray, waking him, and causing him to forget his dream. If only he could remember that dream—

Someone was unlocking the door. He ignored it.

"Howdy, old boy. They tell me you refused your breakfast?" Dr. Hayward's professionally kindly mask hung over his bed.

"I wasn't hungry."

"But we can't have that. You'll get weak, and then I won't be able to get you well completely. Now get up and get your clothes on and I'll order an eggnog for you. Come on, that's a good fellow!"

Unwilling, but still less willing at that moment to enter into any conflict of wills, he got out of bed and slipped on his bathrobe. "That's better," Hayward approved. "Have a cigarette?"

"No, thank you."

The doctor shook his head in a puzzled fashion. "Darned if I can figure you out. Loss of interest in physical pleasures does not fit your type of case."

"What is my type of case?" he inquired in flat tones.

"Tut! Tut!" Hayward tried to appear roguish. "If medicos told their professional secrets, they might have to work for a living."

"What is my type of case?"

"Well—the label doesn't matter, does it? Suppose you tell me. I really know nothing about your case as yet. Don't you think it is about time you talked?"

"I'll play chess with you."

"All right, all right." Hayward made a gesture of impatient concession. "We've played chess every day for a week. If you will talk, I'll play chess."

What could it matter? If he was right, they already understood perfectly that he had discovered their plot; there was nothing to be gained by concealing the obvious. Let them try to argue him out of it. Let the tail go with the hide! To hell with it!

He got out the chessmen and commenced setting them up. "What do you know of my case so far?"

"Very little. Physical examination, negative. Past history, negative. High intelligence, as shown by your record in school and your success in your profession. Occasional fits of moodiness, but nothing exceptional. The only positive information was the incident that caused you to come here for treatment."

"To be brought here, you mean. Why should it cause comment?"

"Well, good gracious, man—if you barricade yourself in your room and insist that your wife is plotting against you, don't you expect people to notice?"

"But she *was* plotting against me—and so are you. White, or black?"

"Black—it's your turn to attack. Why do you think we are plotting against you?"

"It's an involved story, and goes way back into my early childhood. There was an immediate incident, however—" He opened by advancing the white king's knight to KB3. Hayward's eyebrows raised.

"You make a piano attack?"

"Why not? You know that it is not safe for me to risk a gambit with you."

The doctor shrugged his shoulders and answered the opening. "Suppose we start with your early childhood. It may shed more light than more recent incidents. Did you feel that you were being persecuted as a child?"

"No!" He half rose from his chair. "When I was a child I was sure of myself. I knew then, I tell you; I knew! Life was worthwhile, and I knew it. I was at peace with myself and my surroundings. Life was good and I was good and I assumed that the creatures around me were like myself."

"And weren't they?"

"Not at all! Particularly the children. I didn't know what viciousness was until I was turned loose with other children. The little devils! And I was expected to be like them and play with them."

The doctor nodded. "I know. The herd compulsion. Children can be pretty savage at times."

"You've missed the point. This wasn't any healthy roughness; these creatures were different—not like myself at all. They looked like me, but they were not like me. If I tried to say anything to one of them about anything that mattered to me, all I could get was a stare and a scornful laugh. Then they would find some way to punish me for having said it."

Hayward nodded. "I see what you mean. How about grownups?"

"That is somewhat different. Adults don't matter to children at first—or, rather they did not matter to me. They were too big, and they did not bother me, and they were busy with things that did not enter into my considerations. It was only when I noticed that my presence affected them that I began to wonder about them."

"How do you mean?"

"Well, they never did the things when I was around that they did when I was not around."

Hayward looked at him carefully. "Won't that statement take quite a lot of justifying? How do you know what they did when you weren't around?"

He acknowledged the point. "But I used to catch them just stopping. If I came into a room, the conversation would stop suddenly, and then it would pick up about the weather or something equally inane. Then I took to hiding and listening and looking. Adults did not behave the same way in my presence as out of it."

"Your move, I believe. But see here, old man—that was when you were a child. Every child passes through that phase. Now that you are a man, you must see the adult point of view. Children are strange creatures and have to be protected—at least, we do protect them—from many adult interests. There is a whole code of conventions in the matter that—"

"Yes, yes," he interrupted impatiently, "I know all that. Nevertheless, I noticed enough and remembered enough that was never clear to me later. And it put me on my guard to notice the next thing."

"Which was?" He noticed that the doctor's eyes were averted as he adjusted a castle's position.

"The things I saw people doing and heard them talking about were never of any importance. They must be doing something else."

"I don't follow you."

"You don't choose to follow me. I'm telling this to you in exchange for a game of chess."

"Why do you like to play chess so well?"

"Because it is the only thing in the world where I can see all the factors and understand all the rules. Never mind—I saw all around me this enormous plant, cities, farms, factories, churches, schools, homes, railroads, luggage, roller coasters, trees, saxophones, libraries, people and animals. People that looked like me and who should have felt very much like me, if what I was told was the truth. But what did they appear to be doing? 'They went to work to earn the money to buy the food to get the strength to go to work to get the strength to buy the food to earn the money to go to—' until they fell over dead. Any slight variation in the basic pattern did not matter, for they always fell over dead. And everybody tried to tell me that I should be doing the same thing. I knew better!"

The doctor gave him a look apparently intended to denote helpless surrender and laughed. "I can't argue with you. Life does look like that, and maybe it is just that futile. But it is the only life we have. Why not make up your mind to enjoy it as much as possible?"

"Oh, no!" He looked both sulky and stubborn. "You can't peddle nonsense to me by claiming to be fresh out of sense. How do I know? Because all this complex stage setting, all these swarms of actors, could not have been put here just to make idiot noises at each other. Some other explanation, but not that one. An insanity as enormous, as complex, as the one around me had to be planned. I've found the plan!"

"Which is?"

He noticed that the doctor's eyes were again averted.

"It is a play intended to divert me, to occupy my mind and confuse me, to keep me so busy with details that I will not have time to think about the meaning. You are all in it, every one of you." He shook his finger in the doctor's face. "Most of them may be helpless automatons, but you're not. You are one of the conspirators. You've been sent in as a trouble-shooter to try to force me to go back to playing the role assigned to me!"

He saw that the doctor was waiting for him to quiet down.

"Take it easy," Hayward finally managed to say. "Maybe it is all a conspiracy, but why do you think that you have been singled out for special attention? Maybe it is a joke on all of us. Why couldn't I be one of the victims as well as yourself?"

"Got you!" He pointed a long finger at Hayward. "That is the essence of the plot. All of these creatures have been set up to look like me in order to prevent me from realizing that I was the center of the arrangements. But I have noticed the key fact, the mathematically inescapable fact, that I am unique. Here am I, sitting on the inside. The world extends outward from me. I am the center—"

"Easy, man, easy! Don't you realize that the world looks that way to me, too. We are each the center of the universe—"

"Not so! That is what you have tried to make me believe, that I am just one of millions more just like me. Wrong! If they were like me, then I could get into communication with them. I can't. I have tried and tried and I can't. I've sent out my inner thoughts, seeking some one other being who has them, too. What have I gotten back? Wrong answers, jarring incongruities, meaningless obscenity. I've tried. I tell you. God!—how I've tried! But there is nothing out there to speak to me—nothing but emptiness and otherness!"

"Wait a minute. Do you mean to say that you think there is nobody home at my end of the line? Don't you believe that I am alive and conscious?"

He regarded the doctor soberly. "Yes, I think you are probably alive, but you are one of the others—my antagonists. But you have set thousands of others around me whose faces are blank, not lived in, and whose speech is a meaningless reflex of noise."

"Well, then, if you concede that I am an ego, why do you insist that I am so very different from yourself?"

"Why? Wait!" He pushed back from the chess table and strode over to the wardrobe, from which he took out a violin case.

While he was playing, the lines of suffering smoothed out of his face and his expression took a relaxed beatitude. For a while he recaptured the emotions, but not the knowledge, which he had possessed in dreams. The melody proceeded easily from proposition to proposition with inescapable, unforced logic. He finished with a triumphant statement of the essential thesis and turned to the doctor. "Well?"

"Hm-m-m." He seemed to detect an even greater degree of caution in the doctor's manner. "It's an odd bit, but remarkable. 'S pity you didn't take up the violin seriously. You could have made quite a reputation. You could even now. Why don't you do it? You could afford to, I believe."

He stood and stared at the doctor for a long moment, then shook his head as if trying to clear it. "It's no use," he said slowly, "no use at all. There is no possibility of communication. I am alone." He replaced the instrument in its case and returned to the chess table. "My move, I believe?"

"Yes. Guard your queen."

He studied the board. "Not necessary. I no longer need my queen. Check."

The doctor interposed a pawn to parry the attack.

He nodded. "You use your pawn well, but I have learned to anticipate your play. Check again—and mate, I think."

The doctor examined the new situation. "No," he decided, "no—not quite." He retreated from the square under attack. "Not checkmate—stalemate at the worst. Yes, another stalemate."

He was upset by the doctor's visit. He couldn't be wrong, basically, yet the doctor had certainly pointed out logical holes in his position. From a logical standpoint the whole world might be a fraud perpetrated on everybody. But logic meant nothing—logic itself was a fraud, starting with unproved assumptions and capable of proving anything. The world is what it is!—and carries its own evidence of trickery.

But does it? What did he have to go on? Could he lay down a line between known facts and everything else and then make a reasonable interpretation of the world, based on facts alone—an interpretation free from complexities of logic and no hidden assumptions of points not certain. Very well—

First fact, himself. He knew himself directly. He existed.

Second facts, the evidence of his "five senses," everything that he himself saw and heard and smelled and tasted with his physical senses. Subject to their limitations, he must believe his senses. Without them he was entirely solitary, shut up in a locker of bone, blind, deaf, cutoff, the only being in the world.

And that was not the case. He knew that he did not invent the information brought to him by his senses. There had to be something else out there, some otherness that produced the things his senses recorded. All philosophies that claimed that the physical world around him did not exist except in his imagination were sheer nonsense.

But beyond that, what? Were there any third facts on which he could rely? No, not at this point. He could not afford to believe anything that he was told, or that he read, or that was implicitly assumed to be true about the world around him. No, he could not believe any of it, for the sum total of what he had been told and read and been taught in school was so contradictory, so senseless, so wildly insane that none of it could be believed unless he personally confirmed it.

Wait a minute—the very telling of these lies, these senseless contradictions, was a fact in itself, known to him directly. To that extent they were data, probably very important data.

The world as it had been shown to him was a piece of unreason, an idiot's dream. Yet it was on too mammoth a scale to be without some reason. He came wearily back to his original point: Since the world could not be as crazy as it appeared to be, it must necessarily have been arranged to appear crazy in order to deceive him as to the truth.

Why had they done it to him? And what was the truth behind the sham? There must be some clue in the deception itself. What thread ran through it all? Well, in the first place he had been given a superabundance of explanations of the world around him, philosophies, religions, "common sense" explanations. Most of them were so clumsy, so obviously inadequate, or meaningless, that they could hardly have expected him to take them seriously. They must have intended them simply as misdirection.

But there were certain basic assumptions running through all the hundreds of explanations of the craziness around him. It must be these basic assumptions that he was expected to believe. For example, there was the deep-seated assumption that he was a "human being," essentially like millions of others around him and billions more in the past and the future.

That was nonsense! He had never once managed to get into real communication with all those things that looked so much like him but were so different. In the agony of his loneliness, he had deceived himself that Alice understood him and was a being like him. He knew now that he had suppressed and refused to examine thousands of little discrepancies because he could not bear the thought of returning to complete loneliness. He had needed to believe that his wife was a living, breathing being of his own kind who understood his inner thoughts. He had refused to consider the possibility that she was simply, a mirror, an echo—or something unthinkably worse.

He had found a mate, and the world was tolerable, even though dull, stupid, and full of petty annoyance. He was moderately happy and had put away his suspicions. He had accepted, quite docilely, the treadmill he was expected to use, until a slight mischance had momentarily cut through the fraud—then his suspicions had returned with impounded force; the bitter knowledge of his childhood had been confirmed.

He supposed that he had been a fool to make a fuss about it. If he had kept his mouth shut they would not have locked him up. He should have been as subtle and as shrewd as they, kept his eyes and ears open and learned the details of and the reasons for the plot against him. He might have learned how to circumvent it.

But what if they had locked him up—the whole world was an asylum and all of them his keepers.

A key scraped in the lock, and he looked up to see an attendant entering with a tray. "Here's your dinner, sir."

"Thanks, Joe," he said gently. "Just put it down."

"Movies tonight, sir, " the attendant went on. "Wouldn't you like to go? Dr. Hayward said you could—"

"No, thank you. I prefer not to."

"I wish you would, sir." He noticed with amusement the persuasive intentness of the attendant's manner. "I think the doctor wants you to. It's a good movie. There's a Mickey Mouse cartoon—"

"You almost persuade me, Joe," he answered with passive agreeableness. "Mickey's trouble is the same as mine, essentially. However, I'm not going. They need not bother to hold movies tonight."

"Oh, there will be movies in any case, sir. Lots of our other guests will attend."

"Really? Is that an example of thoroughness, or are you simply keeping up the pretense in talking to me? It isn't necessary, Joe, if it's any strain on you. I know the game. If I don't attend, there is no point in holding movies."

He liked the grin with which the attendant answered this thrust. Was it possible that this being was created just as he appeared to be—big muscles, phlegmatic disposition, tolerant, doglike? Or was there nothing going on behind those kind eyes, nothing but robot reflex? No, it was more likely that he was one of them, since he was so closely in attendance on him.

The attendant left and he busied himself at his supper tray, scooping up the already-cut bites of meat with a spoon, the only implement provided. He smiled again at their caution and thoroughness. No danger of that—he would not destroy this body as long as it served him in investigating the truth of the matter. There were still many different avenues of research available before taking that possibly irrevocable step.

After supper he decided to put his thoughts in better order by writing them; he obtained paper. He should start with a general statement of some underlying postulate of the credos that had been drummed into him all his "life." Life? Yes, that was a good one. He wrote:

"I am told that I was born a certain number of years ago and that I will die a similar number of years hence. Various clumsy stories have been offered me to explain to me where I was before birth and what becomes of me after death, but they are rough lies, not intended to deceive, except as misdirection. In every other possible way the world around me assures me that I am mortal, here but a few years, and a few years hence gone completely—nonexistent.

"WRONG—I am immortal. I transcend this little time axis; a seventy-year span on it is but a casual phase in my experience. Second only to the prime datum of my own existence is the emotionally convincing certainty of my own continuity. I may be a closed curve, but, closed or open, I neither have a beginning nor an end. Self-awareness is not relational; it is absolute, and cannot be reached to be destroyed, or created. Memory, however, being a relational aspect of consciousness, may be tampered with and possibly destroyed.

"It is true that most religions which have been offered me teach immortality, but note the fashion in which they teach it. The surest way to lie convincingly is to tell the truth unconvincingly. They did not wish me to believe.

"Caution: Why have they tried so hard to convince me that I am going to die in a few years? There must be a very important reason. I infer that they are preparing me for some sort of a major change. It may be crucially important for me to figure out their intentions about this—probably I have several years in which to reach a decision. Note:

Avoid using the types of reasoning they have taught me."

The attendant was back. "Your wife is here, sir."

"Tell her to go away."

"Please, sir—Dr. Hayward is most anxious that you should see her."

"Tell Dr. Hayward that I said that he is an excellent chess player."

"Yes, sir." The attendant waited for a moment. "Then you won't see her, sir?"

"No, I won't see her."

He wandered around the room for some minutes after the attendant had left, too distraught to return to his recapitulation. By and large they had played very decently with him since they had brought him here. He was glad that they had allowed him to have a room alone, and he certainly had more time free for contemplation than had ever been possible on the outside. To be sure, continuous effort to keep him busy and to distract him was made, but, by being stubborn, he was able to circumvent the rules and gain some hours each day for introspection.

But, damnation!—he did wish they would not persist in using Alice in their attempts to divert his thoughts. Although the intense terror and revulsion which she had inspired in him when he had first rediscovered the truth had now aged into a simple feeling of repugnance and distaste for her company, nevertheless it was emotionally upsetting to be reminded of her, to be forced into making decisions about her.

After all, she had been his wife for many years. Wife? What was a wife? Another soul like one's own, a complement, the other necessary pole to the couple, a sanctuary of understanding and sympathy in the boundless depths of aloneness. That was what he had thought, what he had needed to believe and had believed fiercely for years. The yearning need for companionship of his own kind had caused him to see himself reflected in those beautiful eyes and had made him quite uncritical of occasional incongruities in her responses.

He sighed. He felt that he had sloughed off most of the typed emotional reactions which they had taught him by precept and example, but Alice had gotten under his skin, 'way under, and it still hurt. He had been happy—what if it had been a dope dream? They had given him an excellent, a beautiful mirror to play with—the more fool he to have looked behind it!

Wearily he turned back to his summing up:

"The world is explained in either one of two ways; the commonsense way, which says that the world is pretty much as it appears to be and that ordinary human conduct and motivations are reasonable, and the religio-mystic solution, which states that the world is dream stuff, unreal, insubstantial, with reality somewhere beyond.

"WRONG—both of them. The common-sense scheme has no sense to it of any sort. Life is short and full of trouble. Man born of woman is born to trouble as the sparks fly upward. His days are few and they are numbered. All is vanity and vexation. Those quotations may be jumbled and incorrect, but that is a fair statement of the common-sense world is-as-it-seems in its only possible evaluation. In such a world, human striving is about as rational as the blind darting of a moth against a light bulb. The common-sense world is a blind insanity, out of nowhere, going nowhere, to no purpose.

"As for the other solution, it appears more rational on the surface, in that it rejects the utterly irrational world of common sense. But it is not a rational solution, it is simply a flight from reality of any sort, for it refuses to believe the results of the only available direct communication between the ego and the Outside. Certainly the 'five senses' are poor enough channels of communication, but they are the only channels."

He crumpled up the paper and flung himself from the chair. Order and logic were no good—his answer was right because it smelled right. But he still did not know all the answer. Why the grand scale to the deception, countless creatures, whole continents, an enormously involved and minutely detailed matrix of insane history, insane tradition, insane culture? Why bother with more than a cell and a strait jacket?

It must be, it had to be, because it was supremely important to deceive him completely, because a lesser deception would not do. Could it be that they dare not let him suspect his real identity no matter how difficult and involved the fraud?

He had to know. In some fashion he must get behind the deception and see what went on when he was not looking. He had had one glimpse; this time he must see the actual workings, catch the puppet masters in their manipulations.

Obviously the first step must be to escape from this asylum, but to do it so craftily that they would never see him, never catch up with him, not have a chance to set the stage before him. That would be hard to do. He must excel them in shrewdness and subtlety.

Once decided, he spent the rest of the evening in considering the means by which he might accomplish his purpose. It seemed almost impossible—he must get away without once being seen and remain in strict hiding. They must lose track of him completely in order that they would not know where to center their deceptions. That would mean going without food for several days. Very well—he could do it. He must not give them any warning by unusual action or manner.

The lights blinked twice. Docilely he got up and commenced preparations for bed. When the attendant looked through the peephole he was already in bed, with his face turned to the wall.

Gladness! Gladness everywhere! It was good to be with his own kind, to hear the music swelling out of every living thing, as it always had and always would—good to know that everything was living and aware of him, participating in him, as he participated in them. It was good to be, good to know the unity of many and the diversity of one. There had been one bad thought—the details escaped him—but it was gone—it had never been; there was no place for it.

The early-morning sounds from the adjacent ward penetrated the sleepladen body which served him here and gradually recalled him to awareness of the hospital room. The transition was so gentle that he carried over full recollection of what he had been doing and why. He lay still, a gentle smile on his face, and savored the uncouth, but not unpleasant, languor of the body he wore. Strange that he had ever forgotten, despite their tricks and stratagems. Well, now that he had recalled the key, he would quickly set things right in this odd place. He would call them in at once and announce the new order. It would be amusing to see old Glaroon's expression when he realized that the cycle had ended—

The click of the peephole and the rasp of the door being unlocked guillotined his line of thought. The morning attendant pushed briskly in with the breakfast tray and placed it on the tip table. "Morning, sir. Nice, bright day—want it in bed, or will you get up?"

Don't answer! Don't listen! Suppress this distraction! This is part of their plan—But it was too late, too late. He felt himself slipping, falling, wrenched from reality back into the fraud world in which they had kept him. It was gone, gone completely, with no single association around him to which to anchor memory. There was nothing left but the sense of heart-breaking loss and the acute ache of unsatisfied catharsis.

"Leave it where it is. I'll take care of it."

"Okey-doke." The attendant bustled out, slamming the door, and noisily locked it.

He lay quite still for a long time, every nerve end in his body screaming for relief.

At last he got out of bed, still miserably unhappy, and attempted to concentrate on his plans for escape. But the psychic wrench he had received in being recalled so suddenly from his plane of reality had left him bruised and emotionally disturbed. His mind insisted on rechewing its doubts, rather than engage in constructive thought. Was it possible that the doctor was right, that he was not alone in his miserable dilemma? Was he really simply suffering from paranoia, delusions of self-importance?

Could it be that each unit in this yeasty swarm around him was the prison of another lonely ego—helpless, blind, and speechless, condemned to an eternity of miserable loneliness? Was the look of suffering which he had brought to Alice's face a true reflection of inner torment and not simply a piece of playacting intended to maneuver him into compliance with their plans?

A knock sounded at the door. He said "Come in," without looking up. Their comings and goings did not matter to him.

"Dearest—" A well-known voice spoke slowly and hesitantly.

"Alice!" He was on his feet at once, and facing her. "Who let you in here?"

"Please, dear, please—I had to see you."

"It isn't fair. It isn't fair." He spoke more to himself than to her. Then: "Why did you come?"

She stood up to him with a dignity he had hardly expected. The beauty of her childlike face had been marred by line and shadow, but it shone with an unexpected courage. "I love you," she answered quietly. "You can tell me to go away, but you can't make me stop loving you and trying to help you."

He turned away from her in an agony of indecision. Could it be possible that he had misjudged her? Was there, behind that barrier of flesh and sound symbols, a spirit that truly yearned toward his? Lovers whispering in the dark—*"You do understand, don't you?"*

"Yes, dear heart, I understand."

"Then nothing that happens to us can matter, as long as we are together and understand—" Words, words, rebounding hollowly from an unbroken wall—

No, he couldn't be wrong! Test her again—"Why did you keep me on that job in Omaha?"

"But I didn't make you keep that job. I simply pointed out that we should think twice before—"

"Never mind. Never mind." Soft hands and a sweet face preventing him with mild stubborness from ever doing the thing that his heart told him to do. Always with the best of intentions, the best of intentions, but always so that he had never quite managed to do the silly, unreasonable things that he knew were worth while. Hurry, hurry, hurry, and strive, with an angel-faced jockey to see that you don't stop long enough to think for yourself—

"Why did you try to stop me from going back upstairs that day?"

She managed to smile, although her eyes were already spilling over with tears. "I didn't know it really mattered to you. I didn't want us to miss the train."

It had been a small thing, an unimportant thing. For some reason not clear to him he had insisted on going back upstairs to his study when they were about to leave the house for a short vacation. It was raining, and she had pointed out that there was barely enough time to get to the station. He had surprised himself and her, too, by insisting on his own way, in circumstances in which he had never been known to be stubborn.

He had actually pushed her to one side and forced his way up the stairs. Even then nothing might have come of it had he not—quite unnecessarily—raised the shade of the window that faced toward the rear of the house.

It was a very small matter. It had been raining, hard, out in front. From this window the weather was clear and sunny, with no sign of rain.

He had stood there quite a long while, gazing out at the impossible sunshine and rearranging his cosmos in his mind. He re-examined long-suppressed doubts in the light of this one small but totally unexplainable discrepancy. Then he had turned and had found that she was standing behind him.

He had been trying ever since to forget the expression that he had surprised on her face.

"What about the rain?"

"The rain?" she repeated in a small, puzzled voice. "Why, it was raining, of course. What about it?"

"But it was not raining out my study window."

"What? But of course it was. I did notice the sun break through the clouds for a moment, but that was all."

"Nonsense!"

"But darling, what has the weather to do with you and me? What difference does it make whether it rains or not—to us?" She approached him timidly and slid a small hand between his arm and side. "Am I responsible for the weather?"

"I think you are. Now please go."

She withdrew from him, brushed blindly at her eyes, gulped once, then said in a voice held steady: "All right. I'll go. But remember—you can come home if you want to. And I'll be there, if you want me." She waited a moment, then added hesitantly: "Would you . . . would you kiss me good-bye?"

He made no answer of any sort, neither with voice nor eyes. She looked at him, then turned, fumbled blindly for the door, and rushed through it.

The creature he knew as Alice went to the place of assembly without stopping to change form. "It is necessary to adjourn this sequence. I am no longer able to influence his decisions."

They had expected it, nevertheless they stirred with dismay.

The Glaroon addressed the First for Manipulation. "Prepare to graft the selected memory track at once."

Then, turning to the First for Operations, the Glaroon said: "The extrapolation shows that he will tend to escape within two of his days. This sequence degenerated primarily through your failure to extend that rainfall all around him. Be advised."

"It would be simpler if we understood his motives."

"In my capacity as Dr. Hayward, I have often thought so," commented the Glaroon acidly, "but if we understood his motives, we would be part of *him.* Bear in mind the Treaty! He almost remembered."

The creature known as Alice spoke up. "Could he not have the Taj Mahal next sequence? For some reason he values it."

"You are becoming assimilated!"

"Perhaps, I am not in fear. Will he receive it?"

"It will be considered."

The Glaroon continued with orders: "Leave structures standing until adjournment. New York City and Harvard University are now dismantled. Divert him from those sectors.

"Move!"

The Library of Babel

Jorge Luis Borges

By this art you may contemplate
the variation of the 23 letters . . .
—*The Anatomy of Melancholy,*
Part 2, Sect. II, Mem. IV.

The universe (which others call the Library) is composed of an indefinite, perhaps infinite, number of hexagonal galleries, with enormous ventilation shafts in the middle, encircled by very low railings. From any hexagon the upper or lower stories are visible, interminably. The distribution of the galleries is invariable. Twenty shelves—five long shelves per side—cover all sides except two; their height, which is that of each floor, scarcely exceeds that of an average librarian. One of the free sides gives upon a narrow entrance way, which leads to another gallery, identical to the first and to all the others. To the left and to the right of the entrance way are two miniature rooms. One allows standing room for sleeping; the other, the satisfaction of fecal necessities. Through this section passes the spiral staircase, which plunges down into the abyss and rises up to the heights. In the entrance way hangs a mirror, which faithfully duplicates appearances. People are in the habit of inferring from this mirror that the Library is not infinite (if it really were, why this illusory duplication?); I prefer to dream that the polished surfaces feign and promise infinity. . . .

Light comes from some spherical fruits called by the name of lamps. There are two, running transversally, in each hexagon. The light they emit is insufficient, incessant.

Like all men of the Library, I have traveled in my youth. I have journeyed in search of a book, perhaps of the catalogue of catalogues; now that my eyes can scarcely decipher what I write, I am preparing to die a few leagues from the hexagon in which I was born. Once dead, there will not lack pious hands to hurl me over the banister; my sepulchre shall be the unfathomable air: my body will sink lengthily and will corrupt and dissolve in the wind engendered by the fall, which is infinite. I affirm that the Library is interminable. The idealists argue that the hexagonal halls are a necessary form of absolute space or, at least, of our intuition of space. They contend that a triangular or pentagonal hall is inconceivable. (The mystics claim that to them ecstasy reveals a round chamber containing a great book with a continuous back circling the walls of the room; but their testimony is suspect; their words, obscure. That cyclical book is God.) Let it suffice me, for the time being, to repeat the classic dictum: *The Library is a sphere whose consummate center is any hexagon, and whose circumference is inaccessible.*

Five shelves correspond to each one of the walls of each hexagon; each shelf contains thirty-two books of a uniform format; each book is made up of four hundred and ten pages; each page, of forty lines; each line, of some eighty black letters. There are also letters on the spine of each book; these letters do not indicate or prefigure what the pages will say. I know that such a lack of relevance, at one time, seemed mysterious. Before summarizing the solution (whose disclosure, despite its tragic implications, is perhaps the capital fact of this history), I want to recall certain axioms.

The first: The Library exists *ab aeterno.* No reasonable mind can doubt this truth, whose immediate corollary is the future eternity of the world. Man, the imperfect librarian, may be the work of chance or malevolent demiurges; the universe, with its elegant endowment of shelves, of enigmatic volumes, of indefatigable ladders for the voyager, and of privies for the seated librarian, can only be the work of a god. In order to perceive the distance which exists between the divine and the human, it is enough to compare the rude tremulous symbols which my fallible hand scribbles on the end pages of a book with the organic letters inside: exact, delicate, intensely black, inimitably symmetric.

The second: *The number of orthographic symbols is twenty-five.** This bit of evidence permitted the formulation, three hundred years ago, of a general theory of the Library and the satisfactory resolution of the problem which no conjecture had yet made clear: the formless and chaotic nature of almost all books; one of these books which my father saw in a hexagon of the circuit number fifteen ninety-four was composed of the letters MCV perversely repeated from the first line to the last. Another, very much consulted in this zone, is a mere labyrinth

*The original manuscript of the present note does not contain digits or capital letters. he punctuation is limited to the comma and the period. These two signs, plus the space sign and the twenty-two letters of the alphabet, make up the twenty-five sufficient symbols enumerated by the unknown author.

of letters, but on the next-to-the-last page, one may read *O Time your pyramids*. As is well known: for one reasonable line or one straightforward note there are leagues of insensate cacophony, of verbal farragoes and incoherencies. (I know of a wild region whose librarians repudiate the vain superstitious custom of seeking any sense in books and compare it to looking for meaning in dreams or chaotic lines of one's hands. . . . They admit that the inventors of writing imitated the twenty-five natural symbols, but they maintain that this application is accidental and that books in themselves mean nothing. This opinion—we shall see—is not altogether false.)

For a long time it was believed that these impenetrable books belonged to past or remote languages. It is true that the most ancient men, the first librarians, made use of a language quite different from the one we speak today; it is true that some miles to the right the language is dialectical and that ninety stories up it is incomprehensible. All this, I repeat, is true; but four hundred and ten pages of unvarying MCVs do not correspond to any language, however dialectical or rudimentary it might be. Some librarians insinuated that each letter could influence the next, and that the value of MCV on the third line of page 71 was not the same as that of the same series in another position on another page, but this vague thesis did not prosper. Still other men thought in terms of cryptographs; this conjecture has come to be universally accepted, though not in the sense in which it was formulated by its inventors.

Five hundred years ago, the chief of an upper hexagon* came upon a book as confusing as all the rest but which contained nearly two pages of homogenous lines. He showed his find to an ambulant decipherer, who told him the lines were written in Portuguese. Others told him they were in Yiddish. In less than a century the nature of the language was finally established: it was a Samoyed-Lithuanian dialect of Guarani, with classical Arabic inflections. The contents were also deciphered: notions of combinational analysis, illustrated by examples of variations with unlimited repetition. These examples made it possible for a librarian of genius to discover the fundamental law of the Library. This thinker observed that all the books, however diverse, are made up of uniform elements: the period, the comma, the space, the twenty-two letters of the alphabet. He also adduced a circumstance confirmed by all travelers: *There are not, in the whole vast Library, two identical books*. From all these incontrovertible premises he deduced that the Library is total and that its shelves contain all the possible combinations of the twenty-odd orthographic symbols

*Formerly, for each three hexagons there was one man. Suicide and pulmonary diseases have destroyed this proportion. My memory recalls scenes of unspeakable melancholy: there have been many nights when I have ventured down corridors and polished staircases without encountering a single librarian.

(whose number, though vast, is not infinite); that is, everything which can be expressed, in all languages. Everything is there: the minute history of the future, the autobiographies of the archangels, the faithful catalogue of the Library, thousands and thousands of false catalogues, a demonstration of the fallacy of these catalogues, a demonstration of the fallacy of the true catalogue, the Gnostic gospel of Basilides, the commentary on this gospel, the commentary on the commentary of this gospel, the veridical account of your death, a version of each book in all languages, the interpolations of every book in all books.

When it was proclaimed that the Library comprised all books, the first impression was one of extravagant joy. All men felt themselves lords of a secret, intact treasure. There was no personal or universal problem whose eloquent solution did not exist—in some hexagon. The universe was justified, the universe suddenly expanded to the limitless dimensions of hope. At that time there was much talk of the Vindications: books of apology and prophecy, which vindicated for all time the actions of every man in the world and established a store of prodigious arcana for the future. Thousands of covetous persons abandoned their dear natal hexagons and crowded up the stairs, urged on by the vain aim of finding their Vindication. These pilgrims disputed in the narrow corridors, hurled dark maledictions, strangled each other on the divine stairways, flung the deceitful books to the bottom of the tunnels, and died as they were thrown into space by men from remote regions. Some went mad....

The Vindications do exist. I have myself seen two of these books, which were concerned with future people, people who were perhaps not imaginary. But the searchers did not remember that the calculable possibility of a man's finding his own book, or some perfidious variation of his own book, is close to zero.

The clarification of the basic mysteries of humanity—the origin of the Library and of time—was also expected. It is credible that those grave mysteries can be explained in words: if the language of the philosophers does not suffice, the multiform Library will have produced the unexpected language required and the necessary vocabularies and grammars for this language.

It is now four centuries since men have been wearying the hexagons....

There are official searchers, *inquisitors*. I have observed them carrying out their functions: they are always exhausted. They speak of a staircase without steps where they were almost killed. They speak of galleries and stairs with the local librarian. From time to time they will pick up the nearest book and leaf through its pages, in search of infamous words. Obviously, no one expects to discover anything.

The uncommon hope was followed, naturally enough, by deep

depression. The certainty that some shelf in some hexagon contained precious books and that these books were inaccessible seemed almost intolerable. A blasphemous sect suggested that all searches be given up and that men everywhere shuffle letters and symbols until they succeeded in composing, by means of an improbable stroke of luck, the canonical books. The authorities found themselves obliged to issue severe orders. The sect disappeared, but in my childhood I still saw old men who would hide out in the privies for long periods of time, and, with metal disks in a forbidden dicebox, feebly mimic the divine disorder.

Other men, inversely, thought that the primary task was to eliminate useless works. They would invade the hexagons, exhibiting credentials which were not always false, skim through a volume with annoyance, and then condemn entire bookshelves to destruction: their ascetic, hygenic fury is responsible for the senseless loss of millions of books. Their name is execrated; but those who mourn the "treasures" destroyed by this frenzy, overlook two notorious facts. One: the Library is so enormous that any reduction undertaken by humans is infinitesimal. Two: each book is unique, irreplaceable, but (inasmuch as the Library is total) there are always several hundreds of thousands of imperfect facsimiles—of works which differ only by one letter or one comma. Contrary to public opinion, I dare suppose that the consequences of the depredations committed by the Purifiers have been exaggerated by the horror which these fanatics provoked. They were spurred by the delirium of storming the books in the Crimson Hexagon: books of a smaller than ordinary format, omnipotent, illustrated, magical.

We know, too, of another superstition of that time: the Man of the Book. In some shelf of some hexagon, men reasoned, there must exist a book which is the cipher and perfect compendium of *all the rest:* some librarian has perused it, and it is analogous to a god. Vestiges of the worship of that remote functionary still persist in the language of this zone. Many pilgrimages have sought Him out. For a century they trod the most diverse routes in vain. How to locate the secret hexagon which harbored it? Someone proposed a regressive approach: in order to locate book A, first consult book B, which will indicate the location of A; in order to locate book B, first consult book C, and so on ad infinitum....

I have squandered and consumed my years in adventures of this type. To me, it does not seem unlikely that on some shelf of the universe there lies a total book.* I pray the unknown gods that some

*I repeat: it is enough that a book be possible for it to exist. Only the impossible is excluded. For example: no book is also a stairway, though doubtless there are books that discuss and deny and demonstrate this possibility and others whose structure corresponds to that of a stairway.

man—even if only one man, and though it have been thousands of years ago!—may have examined and read it. If honor and wisdom and happiness are not for me, let them be for others. May heaven exist, though my place be in hell. Let me be outraged and annihilated, but may Thy enormous Library be justified, for one instant, in one being.

The impious assert that absurdities are the norm in the Library and that anything reasonable (even humble and pure coherence) is an almost miraculous exception. They speak (I know) of "the febrile Library, whose hazardous volumes run the constant risk of being changed into others and in which everything is affirmed, denied, and confused as by a divinity in delirium." These words, which not only denounce disorder but exemplify it as well, manifestly demonstrate the bad taste of the speakers and their desperate ignorance. Actually, the Library includes all verbal structures, all the variations allowed by the twenty-five orthographic symbols, but it does not permit of one absolute absurdity. It is pointless to observe that the best book in the numerous hexagons under my administration is entitled *Combed Clap of Thunder;* or that another is called *The Plaster Cramp;* and still another *Axaxaxas Mlö.* Such propositions as are contained in these titles, at first sight incoherent, doubtless yield a cryptographic or allegorical justification. Since they are verbal, these justifications already figure, *ex hypothesi,* in the Library. I cannot combine certain letters, as *dhcmrlchtdj,* which the divine Library has not already foreseen in combination, and which in one of its secret languages does not encompass some terrible meaning. No one can articulate a syllable which is not full of tenderness and fear, and which is not, in one of those languages, the powerful name of some god. To speak is to fall into tautologies. This useless and wordy epistle itself already exists in one of the thirty volumes of the five shelves in one of the uncountable hexagons—and so does its refutation. (An *n* number of possible languages makes use of the same vocabulary; in some of them, the symbol *library* admits of the correct definition *ubiquitous and everlasting system of hexagonal galleries,* but *library* is *bread* or *pyramid* or anything else, and the seven words which define it possess another value. You who read me, are you sure you understand my language?)

Methodical writing distracts me from the present condition of men. But the certainty that everything has been already written nullifies or makes phantoms of us all. I know of districts where the youth prostrate themselves before books and barbarously kiss the pages, though they do not know how to make out a single letter. Epidemics, heretical disagreements, the pilgrimages which inevitably degenerate into banditry, have decimated the population. I believe I have mentioned the suicides, more frequent each year. Perhaps I am deceived by old age and fear, but I suspect that the human species—

the unique human species—is on the road to extinction, while the Library will last on forever: illuminated, solitary, infinite, perfectly immovable, filled with precious volumes, useless, incorruptible, secret.

Infinite I have just written. I have not interpolated this adjective merely from rhetorical habit. It is not illogical, I say, to think that the world is infinite. Those who judge it to be limited, postulate that in remote places the corridors and stairs and hexagons could inconceivably cease—a manifest absurdity. Those who imagine it to be limitless forget that the possible number of books is limited. I dare insinuate the following solution to this ancient problem: *The Library is limitless and periodic.* If an eternal voyager were to traverse it in any direction, he would find, after many centuries, that the same volumes are repeated in the same disorder (which, repeated, would constitute an order: Order itself). My solitude rejoices in this elegant hope.*

Mar del Plata
1941

—*Translated by Anthony Kerrigan*

*Letizia Alvarez de Toledo has observed that the vast Library is useless. Strictly speaking, *one single volume* should suffice: a single volume of ordinary format, printed in nine or ten type body, and consisting of an infinite number of infinitely thin pages. (At the beginning of the seventeenth century, Cavalieri said that any solid body is the superposition of an infinite number of planes.) This silky *vade mecum* would scarcely be handy: each apparent leaf of the book would divide into other analogous leaves. The inconceivable central leaf would have no reverse.

Study Questions

Solaris

1. Suppose that the scientists on Solaris were to discover statistical correlations that enabled them to predict many aspects of the planet's behavior with a high degree of accuracy. Suppose, for example, that they could predict, several days in advance, that the planet would produce a mimoid, symmetriad, or other structure; where it would produce that structure; and even what form that structure would have. Can we say that, to the extent to which they can do this, they understand the planet? If not, why not? What is required to understand the planet in addition to the capacity to predict what it will do?

2. The scientists on Solaris are trying to explain something utterly foreign and unfamiliar in terms of models and concepts at home in the familiar. To attempt to explain the alien by the familar in this way is to impose a structure on it rather than to attempt to understand it in its own terms. And this makes any real understanding impossible."

Discuss this point of view. Ask yourself: (a) what is it to understand something in its own terms? and (b) how do we know when we are doing this? Think of actual examples in which people can be said to impose a structure on something that is foreign to them as opposed to understanding something in its own terms. Do these examples apply in the present case? Explain how they do, if they do, and why they don't, if they don't.

3. "Wherever we go we encounter ourselves." Does Lem's novel provide support for this statement? To answer this you will need to say what this statement means. You may want to distinguish between two or more possible meanings, and to discuss these separately.

They

1. Carefully consider the various bits of evidence that the protagonist of this story offers to support his belief that the world is a kind of stage play arranged for his benefit. Are his reasons convincing, considered one at a time? Are they convincing considered altogether? What arguments could you offer to prove that he is wrong? Write a short dialogue in which you try to persuade him.

The Library of Babel

1. What does Borges's story suggest about the nature of truth and knowledge, and/or our efforts to achieve them? Do you agree? Why or why not?

2. A more difficult question: The Library of Babel contains every sentence that can be written in any language. Does it follow from this that it contains the best possible account of the nature of the universe? To answer this question you will need to consider the difference between sentences and propositions. Roughly, a sentence is a set of words organized according to the rules of syntax. A proposition is what is asserted by a meaningful sentence. For example, the English sentence "Here is the water" is not the same sentence as the Spanish sentence "Aqui esta la agua"; but these two sentences express the same proposition. To answer the question, then, you need to consider whether it follows from the fact that the Library of Babel contains every possible sentence that could be written in a language that it also contains every possible proposition that can be expressed in that language.

Part 2

Trips through Time and Logical Space

Introduction to Part 2

According to the common-sense view of space, the various regions or areas of space coexist. Time-travel stories suggest that time (or space/time) is importantly like this. For if we can travel from the present to the future or to the past, it must be the case that the present, past, and future exist at one time, i.e., that in some strange way they coexist.

This picture of time (or space/time) is not without paradox. To take the classic case, the assumption of "backward" travel seems to allow the possibility that a time traveler—some existing person—may act in a manner that renders his own coming into being impossible (e.g., suppose he kills his father-to-be before his father-to-be impregnates his mother). In this case there could be no time traveler to have traveled backwards in time to begin with. The time-travel writer cannot solve this problem simply by concluding that the time traveler disappears—is annihilated—by such acts. For, among other things, this still leaves us with the problem of explaining all of the years that the time traveler has lived *already.* For this kind of reason, time-travel writers cannot avoid paradoxes simply by creating rules according to which one cannot act in such a way as to render one's own existence impossible. Anything one changes in the past—anything that would have been otherwise but for the time traveler—has in fact been otherwise already. So long as one allows one's time traveler to change anything in the past, then one must explain the consequences of that change in relation to the years that had elapsed "before" the change was implemented.

Travel to the future generates the same sort of problems. The very idea that one can travel to the future suggests that the future is fixed, i.e., that some space/time slice will be in a certain state at a certain time. But once one allows future time travel it becomes increasingly difficult to maintain this point of view. Suppose that time traveler Herman—who is worried about unsafe nuclear-waste storage—visits New York state/year 2080 to check on how things are going. To his dismay, he finds a world whose people are dying of radiation sickness. It seems that the location of certain faulty storage facilities was somehow lost. Herman decides to save the planet by discovering and reporting the location of these facilities "before" it is too late. He travels to the present and spends the bulk of the story performing time-travel maneuvers that enable him to come up with the appropriate TOP SECRET documents. "Shortly thereafter" he returns to the future—this time, New York state/year 2030—with the appropriate information. The facilities are repaired and the planet is saved. The "sequence" of events makes a certain sense until one begins to wonder about such things as what happened to the "original future" that Herman visited. What became of the dying people he spoke to there? What of the lives that were lived between 2030 and 2080, lives overshadowed by the deterioration of the facilities in question. Are they "no longer" part of the future? If not, when/where did Herman go on his original trip?

One could handle such problems by claiming that there are co-existing alternative pasts and futures. One would have to posit an unlimited number of these—one for each potential change—but at least some readers of science fiction are not bothered by this. But even if we accept this unrivaled ontological extravagance, we still must answer the question of what we mean when we talk of traveling to *the* future. For now there can be no such thing as setting one's dial for a certain date/place and expecting to be treated to a unique predecessor to or a unique outcome of the present. In fact, since "the present" may be tampered with by forward- and backward-going travelers (or "has already been" or "will come to be"), it too loses its uniqueness. In fact, if travel to the future is possible, the present is potentially as unlimited as the future; for the present *is* the future from the standpoint of time travelers from the past.

Most philosophers, I suspect, would deny that this description of time as consisting of an indefinite number of coexisting pasts, presents, and futures is coherent. Specifically, they might argue that this picture contains as many implicit paradoxes as any notion of time travel we might arrive at without this theory. Accordingly, they are likely to reject the possibility of time travel on logical grounds; specifically, on the ground that descriptions that could be true, were time travel possible, imply contradictions. This is what makes time-travel paradoxes paradoxical. To illustrate this point, let us return to the simplest example. Let "Lilly" be the name of the daughter of Henry and Mary. Now consider the proposition "Lilly killed Henry before Henry impregnated Mary." Since it is clear that Lilly must exist to do anything, this proposition implies "Lilly existed." On the other hand, if Lilly killed Henry before Henry impregnated Mary, it follows that Henry and Mary had no daughter, i.e., that there was no such person as Lilly. The sentence in question, then, also implies "It is not the case that Lilly existed."

Philosophers generally agree that propositions that imply contradictions are themselves contradictory. But they do not agree on what to say about contradictory sentences (or sets of sentences). Some have said that they are necessarily false (since they assert and deny the same thing, and an assertion and its denial cannot both be true at the same time). Others have said that they are meaningless (since by denying what they assert, they say nothing, i.e., they make no net assertion). Neither of these interpretations, however, are appealing in relation to time-travel stories. The view that descriptions such as "The Connecticut Yankee found himself in the Court of King Arthur" are meaningless is implausible for the reason that we seem to understand them. If we did not understand what they asserted, we would have no idea at all what would count as evidence in their favor. But it is hard to deny that what the Connecticut Yankee experienced counts as evidence in favor of the hypothesis that he traveled in time. A similar argument may be made against the claim that time-travel descriptions are necessarily false, for even those of us who recognize the paradoxes in time-travel stores might find ourselves compelled by the evidence confronting Twain's Connecticut Yankee to conclude that they were indeed in the Court of King Arthur. Yet is it difficult to see how one could find any evidence compelling or overwhelming for a proposition one knows to be necessarily false.

Time-travel stories, then, raise two types of philosophical questions. The first has to do with the nature of time. Specifically it is concerned with the possibility of conceptualizing time in such a way that time travel is possible. Can this be done? If so, how? What rules might be designed to avoid the paradoxes? The second arises if we conclude that time travel cannot be nonparadoxically conceptualized. For now we must explain how it is possible to have evidence for the truth of propositions that assert nothing (are meaningless); or how it is possible to have compelling evidence for a proposition one knows to be necessarily false.

"All You Zombies—"

Robert Heinlein

2217 Time Zone V (EST) 7 Nov 1970—NYC-"Pop's Place": I was polishing a brandy snifter when the Unmarried Mother came in. I noted the time—10:17 P.M. zone five, or Eastern time, November 7th, 1970. Temporal agents always notice time and date; we must.

The Unmarried Mother was a man twenty-five years old, no taller than I am, childish features and a touchy temper. I didn't like his looks—I never had—but he was a lad I was here to recruit, he was my boy. I gave him my best barkeep's smile.

Maybe I'm too critical. He wasn't swish; his nickname came from what he always said when some nosy type asked him his line: "I'm an unmarried mother." If he felt less than murderous he would add: "At four cents a word. I write confession stories."

If he felt nasty, he would wait for somebody to make something of it. He had a lethal style of infighting, like a female cop—one reason why I wanted him. Not the only one.

He had a load on and his face showed that he despised people more than usual. Silently I poured a double shot of Old Underwear and left the bottle. He drank it, poured another.

I wiped the bar top. "How's the 'Unmarried Mother' racket?"

His fingers tightened on the glass and he seemed about to throw it at me; I felt for the sap under the bar. In temporal manipulation you try to figure everything, but there are so many factors that you never take needless risks.

I saw him relax that tiny amount they teach you to watch for in the Bureau's training school. "Sorry," I said. "Just asking, 'How's business?' Make it 'How's the weather?'"

He looked sour. "Business is okay. I write 'em, they print 'em, I eat."

I poured myself one, leaned toward him. "Matter of fact," I said, "you write a nice stick—I've sampled a few. You have an amazingly sure touch with the woman's angle."

It was a slip I had to risk; he never admitted what pen-names he used. But he was boiled enough to pick up only the last: "'Woman's angle!'" he repeated with a snort. "Yeah, I know the woman's angle. I should."

"So?" I said doubtfully. "Sisters?"

"No. You wouldn't believe me if I told you."

"Now, now," I answered mildly, "bartenders and psychiatrists learn that nothing is stranger than truth. Why, son, if you heard the stories I do—well, you'd make yourself rich. Incredible."

"You don't know what *incredible* means!"

"So? Nothing astonishes me. I've always heard worse."

He snorted again. "Want to bet the rest of the bottle?"

"I'll bet a full bottle." I placed one on the bar.

'Well—" I signaled my other bartender to handle the trade. We were at the far end, a single-stool space that I kept private by loading the bar top by it with jars of pickled eggs and other clutter. A few were at the other end watching the fights and somebody was playing the juke box—private as a bed where we were.

"Okay," he began, "to start with, I'm a bastard."

"No distinction around here," I said.

"I mean it," he snapped. "My parents weren't married."

"Still no distinction," I insisted. "Neither were mine."

"When—" He stopped, gave me the first warm look I ever saw on him. "You mean that?"

"I do. A one-hundred-percent bastard. In fact," I added, "no one in my family ever marries. All bastards."

"Oh, that." I showed it to him. "It just looks like a wedding ring; I wear it to keep women off." It is an antique I bought in 1985 from a fellow operative—he had fetched it from pre-Christian Crete. "The Worm Ouroboros . . . the World Snake that eats its own tail, forever without end. A symbol of the Great Paradox."

He barely glanced at it. "If you're really a bastard, you know how it feels. When I was a little girl—"

"Wups!" I said. "Did I hear you correctly?"

"Who's telling this story? When I was a little girl—Look, ever hear of Christine Jorgenson? Or Roberta Cowell?"

"Uh, sex-change cases? You're trying to tell me—"

"Don't interrupt or swelp me, I won't talk. I was a foundling, left at an orphanage in Cleveland in 1945 when I was a month old. When I was a little girl, I envied kids with parents. Then, when I learned about sex—and, believe me, Pop, you learn fast in an orphanage—"

"I know."

"—I made a solemn vow that any kid of mine would have both a pop and a mom. It kept me 'pure,' quite a feat in that vicinity—I had to learn to fight to manage it. Then I got older and realized I stood darn little chance of getting married—for the same reason I hadn't been adopted." He scowled. "I was horse-faced and buck-toothed, flat-chested and straight-haired."

"You don't look any worse than I do."

"Who cares how a barkeep looks? Or a writer? But people wanting to adopt pick little blue-eyed golden-haired morons. Later on, the boys want bulging breasts, a cute face, and an Oh-you-wonderful-male manner." He shrugged. "I couldn't compete. So I decided to join the W.E.N.C.H.E.S."

"Eh?"

"Women's Emergency National Corps, Hospitality & Entertainment Section, what they now call 'Space Angels'—Auxiliary Nursing Group, Extraterrestrial Legions."

I knew both terms, once I had them chronized. We use still a third name, it's that elite military service corps: Women's Hospitality Order Refortifying & Encouraging Spacemen. Vocabulary shift is the worst hurdle in time-jumps—did you know that "service station" once meant a dispensary for petroleum fractions? Once on an assignment in the Churchill Era, a woman said to me, "Meet me at the service station next door"—which is not what it sounds; a "service station" (then) wouldn't have a bed in it.

He went on: "It was when they first admitted you can't send men into space for months and years and not relieve the tension. You remember how the wowsers screamed?—that improved my chance, since volunteers were scarce. A gal had to be respectable, preferably virgin (they like to train them from scratch), above average mentally, and stable emotionally. But most volunteers were old hookers, or neurotics who would crack up ten days off Earth. So I didn't need looks; if they accepted me, they would fix my buck teeth, put a wave in my hair, teach me to walk and dance and how to listen to a man pleasingly, and everything else—plus training for the prime duties. They would even use plastic surgery if it would help—nothing too good for Our Boys.

"Best yet, they made sure you didn't get pregnant during your enlistment—and you were almost certain to marry at the end of your hitch. Same way today, A.N.G.E.L.S. marry spacers—they talk the same language.

"When I was eighteen I was placed as a 'mother's helper.' This family simply wanted a cheap servant but I didn't mind as I couldn't enlist till I was twenty-one. I did housework and went to night school—pretending to continue my high school typing and shorthand but going to a charm class instead, to better my chances for enlistment.

"Then I met this city slicker with his hundred-dollar bills." He scowled. "The no-good actually did have a wad of hundred-dollar bills. He showed me one night, told me to help myself.

"But I didn't. I liked him. He was the first man I ever met who was nice to me without trying games with me. I quit night school to see him oftener. It was the happiest time of my life.

"Then one night in the park the games began."

He stopped. I said, "And then?"

"And then *nothing!* I never saw him again. He walked me home and told me he loved me—and kissed me good-night and never came back." He looked grim. "If I could find him, I'd kill him!"

"Well," I sympathized, "I know how you feel. But killing him—just for doing what comes naturally—hmm . . . Did you struggle?"

"Huh? What's that got to do with it?"

"Quite a bit. Maybe he deserves a couple of broken arms for running out on you, but—"

"He deserves worse than that! Wait till you hear. Somehow I kept anyone from suspecting and decided it was all for the best. I hadn't really loved him and probably would never love anybody—and I was more eager to join the W.E.N.C.H.E.S. than ever. I wasn't disqualified, they didn't insist on virgins. I cheered up.

"It wasn't until my skirts got tight that I realized."

"Pregnant?"

"He had me higher 'n a kite! Those skinflints I lived with ignored it as long as I could work—then kicked me out and the orphanage wouldn't take me back. I landed in a charity ward surrounded by other big bellies and trotted bedpans until my time came.

"One night I found myself on an operating table, with a nurse saying, 'Relax. Now breathe deeply.'

"I woke up in bed, numb from the chest down. My surgeon came in. 'How do you feel?' he says cheerfully.

"'Like a mummy.'

"'Naturally. You're wrapped like one and full of dope to keep you numb. You'll get well—but a Caesarean isn't a hangnail.'

"'Caesarean' I said. 'Doc—*did I lose the baby?'*

"'Oh, no. Your baby's fine.'

"'Oh. Boy or girl?'

"'A healthy little girl. Five pounds, three ounces.'

"I relaxed. It's something, to have made a baby. I told myself I would go somewhere and tack 'Mrs.' on my name and let the kid think her papa was dead—no orphanage for *my* kid!

"But the surgeon was talking. 'Tell me, uh—' He avoided my

name. '—did you ever think your glandular setup was odd?'

"I said, 'Huh? Of course not. What are you driving at?'

"He hesitated. 'I'll give you this in one dose, then a hypo to let you sleep off your jitters. You'll have 'em.'

"'Why?' I demanded.

"'Ever hear of that Scottish physician who was female until she was thirty-five?—then had surgery and became legally and medically a man? Got married. All okay.'

"'What's that got to do with me?'

"'That's what I'm saying. You're a man.'

"I tried to sit up. *'What?'*

"'Take it easy. When I opened you, I found a mess. I sent for the Chief of Surgery while I got the baby out, then we held a consultation with you on the table—and worked for hours to salvage what we could. You had two full sets of organs, both immature, but with the female set well enough developed for you to have a baby. They could never be any use to you again, so we took them out and rearranged things so that you can develop properly as a man.' He put a hand on me. 'Don't worry. You're young, your bones will readjust, we'll watch your glandular balance—and make a fine young man out of you.'

"I started to cry. 'What about my *baby?'*

"'Well, you can't nurse her, you haven't milk enough for a kitten. If I were you, I wouldn't see her—put her up for adoption.'

"*'No!'*

"He shrugged. 'The choice is yours; you're her mother—well, her parent. But don't worry now; we'll get you well first.'

"Next day they let me see the kid and I saw her daily—trying to get used to her. I had never seen a brand-new baby and had no idea how awful they look—my daughter looked like an orange monkey. My feelings changed to cold determination to do right by her. But four weeks later that didn't mean anything."

"Eh?"

"She was snatched."

"Snatched?"

The Unmarried Mother almost knocked over the bottle we had bet. "Kidnapped—stolen from the hospital nursery!" He breathed hard. "How's that for taking the last a man's got to live for?"

"A bad deal," I agreed. "Let's pour you another. No clues?"

"Nothing the police could trace. Somebody came to see her, claimed to be her uncle. While the nurse had her back turned, he walked out with her."

"Description?"

"Just a man, with a face-shaped face, like yours or mine." He frowned. "I think it was the baby's father. The nurse swore it was an older man but he probably used makeup. Who else would swipe my baby? Childless women pull such stunts—but whoever heard of a man doing it?"

"What happened to you then?"

"Eleven more months of that grim place and three operations. In four months I started to grow a beard; before I was out I was shaving regularly . . . and no longer doubted that I was male." He grinned wryly. "I was staring down nurses' necklines."

"Well," I said, "seems to me you came though okay. Here you are, a normal man, making good money, no real troubles. And the life of a female is not an easy one."

He glared at me. "A lot you know about it!"

"So?"

"Ever hear the expression 'a ruined woman'?"

"Mmm, years ago. Doesn't mean much today."

"I was as ruined as a woman can be; that bum *really* ruined me—I was no longer a woman . . . and I didn't know *how* to be a man."

"Takes getting used to, I suppose."

"You have no idea. I don't mean learning how to dress, or not walking into the wrong rest room; I learned those in the hospital. But how could I *live?* What job could I get? Hell, I couldn't even drive a car. I didn't know a trade; I couldn't do manual labor—too much scar tissue, too tender.

"I hated him for having ruined me for the W.E.N.C.H.E.S., too, but I didn't know how much until I tried to join the Space Corps instead. One look at my belly and I was marked unfit for military service. The medical officer spent time on me just from curiosity; he had read about my case.

"So I changed my name and came to New York. I got by as a fry cook, then rented a typewriter and set myself up as a public stenographer—what a laugh! In four months I typed four letters and one manuscript. The manuscript was for *Real Life Tales* and a waste of paper, but the goof who wrote it sold it. Which gave me an idea; I bought a stack of confession magazines and studied them." He looked cynical. "Now you know how I get the authentic woman's angle on an unmarried-mother story . . . through the only version I haven't sold—the true one. Do I win the bottle?"

I pushed it towards him. I was upset myself, but there was work to do. I said, "Son, you still want to lay hands on that so-and-so?"

His eyes lighted up—a feral gleam.

"Hold it!" I said. "You wouldn't kill him?"

He chuckled nastily. "Try me."

"Take it easy. I know more about it than you think I do. I can help you. I know where he is."

He reached across the bar. *"Where is he?"*

I said softly, "Let go my shirt, sonny—or you'll land in the alley and we'll tell the cops you fainted." I showed him the sap.

He let go. "Sorry. But where is he?" He looked at me. "And how do you know so much?"

"All in good time. There are records—hospital records, orphanage records, medical records. The matron of your orphanage was Mrs. Fetherage—right? She was followed by Mrs. Gruenstein—right? Your name, as a girl, was Jane—right? And you didn't tell me any of this—right?"

I had him baffled and a bit scared. "What's this? You trying to make trouble for me?"

"No indeed. I've your welfare at heart. I can put this character in your lap. You do to him as you see fit—and I guarantee that you'll get away with it. But I don't think you'll kill him. You'd be nuts to—and you aren't nuts. Not quite."

He brushed it aside. "Cut the noise. *Where is he?"*

I poured him a short one; he was drunk but anger was offsetting it. "Not so fast. I do something for you—you do something for me."

"Uh . . . what?"

"You don't like your work. What would you say to high pay, steady work, unlimited expense account, your own boss on the job, and lots of variety and adventure?"

He stared. "I'd say, 'Get those goddam reindeer off my roof!' Shove it, Pop—there's no such job."

"Okay, put it this way: I hand him to you, you settle with him, then try my job. If it's not all I claim—well, I can't hold you."

He was wavering; the last drink did it. "When d'yuh d'liver 'im?" he said thickly.

He shoved out his hand. "It's a deal!"

"If it's a deal—*right now!"*

I nodded to my assistant to watch both ends, noted the time—2300—started to duck through the gate under the bar—when the juke box blared out: "I'm My Own Grandpaw!" The service man had orders to load it with Americana and classics because I couldn't stomach the "music" of 1970, but I hadn't known that tape was in it. I called out, "Shut that off! Give the customer his money back." I added, "Storeroom, back in a moment," and headed there with my Unmarried Mother following.

It was down the passage across from the johns, a steel door to which no one but my day manager and myself had a key; inside was a door to an inner room to which only I had a key. We went there.

He looked blearily around at windowless walls. "Where is 'e?"

"Right away." I opened a case, the only thing in the room; it was a U.S.F.F. Co-ordinates Transformer Field Kit, series 1992, Mod. II—a beauty, no moving parts, weight twenty-three kilos fully charged, and shaped to pass as a suitcase. I had adjusted it precisely earlier that day; all I had to do was to shake out the metal net which limits the transformation field.

Which I did. "What's that?" he demanded.

"Time machine," I said and tossed the net over us.

"Hey!" he yelled and stepped back. There is a technique to this; the net has to be thrown so that the subject will instinctively step back *onto* the metal mesh, then you close the net with both of you inside completely—else you might leave shoe soles behind or a piece of foot, or scoop up a slice of floor. But that's all the skill it takes. Some agents con a subject into the net; I tell the truth and use that instant of utter astonishment to flip the switch. Which I did.

1030-VI-3 April 1963—Cleveland, Ohio-Apex Bldg.: "Hey!" he repeated. "Take this damn thing off!"

"Sorry," I apologized and did so, stuffed the net into the case, closed it. "You said you wanted to find him."

"But—you said that was a time machine!"

I pointed out a window. "Does that look like November? Or New York?" While he was gawking at new buds and spring weather, I reopened the case, took out a packet of hundred-dollar bills, checked that the numbers and signatures were compatible with 1963. The Temporal Bureau doesn't care how much you spend (it costs nothing) but they don't like unnecessary anachronisms. Too many mistakes, and a general court-martial will exile you for a year in a nasty period, say 1974 with its strict rationing and forced labor. I never make mistakes; the money was okay.

He turned around and said, "What happened?"

"He's here. Go outside and take him. Here's expense money." I shoved it at him and added, "Settle him, then I'll pick you up."

Hundred-dollar bills have a hypnotic effect on a person not used to them. He was thumbing them unbelievingly as I eased him into the hall, locked him out. The next jump was easy, a small shift in era.

7100-VI-10 March 1964—Cleveland-Apex Bldg.: There was a notice under the door saying that my lease expired next week; otherwise the room looked as it had a moment before. Outside, trees were bare and snow threatened; I hurried, stopping only for contemporary money and a coat, hat, and topcoat I had left there when I leased the room. I hired a car, went to the hospital. It took twenty minutes to bore the nursery attendant to the point where I could swipe the baby without being noticed. We went back to the Apex Building. This dial setting was more involved, as the building did not yet exist in 1945. But I had precalculated it.

0100-VI-20 Sept 1945—Cleveland-Skyview Motel: Field kit, baby, and I arrived in a motel outside town. Earlier I had registered as "Gregory Johnson, Warren, Ohio," so we arrived in a room with curtains closed, windows locked, and doors bolted, and the floor cleared to allow for waver as the machine hunts. You can get a nasty bruise from a chair where it shouldn't be—not the chair, of course, but backlash from the field.

No trouble. Jane was sleeping soundly; I carried her out, put her in a grocery box on the seat of a car I had provided earlier, drove to the orphanage, put her on the steps, drove two blocks to a "service station" (the petroleum-products sort) and phoned the orphanage, drove back in time to see them taking the box inside, kept going and abandoned the car near the motel—walked to it and jumped foward to the Apex Building in 1963.

2200-VI-24 April 1963—Cleveland-Apex Bldg.: I had cut the time rather fine—temporal accuracy depends on span, except on return to zero. If I had it right, Jane was discovering, out in the park this balmy spring night, that she wasn't quite as "nice" a girl as she had thought. I grabbed a taxi to the home of those skinflints, had the hackie wait around a corner while I lurked in shadows.

Presently I spotted them down the street, arms around each other. He took her up on the porch and made a long job of kissing her goodnight—longer than I thought. Then she went in and he came down the walk, turned away. I slid into step and hooked an arm in his. "That's all, son," I announced quietly. "I'm back to pick you up."

"You!" He gasped and caught his breath.

"Me. Now you know who *he* is—and after you think it over you'll know who you are . . . and if you think hard enough, you'll figure out who the baby is . . . and who *I* am."

He didn't answer, he was badly shaken. It's a shock to have it proved to you that you can't resist seducing yourself. I took him to the Apex Building and we jumped again.

2300-VIII-12 Aug 1985—Sub Rockies Base: I woke the duty sergeant, showed my I.D., told the sergeant to bed my companion down with a happy pill and recruit him in the morning. The sergeant looked sour, but rank is rank, regardless of era; he did what I said—thinking, no doubt, that the next time we met he might be the colonel and I the sergeant. Which can happen in our corps. "What name?" he asked.

I wrote it out. He raised his eyebrows. "Like so, eh? *Hmmm—"*

"You just do your job, Sergeant." I turned to my companion.

"Son, your troubles are over. You're about to start the best job a man ever held—and you'll do well. *I know."*

"That you will!" agreed the sergeant. "Look at me—born in 1917—

still around, still young, still enjoying life." I went back to the jump room, set everything on preselected zero.

2301-V-7 Nov 1970—NYC-"Pop's Place": I came out of the storeroom carrying a fifth of Drambuie to account for the minute I had been gone. My assistant was arguing with the customer who had been playing "I'm My Own Grandpaw!" I said, "Oh, let him play it, then unplug it." I was very tired.

It's rough, but somebody must do it and it's very hard to recruit anyone in the later years, since the Mistake of 1972. Can you think of a better source than to pick people all fouled up where they are and give them well-paid, interesting (even though dangerous) work in a necessary cause? Everybody knows now why the Fizzle War of 1963 fizzled. The bomb with New York's number on it didn't go off, a hundred other things didn't go as planned—all arranged by the likes of me.

But not the Mistake of '72; that one is not our fault—and can't be undone; there's no paradox to resolve. A thing either is, or it isn't, now and forever amen. But there won't be another like it; an order dated "1992" takes precedence any year.

I closed five minutes early, leaving a letter in the cash register telling my day manager that I was accepting his offer to buy me out, so see my lawyer as I was leaving on a long vacation. The Bureau might or might not pick up his payments, but they want things left tidy. I went to the room back of the storeroom and forward to 1993.

2200-VII-12 Jan 1993—Sub Rockies Annex-HQ Temporal DOL: I checked in with the duty officer and went to my quarters, intending to sleep for a week. I had fetched the bottle we bet (after all, I won it) and took a drink before I wrote my report. It tasted foul and I wondered why I had ever liked Old Underwear. But it was better than nothing; I don't like to be cold sober, I think too much. But I don't really hit the bottle either; other people have snakes—I have people.

I dictated my report; forty recruitments all okayed by the Psych Bureau—counting my own, which I knew would be okayed. I was here, wasn't I? Then I taped a request for assignment to operations; I was sick of recruiting. I dropped both in the slot and headed for bed.

My eye fell on "The By-Laws of Time," over my bed:

Never Do Yesterday What Should Be Done Tomorrow.
If at Last You Do Succeed, Never Try Again.
A Stitch in Time Saves Nine Billion.
A Paradox May be Paradoctored.
It Is Earlier When You Think.
Ancestors Are Just People.
Even Jove Nods.

They didn't inspire me the way they had when I was a recruit; thirty subjective-years of time-jumping wears you down. I undressed and when I got down to the hide I looked at my belly. A Caesarean leaves a big scar but I'm so hairy now that I don't notice it unless I look for it.

Then I glanced at the ring on my finger.

The Snake That Eats Its Own Tail, Forever and Ever . . . I *know* where I came from—but *where did all you zombies come from?*

I felt a headache coming on, but a headache powder is one thing I do not take. I did once—and you all went away.

So I crawled into bed and whistled out the light.

You aren't really there at all. There isn't anybody but me—Jane—here alone in the dark.

I miss you dreadfully!

The Weed of Time

Norman Spinrad

I, me, the spark of mind that is my consciousness, dwells in a locus that is neither place nor time. The objective duration of my life-span is one hundred and ten years, but from my own locus of consciousness, I am immortal—my awareness of my own awareness can never cease to be. I am an infant am a child am a youth am an old, old man dying on clean white sheets. I am all these me's, have always been all these me's will always be all these me's in the place where my mind dwells in an eternal moment divorced from time....

A century and a tenth is my eternity. My life is like a biography in a book: immutable, invariant, fixed in length, limitless in duration. On April 3, 2040, I am born. On December 2, 2150, I die. The events in between take place in a single instant. Say that I range up and down them at will, experiencing each of them again and again and again eternally. Even this is not really true; I experience all moments in my century and a tenth simultaneously, once and forever . . . How can I tell my story? How can I make you understand? The language we have in common is based on concepts of time which we do not share.

For me, time as you think of it does not exist. I do not move from moment to moment sequentially like a blind man groping his way down a tunnel. I am at all points in the tunnel simultaneously, and my eyes are open wide. Time is to me, in a sense, what space is to you, a field over which I move in more directions than one.

How can I tell you? How can I make you understand? We are all of us men born of women but in a way you have less in common with me than you do with an ape or an amoeba. Yet I *must* tell you, somehow. It is too late for me, will be too late, has been too late. I am trapped in this eternal hell and I can never escape, not even into death. My life is immutable, invariant, for I have eaten of Temp, the Weed of Time. But you must not! You must listen! You must understand! Shun the Weed of Time! I must try to tell you in my own way. It is pointless to try to start at the beginning. There is no beginning. There is no end. Only significant time-loci. Let me describe these loci. Perhaps I can make you understand....

September 8, 2050. I am ten years old. I am in the office of Dr. Phipps, who is the director of the mental hospital in which I have been for the past eight years. On June 12, 2053, they will finally understand that I am not insane. It is all they will understand, but it will be enough for them to release me. But on September 8, 2050, I am in a mental hospital.

September 8, 2050, is the day the first expedition returns from Tau Ceti. The arrival is to be televised, and that is why I am in Dr. Phipps' office watching television with the director. The Tau Ceti expedition is the reason I am in the hospital. I have been babbling about it for the previous ten years. I have been demanding that the ship be quarantined, that the plant samples it will bring back be destroyed, not allowed to grow in the soil of Earth. For most of my life this has been regarded as an obvious symptom of schizophrenia—after all, before July 12, 2048, the ship has not left for Tau Ceti, and until today it has not returned.

But on September 8, 2050, they wonder. This is the day I have been babbling about since I emerged from my mother's womb and now it is happening. So now I am alone with Dr. Phipps as the image of the ship on the television set lands on the image of a wide concrete apron....

"Make them understand!" I shout, knowing that it is futile. "Stop them, Dr. Phipps, stop them!"

Dr. Phipps stares at me uneasily. His small blue eyes show a mixture of pity, confusion and fright. He is all too familiar with my case. Sharing his desk top with the portable television set is a heavy oak-tag folder filled with my case history, filled with hundreds of therapy session records. In each of these records, this day is mentioned: September 8, 2050. I have repeated the same story over and over and over again. The ship will leave for Tau Ceti on July 12, 2048. It will return on September 8, 2050. The expedition will report that Tau Ceti has twelve planets. . . . The fifth alone is Earthlike and bears plant and animal life. . . . The expedition will bring back samples and seeds of a small Cetan plant with broad green leaves and small purple flowers. . . . The plant will be named *tempis ceti*. . . . It will become known as Temp. . . . Before the properties of the plant are fully understood, seeds will somehow become scattered and Temp will flourish in the soil of the Earth. . . . Somewhere, somehow, people will begin to eat the leaves of the Temp plant. They will become changed. They will babble of the future, and they will be considered mad—until the future events of which they speak begin to come to pass. . . .

Then the plant will be outlawed as a dangerous narcotic. Eating Temp will become a crime. . . . But as with all forbidden fruit, Temp will continue to be eaten. . . . And finally, Temp addicts will become the most sought-after criminals in the world. The governments of the Earth will attempt to milk the secrets of the future from their tortured minds. . . .

All this is in my case history, with which Dr. Phipps is familiar. For eight years, this has been considered only a remarkably consistent psychotic delusion.

But now it is September 8, 2050. As I have predicted, the ship has returned from Tau Ceti. Dr. Phipps stares at me woodenly as the gangplank is erected and the crew begins to debark. I can see his jaw tense as the reporters gather around the Captain, a tall, lean man carrying a small sack.

The Captain shakes his head in confusion as the reporters besiege him. "Let me make a short statement first," he says crisply. "Save wear and tear on all of us."

The Captain's thin, hard, pale face fills the television screen. "The expedition is a success," he says. "The Tau Ceti system was found to have twelve planets, and the fifth is Earthlike and bears plant and simple animal life. Very peculiar animal life. . . . "

"What do you mean peculiar?" a reporter shouts.

The Captain frowns and shrugs his wide shoulders. "Well, for one thing, they all seem to be herbivores and they seem to live off one species of plant which dominates the planetary flora. No predators. And it's not hard to see why. I don't quite know how to explain this, but all the critters seem to know what the other animals will do before they do it. And what we were going to do, too. We had one hell of a time taking specimens. We think it has something to do with the plant. Does something strange to their time sense."

"What makes you say that?" a reporter asks.

"Well, we fed some of the stuff to our lab animals. Same thing seemed to happen. It became virtually impossible to lay a hand on 'em. They seemed to be living a moment in the future, or something. That's why Dr. Lominov has called the plant *tempis ceti.*"

"What's this *tempis* look like?" a reporter says.

"Well, it's sort of . . . " the Captain begins. "Wait a minute," he says, "I've got a sample right here."

He reaches into the small sack and pulls something out. The camera zooms in on the Captain's hand.

He is holding a small plant. The plant has broad green leaves and small purple blossoms.

Dr. Phipp's hands begin to tremble uncontrollably. He stares at me. He stares and stares and stares....

May 12, 2062. I am in a small room. Think of it as a hospital room, think of it as a laboratory, think of it as a cell; it is all three. I have been here for three months.

I am seated on a comfortable lounge chair. Across a table from me sits a man from an unnamed government intelligence bureau. On the table is a tape recorder. It is running. The man seated opposite is frowning in exasperation.

"The subject is December 2081," he says. "You will tell me all you know of the events of December 2081."

I stare at him silently, sullenly. I am tired of all the men from intelligence sections, economic councils, scientific bureaus, with their endless, futile demands.

"Look," the man snaps, "we know better than to appeal to your nonexistent sense of patriotism. We are all too well aware that you don't give a damn about what the knowledge you have can mean to your country. But just remember this: you're a convicted criminal. Your sentence is indeterminate. Cooperate, and you'll be released in two years. Clam up, and we'll hold you here till you rot or until you get it through your head that the only way for you to get out is to talk. The subject is the month of December in the year 2081. Now, *give!*"

I sigh. I know that it is no use trying to tell any of them that knowledge of the future is useless, that the future cannot be changed because it was not changed because it will not be changed. They will not accept the fact that choice is an illusion caused by the fact that future time-loci are hidden from those who advance sequentially along the timestream one moment after the other in blissful ignorance. They refuse to understand that moments of future time are no different from moments of past or present time: fixed, immutable, invariant. They live in the illusion of sequential time.

So I begin to speak of the month of December in the year 2081. I know they will not be satisfied until I have told them all I know of the years between this time-locus and December 2, 2150. I know they will not be satisfied because they are not satisfied, have not been satisfied, will not be satisfied....

So I tell them of that terrible December nine years in their future....

December 2, 2150. I am old, old, a hundred and ten years old. My age-ruined body lies on the clean white sheets of a hospital bed, lungs, heart, blood vessels, organs, all failing. Only my mind is forever untouched, the mind of an infant-child-youth-man-ancient. I am, in a sense, dying. Beyond this day, December 2, 2150, my body no longer exists as a living organism. Time to me forward of this date is as blank to me as time beyond April 3, 2040, is in the other temporal direction.

In a sense, I am dying. But in another sense, I am immortal. The spark of my consciousness will not go out. My mind will not come to an end, for it has neither end nor beginning. I exist in one moment that lasts forever and spans one hundred and ten years.

Think of my life as a chapter in a book, the book of eternity, a book with no first page and no last. The chapter that is my life-span is one hundred and ten pages long. It has a starting point and an ending point, but the chapter exists as long as the book exists, the infinite book of eternity. . . .

Or, think of my life as a ruler one hundred and ten inches long. The ruler "begins" at one and "ends" at one hundred and ten, but "begins" and "ends" refer to length, not duration.

I am dying. I experience dying always, but I never experience death. Death is the absence of experience. It can never come for me.

December 2, 2150, is but a significant time-locus for me, a dark wall, an end point beyond which I cannot see. The other wall has the time-locus April 3, 2040. . . .

April 3, 2040. Nothingness abruptly ends, non-nothingness abruptly begins. I am born.

What is it like for me to be born? How can I tell you? How can I make you understand? My life, my whole life-span of one hundred and ten years comes into being at once, in an instant. At the "moment" of my birth I am at the moment of my death and all moments in between. I emerge from my mother's womb and I see my life as one sees a painting, a painting of some complicated landscape: all at once, whole, a complete gestalt. I see my strange, strange infancy, the incomprehension as I emerge from the womb speaking perfect English, marred only by my undeveloped vocal apparatus, as I emerge from my mother's womb demanding that the ship from Tau Ceti in the time-locus September 8, 2050, be quarantined, knowing that my demand will be futile because it was futile, will be futile, is futile, knowing that at the moment of my birth I am have been will be all that I ever was/am/will be and that I cannot change a moment of it.

I emerge from my mother's womb and I am dying in clean white sheets and I am in the office of Dr. Phipps watching the ship land and I am in the government cell for two years babbling of the future and I am in a clearing in some woods where a plant with broad green leaves and small purple flowers grow and I am picking the plant and eating it as I know I will do have done am doing....

I emerge from my mother's womb and I see the gestalt-painting of my life-span, a pattern of immutable events painted on the stationary and eternal canvas of time....

But I do not merely *see* the "painting," I *am* the "painting" and I am the painter and I am also outside the painting viewing the whole and I am none of these.

And I see the immutable time-locus that determines all the rest—March 4, 2060. Change that and the painting dissolves and I live in time like any other man, moment after blessed moment, freed from this all-knowing hell. But change itself is illusion.

March 4, 2060, in a wood not too far from where I was born. But knowledge of the horror that day brings, has brought, will bring can change nothing. I will do as I am doing will do did because I did it will do it am doing it....

April 3, 2040, and I emerge from my mother's womb, an infant-child-youth-man-ancient, in a government cell in a mental hospital dying in clean white sheets....

March 4, 2060. I am twenty. I am in a clearing in the woods. Before me grows a small plant with broad green leaves and purple blossoms—Temp, the Weed of Time, which has haunted, haunts, will haunt my never-ending life. I know what I am doing will do have done because I will do have done am doing it.

How can I explain? How can I make you understand that this moment is unavoidable, invariant, that though I have known, do know, will know its dreadful consequences, I can do nothing to alter it?

The language is inadequate. What I have told you is an unavoidable half-truth. All actions I perform in my one-hundred-and-ten-year life-span occur simultaneously. But even that statement only hints around the truth, for *simultaneously* means "at the same time" and *time* as you understand the word has no relevance to my life. But let me approximate:

Let me say that all actions I have ever performed, will perform, do perform, occur simultaneously. Thus no knowledge inherent in any particular time-locus can effect any action performed at any other locus in time. Let me construct another useful lie. Let me say that for me action and perception are totally independent of each other. At the moment of my birth, I did everything I ever would do in my life, instantly, blindly, in one total gestalt. Only in the next "moment" do I perceive the results of all those myriad actions, the horror that March 4, 2060, will make has made is making of my life.

Or . . . they say that at the moment of death, one's entire life flashes instantaneously before one's eyes. At the moment of my birth, my whole life flashed before me, not merely before my eyes, but in reality. I cannot change any of it because change is something that exists only as a function of the relationship between different moments in time and for me life is one eternal moment that is one hundred and ten years long....

So this awful moment is invariant, inescapable.

March 4, 2060. I reach down, pluck the Temp plant. I pull off a broad green leaf, put it in my mouth. It tastes bittersweet, woody, unpleasant. I chew it, bolt it down.

The Temp travels to my stomach, is digested, passes into my bloodstream, reaches my brain. There changes occur which better men than I are powerless, will be powerless to understand, at least up till December 2, 2150, beyond which is blankness. My body remains in the objective timestream, to age, grow old, decay, die. But my mind is abstracted out of time to experience all moments as one.

It is like a *déjà vu*. Because this happened on March 4, 2060, I have already experienced it in the twenty years since my birth. Yet this is the beginning point for my Temp-consciousness in the objective timestream. But the objective timestream has no relevance to what happens....

The language, the very thought patterns are inadequate. Another useful lie: in the objective timestream I was a normal human being until this dire March 4, experiencing each moment of the previous twenty years sequentially, in order, moment, after moment, after moment. ...

Now on March 4, 2060, my consciousness expands in two directions in the timestream to fill my entire life-span: forward to December 2, 2150, and my death, backwards to April 3, 2040, and my birth. As this time-locus of March 4 "changes" my future, so too it "changes" my past, expanding my Temp-consciousness to both extremes of my life-span.

But once the past is changed, the previous past has never existed and I emerge from my mother's womb an infant-child-youth-man-ancient in a government cell in a mental hospital dying in clean white sheets.... And—

I, me, the spark of mind that is my consciousness, dwells in a locus that is neither place nor time. The objective duration of my life-span is one hundred and ten years, but from my own locus of consciousness, I am immortal—my awareness of my own awareness can never cease to be. I am an infant child am a youth am an old, old man dying on clean white sheets. I am all these me's, have always been all these me's will always be all these me's in the place where my mind dwells in an eternal moment divorced from time....

Study Questions

"All You Zombies—"

1. Carefully describe the steps by which the protagonist of Heinlein's story becomes his own father and mother. Is he also his own grandfather and grandmother? Why?

2. Using Heinlein's style of reasoning, show how an entire population could come to be with only one natural birth. Derive some other exotic consequence.

3. Try to write a set of rules for time-travel stories that eliminate the possibility of deriving contradictions from time-travel descriptions. Good luck.

The Weed of Time

1. Theologians sometimes write that God sees all time at once—as if it were spread out in space or illustrated in a mural. Is Temp consciousness like this? Do we see our entire lifetime as if it were portrayed in a mural? What, in addition to this, does Temp consciousness involve?

2. How does it come to be that the protagonist of Spinrad's story is born with Temp consciousness? Given that he has Temp consciousness, is his response to having it a rational one?

3. If there is no difference between past, present, and future—if all coexist—what sense can be made of the notion of causality? In view of the picture of time presented in the story, what sense if any can be made of the claim that eating Temp causes Temp consciousness? Given this picture, can the concept of causality be altered (or replaced by some related notion) in a manner that enables us to make sense of the way in which events are related to one another?

Part 3

The Elusive Self

Introduction to Part 3

One might suppose that there is nothing with which we can be more intimately acquainted than ourselves. Yet when we attempt to say just what we mean by this deceptively simple word *self,* we are confronted with unanticipated difficulties. We begin with the feeling that the word refers to *something,* but we have difficulty saying to what it refers. Is it something that we experience? Many philosophers since Hume maintain that it is not; at least, that it cannot be experienced in the ways that we experience rivers and trees. We do not observe the self in the sense in which we observe material objects. As Hume argued, all that we experience when we look for the self "within" are thoughts, perceptions, sensations, images, and so forth. Never do we perceive that which thinks the thoughts or has the images. Nor do we perceive that about us that makes us the selves we are, i.e., that about me that distinguishes me from you and enables me to say that I am the same person now that I was two hours ago.

Sometimes in philosophy what seems to be one question—e.g., what is the nature of the self?—turns out to be many. Thus we can distinguish between at least four importantly different questions about the nature of the self that have been of concern to philosophers. Each question arises in relation to a different philosophical problem. The first question arises in relation to the alleged uniqueness of the self. An important theme in the Western tradition is that there is something fundamental about each of us that makes us different from anyone else. This difference—whatever it is—is what makes you, you and what makes me, me. Since we are thought to be unique, moreover, we are also thought to be irreplaceable; and this irreplaceability is sometimes thought to be a source of our worth. But what, we might ask, is this unique something that makes me, me and makes you, you? And what is so valuable about it?

The common sense of our time and place tells us not only that we are unique, but also that we endure, i.e., that we retain our identity despite the fact that we undergo constant changes, no matter how dramatic these changes may be. We grow, we age, most of the cells in our bodies are replaced every seven years. Parts of us—even parts of our brain—may be replaced by rubber, wire, or silicon chips. We may change our sex, our beliefs, our values, our character traits. We may undergo religious conversions and/or lose our religion; we may change from careerists to moral crusaders or from moral crusaders to careerists. We may have our character overhauled by EST, scientology, behavioral therapy, or psychoanalysis. And yet, despite all this, we remain the same person; that is, we think of these changes as changes *of* one and the same self. What makes it the same? On what basis do we say that despite all of these changes, we remain one through time? Philosophers call this the problem of personal identity.

The problem of personal identity concerns the basis of the unity of the self over time. But one might also wonder what it is that makes the self one self at any given point in time. At the present moment I am writing, conducting an internal dialogue, and shaking my leg a bit to dispel nervousness. Also there is a slight itch in the back of my head and a bit of soreness behind my eyes and in my throat. In addition, my heart is beating, my lungs inhaling and exhaling air, many of my muscle groups are tense, others relaxed, and untold numbers of my neurons are firing. What makes us say that all of these states and actions are *my* states and actions? What is this "me" to which these actings and endurings are attributed? Why do we suppose that there is *one* being that has and does all of these things instead of supposing that there are simply a number of interrelated processes going on? This is the question of the unity of self.

Finally, there are questions concerning the *true* or *real* self. All of us modify our behavior in relation to our circumstances. Where we do this in order to conform to social expectations, we speak of taking on social roles. Where we do this to project a certain image of ourselves, we speak of assuming social masks. It is often said that what we do in our roles and disguised by our masks is not expressive of our true selves. Those who speak this way think of the true self as *standing behind* one's roles and masks. Indeed, the true self may be so well concealed behind the masks and roles that it is entirely lost to consciousness. In this view our health as a person—our freedom—consists in the discovery (recovery) of this self, and in its development. In some theories this self is thought to be utterly unique and personal. Here, I find my true self when I find "the real me." In other theories this true self is impersonal or universal. I come to it by transcending all illusions about my uniqueness and by recognizing that in me which is in everyone else as well. This latter view of the true self is typically associated with Eastern thought and with Western mysticism, but a case can be made that something very much like it is present in major Western thinkers who are not mystics. (Kant, for example, identifies the true self with the noumenal self; but insofar as we act as noumenal selves, in his view, there appears to be no way to separate any one of us from any other.) In any case, the philosophical question is whether we can provide an intelligible account of the true self, conceived in either way. One source of apparent difficulty here is that in both conceptions the true self may be hidden and inactive, and so long as it is in this position the actions, thoughts, and feelings of the person cannot in any obvious and straightforward way be attributed to it. An intelligible account of the true self must face this problem squarely and work out an acceptable account of the relationship between the true self and its counterpart.

For those of us raised in the Judeo-Christian tradition there is a temptation to attempt to answer each of these questions in the same way, namely, in relation to the soul. Thus we might say that it is differences in our souls that make you, you and me, me; and it is in virtue of possessing the same soul that I am who I am through all of my changes. Similarly, we might say that all of my states and actions are *my* states and actions in virtue of their relation to my soul; and that the real or essential me is "how I am in my soul." If these explanations are to succeed in explaining anything at all, however, they must include an account of the nature of the soul in relation to which we can see how the soul is capable of filling these various roles assigned to it. We need to know what differs in two souls such that one makes you, you and the other makes me, me; what is this soul that remains the same through all of my other changes; and so forth. Without answers to such questions, attempts to explain the self in terms of the soul simply push the problems back a step, for the soul is no less mysterious than the self is. Indeed, such attempts may do damage, for they suggest that each of our questions about the self may have the same kind of answer, and this seems unlikely. In any case, philosophers have offered importantly different types of answers to them.

Both stories in this section raises at least one important philosophical question about the self. Philip K. Dick's "Impostor" raises an intriguing question about the nature of personal identity. Suppose we were capable of completely and precisely duplicating human beings such that the created being has every characteristic of the model except his history. In this case the created being will not only look like and act like the original, he will believe that he is the original as well. Most of us would be reluctant to agree. For example, we would be reluctant to prosecute the duplicate for a crime committed by the model; and we would be reluctant to say that the family of the model ought to accept the duplicate as the model (even where the model died in being duplicated). Why? What is the difference? Is it something "inside"? Presumably, the duplicate believes just what the original believes, desires just what the original desires, and is disposed to feel just what the original is disposed to feel (immediately after his creation, at least). It might be said that there is an important difference in the sphere of memory since the memories of the model are just that—memories of real events—while the memories of the duplicate are not. But in this case the important difference is that the original actually witnessed or participated in certain events while the duplicate did not. That is, the real difference is not "internal" at all. What is important, rather, is the histories of the beings in question. But to say this is not to explain the mystery of personal identity. For we now want to know: What makes all of these events constitutive of *my* history, i.e., what makes them all events in which one and the same person has participated?

Fritz Leiber's brilliant story "Catch That Zeppelin" is, among other things, another challenge to the notion of the unique self. Few people, it would seem, have more fully expressed or developed their uniqueness than Adolph Hitler (which ought to make us suspicious of any simple platitudes to the effect that our worth resides in our uniqueness; this is not self-explanatory). But does the fact that Hitler has expressed his uniqueness as a leader of the Nazis imply that he has expressed or fulfilled his essence in that capacity? Leiber asks us to consider another possibility. His premise is that under other conditions—in a prosperous post-World War I Germany—the man who became the leader of the Nazi Party might have become a contented, life-loving, proud father and middle-class businessman. What then is the relation between this possible Hitler and the actual Hitler? Could it be said that one is an expression of the real or essential Hitlerian self while the other is not? This seems unlikely. Each Hitler comes to be who he is by the choices he makes (choice, at least, plays an important part in this process). But choice options are limited by circumstances. The options among which Hitler the dictator chose on the road to becoming Hitler the dictator did not exist in the world inhabited by Hitler the businessman. And the options among which Hitler the businessman chose in becoming a Zeppelin salesman did not exist in the world inhabited by Hitler the dictator. Since historical circumstances played an important role in the coming to be of each, neither can be described as an inevitable expression of a personal essence.

Still, it might be said that either Hitler could be the expression of such an essence. After all, something must explain why Hitler chose the options he chose in his historical situation. Admittedly, he would have made other choices were he presented with different options. But in this case we could explain these choices too in relation to his essence. On this view the essential self does not determine who we will become *per se,* but does determine who we will become given a certain range of options.

But is this plausible? It might be said, on the contrary, that we make ourselves who we are by our choices and actions. These choices and actions both transform (or reinforce) our character and delimit our future options. If I choose to become a policeman, for example, my experience and activities in that capacity will both shape my character and delimit my possibilities in ways that will shape it in the future. To say that important choices express some essence is to suggest that the basis on which we chose remains constant through all of this apparent self-transformation. That is, it is to suggest in effect that there is no such thing as significant self-transformation. I leave it to the reader to evaluate this position.

Catch That Zeppelin!

Fritz Leiber

This year on a trip to New York City to visit my son, who is a social historian at a leading municipal university there, I had a very unsettling experience. At black moments, of which at my age I have quite a few, it still makes me distrust profoundly those absolute boundaries in Space and Time which are our sole protection against Chaos, and fear that my mind—no, my entire individual existence—may at any moment at all and without any warning whatsoever be blown by a sudden gust of Cosmic Wind to an entirely different spot in a Universe of Infinite Possibilities. Or, rather, into another Universe altogether. And that my mind and individuality will be changed to fit.

But at other moments, which are still in the majority, I believe that my unsettling experience was only one of those remarkably vivid waking dreams to which old people become increasingly susceptible, generally waking dreams about the past, and especially waking dreams about a past in which at some crucial point one made an entirely different and braver choice than one actually did, or in which the whole world made such a decision, with a completely different future resulting. Golden glowing might-have-beens nag increasingly at the minds of some older people.

In line with this interpretation I must admit that my whole unsettling experience was structured very much like a dream. It began with startling flashes of a changed world. It continued into a longer period when I completely accepted the changed world and delighted in it and, despite fleeting quivers of uneasiness, wished I could bask in its glow forever. And it ended in horrors, or nightmares, which I hate to mention, let alone discuss, until I must.

Opposing this dream notion, there are times when I am completely convinced that what happened to me in Manhattan and in a certain famous building there was no dream at all, but absolutely real, and that I did indeed visit another Time Stream.

Finally, I must point out that what I am about to tell you I am necessarily describing in retrospect, highly aware of several transitions involved, and whether I want to or not, commenting on them and making deductions that never once occurred to me at the time.

No, at the time it happened to me—and now at this moment of writing I am convinced that it did happen and was absolutely real—one instant simply succeeded another in the most natural way possible. I questioned nothing.

As to why it all happened to me, and what particular mechanism was involved, well, I am convinced that every man or woman has rare brief moments of extreme sensitivity, or rather vulnerability, when his mind and entire being may be blown by the Change Winds to Somewhere Else. And then, by what I call the Law of the Conservation of Reality, blown back again.

I was walking down Broadway somewhere near 34th Street. It was a chilly day, sunny despite the smog—a bracing day—and I suddenly began to stride along more briskly than is my cautious habit, throwing my feet ahead of me with a faint suggestion of the goose step. I also threw back my shoulders and took deep breaths, ignoring the fumes which tickled my nostrils. Beside me, traffic growled and snarled, rising at times to a machine-gun rata-tat-tat. While pedestrians were scuttling about with that desperate ratlike urgency characteristic of all big American cities, but which reaches its ultimate in New York, I cheerfully ignored that too. I even smiled at the sight of a ragged bum and a fur-coated gray-haired society lady both independently dodging across the street through the hurtling traffic with a cool practiced skill one sees only in America's biggest metropolis.

Just then I noticed a dark, wide shadow athwart the street ahead of me. It could not be that of a cloud, for it did not move. I craned my neck sharply and looked straight up like the veriest yokel, a regular *Hans-Kopf-in-die-Luft* (Hans-Head-in-the-Air, a German figure of comedy).

My gaze had to climb up the giddy 102 stories of the tallest building in the world, the Empire State. My gaze was strangely accompanied by the vision of a gigantic, long-fanged ape making the same ascent with a beautiful girl in one paw—oh, yes, I was recollecting the charming American fantasy-film *King Kong,* or as they name it in

Sweden, *Kong King.*

And then my gaze clambered higher still up the 222-foot sturdy tower, to the top of which was moored the nose of the vast, breathtakingly beautiful, streamlined, silvery shape which was making the shadow.

Now here is a most important point. I was not at the time in the least startled by what I saw. I knew at once that it was simply the bow section of the German Zeppelin *Ostwald,* named for the great German pioneer of physical chemistry and electrochemistry, and queen of the mighty passenger and light-freight fleet of luxury airliners, working out of Berlin, Baden-Baden, and Bremerhaven. That matchless Armada of Peace, each titanic airship named for a world-famous German scientist—the *Mach,* the *Nernst,* the *Humboldt,* the *Fritz Haber,* the French-named *Antoine Henri Becquerel,* the American-named *Edison,* the Polish-named *Sklodowska,* the American-Polish *T. Sklodowska Edison,* and even the Jewish-named *Einstein!* The great humanitarian navy in which I held a not unimportant position as international sales consultant and *Fachman*—I mean expert. My chest swelled with justified pride at this *edel*—noble—achievement of *der Vaterland.*

I knew also without any mind-searching or surprise that the length of the *Ostwald* was more than one half the 1,472-foot height of the Empire State Building plus its mooring tower, thick enough to hold an elevator. And my heart swelled again with the thought that the Berlin *Zeppelinturm* (dirigible tower) was only a few meters less high. Germany, I told myself, need not strain for mere numerical records—her sweeping scientific and technical achievements speak for themselves to the entire planet.

All this literally took little more than a second, and I never broke my snappy stride. As my gaze descended, I cheerfully hummed under my breath *Deutschland, Deutschland uber Alles.*

The Broadway I saw was utterly transformed, though at the time this seemed every bit as natural as the serene presence of the *Ostwald* high overhead, vast ellipsoid held aloft by helium. Silvery electric trucks and buses and private cars innumerable purred along far more evenly and quietly, and almost as swiftly, as had the noisy, stenchful, jerky gasoline-powered vehicles only moments before, though to me now the latter were completely forgotten. About two blocks ahead, an occasional gleaming electric car smoothly swung into the wide silver arch of a quick-battery-change station, while others emerged from under the arch to rejoin the almost dreamlike stream of traffic.

The air I gratefully inhaled was fresh and clean, without trace of smog.

The somewhat fewer pedestrians around me still moved quite swiftly, but with a dignity and courtesy largely absent before, with the numerous blackamoors among them quite as well dressed and exuding the same quiet confidence as the Caucasians.

The only slightly jarring note was struck by a tall, pale, rather emaciated man in black dress and with unmistakably Hebraic features. His somber clothing was somewhat shabby, though well kept, and his thin shoulders were hunched. I got the impression he had been looking closely at me, and then instantly glancing away as my eyes sought his. For some reason I recalled what my son had told me about the City College of New York—CCNY—being referred to surreptitiously and jokingly as Christian College Now Yiddish. I couldn't help chuckling a bit at that witticism, though I am glad to say it was a genial little guffaw rather than a malicious snicker. Germany in her well-known tolerance and noble-mindedness has completely outgrown her old, disfiguring anti-Semitism—after all, we must admit in all fairness that perhaps a third of our great men are Jews or carry Jewish genes, Haber and Einstein among them—despite what dark, and yes, wicked memories may lurk in the subconscious minds of oldsters like myself and occasionally briefly surface, into awareness like submarines bent on ship murder.

My happily self-satisfied mood immediately reasserted itself, and with a smart, almost military gesture I brushed to either side with a thumbnail the short, horizontal black mustache which decorates my upper lip, and I automatically swept back into place the thick comma of black hair (I confess I dye it) which tends to fall down across my forehead.

I stole another glance at the *Ostwald,* which made me think of the matchless amenities of that wondrous deluxe airliner: the softly purring motors that powered its propellers—electric motors, naturally, energized by banks of lightweight TSE batteries and as safe as its helium; the Grand Corridor running the length of the passenger deck from the Bow Observatory to the stern's like-windowed Games Room, which becomes the Grand Ballroom at night; the other peerless rooms letting off that corridor—the *Gesellschaftsraum der Kapitan* (Captain's Lounge) with its dark woodwork, manly cigar smoke and *Damentische* (Tables for Ladies), the Premier Dining Room with its linen napery and silver-plated aluminum dining service, the Ladies' Retiring Room always set out profusely with fresh flowers, the Schwartzwald bar, the gambling casino with its roulette, baccarat, chemmy, blackjack *(vingt-et-un),* its tables for skat and bridge and dominoes and sixty-six, its chess tables presided over by the delightfully eccentric world's champion, Nimzowitch, who would defeat you blindfold, but always brilliantly, simultaneously or one at a time, in charmingly baroque brief games for only two gold pieces per person per game (one gold piece to nutsy Nimzy, one to the DLG), and the supremely luxurious staterooms with costly veneers of mahogany over balsa; the hosts of attentive stewards, either as short and skinny as jockeys or else actual dwarfs, both types chosen to save weight; and the titanium elevator rising through the countless bags of helium to the two-decked Zenith Observatory, the sun deck wind-screened but roofless to let in the ever-changing clouds, the mysterious fog, the rays of the stars and good old Sol, and all the heavens. Ah, where else on land or sea could you buy such high living?

I called to mind in detail the single cabin which was always mine when I sailed on the *Ostwald—meine Stammkabine.* I visualized the Grand Corridor thronged with wealthy passengers in evening dress, the handsome officers, the unobtrusive ever-attentive stewards, the gleam of white shirt fronts, the glow of bare shoulders, the muted dazzle of jewels, the music of conversations like string quartets, the lilting low laughter that traveled along.

Exactly on time I did a neat *"Links, marschieren!"* ("To the left, march!") and passed through the impressive portals of the Empire State and across its towering lobby to the mutedly silver-glowing date: 6 May 1937 and the time of day: 1:07 P.M. Good!—since the *Ostwald* did not cast off until the tick of three P.M., I would be left plenty of time for a leisurely lunch and good talk with my son, if he had remembered to meet me—and there was actually no doubt of that, since he is the most considerate and orderly minded of sons, a real German mentality, though I say it myself.

I headed for the express bank, enjoying my passage through the clusters of high-class people who thronged the lobby without any unseemly crowding, and placed myself before the doors designated "Dirigible Departure Lounge" and in briefer German *"Zum Zeppelin."*

The elevator hostess was an attractive Japanese girl in skirt of dull silver with the DLG, Double Eagle and Dirigible insignia of the German Airship Union emblazoned on the left breast of her mutedly silver jacket. I noted with unvoiced approval that she appeared to have an excellent command of both German and English and was uniformly courteous to the passengers in her smiling but unemotional Nipponese fashion, which is so like our German scientific precision of speech, though without the latter's warm underlying passion. How good that our two federations, at opposite sides of the globe, have strong commercial and behavioral ties!

My fellow passengers in the lift, chiefly Americans and Germans, were of the finest type, very well dressed—except that just as the doors were about to close, there pressed in my doleful Jew in black. He seemed ill at ease, perhaps because of his shabby clothing. I was surprised, but made a point of being particularly polite towards him, giving him a slight bow and brief but friendly smile, while flashing my eyes. Jews have as much right to the acme of luxury travel as any other people on the planet, if they have the money—and most of them do.

During our uninterrupted and infinitely smooth passage upward, I touched my outside left breast pocket to reassure myself that my ticket—first class on the *Ostwald!*—and my papers were there. But actually I got far more reassurance and even secret joy from the feel and thought of the documents in my tightly zippered inside left breast pocket: the signed preliminary agreements that would launch America herself into the manufacture of passenger zeppelins. Modern Germany is always generous in sharing her great technical achievements with responsible sister nations, supremely confident that the genius of her scientists and engineers will continue to keep her well ahead of all other lands; and after all, the genius of two Americans, father and son, had made vital though indirect contributions to the development of safe airship travel (and not forgetting the part played by the Polish-born wife of the one and mother of the other).

The obtaining of those documents had been the chief and official reason for my trip to New York City, though I had been able to combine it most pleasurably with a long overdue visit with my son, the social historian, and with his charming wife.

These happy reflections were cut short by the jarless arrival of our elevator at its lofty terminus on the 100th floor. The journey old lovesmitten King Kong had made only after exhausting exertion we had accomplished effortlessly. The silvery doors spread wide. My fellow passengers hung back for a moment in awe and perhaps a little trepidation at the thought of the awesome journey ahead of them, and I—seasoned airship traveler that I am—was the first to step out, favoring with a smile and nod of approval my pert yet cool Japanese fellow employee of the lower echelons.

Hardly sparing a glance toward the great, fleckless window confronting the doors and showing a matchless view of Manhattan from an elevation of 1,250 feet minus two stories, I briskly turned, not right to the portals of the Departure Lounge and tower elevator, but left to those of the superb German restaurant *Krahenest* (Crow's Nest).

I passed between the flanking three-foot-high bronze statuettes of Thomas Edison and Marie Sklodowska Edison niched in one wall and those of Count von Zeppelin and Thomas Sklodowska Edison facing them from the other, and entered the select precincts of the finest German dining place outside the Fatherland. I paused while my eyes traveled searchingly around the room with its restful, dark wood paneling deeply carved with beautiful representations of the Black Forest and its grotesque supernatural denizens—kobolds, elves, gnomes, dryads (tastefully sexy) and the like. They interested me since I am what Americans call a Sunday painter, though almost my sole subject matter is zeppelins seen against blue sky and airy, soaring clouds.

The *Oberkellner* came hurrying toward me with menu tucked under his left elbow and saying, *"Mein Herr!* Charmed to see you once more! I have a perfect table-for-one with porthole looking out across the Hudson."

But just then a youthful figure rose springily from behind a table set against the far wall, and a dear and familiar voice rang out to me with *"Hier, Papa!"*

"Nein, Herr Ober," I smilingly told the head waiter as I walked past him, *"heute hab ich ein Gesellschafter. Mein Sohn."*

I confidently made my way between tables occupied by well-dressed folk, both white and black.

My son wrung my hand with fierce family affection, though we had last parted only that morning. He insisted that I take the wide, dark, leather-upholstered seat against the wall, which gave me a fine view of the entire restaurant, while he took the facing chair.

"Because during this meal I wish to look only on you, Papa," he assured me with manly tenderness. "And we have at least an hour and a half together, Papa—I have checked your luggage through, and it is likely already aboard the *Ostwald."* Thoughtful, dependable boy!

"And now, Papa, what shall it be?" he continued after we had settled ourselves. "I see that today's special is *Sauerbraten mit Spatzel* and sweet-sour red cabbage. But there is also *Paprikahuhn* and—"

"Leave the chicken to flaunt her paprika in lonely red splendor today," I interrupted him. "Sauerbraten sounds fine."

Ordered by my Herr Ober, the aged wine waiter had already approached our table. I was about to give him directions when my son took upon himself that task with an authority and a hostfulness that warmed my heart. He scanned the wine menu rapidly but thoroughly.

"The Zinfandel 1933," he ordered with decision, though glancing my way to see if I concurred with his judgment. I smiled and nodded.

"And perhaps *ein Tropfchen Schnapps* to begin with?" he suggested.

"A brandy?—yes!" I replied. "And not just a drop, either. Make it a double. It is not every day I lunch with that distinguished scholar, my son."

"Oh, Papa," he protested, dropping his eyes and almost blushing. Then firmly to the bent-backed, white-haired wine waiter, *"Schnapps also. Doppel."* The old waiter nodded his approval and hurried off.

We gazed fondly at each other for a few blissful seconds. Then I said, "Now tell me more fully about your achievements as a social historian on an exchange of professorship in the New World. I know we have spoken about this several times, but only rather briefly and generally when various of your friends were present, or at least your lovely wife. Now I would like a more leisurely man-to-man account of your great work. Incidentally, do you find the scholarly apparatus—

books, *und so weiter* (et cetera)—of the Municipal Universities of New York City adequate to your needs after having enjoyed those of Baden-Baden University and the institutions of high learning in the German Federation?"

"In some respects they are lacking," he admitted. "However, for my purposes they have proved completely adequate." Then once more he dropped his eyes and almost blushed. "But, Papa, you praise my small efforts far too highly." He lowered his voice. "They do not compare with the victory for international industrial relations you yourself have won in a fortnight."

"All in a day's work for the DLG," I said self-deprecatingly, though once again lightly touching my left chest to establish contact with those most important documents safely stowed in my inside left breast pocket. "But now, no more polite fencing!" I went on briskly. "Tell me all about those 'small efforts,' as you modestly refer to them."

His eyes met mine. "Well, Papa," he began in suddenly matter-of-fact fashion, "all my work these last two years has been increasingly dominated by a firm awareness of the fragility of the underpinnings of the good world-society we enjoy today. If certain historically minute key-events, or cusps, in only the past one hundred years had been decided differently—if another course had been chosen than the one that was—then the whole world might now be plunged in wars and worse horrors than we ever dream of. It is a chilling insight, but it bulks continually larger in my entire work, my every paper."

I felt the thrilling touch of inspiration. At that moment the wine waiter arrived with our double brandies in small goblets of cut glass. I wove the interruption into the fabric of my inspiration. "Let us drink then to what you name your chilling insight," I said. *"Prosit!"*

The bite and spreading warmth of the excellent schnapps quickened my inspiration further. "I believe I understand exactly what you're getting at . . . " I told my son. I set down my half-emptied goblet and pointed at something over my son's shoulder.

He turned his head around, and after one glance back at my pointing finger, which intentionally waggled a tiny bit from side to side, he realized that I was not indicating the entry of the *Krahenest,* but the four sizable bronze statuettes flanking it.

"For instance," I said, "if Thomas Edison and Marie Sklodowska had not married, and especially if they had not had their supergenius son, then Edison's knowledge of electricity and hers of radium and other radioactives might never have been joined. There might never have been developed the fabulous T. S. Edison battery, which is the prime mover of all today's surface and air traffic. Those pioneering electric trucks introduced by the *Saturday Evening Post* in Philadelphia might have remained an expensive freak. And the gas helium might never have been produced industrially to supplement earth's meager subterranean supply."

My son's eyes brightened with the flame of pure scholarship. "Papa," he said eagerly, "you are a genius yourself! You have precisely hit on what is perhaps the most important of those cusp-events I referred to. I am at this moment finishing the necessary research for a long paper on it. Do you know, Papa, that I have firmly established by researching Parisian records that there was in 1894 a close personal relationship between Marie Sklodowska and her fellow radium researcher Pierre Curie, and that she might well have become Madame Curie—or perhaps Madame Becquerel, for he too was in that work—if the dashing and brilliant Edison had not most opportunely arrived in Paris in December, 1894, to sweep her off her feet and carry her off to the New World to even greater achievements?

"And just think, Papa," he went on, his eyes aflame, "what might have happened if their son's battery had not been invented—the most difficult technical achievement, hedged by all sorts of seemingly scientific impossibilities, in the entire millennium-long history of industry. Why, Henry Ford might have manufactured automobiles powered by steam or by exploding natural gas or conceivably even vaporized liquid gasoline, rather than the mass-produced electric cars which have been such a boon to mankind everywhere—not our smokeless cars, but cars spouting all sorts of noxious fumes to pollute the environment."

Cars powered by the danger-fraught combustion of vaporized liquid gasoline!—it almost made me shudder and certainly it was a fantastic thought, yet not altogether beyond the bounds of possibility, I had to admit.

Just then I noticed my gloomy, black-clad Jew sitting only two tables away from us, though how he had got himself into the exclusive *Krahenest* was a wonder. Strange that I had missed his entry—probably immediately after my own, while I had eyes only for my son. His presence somehow threw a dark though only momentary shadow over my bright mood. Let him get some good German food inside him and some fine German wine, I thought generously—it will fill that empty belly of his and even put a bit of a good German smile into those sunken Yiddish cheeks! I combed my little mustache with my thumbnail and swept the errant lock of hair off my forehead.

Meanwhile my son was saying, "Also, Father, if electric transport had not been developed, and if during the last decade relations between Germany and the United States had not been so good, then we might never have gotten from the wells in Texas the supply of natural helium our Zeppelins desperately needed during the brief but vital period before we had put the artificial creation of helium onto an industrial footing. My researchers at Washington have revealed that there was a strong movement in the U.S. military to ban the sale of helium to any other nation, Germany in particular. Only the powerful influence of Edison, Ford, and a few other key Americans, instantly brought to bear, prevented that stupid injunction. Yet if it had gone through, Germany might have been forced to use hydrogen instead of helium to float her passenger dirigibles. That was another crucial cusp."

"A hydrogen-supported Zeppelin!—ridiculous! Such an airship would be a floating bomb, ready to be touched off by the slightest spark," I protested.

"Not ridiculous, Father," my son calmly contradicted me, shaking his head. "Pardon me for trespassing in your field, but there is an inescapable imperative about certain industrial developments. If there is not a safe road of advance, then a dangerous one will invariably be taken. You must admit, Father, that the development of commercial airships was in its early stages a most perilous venture. During the 1920s there were the dreadful wrecks of the American dirigibles *Roma, Shenandoah,* which broke in two, *Akron,* and *Macon,* the British *R-38* which also broke apart in the air, and *R-101,* the French *Dixmude,* which disappeared in the Mediterranean, Mussolini's *Italia,* which crashed trying to reach the North Pole, and the Russian *Maxim Gorky,* struck down by a plane, with a total loss of no fewer than 340 crew members for the nine accidents. If that had been followed by the explosions of two or three hydrogen Zeppelins, world industry might well have abandoned forever the attempts to create passenger airships and turned instead to the development of large propeller-driven, heavier-than-air craft."

Monster airplanes, in danger every moment of crash from engine failure, competing with good old unsinkable Zeppelins?—impossible, at least at first thought. I shook my head, but not with as much conviction as I might have wished. My son's suggestion was really a valid one.

Besides, he had all his facts at his fingertips and was complete master of his subject, as I also had to allow. Those nine fearful airship disasters he mentioned had indeed occurred, as I knew well, and might have tipped the scale in favor of long-distance passenger and troop-carrying airplanes, had it not been for helium, the T. S. Edison battery, and German genius.

Fortunately I was able to dump from my mind these uncomfortable speculations and immerse myself in admiration of my son's multi-sided scholarship. That boy was a wonder!—a real chip off the old block, and, yes, a bit more.

"And now, Dolfy," he went on, using my nickname (I did not mind), "may I turn to an entirely different topic? Or rather to a very different example of my hypothesis of historical cusps?"

I nodded mutely. My mouth was busily full with fine Sauerbraten and those lovely, tiny German dumplings, while my nostrils enjoyed the unique aroma of sweet-sour red cabbage. I had been so engrossed in my son's revelations that I had not consciously noted our luncheon being served. I swallowed, took a slug of the good, red Zinfandel, and said, "Please go on."

"It's about the consequences of the American Civil War, Father," he said surprisingly. "Did you know that in the decade after that bloody conflict, there was a very real danger that the whole cause of Negro freedom and rights—for which the war was fought, whatever they say—might well have been completely smashed? The fine work of Abraham Lincoln, Thaddeus Stevens, Charles Sumner, the Freedmen's Bureau, and the Union League Clubs put to naught? And even the Ku Klux Klan underground allowed free reign rather than being sternly repressed? Yes, Father, my thoroughgoing researchings have convinced me such things might easily have happened, resulting in some sort of re-enslavement of the Blacks, with the whole war to be refought at an indefinite future date, or at any rate Reconstruction brought to a dead halt for many decades—with what disastrous effects on the American character, turning its deep simple faith in freedom to hypocrisy, it is impossible to exaggerate. I have published a sizable paper on this subject in the *Journal of Civil War Studies.*"

I nodded somberly. Quite a bit of this new subject matter of his was *terra incognita* to me; yet I knew enough of American history to realize he had made a cogent point. More than ever before, I was impressed by his multifaceted learning—he was indubitably a figure in the great tradition of German scholarship, a profound thinker, broad and deep. How fortunate to be his father. Not for the first time, but perhaps with the greatest sincerity yet, I thanked God and the Laws of Nature that I had early moved my family from Braunau, Austria, where I had been born in 1899, to Baden-Baden, where he had grown up in the ambience of the great new university on the edge of the Black Forest and only 150 kilometers from Count Zeppelin's dirigible factory in Württemberg, at Friedrichshafen on Lake Constance.

I raised my glass of Kirschwasser to him in a solemn, silent toast—we had somehow got to that stage in our meal—and downed a sip of the potent, fiery, white, cherry brandy.

He leaned toward me and said, "I might as well tell you, Dolf, that my big book, at once popular and scholarly, my *Meisterwerk,* to be titled *If Things Had Gone Wrong,* or perhaps *If Things Had Turned for the Worse,* will deal solely—though illuminated by dozens of diverse examples—with my theory of historical cusps, a highly speculative concept but firmly rooted in fact." He glanced at his wristwatch, muttered, "Yes, there's still time for it. So now—" His face grew grave, his voice clear though small—"I will venture to tell you about one more cusp, the most disputable and yet most crucial of them all." He paused.

"I warn you, dear Dolf, that this cusp may cause you pain."

"I doubt that," I told him indulgently. "Anyhow, go ahead."

"Very well. In November of 1918, when the British had broken the Hindenburg Line and the weary German army was defiantly dug in along the Rhine, and just before the Allies, under Marshal Foch, launched the final crushing drive which would cut a bloody swath across the heartland to Berlin—"

I understood his warning at once. Memories flamed in my mind like the sudden blinding flares of the battlefield with their deafening thunder. The company I had commanded had been among the most desperately defiant of those he mentioned, heroically nerved for a last-ditch resistance. And then Foch had delivered that last vast blow, and we had fallen back and back and back before the overwhelming numbers of our enemies with their field guns and tanks and armored cars innumerable and above all their huge aerial armadas of De Haviland and Handley-Page and other big bombers escorted by insect-buzzing fleets of Spads and other fighters shooting to bits our last Fokkers and Pfalzes and visiting on Germany a destruction greater far than our Zeps had worked on England. Back, back, endlessly reeling and regrouping, across the devastated German countryside, a dozen times decimated yet still defiant until the end came at last amid the ruins of Berlin, and the most bold among us had to admit we were beaten and we surrendered unconditionally—

These vivid, fiery recollections came to me almost instantaneously.

I heard my son continuing, "At that cusp moment in November, 1918, Dolf, there existed a very strong possibility—I have established this beyond question—that an immediate armistice would be offered and signed, and the war ended inconclusively. President Wilson was wavering, the French were very tired, and so on.

"And if that had happened in actuality—harken closely to me now, Dolf—then the German temper entering the decade of the 1920s would have been entirely different. She would have felt she had not been really licked, and there would inevitably have been a secret recrudescence of pan-German militarism. German scientific humanism would not have won its total victory over the Germany of the—yes!—Huns.

"As for the Allies, self-tricked out of the complete victory which lay within their grasp, they would in the long run have treated Germany far less generously than they did after their lust for revenge had been sated by that last drive to Berlin. The League of Nations would not have become the strong instrument for world peace that it is today; it might well have been repudiated by America and certainly secretly detested by Germany. Old wounds would not have healed because, paradoxically, they would not have been deep enough.

"There, I've said my say. I hope it hasn't bothered you too badly, Dolf."

I let out a gutsy sigh. Then my wincing frown was replaced by a brow serene. I said deliberately, "Not one bit, my son, though you have certainly touched my own old wounds to the quick. Yet I feel in my bones that your interpretation is completely valid. Rumors of an armistice were indeed running like wildfire through our troops in that black autumn of 1918. And I know only too well that if there had been an armistice at that time, then officers like myself would have believed that the German soldier had never really been defeated, only betrayed by his leaders and by Red incendiaries, and we would have begun to conspire endlessly for a resumption of the war under happier circumstances. My son, let us drink to our amazing cusps."

Our tiny glasses touched with a delicate ting, and the last drops went down of biting, faintly bitter Kirschwasser. I buttered a thin slice of pumpernickel and nibbled it—always good to finish off a meal with bread. I was suddenly filled with an immeasurable content. It was a golden moment, which I would have been happy to have go on forever, while I listened to my son's wise words and fed my satisfaction in him. Yes, indeed, it was a golden nugget of pause in the terrible rush of time—the enriching conversation, the peerless food and drink, the darkly pleasant surroundings—

At that moment I chanced to look at my discordant Jew two tables away. For some weird reason he was glaring at me with naked hate, though he instantly dropped his gaze—

But even that strange and disquieting event did not disrupt my mood of golden tranquillity, which I sought to prolong by saying in summation, "My dear son, this has been the most exciting though eerie lunch I have ever enjoyed. Your remarkable cusps have opened to me a fabulous world in which I can nevertheless utterly believe. A horridly fascinating world of sizzling hydrogen Zeppelins, of countless evil-smelling gasoline cars built by Ford instead of his electrics, of re-enslaved American blackamoors, of Madame Becquerels or Curies, a world without the T. S. Edison battery and even T. S. himself, a world in which German scientists are sinister pariahs instead of tolerant, humanitarian, great-souled leaders of world thought, a world in which a mateless old Edison tinkers forever at a powerful storage battery he cannot perfect, a world in which Woodrow Wilson doesn't insist on Germany being admitted at once to the League of Nations, a world of festering hatreds reeling toward a second and worse world war. Oh, altogether an incredible world, yet one in which you have momentarily made me believe, to the extent that I do actually have the fear that time will suddenly shift gears and we will be plunged into that bad dream world, and our real world will become a dream—"

I suddenly chanced to see the face of my watch—

At the same time my son looked at his own left wrist—

"Dolf," he said, springing up in agitation, "I do hope that with my stupid chatter I haven't made you miss—"

I had sprung up too—

"No, no, my son," I heard myself say in a fluttering voice, "but it's true I have little time in which to catch the *Ostwald. Auf Wiedersehn, mein Sohn, auf Wiedersehn!*"

And with that I was hastening, indeed almost running, or else sweeping through the air like a ghost—leaving him behind to settle our reckoning—across a room that seemed to waver with my feverish agitation, alternately darkening and brightening like an electric bulb with its fine tungsten filament about to fly to powder and wink out forever—

Inside my head a voice was saying in calm yet death-knell tones, "The lights of Europe are going out. I do not think they will be rekindled in my generation—"

Suddenly the only important thing in the world for me was to catch the *Ostwald,* get aboard her before she unmoored. That and only that would reassure me that I was in my rightful world. I would touch and feel the *Ostwald,* not just talk about her—

As I dashed between the four bronze figures, they seemed to hunch down and become deformed, while their faces became those of grotesque, aged witches—four evil kobolds leering up at me with a horrid knowledge bright in their eyes—

While behind me I glimpsed in pursuit a tall, black, white-faced figure, skeletally lean—

The strangely short corridor ahead of me had a blank end—the Departure Lounge wasn't there—

I instantly jerked open the narrow door to the stairs and darted nimbly up them as if I were a young man again and not 48 years old—

On the third sharp turn I risked a glance behind and down—

Hardly a flight behind me, taking great pursuing leaps, was my dreadful Jew—

I tore open the door to the 102nd floor. There at last, only a few feet away, was the silver door I sought of the final elevator and softly glowing above it the words, *"Zum Zeppelin."* At last I would be shot aloft to the *Ostwald* and reality.

But the sign began to blink as the *Krahenest* had, while across the door was pasted askew a white cardboard sign which read "Out of Order."

I threw myself at the door and scrabbled at it, squeezing my eyes several times to make my vision come clear. When I finally fully opened them, the cardboard sign was gone.

But the silver door was gone too, and the words above it forever. I was scrabbling at seamless pale plaster.

There was a touch on my elbow. I spun around.

"Excuse me, sir, but you seem troubled," my Jew said solicitously.

"Is there anything I can do?"

I shook my head, but whether in negation or rejection or to clear it, I don't know. "I'm looking for the *Ostwald,*" I gasped, only now realizing I'd winded myself on the stairs. "For the zeppelin," I explained when he looked puzzled.

I may be wrong, but it seemed to me that a look of secret glee flashed deep in his eyes, though his general sympathetic expression remained unchanged.

"Oh, the Zeppelin," he said in a voice that seemed to me to have become sugary in its solicitude. "You must mean the *Hindenburg.*"

Hindenburg?—I asked myself. There was no Zeppelin named *Hindenburg*. Or was there? Could it be that I was mistaken about such a simple and, one would think, immutable matter? My mind had been getting very foggy the last minute or two. Desperately I tried to assure myself that I was indeed myself and in my right world. My lips worked and I muttered to myself, *Bin Adolf Hitler, Zeppelin Fachman...*

"But the *Hindenburg* doesn't land here, in any case," my Jew was telling me, "though I think some vague intention once was voiced about topping the Empire State with a mooring mast for dirigibles. Perhaps you saw some news story and assumed—"

His face fell, or he made it seem to fall. The sugary solicitude in his voice became unendurable as he told me, "But apparently you can't have heard today's tragic news. Oh, I do hope you weren't seeking the *Hindenburg* so as to meet some beloved family member or close friend. Brace yourself, sir. Only hours ago, coming in for her landing at Lakehurst, New Jersey, the *Hindenburg* caught fire and burned up entirely in a matter of seconds. Thirty or forty at least of her passengers and crew were burned alive. Oh, steady yourself, sir."

"But the *Hindenburg*—I mean the *Ostwald!*—couldn't burn like that," I protested. "She's a helium Zeppelin."

He shook his head. "Oh, no. I'm no scientist, but I know the *Hindenburg* was filled with hydrogen—a wholly typical bit of reckless German risk-running. At least we've never sold helium to the Nazis, thank God."

I stared at him, wavering my face from side to side in feeble denial.

While he stared back at me with obviously a new thought in mind.

"Excuse me once again," he said, "but I believe I heard you start to say something about Adolf Hitler. I suppose you know that you bear a certain resemblance to that execrable dictator. If I were you, sir, I'd shave my mustache."

I felt a wave of fury at this inexplicable remark with all its baffling references, yet withal a remark delivered in the unmistakable tones of an insult. And then all my surroundings momentarily reddened and flickered, and I felt a tremendous wrench in the inmost core of my being, the sort of wrench one might experience in transiting timelessly from one universe into another parallel to it. Briefly I became a man still named Adolf Hitler, same as the Nazi dictator and almost the same age, a German-American born in Chicago, who had never visited Germany or spoke German, whose friends teased him about his chance resemblance to the other Hitler, and who used stubbornly to say, "No, I won't change my name! Let that *Fuehrer* bastard across the Atlantic change his! Ever hear about the British Winston Churchill writing the American Winston Churchill, who wrote *The Crisis* and other novels, and suggesting he change his name to avoid confusion, since the Englishman had done some writing too? The American wrote back it was a good idea, but since he was three years older, he was senior and so the Britisher should change *his* name. That's exactly how I feel about that son of a bitch Hitler."

The Jew still stared at me sneeringly. I started to tell him off, but then I was lost in a second weird, wrenching transition. The first had been directly from one parallel universe to another. The second was also in time—I aged 14 or 15 years in a single infinite instant while transiting from 1937 (where I had been born in 1889 and was 48) to 1973 (where I had been born in 1910 and was 63). My name changed back to my truly own (but what is that?), and I no longer looked one bit like Adolf Hitler the Nazi dictator (or dirigible expert?), and I had a married son who was a sort of social historian in a New York City municipal university, and he had many brilliant theories, but none of historical cusps.

And the Jew—I mean the tall, thin man in black, with possibly Semitic features—was gone. I looked around but there was no one there.

I touched my outside left breast pocket, then my hand darted tremblingly underneath. There was no zipper on the pocket inside and no precious documents, only a couple of grimy envelopes with notes I'd scribbled on them in pencil.

I don't know how I got out of the Empire State Building. Presumably by elevator. Though all my memory holds for that period is a persistent image of King Kong tumbling down from its top like a ridiculous yet poignantly pitiable giant teddy bear.

I do recollect walking in a sort of trance for what seemed hours through a Manhattan stinking with monoxide and carcinogens innumerable, half waking from time to time (usually while crossing streets that snarled, not purred) and then relapsing into trance. There were big dogs.

When I at last fully came to myself, I was walking down a twilit Hudson Street at the north end of Greenwich Village. My gaze was fixed on a distant and unremarkable pale-gray square of building top. I guessed it must be that of the World Trade Center, 1,350 feet tall.

And then it was blotted out by the grinning face of my son, the professor.

"Justin!" I said.

"Fritz!" he said. "We'd begun to worry a bit. Where did you get off to, anyhow? Not that it's a damn bit of my business. If you had an assignation with a go-go girl, you needn't tell me."

"Thanks," I said. "I do feel tired, I must admit, and somewhat cold. But no, I was just looking at some of my old stamping grounds," I told him, "and taking longer than I realized. Manhattan's changed during my years on the West Coast, but not all that much."

"It's getting chilly," he said. "Let's stop in that place ahead with the black front. It's the White Horse. Dylan Thomas used to drink there. He's supposed to have scribbled a poem on the wall of the can, only they painted it over. But it has the authentic sawdust."

"Good," I said, "only we'll make mine coffee, not ale. Or if I can't get coffee, then cola."

I am not really a *Prosit!*-type person.

Impostor

Philip K. Dick

"One of these days I'm going to take time off," Spence Olham said at first-meal. He looked around at his wife. "I think I've earned a rest. Ten years is a long time."

"And the Project?"

"The war will be won without me. This ball of clay of ours isn't really in much danger." Olham sat down at the table and lit a cigarette. "The news machines alter dispatches to make it appear the Outspacers are right on top of us. You know what I'd like to do on my vacation? I'd like to take a camping trip in those mountains outside of town, where we went that time. Remember? I got poison oak and you almost stepped on a gopher snake."

"Sutton Wood?" Mary began to clear away the food dishes. "The Wood was burned a few weeks ago. I thought you knew. Some kind of a flash fire."

Olham sagged. "Didn't they even try to find the cause?" His lips twisted. "No one cares any more. All they can think of is the war." He clamped his jaws together, the whole picture coming up in his mind, the Outspacers, the war, the needle ships.

"How can we think about anything else?"

Olham nodded. She was right, of course. The dark little ships out of Alpha Centauri had by-passed the Earth cruisers easily, leaving them like helpless turtles. It had been one-way fights, all the way back to Terra.

All the way, until the protec-bubble was demonstrated at Westinghouse Labs. Thrown around the major Earth cities and finally the planet itself, the bubble was the first real defense, the first legitimate answer to the Outspacers—as the news machines labelled them.

But to win the war, that was another thing. Every lab, every project was working night and day, endlessly, to find something more: a weapon for positive combat. His own project, for example. All day long, year after year.

Olham stood up, putting out his cigarette. "Like the Sword of Damocles. Always hanging over us. I'm getting tired. All I want to do is take a long rest. But I guess everybody feels that way."

He got his jacket from the closet and went out on the front porch. The shoot would be along any moment, the fast little bug that would carry him to the Project.

"I hope Nelson isn't late." He looked at his watch. "It's almost seven."

"Here the bug comes," Mary said, gazing between the rows of houses. The sun glittered behind the roofs, reflecting against the heavy lead plates. The settlement was quiet; only a few people were stirring. "I'll see you later. Try not to work beyond your shift, Spence."

Olham opened the car door and slid inside, leaning back against the seat with a sigh. There was an older man with Nelson.

"Well?" Olham said, as the bug shot ahead. "Heard any interesting news?"

"The usual," Nelson said. "A few Outspace ships hit, another asteroid abandoned for strategic reasons."

"It'll be good when we get the Project into final stage. Maybe it's just the propaganda from the news machines, but in the last month I've got weary of all this. Everything seems so grim and serious, no colour to life."

"Do you think the war is in vain?" the older man said suddenly. "You are an integral part of it, yourself."

"This is Major Peters," Nelson said. Olham and Peters shook hands. Olham studied the older man.

"What brings you along so early?" he said. "I don't remember seeing you at the Project before."

"No, I'm not with the Project," Peters said, "but I know something about what you're doing. My own work is altogether different."

A look passed between him and Nelson. Olham noticed it and he frowned. The bug was gaining speed, flashing across the barren, lifeless ground toward the distant rim of the Project buildings.

"What is your business?" Olham said. "Or aren't you permitted to talk about it?"

"I'm with the government," Peters said. "With FSA, the Security Organ."

"Oh?" Olham raised an eyebrow. "Is there any enemy infiltration in this region?"

"As a matter of fact I'm here to see you, Mr. Olham."

Olham was puzzled. He considered Peters' words, but he could make nothing of them. "To see me? Why?"

"I'm here to arrest you as an Outspace spy. That's why I'm up so early this morning. *Grab him, Nelson—*"

The gun drove into Olham's ribs. Nelson's hands were shaking, trembling with released emotion, his face pale. He took a deep breath and let it out again.

"Shall we kill him now?" he whispered to Peters. "I think we should kill him now. We can't wait."

Olham stared into his friend's face. He opened his mouth to speak, but no words came. Both men were staring at him steadily, rigid and grim with fright. Olham felt dizzy. His head ached and spun.

"I don't understand," he murmured.

At that moment the shoot car left the ground and rushed up, heading into space. Below them the Project fell away, smaller and smaller, disappearing. Olham shut his mouth.

"We can wait a little," Peters said. "I want to ask him some questions first."

Olham gazed dully ahead as the bug rushed through space.

"The arrest was made all right," Peters said into the vidscreen. On the screen the features of the Security Chief showed. "It should be a load off everyone's mind."

"Any complications?"

"None. He entered the bug without suspicion. He didn't seem to think my presence was too unusual."

"Where are you now?"

"On our way out, just inside the protec-bubble. We're moving at maximum speed. You can assume that the critical period is past. I'm glad the take-off jets in this craft were in good working order. If there had been any failures at that point—"

"Let me see him," the Security Chief said. He gazed directly at Olham where he sat, his hands in his lap, staring ahead.

"So that's the man." He looked at Olham for a time. Olham said nothing. At last the chief nodded to Peters. "All right. That's enough." A faint trace of disgust wrinkled his features. "I've seen all I want. You've done something that will be remembered for a long time. They're preparing some sort of citation for both of you."

"That's not necessary," Peters said.

"How much danger is there now? Is there still much chance that—"

"There is some chance, but not too much. According to my understanding, it requires a verbal key phrase. In any case we'll have to take the risk."

"I'll have the Moon base notified you're coming."

"No," Peters shook his head. "I'll land the ship outside, beyond the base. I don't want it in jeopardy."

"Just as you like." The chief's eyes flickered as he glanced again at Olham. Then his image faded. The screen blanked.

Olham shifted his gaze to the window. The ship was already through the protec-bubble, rushing with greater and greater speed all the time. Peters was in a hurry; below him, rumbling under the floor, the jets were wide open. They were afraid, hurrying frantically, because of him.

Next to him on the seat, Nelson shifted uneasily. "I think we should do it now," he said. "I'd give anything if we could get it over with."

"Take it easy," Peters said. "I want you to guide the ship for a while so I can talk to him."

He slid over beside Olham, looking into his face. Presently he reached out and touched him gingerly, on the arm and then on the cheek.

Olham said nothing, *If I could let Mary know,* he thought again. *If I could find some way of letting her know.* He looked around the ship. How? The vidscreen? Nelson was sitting by the board, holding the gun. There was nothing he could do. He was caught, trapped.

But why?

"Listen," Peters said. "I want to ask you some questions. You know where we're going. We're moving Moonward. In an hour we'll land on the far side, on the desolate side. After we land you'll be turned over immediately to a team of men waiting there. Your body will be destroyed at once. Do you understand that?" He looked at his watch. "Within two hours your parts will be strewn over the landscape. There won't be anything left of you."

Olham struggled out of his lethargy. "Can't you tell me—"

"Certainly, I'll tell you." Peters nodded. "Two days ago we received a report that an Outspace ship had penetrated the protec-bubble. The ship let off a spy in the form of a humanoid robot. The robot was to destroy a particular human being and take his place."

Peters looked calmly at Olham.

"Inside the robot was a U-bomb. Our agent did not know how the bomb was to be detonated, but he conjectured that it might be by a particular spoken phrase, a certain group of words. The robot would live the life of the person he killed, entering into his usual activities, his job, his social life. He had been constructed to resemble that person. No one would know the difference."

Olham's face went sickly chalk.

"The person whom the robot was to impersonate was Spence

Olham, a high-ranking official at one of the Research projects. Because this particular project was approaching crucial stage, the presence of an animate bomb, moving toward the centre of the Project—"

Olham stared down at his hands. *"But I'm Olham!"*

"Once the robot had located and killed Olham, it was a simple matter to take over his life. The robot was probably released from the ship eight days ago. The substitution was probably accomplished over the last weekend, when Olham went for a short walk in the hills."

"But I'm Olham." He turned to Nelson, sitting at the controls. "Don't you recognize me? You've known me for twenty years. Don't you remember how we went to college together?" He stood up. "You and I were at the University. We had the same room." He went toward Nelson.

"Stay away from me!" Nelson snarled.

"Listen. Remember our second year? Remember that girl. What was her name—" He rubbed his forehead. "The one with the dark hair. The one we met over at Ted's place."

"Stop!" Nelson waved the gun frantically. "I don't want to hear any more. You killed him! You . . . machine."

Olham looked at Nelson. "You're wrong. I don't know what happened, but the robot never reached me. Something must have gone wrong. Maybe the ship crashed." He turned to Peters. "I'm Olham. I know it. No transfer was made. I'm the same as I've always been."

He touched himself, running his hands over his body. "There must be some way to prove it. Take me back to Earth. An X-ray examination, a neurological study, anything like that will show you. Or maybe we can find the crashed ship."

Neither Peters nor Nelson spoke.

"I am Olham," he said again. "I know I am. But I can't prove it."

"The robot," Peters said, "would be unaware that he was not the real Spence Olham. He would become Olham in mind as well as in body. He was given an artificial memory system, false recall. He would look like him, have his memories, his thoughts and interests, perform his job.

"But there would be one difference. Inside the robot is a U-bomb, ready to explode at the trigger phrase." Peters moved a little away. "That's the one difference. That's why we're taking you to the Moon. They'll disassemble you and remove the bomb. Maybe it will explode, but it won't matter, not there."

Olham sat down slowly.

"We'll be there soon," Nelson said.

He lay back, thinking frantically, as the ship dropped slowly down. Under them was the pitted surface of the Moon, the endless expanse of ruin. What could he do? What would save him?

"Get ready," Peters said.

In a few minutes he would be dead. Down below he could see a tiny dot, a building of some kind. There were men in the building, the demolition team, waiting to tear him to bits. They would rip him open, pull off his arms and legs, break him apart. When they found no bomb they would be surprised; they would know, but it would be too late.

Olham looked around the small cabin. Nelson was still holding the gun. There was no chance there. If he could get to a doctor, have an examination made—that was the only way. Mary could help him. He thought frantically, his mind racing. Only a few minutes, just a little time left. If he could contact her, get word to her some way.

"Easy," Peters said. The ship came down slowly, bumping on the rough ground. There was silence.

"Listen," Olham said thickly. "I can prove I'm Spence Olham. Get a doctor. Bring him here—"

"There's the squad." Nelson pointed. "They're coming." He glanced nervously at Olham. "I hope nothing happens."

"We'll be gone before they start work," Peters said. "We'll be out of here in a moment." He put on his pressure suit. When he had finished he took the gun from Nelson. "I'll watch him for a moment."

Nelson put on his pressure suit, hurrying awkwardly. "How about him?" He indicated Olham. "Will he need one?"

"No," Peters shook his head. "Robots probably don't require oxygen."

The group of men were almost to the ship. They halted, waiting. Peters signalled to them.

"Come on!" He waved his hand and the men approached warily; stiff, grotesque figures in their inflated suits.

"If you open the door," Olham said, "it means my death. It will be murder."

"Open the door," Nelson said. He reached for the handle.

Olham watched him. He saw the man's hand tighten around the metal rod. In a moment the door would swing back, the air in the ship would rush out. He would die, and presently they would realize their mistake. Perhaps at some other time, when there was no war, men might not act this way, hurrying an individual to his death because they were afraid. Everyone was frightened, everyone was willing to sacrifice the individual because of the group fear.

He was being killed because they could not wait to be sure of his guilt. There was not enough time.

He looked at Nelson. Nelson had been his friend for years. They had gone to school together. He had been best man at his wedding. Now Nelson was going to kill him. But Nelson was not wicked; it was not his fault. It was the times. Perhaps it had been the same way during the plagues. When men had shown a spot they probably had been killed, too, without a moment's hesitation, without proof, on suspicion alone. In times of danger there was no other way.

He did not blame them. But he had to live. His life was too precious to be sacrificed. Olham thought quickly. What could he do? Was there anything? He looked around.

"Here goes," Nelson said.

"You're right," Olham said. The sound of his own voice surprised him. It was the strength of desperation. "I have no need of air. Open the door."

They paused, looking at him in curious alarm.

"Go ahead. Open it. It makes no difference." Olham's hand disappeared inside his jacket. "I wonder how far you two can run?"

"Run?"

"You have fifteen seconds to live." Inside his jacket his fingers twisted, his arm suddenly rigid. He relaxed, smiling a little. "You were wrong about the trigger phrase. In that respect you were mistaken. Fourteen seconds, now."

Two shocked faces stared at him from the pressure suits. Then they were struggling, running, tearing the door open. The air shrieked out, spilling into the void. Peters and Nelson bolted out of the ship. Olham came after them. He grasped the door and dragged it shut. The automatic pressure system chugged furiously, restoring the air. Olham let his breath out with a shudder.

One more second.....

Beyond the window the two men had joined the group. The group scattered, running in all directions. One by one they threw themselves down, prone on the ground. Olham seated himself at the control board. He moved the dials into place. As the ship rose up into the air the men below scrambled to their feet and stared up, their mouths open.

"Sorry," Olham murmured, "but I've got to get back to Earth."

He headed the ship back the way it had come.

It was night. All around the ship crickets chirped, disturbing the chill darkness. Olham bent over the vidscreen. Gradually the image formed; the call had gone through without trouble. He breathed a sigh of relief.

"Mary," he said. The woman stared at him. She gasped.

"Spence! Where are you? What's happened?"

"I can't tell you. Listen, I have to talk fast. They may break this call off any minute. Go to the Project grounds and get Dr. Chamberlain. If he isn't there, get any doctor. Bring him to the house and have him stay there. Have him bring equipment, X-ray, fluoroscope, everything."

"But—"

"Do as I say. Hurry. Have him get it ready in an hour." Olham leaned toward the screen. "Is everything all right? Are you alone?"

"Alone?"

"Is anyone with you? Has . . . has Nelson or anyone contacted you?"

"No, Spence. I don't understand."

"All right. I'll see you at the house in an hour. And don't tell anyone anything. Get Chamberlain there on any pretext. Say you're very ill."

He broke the connection and looked at his watch. A moment later he left the ship, stepping down into the darkness. He had a half-mile to go.

He began to walk.

One light showed in the window, the study light. He watched it, kneeling against the fence. There was no sound, no movement of any kind. He held his watch up and read it by starlight. Almost an hour had passed.

Along the street a shoot bug came. It went on.

Olham looked toward the house. The doctor should have already come. He should be inside, waiting with Mary. A thought struck him. Had she been able to leave the house? Perhaps they had intercepted her. Maybe he was moving into a trap.

But what else could he do?

With a doctor's records, photographs and reports, there was a chance, a chance of proof. If he could be examined, if he could remain alive long enough for them to study him. . . .

He could prove it that way. It was probably the only way. His one hope lay inside the house. Dr. Chamberlain was a respected man. He was the staff doctor for the Project. He would know; his word on the matter would have meaning. He could overcome their hysteria, their madness, with facts.

Madness—that was what it was. If only they could wait, act slowly, take their time. But they could not wait. He had to die, die at once, without proof, without any kind of trial or examination. The simplest test would tell, but they had not time for the simplest test. They could think only of the danger. Danger, and nothing more.

He stood up and moved toward the house. He came up on the porch. At the door he paused, listening. Still no sound. The house was absolutely still.

Too still.

Olham stood on the porch, unmoving. They were trying to be silent inside. Why? It was a small house; only a few feet away, beyond the door, Mary and Dr. Chamberlain should be standing. Yet he could hear nothing, no sound of voices, nothing at all. He looked at the door. It was a door he had opened and closed a thousand times, every morning and every night.

He put his hand on the knob. Then, all at once, he reached out and touched the bell instead. The bell pealed, off some place in the back of the house. Olham smiled. He could hear movement.

Mary opened the door. As soon as he saw her face he knew.

He ran, throwing himself into the bushes. A Security officer shoved Mary out of the way, firing past her. The bushes burst apart. Olham wriggled around the side of the house. He leaped up and ran, racing frantically into the darkness. A searchlight snapped on, a beam of light circling past him.

He crossed the road and squeezed over a fence. He jumped down and made his way across a backyard. Behind him men were coming. Security officers, shouting to each other as they came. Olham gasped for breath, his chest rising and falling.

Her face—he had known at once. The set lips, the terrified, wretched eyes. Suppose he had gone ahead, pushed open the door and entered! They had tapped the call and come at once, as soon as he had broken off. Probably she believed their account. No doubt she thought he was the robot, too.

Olham ran on and on. He was losing the officers, dropping them behind. Apparently they were not much good at running. He climbed a hill and made his way down the other side. In a moment he would be back at the ship. But where to, this time? He slowed down, stopping. He could see the ship already, outlined against the sky, where he had parked it. The settlement was behind him; he was on the outskirts of the wilderness between the inhabited places, where the forests and desolation began. He crossed a barren field and entered the trees.

As he came toward it, the door of the ship opened.

Peters stepped out, framed against the light. In his arms was a heavy boris-gun. Olham stopped, rigid. Peters stared around him, into the darkness. "I know you're there, some place," he said. "Come on up here, Olham. There are Security men all around you."

Olham did not move.

"Listen to me. We will catch you very shortly. Apparently you still do not believe you're the robot. Your call to the woman indicates that you are still under the illusion created by your artifical memories.

"But you *are* the robot. You are the robot, and inside you is the bomb. Any moment the trigger phrase may be spoken, by you, by someone else, by anyone. When that happens the bomb will destroy everything for miles around. The Project, the woman, all of us will be killed. Do you understand?"

Olham said nothing. He was listening. Men were moving toward him, slipping through the woods.

"If you don't come out, we'll catch you. It will be only a matter of time. We no longer plan to remove you to the Moon-base. You will be destroyed on sight and we will have to take the chance that the bomb will detonate. I have ordered every available Security officer into the area. The whole county is being searched, inch by inch. There is no place you can go. Around this wood is a cordon of armed men. You have about six hours left before the last inch is covered."

Olham moved away. Peters went on speaking; he had not seen him at all. It was too dark to see anyone. But Peters was right. There was no place he could go. He was beyond the settlement, on the outskirts where the woods began. He could hide for a time, but eventually they would catch him.

Only a matter of time.

Olham walked quietly through the wood. Mile by mile, each part of the county was being measured off, laid bare, searched, studied, examined. The cordon was coming all the time, squeezing him into a smaller and smaller space.

What was there left? He had lost the ship, the one hope of escape. They were at his home; his wife was with them, believing, no doubt, that the real Olham had been killed. He clenched his fists. Some place there was a wrecked Outspace needle-ship, and in it the remains of the robot. Somewhere nearby the ship had crashed, crashed and broken up.

And the robot lay inside, destroyed.

A faint hope stirred him. What if he could find the remains? If he could show them the wreckage, the remains of the ship, the robot....

But where? Where would he find it?

He walked on, lost in thought. Some place, not too far off, probably. The ship would have landed close to the Project; the robot would have expected to go the rest of the way on foot. He went up the side of a hill and looked around. Crashed and burned. Was there some clue, some hint? Had he read anything, heard anything? Some place close by, within walking distance. Some wild place, a remote spot where there would be no people.

Suddenly Olham smiled. Crashed and burned....

Sutton Wood.

He increased his pace.

It was morning. Sunlight filtered down through the broken trees onto the man crouching at the edge of the clearing. Olham glanced up from time to time, listening. They were not far off, only a few minutes away. He smiled.

Down below him, strewn across the clearing and into the charred stumps that had been Sutton Wood, lay a tangled mass of wreckage. In the sunlight it glittered a little, gleaming darkly. He had not had too much trouble finding it. Sutton Wood was a place he knew well; he had climbed around it many times in his life, when he was younger. He had known where he would find the remains. There was one peak that jutted up suddenly, without warning.

A descending ship, unfamiliar with the Wood, had little chance of missing it. And now he squatted, looking down at the ship, or what remained of it.

Olham stood up. He could hear them, only a little distance away, coming together, talking in low tones. He tensed himself. Everything depended on who first saw him. If it were Nelson, he had no chance. Nelson would fire at once. He would be dead before they saw the ship. But if he had time to call out, hold them off for a moment.... That was all he needed. Once they saw the ship he would be safe.

But if they fired first....

A charred branch cracked. A figure appeared, coming forward uncertainly. Olham took a deep breath. Only a few seconds remained, perhaps the last seconds in his life. He raised his arms, peering intently.

It was Peters.

"Peters!" Olham waved his arms. Peters lifted his gun, aiming. "Don't fire!" His voice shook. "Wait a minute. Look past me, across the clearing."

"I've found him," Peters shouted. Security men came pouring out of the burned woods around him.

"Don't shoot. Look past me. The ship, the needle-ship. The Outspace ship. Look!"

Peters hesitated. The gun wavered.

"It's down there," Olham said rapidly. "I knew I'd find it here. The burned wood. Now you believe me. You'll find the remains of the robot in the ship. Look, will you?"

"There is something down there," one of the men said nervously.

"Shoot him!" a voice said. It was Nelson.

"Wait." Peters turned sharply. "I'm in charge. Don't anyone fire. Maybe he's telling the truth."

"Shoot him," Nelson said. "He killed Olham. Any minute he may kill us all. If the bomb goes off—"

"Shut up." Peters advanced toward the slope. He stared down. "Look at that." He waved two men up to him. "Go down there and see what that is."

The men raced down the slope, across the clearing. They bent down, poking in the ruins of the ship.

"Well?" Peters called.

Olham held his breath. He smiled a little. It must be there; he had not had time to look, himself, but it had to be there. Suddenly doubt assailed him. Suppose the robot had lived long enough to wander away? Suppose his body had been completely destroyed, burned to ashes by the fire?

He licked his lips. Perspiration came out on his forehead. Nelson was staring at him, his face still livid. His chest rose and fell.

"Kill him," Nelson said. "Before he kills us."

The two men stood up.

"What have you found?" Peters said. He held the gun steady. "Is there anything there?"

"Looks like something. It's a needle-ship, all right. There's something beside it."

"I'll look." Peters strode past Olham. Olham watched him go down the hill and up to the men. The others were following after him, peering to see.

"It's a body of some sort," Peters said. "Look at it!"

Olham came along with them. They stood around in a circle, staring down.

On the ground, bent and twisted into a strange shape, was a grotesque form. It looked human, perhaps; except that it was bent so strangely, the arms and legs flung off in all directions. The mouth was open, the eyes stared glassily.

"Like a machine that's run down," Peters murmured.

Olham smiled feebly. "Well?" he said.

Peters looked at him. "I can't believe it. You were telling the truth all the time."

"The robot never reached me," Olham said. He took out a cigarette and lit it. "It was destroyed when the ship crashed. You were all too busy with the war to wonder why an out-of-the-way woods would suddenly catch fire and burn. Now you know."

He stood smoking, watching the men. They were dragging the grotesque remains from the ship. The body was stiff, the arms and legs rigid.

"You'll find the bomb, now," Olham said. The men laid the body on the ground. Peters bent down.

"I think I see the corner of it." He reached out, touching the body.

The chest of the corpse had been laid open. Within the gaping tear something glinted, something metal. The men stared at the metal without speaking.

"That would have destroyed us all, if it had lived," Peters said. "That metal box, there."

There was silence.

"I think we owe you something," Peters said to Olham. "This must have been a nightmare to you. If you hadn't escaped, we would have—" He broke off.

Olham put out his cigarette. "I knew, of course, that the robot had never reached me. But I had no way of proving it. Sometimes it isn't possible to prove a thing right away. That was the whole trouble. There wasn't any way I could demonstrate that I was myself."

"How about a vacation?" Peters said. "I think we might work out a month's vacation for you. You could take it easy, relax."

"I think right now I want to go home," Olham said.

"All right, then," Peters said. "Whatever you say."

Nelson had squatted down on the ground, beside the corpse. He reached out toward the glint of metal visible within the chest.

"Don't touch it," Olham said. "It might still go off. We'd better let the demolition squad take care of it later on."

Nelson said nothing. Suddenly he grabbed hold of the metal, reaching his hand inside the chest. He pulled.

"What are you doing?" Olham cried.

Nelson stood up. He was holding on to the metal object. His face was blank with terror. It was a metal knife, an Outspace needle-knife, covered with blood.

"This killed him," Nelson whispered. "My friend was killed with this." He looked at Olham. "You killed him with this and left him beside the ship."

Olham was trembling. His teeth chattered. He looked from the knife to the body. "This can't be Olham," he said. His mind spun, everything was whirling. "Was I wrong?"

He gaped.

"But if that's Olham, then I must be—"

He did not complete the sentence, only the first phrase. The blast was visible all the way to Alpha Centauri.

Study Questions

Catch That Zeppelin

1. Some people argue that we are entirely a product of our heredity and our environment, i.e., that given our genetic makeup, our environment makes us who we are. Does Leiber's story presuppose this view? In order for his story to make sense, does he need to assume that given Hitler's genetic material and given his history up to the "cusp" in World War I, one chain of historical events would necessarily have made him the leader of the Nazi Party and that the other would necessarily have made him Hitler the Zeppelin salesman? What other interpretation is possible?

2. Since circumstances play so great a role in who we become, does it follow that we ought not to hold people responsible for who they become? Is there a way to acknowledge the force of circumstance without concluding that we have no responsibility for what we are?

3. What characteristics does the historical Hitler have in common with Hitler the Zeppelin Company executive? Is it plausible that—given the different circumstances Leiber describes—someone with these characteristics might have gone in each of the directions Leiber suggests? If so, should we say that these characteristics constitute his "essential self"? What would we gain by talking this way? Would it help us to explain anything? Would it suggest anything that we believe to be false?

Impostor

1. As we suggested in the introduction to this section, philosophers sometimes wonder about the nature of personal identity, i.e., of the permanence of the self through change. Typically, the problem is posed by asking on what basis we say that we are the same person through time. Is there something about *us*—as opposed to our history (what we have done and experienced)—that makes us one and the same person through time? Consider this question in relation to "Impostor." Was there something about the real Olham—distinct from his history—that differentiates him from the Impostor? Suppose that the Impostor's body were organic and an exact duplicate of his own (and that they were both living). Would there then be something—distinct from their histories—

that made each a separate self? If so, what?

2. Suppose we had the capacity completely to duplicate a person down to the last brain cell. And suppose that we used this technology to replace people who die accidentally, i.e., suppose we could and did produce exact replicas of what they were immediately before their deaths. Finally, suppose it is the practice of our society to treat these replicas as if they were continuations of the original (which is exactly how they would *feel*).
Would we be fooling ourselves? Is there one self here (resurrected, as it were) or are there two? What is it that we are counting? Will the result be the same if the original is not dead?

3. Suppose that we choose to produce copies of living persons. Each would have the same memories, personalities, and so forth, and think of herself as the same person (at least until informed of her origin). Could we now say that each person (self) is unique in some important sense? If our uniqueness is the foundation of our value, does it follow that duplicate persons have less value (have less worth, deserve less respect, have fewer rights)? Do they?

Part 4

Persons, Minds, and the Essentially Human

Introduction to Part 4

Human beings generally find nothing repugnant in the idea of pulverizing stone for building material or grinding wheat for food. In fact, most of us are not much bothered by the slaughter of cattle, pigs, and fish for meat or skins. But we do think that there is something wrong with treating persons in this way. This suggests that we think that there is something that distinguishes persons from other kinds of beings in the universe in virtue of which persons are entitled to special treatment. But who are persons anyway? Only human beings? What of androids and aliens? Might they not have intelligence, feelings, imagination, hopes, desires, and dreams? If so, are they not also persons and entitled to the respect to which (other) persons are entitled? If not, why not? What is so special about us?

According to one view, human beings are distinguished from other inhabitants of the universe in virtue of having souls. It is this that entitles us to special treatment. The more familiar versions of this view are religious. In this case the special treatment to which we are entitled as persons is that treatment to which we are entitled by divine law. This strategy, of course, is rejected by philosophers who are atheists or agnostics. And it is rejected by some philosophers who are theistic as well. Since the theory of personhood is supposed to explain why it is that human beings deserve special treatment—e.g., why human beings deserve rights—many philosophers believe that it is important to find a theory that can be shared by those who hold importantly different religious views.

Who, then, are persons? Well, to begin with, we are. To discover what it is about a being that makes it a person we may ask what it is about us that makes us persons. In effect, this is to ask what it is about us that entitles us to special treatment.

One major historical tendency has been to answer this question in relation to what were thought to be certain distinctively human capacities. The most important candidate here is the capacity to reason. Although different philosophers have meant different things by "reason," those who connect being a person to having reason take reason to include the capacity to make and to act upon value judgments, i.e., the capacity to understand the good life (or the moral life) and to organize one's life according to this understanding (at least to some degree). It is a consequence of this view that any being of comparable capacities has comparable claims to personhood, be he or she android or alien.

A less generous account of what it is to be a person would require that a being have feelings as well as the capacity to organize its choices on the basis of values. The term "feelings" here is to be understood in a wide sense that includes both sensations and emotions. Some would argue that a being incapable of feeling is not entitled to the special treatment we reserve for persons despite the fact that it has and acts on values. Of course, if it is maintained by defenders of the first view that having and acting on values logically presupposes having feelings, there will be no difference between these two views. But some philosophers maintain that it is possible to have and to act on values without having feelings.

Whichever of these views we adopt, we will not be able to distinguish persons from nonpersons unless we are able to say what it means to have the capacities in question. That is, we need to be able to say what it is to decide, choose, prefer, and think, on the one hand, and to have sensations and emotions on the other. Pursued deeply, then, the question "What is it to be a person?" gives rise to questions in the philosophy of mind. How we decide these latter questions will importantly affect how we decide the former.

Can a machine made of plastic and metal think or feel? Can an alien made primarily of silicon? Different philosophical theories of mind commit us to different answers to these questions. According to one historically influential theory—psychophysical dualism—thinking and feeling are activities of a special nonmaterial substance called "mind." This substance differs from physical substance in that it lacks characteristics essential to the physical. Specifically, it lacks spatial location, size, shape, and mass; nor do its "products" (e.g., thoughts and feelings) have these properties. Because it is a separate substance, moreover, the mind is *in principle* capable of existing without the body, i.e., as a disembodied spirit. Still, the minds with which we are familiar happen to be embodied. Furthermore they interact with bodies causally: mental states cause physical states and physical states cause mental states. And it may be that, though minds can exist without bodies in principle, the world is in fact so structured that minds cannot exist without bodies in actuality.

Where does this leave us in relation to the question of whether beings of metal, steel, and glass can think and feel? In fact, it leaves the question open. After all, how would a dualist know that a mind is connected up to a body? He claims to know this in his own case by direct experience. He has direct access to his own thoughts and feelings. And he claims to know this in the case of other humans on the basis of the similarities between their behavior and physiological makeup and his own. Critics of dualism have challenged the dualists' right to make this inference. But even if we grant him this right in this case of other human beings, it is clear that his right diminishes to the degree that the being under consideration differs from him in relevant respects, e.g., in its material, its structure, or its behavior. In the case of such beings, it would *appear* that the dualist must remain agnostic. This conclusion is all the more plausible in view of the fact that we can create machines that behave very much like human beings do, to which few dualists would want to attribute a mind.

One main alternative to dualism is philosophical behaviorism. According to the behaviorist, to have a thought, feeling, or sensation is simply to behave or to be disposed to behave in a certain way. This behavior includes sincere verbal behavior. To have a pain, for example, is to be disposed to do such things as grimace, groan, and sincerely say "I am in pain." The behaviorist denies that terms like *pain, thought,* and so forth, refer to private events, i.e., events to which only the experiencer has direct access. Were we to maintain *that* view, the behaviorist insists, we would have no way of knowing whether a term such as *pain* means the same thing to each of us. Each of us might be using it to refer to a *different* private event. Some behaviorists write as if there are no such things as "raw feels" at all; others insist only and somewhat more sanely that terms like *pain, thought,* etc., do not refer to them. In either case a behaviorist *might* say that a being of metal, plastic, or silicon thinks, feels pain, and so forth, so long as it is disposed to behave in certain ways. Indeed, she is committed to this view unless she can provide good reason to limit her analysis of these terms to protoplasmic life forms. (Some behaviorists do argue that they are properly so limited, but that is too long a tale to tell here.)

Some philosophers and scientists impressed with progress in neurophysiology are attracted to a third view, namely, the view that mental states are nothing but brain states. In the context of the laboratory, this seems a natural thing to say. Its defenders, however, have had difficulty specifying a sense of "are nothing but" ("are identical with") in which it is true. The main problem is that mental states have a number of properties that brain states do not. Thoughts may be witty or profound; afterimages may be round and green; pains may be sharp or dull. Brain states have none of these features. Defenders of the thesis that mental states are brain states have attempted to deal with these problems in a variety of ways, and philosophers are divided on the success of their replies to these criticisms.

It is difficult to see how someone who supports the identity thesis could maintain that creatures of metal and plastic or silicon have thoughts and feelings; they do not, after all, have brain states of the appropriate kind. On the other hand, most of us would agree that it is at least *in principle* possible to replace a damaged part of the human brain with, e.g., a silicon chip to restore function. This being the case, the relation between a given mental state **M** and a corresponding brain state **B** seems inaccurately described as identity; for in theory, many different brain structures could give rise to **M.** Indeed, we could in theory replace an entire brain with circuitry, bit by bit, testing for function after each substitution (e.g., after replacing the pain centers with functional equivalents, we test for pain response; after we replace the memory centers, we test for memory response, etc.). The new brain might be entirely different from the old in structure and material, but do everything the old brain could do.

In response to this sort of objection, some identity theorists have amended their position. Instead of holding that every mental state is some particular brain state, they now hold simply that every mental state is identical to some brain state. Thus, although no one specific brain state may obtain every time I think "2 + 2 = 4," that thought is always identical to some state of my brain, i.e., whenever I think that thought there is something going on in my brain that is that thought. This view, then, requires us to be in a position to say that various mental states are independent of their relation to brain states. For, if we cannot say what thinking is, we cannot say that any number of brain states might be identical to it (identical to *what?*). In deciding what "prescientific" account of mental states to adopt, the identity theorist has a number of options. Thus, for example, he may accept or reject the view that a term like *pain* refers to a raw feeling and/or that terms like *thought* and *anger* refer to dispositions to behave.

The most recent philosophical theory of mind is called functionalism. As the name suggests, functionalists hold that mental states are functional states, i.e., that they are means by which an organism or being achieves a particular result. To say that thought is a functional state is to say that thought is what an organism does to solve problems, make decisions, and so forth. The specific nature of that activity—i.e., what a being does specifically to achieve these ends—is an open question. The functionalist is willing to attribute thought to anything that is capable of solving problems, choice to anything capable of making nonrandom selections and seeing to anything capable of discriminating between visual stimuli. It does not matter how these results are achieved. On a functionalist view, then, we may attribute thoughts and feelings to beings of metal, plastic, and silicon so long as they are capable of doing such things. Indeed, we may attribute beliefs to thermostats and sight to electric eyes.

Recall that the question of the nature of thoughts and feelings arose because we were trying to understand certain theories of what it is to be a person. To be a person, it was said, is to be capable of organizing one's life in accordance with one's values, and perhaps to have feelings as well. Thus the capacity for thought and for feeling was said to be a necessary condition for being a person. Some philosophers, however, would add to this a further condition, namely, the capacity for freedom.

Of course it could be said that choice implies freedom. If this is so, the earlier account of what it is to be a person already includes the freedom requirement. On a more narrow account of choice, however, to choose is simply to make a selection on the basis of criteria. This can be done by machines that no one would want to describe as free (e.g., orange sorters). In general, many people resist talking of freedom where the choices a being makes are choices that it is *programmed* to make, and where it has no capacity to make any other sort of choices. Since they believe that this description fits machines, they deny that machines have the capacity for freedom, and hence that machines can be persons. Notice that the word *capacity* is all-important here. Given a properly controlled environment, it is also possible to "program" human beings such that they adopt and act on certain values without question. The differences between human beings and machines, it is argued, is that humans have the *capacity* to act otherwise. Just what this capacity involves is a deep and complex question. Very roughly, however, we might say that it requires the capacity to form new values in a manner that is not open to a machine with a *fixed* value-formation program.

Closely related to the question "What is it to be a person?" is the question "What is it to be human?" But these questions are not identical. According to the criteria outlined earlier, it is possible for a robot or an alien to be a person, but no one would claim that robots or aliens who so qualify are human for that reason. A not very interesting way to answer the question "What is it to be human?" is to identify being human with being a member of the species Homo sapiens. A more interesting approach is to ask whether there are any important nonbiological characteristics of members of this species that importantly distinguish them from some or all other beings entitled to be treated as persons. This latter approach would allow the possibility that non-Homo sapiens are human in some important sense; or, if you prefer, that they are humanoid (although either description reflects a certain biocentrism; as if all beings like us in the relevant way should be named after us). In any case, what we are after here are those characteristics that enable human beings to participate in a distinctively human form of life. Roughly, then, we might say that any being is human (or humanoid) to the degree that it is endowed with the capacity to participate as a full member of a human community.

Precisely what it is so to participate is difficult to say. Human cultures are and have been very different from one another. And in some sense of "fully participate" it may be that people of certain cultures would be incapable of full participation in the life of others. Adaptability, after all, has its limits. Still, it appears to be the case that any normal human infant can be brought up to be a full participant in any human culture. To identify what is essentially human is to identify the *potentials* in virtue of which this is so. To do this we need to discover what (if anything) is common to all human social organizations and what characteristics a being must have to participate in them.

Given the extraordinary variability of human social forms, any account of these matters is bound to be very general. Brian Aldiss's "Who Can Replace a Man?" and Isaac Asimov's "The Bicentennial

Man" are based on theories of what these characteristics might be. James Causey's "The Show Must Go On" is not based on such a theory, but his picture of the human response to androids suggests one.

Aldiss and Asimov describe a future in which machines with thoughts and feelings are used virtually as slaves by human beings. Causey describes a future in which androids have been emancipated but, under special circumstances, still may be used as tools. As you read these stories, ask yourself whether the robots and androids in these stories are treated unjustly. Do they have thoughts and feelings? If so, ought they to be treated as persons? What difference, if any, does it make that they are not human?

The Bicentennial Man

Isaac Asimov

The Three Laws of Robotics

1. A robot may not injure a human being, or, through inaction, allow a human being to come to harm.
2. A robot must obey the orders given it by human beings except where such orders would conflict with the First Law.
3. A robot must protect its own existence as long as such protection does not conflict with the First or Second Law.

1

Andrew Martin said, "Thank you," and took the seat offered him. He didn't look driven to the last resort, but he had been.

He didn't, actually, look anything, for there was smooth blankness to his face, except for the sadness one imagined one saw in his eyes. His hair was smooth, light brown, rather fine; and he had no facial hair. He looked freshly and cleanly shaved. His clothes were distinctly old-fashioned, but neat, and predominantly a velvety red-purple in color.

Facing him from behind the desk was the surgeon. The nameplate on the desk included a fully identifying series of letters and numbers which Andrew didn't bother with. To call him Doctor would be quite enough.

"When can the operation be carried through, Doctor?" he asked.

Softly, with that certain inalienable note of respect that a robot always used to a human being, the surgeon said, "I am not certain, sir, that I understand how or upon whom such an operation could be performed."

There might have been a look of respectful intransigence on the surgeon's face, if a robot of his sort, in lightly bronzed stainless steel, could have such an expression—or any expression.

Andrew Martin studied the robot's right hand, his cutting hand, as it lay motionless on the desk. The fingers were long and were shaped into artistically metallic, looping curves so graceful and appropriate that one could imagine a scalpel fitting them and becoming, temporarily, one piece with them. There would be no hesitation in his work, no stumbling, no quivering, no mistakes. That confidence came with specialization, of course, a specialization so fiercely desired by humanity that few robots were, any longer, independently brained. A surgeon, of course, would have to be. But this one, though brained, was so limited in his capacity that he did not recognize Andrew, had probably never heard of him.

"Have you ever thought you would like to be a man?" Andrew asked.

The surgeon hesitated a moment, as though the question fitted nowhere in his allotted positronic pathways. "But I am a robot, sir."

"Would it be better to be a man?"

"It would be better, sir, to be a better surgeon. I could not be so if I were a man, but only if I were a more advanced robot. I would be pleased to be a more advanced robot."

"It does not offend you that I can order you about? That I can make you stand up, sit down, move right or left, by merely telling you to do so?"

"It is my pleasure to please you, sir. If your orders were to interfere with my functioning with respect to you or to any other human being, I would not obey you. The First Law, concerning my duty to human safety, would take precedence over the Second Law relating to obedience. Otherwise, obedience is my pleasure. Now, upon whom I am to perform this operation?"

"Upon me," Andrew said.

"But that is impossible. It is patently a damaging operation."

"That does not matter," said Andrew, calmly.

"I must not inflict damage," said the surgeon.

"On a human being, you must not," said Andrew, "but I, too, am a robot."

2

Andrew had appeared much more a robot when he had first been manufactured. He had then been as much a robot in appearance as any that had ever existed—smoothly designed and functional.

He had done well in the home to which he had been brought in those days when robots in households, or on the planet altogether, had been a rarity. There had been four in the home: Sir and Ma'am and Miss and Little Miss. He knew their names, of course, but he never used them. Sir was Gerald Martin.

His own serial number was NDR- . . . He eventually forgot the numbers. It had been a long time, of course; but if he had wanted to remember, he could not have forgotten. He had not wanted to remember.

Little Miss had been the first to call him Andrew, because she could not use the letters, and all the rest followed her in doing so.

Little Miss . . . She had lived for ninety years and was long since dead. He had tried to call her Ma'am once, but she would not allow it. Little Miss she had been to her last day.

Andrew had been intended to perform the duties of a valet, a butler, even a lady's maid. Those were the experimental days for him, and indeed, for all robots anywhere save in the industrial and exploratory factories and stations off Earth.

The Martins enjoyed him, and half the time he was prevented from doing his work because Miss and Little Miss wanted to play with him. It was Miss who first understood how this might be arranged. "We order you to play with us and you must follow orders."

"I am sorry, Miss, but a prior order from Sir must surely take precedence."

But she said, "Daddy just said he *hoped* you would take care of the cleaning. That's not much of an order. I *order* you."

Sir did not mind. Sir was fond of Miss and of Little Miss, even more than Ma'am was; and Andrew was fond of them, too. At least, the effect they had upon his actions were those which in a human being would have been called the result of fondness. Andrew thought of it as fondness for he did not know any other word for it.

It was for Little Miss that Andrew had carved a pendant out of wood. She had ordered him to. Miss, it seemed, had received an ivorite pendant with scrollwork for her birthday and Little Miss was unhappy over it. She had only a piece of wood, which she gave Andrew together with a small kitchen knife.

He had done it quickly and Little Miss had said, "That's *nice,* Andrew. I'll show it to Daddy."

Sir would not believe it. "Where did you really get this, Mandy?" Mandy was what he called Little Miss. When Little Miss assured him she was really telling the truth, he turned to Andrew. "Did you do this, Andrew?"

"Yes, Sir."

"The design, too?"

"Yes, Sir."

"From what did you copy the design?"

"It is a geometric representation, Sir, that fits the grain of the wood."

The next day, Sir brought him another piece of wood—a larger one—and an electric vibro-knife. "Make something out of this, Andrew. Anything you want to," he said.

Andrew did so as Sir watched, then looked at the product a long time. After that, Andrew no longer waited on tables. He was ordered to read books on furniture design instead, and he learned to make cabinets and desks.

"These are amazing productions, Andrew," Sir soon told him.

"I enjoy doing them, Sir," Andrew admitted.

"Enjoy?"

"It makes the circuits of my brain somehow flow more easily. I have heard you use the word *enjoy* and the way you use it fits the way I feel. I enjoy doing them, Sir."

3

Gerald Martin took Andrew to the regional offices of the United States Robots and Mechanical Men Corporation. As a member of the Regional Legislature he had no trouble at all in gaining an interview with the chief robopsychologist. In fact, it was only as a member of the Regional Legislature that he qualified as a robot owner in the first place—in those early days when robots were rare.

Andrew did not understand any of this at the time. But in later years, with greater learning, he could review that early scene and understand it in its proper light.

The robopsychologist, Merton Mansky, listened with a growing frown and more than once managed to stop his fingers at the point beyond which they would have irrevocably drummed on the table. He had drawn features and a lined forehead, but he might actually have been younger than he looked.

"Robotics is not an exact art, Mr. Martin," Mansky explained. "I cannot explain it to you in detail, but the mathematics governing the plotting of the positronic pathways is far too complicated to permit of any but approximate solutions. Naturally, since we build everything around the Three Laws, those are incontrovertible. We will, of course, replace your robot—"

"Not at all," said Sir. "There is no question of failure on his part. He performs his assigned duties perfectly. The point is he also carves wood in exquisite fashion and never the same twice. He produces works of art."

Mansky looked confused. "Strange. Of course, we're attempting generalized pathways these days. Really creative, you think?"

"See for yourself." Sir handed over a little sphere of wood on which there was a playground scene in which the boys and girls were almost too small to make out, yet they were in perfect proportion and they blended so naturally with the grain that it, too, seemed to have been carved.

Mansky was incredulous. "*He* did that?" He handed it back with a shake of his head. "The luck of the draw. Something in the pathways."

"Can you do it again?"

"Probably not. Nothing like this has ever been reported."

"Good! I don't in the least mind Andrew's being the only one."

"I suspect that the company would like to have your robot back for study," Mansky said.

"Not a chance!" Sir said with sudden grimness. "Forget it." He turned to Andrew, "Let's go home, now."

"As you wish, Sir," said Andrew.

4

Miss was dating boys and wasn't about the house much. It was Little Miss, not as little as she once was, who filled Andrew's horizon now. She never forgot that the very first piece of wood carving he had done had been for her. She kept it on a silver chain about her neck.

It was she who first objected to Sir's habit of giving away Andrew's work. "Come on, Dad, if anyone wants one of them, let him pay for it. It's worth it."

"It isn't like you to be greedy, Mandy."

"Not for us, Dad. For the artist."

Andrew had never heard the word before, and when he had a moment to himself he looked it up in the dictionary.

Then there was another trip, this time to Sir's lawyer.

"What do you think of this, John?" Sir asked.

The lawyer was John Feingold. He had white hair and a pudgy belly, and the rims of his contact lenses were tinted a bright green. He looked at the small plaque Sir had given him. "This is beautiful. But I've already heard the news. Isn't this a carving made by your robot?

The one you've brought with you."

"Yes, Andrew does them. Don't you, Andrew?"

"Yes, Sir," said Andrew.

"How much would you pay for that, John?" Sir asked.

"I can't say. I'm not a collector of such things."

"Would you believe I have been offered two hundred and fifty dollars for that small thing. Andrew has made chairs that have sold for five hundred dollars. There's two hundred thousand dollars in the bank from Andrew's products."

"Good heavens, he's making you rich, Gerald."

"Half rich," said Sir. "Half of it is in an account in the name of Andrew Martin."

"The robot?"

"That's right, and I want to know if it's legal."

"Legal . . . ?" Feingold's chair creaked as he leaned back in it. "There are no precedents, Gerald. How did your robot sign the necessary papers?"

"He can sign his name. Now, is there anything further that ought to be done?"

"Um." Feingold's eyes seemed to turn inward for a moment. Then he said, "Well, we can set up a trust to handle all finances in his name and that will place a layer of insulation between him and the hostile world. Beyond that, my advice is you do nothing. No one has stopped you so far. If anyone objects, let *him* bring suit."

"And will you take the case if the suit is brought?"

"For a retainer, certainly."

"How much?"

"Something like that," Feingold said, and pointed to the wooden plaque.

"Fair enough," said Sir.

Feingold chuckled as he turned to the robot. "Andrew, are you pleased that you have money?"

"Yes, sir."

"What do you plan to do with it?"

"Pay for things, sir, which otherwise Sir would have to pay for. It would save him expense, sir."

5

Such occasions arose. Repairs were expensive, and revisions were even more so. With the years, new models of robots were produced and Sir saw to it that Andrew had the advantage of every new device, until he was a model of metallic excellence. It was all done at Andrew's expense. Andrew insisted on that.

Only his positronic pathways were untouched. Sir insisted on that.

"The new models aren't as good as you are, Andrew," he said. "The new robots are worthless. The company has learned to make the pathways more precise, more closely on the nose, more deeply on the track. The new robots don't shift. They do what they're designed for and never stray. I like you better."

"Thank you, Sir."

"And it's your doing, Andrew, don't you forget that. I am certain Mansky put an end to generalized pathways as soon as he had a good look at you. He didn't like the unpredictability. Do you know how many times he asked for you back so he could place you under study? Nine times! I never let him have you, though; and now that he's retired, we may have some peace."

So Sir's hair thinned and grayed and his face grew pouchy, while Andrew looked even better than he had when he first joined the family. Ma'am had joined an art colony somewhere in Europe, and Miss was a poet in New York. They wrote sometimes, but not often. Little Miss was married and lived not far away. She said she did not want to leave Andrew. When her child, Little Sir, was born, she let Andrew hold the bottle and feed him.

With the birth of a grandson, Andrew felt that Sir had finally had someone to replace those who had gone. Therefore, it would not be so unfair now to come to him with the request.

"Sir, it is kind of you to have allowed me to spend my money as I wished."

"It was your money, Andrew."

"Only by your voluntary act, Sir. I do not believe the law would have stopped you from keeping it all."

"The law won't persuade me to do wrong, Andrew."

"Despite all expenses, and despite taxes, too, Sir, I have nearly six hundred thousand dollars."

"I know that, Andrew."

"I want to give it to you, Sir."

"I won't take it, Andrew."

"In exchange for something you can give me, Sir."

"Oh? What is that, Andrew?"

"My freedom, Sir."

"Your—"

"I wish to buy my freedom, Sir."

6

It wasn't that easy. Sir had flushed, had said, "For God's sake!" Then he had turned on his heel and stalked away.

It was Little Miss who finally brought him round, defiantly and harshly—and in front of Andrew. For thirty years no one had ever hesitated to talk in front of Andrew, whether or not the matter involved Andrew. He was only a robot.

"Dad, why are you taking this as a personal affront? He'll still be here. He'll still be loyal. He can't help that; it's built in. All he wants is a form of words. He wants to be called free. Is that so terrible? Hasn't he earned this chance? Heavens, he and I have been talking about it for years!"

"Talking about it for years, have you?"

"Yes, and over and over again he postponed it for fear he would hurt you. I *made* him put the matter up to you."

"He doesn't know what freedom is. He's a robot."

"Dad, you don't know him. He's read everything in the library. I don't know what he feels inside, but I don't know what *you* feel inside either. When you talk to him you'll find he reacts to the various abstractions as you and I do, and what else counts? If someone else's reactions are like your own, what more can you ask for?"

"The law won't take that attitude," Sir said, angrily. "See here, you!" He turned to Andrew with a deliberate grate in his voice. "I can't free you except by doing it legally. If this gets into the courts, you not only won't get your freedom but the law will take official cognizance of your money. They'll tell you that a robot has no right to earn money. Is this rigmarole worth losing your money?"

"Freedom is without price, Sir," said Andrew. "Even the chance of freedom is worth the money."

7

It seemed the court might also take the attitude that freedom was without a price, and might decide that for no price, however great, could a robot buy its freedom.

The simple statement of the regional attorney who represented those who had brought a class action to oppose the freedom was this: "The word *freedom* has no meaning when applied to a robot. Only a human being can be free." He said it several times, when it seemed appropriate; slowly, with his hand coming down rhythmically on the desk before him to mark the words.

Little Miss asked permission to speak on behalf of Andrew.

She was recognized by her full name, something Andrew had never heard pronounced before: "Amanda Laura Martin Charney may approach the bench."

"Thank you, Your Honor. I am not a lawyer and I don't know the proper way of phrasing things, but I hope you will listen to my meaning and ignore the words.

"Let's understand what it means to be free in Andrew's case. In some ways, he *is* free. I think it's at least twenty years since anyone in the Martin family gave him an order to do something that we felt he might not do of his own accord. But we can, if we wish, give him an order to do anything, couching it as harshly as we wish, because he is a machine that belongs to us. Why should we be in a position to do so, when he has served us so long, so faithfully, and has earned so much money for us? He owes us nothing more. The debt is entirely on the other side.

"Even if we were legally forbidden to place Andrew in involuntary servitude, he would still serve us voluntarily. Making him free would be a trick of words only, but it would mean much to him. It would give him everything and cost us nothing."

For a moment the judge seemed to be suppressing a smile. "I see your point, Mrs. Charney. The fact is that there is no binding law in this respect and no precedent. There is, however, the unspoken assumption that only a man may enjoy freedom. I can make new law here, subject to reversal in a higher court; but I cannot lightly run counter to that assumption. Let me address the robot. Andrew!"

"Yes, Your Honor."

It was the first time Andrew had spoken in court, and the judge seemed astonished for a moment at the human timbre of his voice.

"Why do you want to be free, Andrew? In what way will this matter to you?"

"Would *you* wish to be a slave, Your Honor," Andrew asked.

"But you are not a slave. You are a perfectly good robot—a genius of a robot, I am given to understand, capable of an artistic expression that can be matched nowhere. What more could you do if you were free?"

"Perhaps no more than I do now, Your Honor, but with greater joy. It has been said in this courtroom that only a human being can be free. It seems to me that only someone who *wishes* for freedom can be free. I wish for freedom."

And it was that statement that cued the judge. The crucial sentence in his decision was "There is no right to deny freedom to any object with a mind advanced enough to grasp the concept and desire the state."

It was eventually upheld by the World Court.

8

Sir remained displeased, and his harsh voice made Andrew feel as if he were being short-circuited. "I don't want your damned money, Andrew. I'll take it only because you won't feel free otherwise. From now on, you can select your own jobs and do them as you please. I will give you no orders, except this one: Do as you please. But I am still responsible for you. That's part of the court order. I hope you understand that."

Little Miss interrupted. "Don't be irascible, Dad. The responsibility is no great chore. You know you won't have to do a thing. The Three Laws still hold."

"Then how is he free?"

"Are not human beings bound by their laws, Sir?" Andrew replied.

"I'm not going to argue." Sir left the room, and Andrew saw him only infrequently after that.

Little Miss came to see him frequently in the small house that had been built and made over for him. It had no kitchen, of course, nor bathroom facilities. It had just two rooms; one was a library and one was a combination storeroom and workroom. Andrew accepted many commissions and worked harder as a free robot than he ever had before, till the cost of the house was paid for and the structure was signed over to him.

One day Little Sir—no, "George!"—came. Little Sir had insisted on that after the court decision. "A free robot doesn't call anyone Little Sir," George had said. "I call you Andrew. You must call me George."

His preference was phrased as an order, so Andrew called him George—but Little Miss remained Little Miss.

One day when George came alone, it was to say that Sir was dying. Little Miss was at the bedside, but Sir wanted Andrew as well.

Sir's voice was still quite strong, though he seemed unable to move much. He struggled to raise his hand.

"Andrew," he said, "Andrew—don't help me, George. I'm only dying; I'm not crippled. Andrew, I'm glad you're free. I just wanted to tell you that."

Andrew did not know what to say. He had never been at the side of someone dying before, but he knew it was the human way of ceasing to function. It was an involuntary and irreversible dismantling, and Andrew did not know what to say that might be appropriate. He could only remain standing, absolutely silent, absolutely motionless.

When it was over, Little Miss said to him, "He may not have seemed friendly to you toward the end, Andrew, but he was old, you know; and it hurt him that you should want to be free."

Then Andrew found the words. "I would never have been free without him, Little Miss."

9

Only after Sir's death did Andrew begin to wear clothes. He began with an old pair of trousers at first, a pair that George had given him.

George was married now, and a lawyer. He had joined Feingold's firm. Old Feingold was long since dead, but his daughter had carried on. Eventually the firm's name became Feingold and Martin. It remained so even when the daughter retired and no Feingold took her place. At the same time Andrew first put on clothes, the Martin name had just been added to the firm.

George had tried not to smile the first time he saw Andrew attempting to put on trousers, but to Andrew's eyes the smile was clearly there. George showed Andrew how to manipulate the static charge to allow the trousers to open, wrap about his lower body, and move shut. George demonstrated on his own trousers, but Andrew was quite aware it would take him a while to duplicate that one flowing motion.

"But why do you want trousers, Andrew? Your body is so beautifully functional it's a shame to cover it—especially when you needn't worry about either temperature control or modesty. And the material doesn't cling properly—not on metal."

Andrew held his ground. "Are not human bodies beautifully functional, George? Yet you cover yourselves."

"For warmth, for cleanliness, for protection, for decorativeness. None of that applies to you."

"I feel bare without clothes. I feel different, George," Andrew responded.

"Different! Andrew, there are millions of robots on Earth now. In this region, according to the last census, there are almost as many robots as there are men."

"I know, George. There are robots doing every conceivable type of work."

"And none of them wear clothes."

"But none of them are free, George."

Little by little, Andrew added to his wardrobe. He was inhibited by George's smile and by the stares of the people who commissioned work.

He might be free, but there was built into Andrew a carefully detailed program concerning his behavior to people, and it was only by the tiniest steps that he dared advance; open disapproval would set him back months. Not everyone accepted Andrew as free. He was incapable of resenting that, and yet there was a difficulty about his thinking process when he thought of it. Most of all, he tended to avoid putting on clothes—or too many of them—when he thought Little Miss might come to visit him. She was older now and was often away in some warmer climate, but when she returned the first thing she did was visit him.

On one of her visits, George said, ruefully, "She's got me, Andrew. I'll be running for the legislature next year. 'Like grandfather,' she says, 'like grandson.'"

"Like grandfather..." Andrew stopped, uncertain.

"I mean that I, George, the grandson, will be like Sir, the grandfather, who was in the legislature once."

"It would be pleasant, George, if Sir were still—" He paused, for he did not want to say, "in working order." That seemed inappropriate.

"Alive," George said. "Yes, I think of the old monster now and then, too."

Andrew often thought about this conversation. He had noticed his own incapacity in speech when talking with George. Somehow the language had changed since Andrew had come into being with a built-in vocabulary. Then, too, George used a colloquial speech, as Sir and Little Miss had not. Why should he have called Sir a monster when surely that word was not appropriate. Andrew could not even turn to his own books for guidance. They were old, and most dealt with woodworking, with art, with furniture design. There were none on language, none on the ways of human beings.

Finally, it seemed to him that he must seek the proper books; and as a free robot, he felt he must not ask George. He would go to town and use the library. It was a triumphant decision and he felt his electropotential grow distinctly higher until he had to throw in an impedance coil.

He put on a full costume, including even a shoulder chain of wood. He would have preferred the glitter plastic, but George had said that wood was much more appropriate and that polished cedar was considerably more valuable as well.

He had placed a hundred feet between himself and the house before gathering resistance brought him to a halt. He shifted the impedance coil out of circuit, and when that did not seem to help enough he returned to his home and on a piece of notepaper wrote neatly, "I have gone to the library," and placed it in clear view on his worktable.

10

Andrew never quite got to the library.

He had studied the map. He knew the route, but not the appearance of it. The actual landmarks did not resemble the symbols on the map and he would hesitate. Eventually, he thought he must have somehow gone wrong, for everything looked strange.

He passed an occasional field-robot, but by the time he decided he should ask his way none were in sight. A vehicle passed and did not stop.

Andrew stood irresolute, which meant calmly motionless, for coming across the field toward him were two human beings.

He turned to face them, and they altered their course to meet him. A moment before, they had been talking loudly. He had heard their voices. But now they were silent. They had the look that Andrew associated with human uncertainty; and they were young, but not very young. Twenty, perhaps? Andrew could never judge human age.

"Would you describe to me the route to the town library, sirs?"

One of them, the taller of the two, whose tall hat lengthened him still farther, almost grotesquely, said, not to Andrew, but to the other, "It's a robot."

The other had a bulbous nose and heavy eyelids. He said, not to Andrew but to the first, "It's wearing clothes."

The tall one snapped his fingers. "It's the free robot. They have a robot at the old Martin place who isn't owned by anybody. Why else would it be wearing clothes?"

"Ask it," said the one with the nose.

"Are you the Martin robot?" asked the tall one.

"I am Andrew Martin, sir," Andrew said.

"Good. Take off your clothes. Robots don't wear clothes." He said to the other, "That's disgusting. Look at him!"

Andrew hesitated. He hadn't heard an order in that tone of voice in so long that his Second Law circuits had momentarily jammed.

The tall one repeated, "Take off your clothes. I order you."

Slowly, Andrew began to remove them.

"Just drop them," said the tall one.

The nose said, "If it doesn't belong to anyone, it could be ours as much as someone else's."

"Anyway," said the tall one, "who's to object to anything we do. We're not damaging property." He turned to Andrew. "Stand on your head."

"The head is not meant—" Andrew began.

"That's an order. If you don't know how, try anyway."

Andrew hesitated again, then bent to put his head on the ground. He tried to lift his legs but fell, heavily.

The tall one said, "Just lie there." He said to the other, "We can take him apart. Ever take a robot apart?"

"Will he let us?"

"How can he stop us?"

There was no way Andrew could stop them, if they ordered him in a forceful enough manner not to resist. The Second Law of obedience took precedence over the Third Law of self-preservation. In any case, he could not defend himself without possibly hurting them, and that would mean breaking the First Law. At that thought, he felt every motile unit contract slightly and he quivered as he lay there.

The tall one walked over and pushed at him with his foot. "He's heavy. I think we'll need tools to do the job."

The nose said, "We could order him to take himself apart. It would be fun to watch him try."

"Yes," said the tall one, thoughtfully, "but let's get him off the road. If someone comes along—"

It was too late. Someone had, indeed, come along and it was George. From where he lay, Andrew had seen him topping a small rise in the middle distance. He would have liked to signal him in some way, but the last order had been "Just lie there!"

George was running now, and he arrived on the scene somewhat winded. The two young men stepped back a little and then waited thoughtfully.

"Andrew, has something gone wrong?" George asked, anxiously.

Andrew replied, "I am well, George."

"Then stand up. What happened to your clothes?"

"That your robot, Mac?" the tall young man asked.

George turned sharply. "He's no one's robot. What's been going on here."

"We politely asked him to take his clothes off. What's that to you, if you don't own him."

George turned to Andrew. "What were they doing, Andrew?"

"It was their intention in some way to dismember me. They were about to move me to a quiet spot and order me to dismember myself."

George looked at the two young men, and his chin trembled.

The young men retreated no farther. They were smiling.

The tall one said, lightly, "What are you going to do, pudgy? Attack us?"

George said, "No. I don't have to. This robot has been with my family for over seventy-five years. He knows us and he values us more than he values anyone else. I am going to tell him that you two are threatening my life and that you plan to kill me. I will ask him to defend me. In choosing between me and you two, he will choose me. Do you know what will happen to you when he attacks you?"

The two were backing away slightly, looking uneasy.

George said, sharply, "Andrew, I am in danger and about to come to harm from these young men. Move toward them!"

Andrew did so, and the young men did not wait. They ran.

"All right, Andrew, relax," George said. He looked unstrung. He was far past the age where he could face the possibility of a dustup with one young man, let alone two.

"I couldn't have hurt them, George. I could see they were not attacking you."

"I didn't order you to attack them. I only told you to move toward them. Their own fears did the rest."

"How can they fear robots?"

"It's a disease of mankind, one which has not yet been cured. But never mind that. What the devil are you doing here, Andrew? Good thing I found your note. I was just on the point of turning back and hiring a helicopter when I found you. How did you get it into your head to go to the library? I would have brought you any books you needed."

"I am a—" Andrew began.

"Free robot. Yes, yes. All right, what did you want in the library?"

"I want to know more about human beings, about the world, about everything. And about robots, George. I want to write a history about robots."

George put his arm on the other's shoulder. "Well, let's walk home. But pick up your clothes first. Andrew, there are a million books on robotics and all of them include histories of the science. The world is growing saturated not only with robots but with information about robots."

Andrew shook his head, a human gesture he had lately begun to adopt. "Not a history of robotics, George. A history of *robots,* by a robot. I want to explain how robots feel about what has happened since the first ones were allowed to work and live on Earth."

George's eyebrows lifted, but he said nothing in direct response.

11

Little Miss was just past her eighty-third birthday, but there was nothing about her that was lacking in either energy or determination. She gestured with her cane oftener than she propped herself up with it.

She listened to the story in a fury of indignation. "George, that's horrible. Who were those young ruffians?"

"I don't know. What difference does it make? In the end they did not do any damage."

"They might have. You're a lawyer, George; and if you're well off, it's entirely due to the talents of Andrew. It was the money *he* earned that is the foundation of everything we have. He provides the continuity for this family, and I will *not* have him treated as a wind-up toy."

"What would you have me do, Mother?" George asked.

"I said you're a lawyer. Don't you listen? You set up a test case somehow, and you force the regional courts to declare for robot rights and get the legislature to pass the necessary bills. Carry the whole thing to the World Court, if you have to. I'll be watching, George, and I'll tolerate no shirking."

She was serious, so what began as a way of soothing the fearsome old lady became an involved matter with enough legal entanglement to make it interesting. As senior partner of Feingold and Martin, George plotted strategy. But he left the actual work to his junior partners, with much of it a matter for his son, Paul, who was also a member of the firm and who reported dutifully nearly every day to his grandmother. She, in turn, discussed the case every day with Andrew.

Andrew was deeply involved. His work on his book on robots was delayed and delayed again, as he pored over the legal arguments and even, at times, made very diffident suggestions. "George told me that day I was attacked that human beings have always been afraid of robots," he said one day. "As long as they are, the courts and the legislatures are not likely to work hard on behalf of robots. Should not something be done about public opinion?"

So while Paul stayed in court, George took to the public platform. It gave him the advantage of being informal, and he even went so far sometimes as to wear the new, loose style of clothing which he called drapery.

Paul chided him, "Just don't trip over it on stage, Dad."

George replied, despondently, "I'll try not to."

He addressed the annual convention of holo-news editors on one occasion and said, in part: "If, by virtue of the Second Law, we can demand of any robot unlimited obedience in all respects not involving harm to a human being, then any human being, *any* human being, has a fearsome power over any robot, *any* robot. In particular, since Second Law supersedes Third Law, *any* human being can use the law of obedience to overcome the law of self-protection. He can order any robot to damage itself or even to destroy itself for any reason, or for no reason.

"Is this just? Would we treat an animal so? Even an inanimate object which had given us good service has a claim on our consideration. And a robot is not insensitive; it is not an animal. It can think well enough so that it can talk to us, reason with us, joke with us. Can we treat them as friends, can we work together with them, and not give them some of the fruits of that friendship, some of the benefits of co-working?

"If a man has the right to give a robot any order that does not involve harm to a human being, he should have the decency never to give a robot any order that involves harm to a robot, unless human safety absolutely requires it. With great power goes great responsibility, and if the robots have Three Laws to protect men, is it too much to ask that men have a law or two to protect robots?"

Andrew was right. It was the battle over public opinion that held the key to courts and legislature. In the end, a law was passed that set up conditions under which robot-harming orders were forbidden. It was endlessly qualified and the punishments for violating the law were totally inadequate, but the principle was established. The final passage by the World Legislature came through on the day of Little Miss' death.

That was no coincidence. Little Miss held on to life desperately during the last debate and let go only when word of victory arrived. Her last smile was for Andrew. Her last words were, "You have been good to us, Andrew." She died with her hand holding his, while her son and his wife and children remained at a respectful distance from both.

12

Andrew waited patiently when the receptionist-robot disappeared into the inner office. The receptionist might have used the holographic chatterbox, but unquestionably it was perturbed by having to deal with another robot rather than with a human being.

Andrew passed the time revolving the matter in his mind: Could "unroboted" be used as an analog of "unmanned," or had unmanned become a metaphoric term sufficiently divorced from its original meaning to be applied to robots—or to women for that matter? Such problems frequently arose as he worked on his book on robots. The trick of thinking out sentences to express all complexities had undoubtedly increased his vocabulary.

Occasionally, someone came into the room to stare at him and he did not try to avoid the glance. He looked at each calmly, and each in turn looked away.

Paul Martin finally emerged. He looked surprised, or he would have if Andrew could have made out his expression with certainty. Paul had taken to wearing the heavy makeup that fashion was dictating for both sexes. Though it made sharper and firmer the somewhat bland lines of Paul's face, Andrew disapproved. He found that disapproving of human beings, as long as he did not express it verbally, did not make him very uneasy. He could even write the disapproval. He was sure it had not always been so.

"Come in, Andrew. I'm sorry I made you wait, but there was something I *had* to finish. Come in, you had said you wanted to talk to me, but I didn't know you meant here in town."

"If you are busy, Paul, I am prepared to continue to wait."

Paul glanced at the interplay of shifting shadows on the dial on the wall that served as timepiece and said, "I can make some time. Did you come alone?"

"I hired an automatobile."

"Any trouble?" Paul asked, with more than a trace of anxiety.

"I wasn't expecting any. My rights are protected."

Paul looked all the more anxious for that. "Andrew, I've explained that the law is unenforceable, at least under most conditions. And if you insist on wearing clothes, you'll run into trouble eventually; just like that first time."

"And *only* time, Paul. I'm sorry you are displeased."

"Well, look at it this way: you are virtually a living legend, Andrew, and you are too valuable in many different ways for you to have any right to take chances with yourself. By the way, how's the book coming?"

"I am approaching the end, Paul. The publisher is quite pleased."

"Good!"

"I don't know that he's necessarily pleased with the book as a book. I think he expects to sell many copies because it's written by a robot and that's what pleases him."

"Only human, I'm afraid."

"I am not displeased. Let it sell for whatever reason, since it will mean money and I can use some."

"Grandmother left you—"

"Little Miss was generous, and I'm sure I can count on the family to help me out further. But it is the royalties from the book on which I am counting to help me through the next step."

"What next step is that?"

"I wish to see the head of U.S. Robots and Mechanical Men Corporation. I have tried to make an appointment; but so far I have not been able to reach him. The Corporation did not cooperate with me in the writing of the book, so I am not surprised, you understand."

Paul was clearly amused. "Cooperation is the last thing you can expect. They didn't cooperate with us in our great fight for robot rights. Quite the reverse, and you can see why. Give a robot rights and people may not want to buy them."

"Nevertheless," said Andrew, "if *you* call them, you may be able to obtain an interview for me."

"I'm no more popular with them than you are, Andrew."

"But perhaps you can hint that by seeing me they may head off a campaign by Feingold and Martin to strengthen the rights of robots further."

"Wouldn't that be a lie, Andrew?"

"Yes, Paul, and I can't tell one. That is why you must call."

"Ah, you can't lie, but you can urge me to tell a lie, is that it? You're getting more human all the time, Andrew."

13

The meeting was not easy to arrange, even with Paul's supposedly weighted name. But it finally came about. When it did, Harley Smythe-Robertson, who, on his mother's side, was descended from the original founder of the corporation and who had adopted the hyphenation to indicate it, looked remarkably unhappy. He was approaching retirement age and his entire tenure as president had been devoted to the matter of robot rights. His gray hair was plastered thinly over the top of his scalp; his face was not made up, and he eyed Andrew with brief hostility from time to time.

Andrew began the conversation. "Sir, nearly a century ago, I was told by a Merton Mansky of this corporation that the mathematics governing the plotting of the positronic pathways was far too complicated to permit of any but approximate solutions and that, therefore, my own capacities were not fully predictable."

"That was a century ago." Smythe-Robertson hesitated, then said icily, "*Sir.* It is true no longer. Our robots are made with precision now and are trained precisely to their jobs."

"Yes," said Paul, who had come along, as he said, to make sure that the corporation played fair, "with the result that my receptionist must be guided at every point once events depart from the conventional, however slightly."

"You would be much more displeased if it were to improvise," Smythe-Robertson said.

"Then you no longer manufacture robots like myself which are flexible and adaptable."

"No longer."

"The research I have done in connection with my book," said Andrew, "indicates that I am the oldest robot presently in active operation."

"The oldest presently," said Smythe-Robertson, "and the oldest ever. The oldest that will ever be. No robot is useful after the twenty-fifth year. They are called in and replaced with newer models."

"No robot as presently manufactured is useful after the *twentieth* year," said Paul, with a note of sarcasm creeping into his voice. "Andrew is quite exceptional in this respect."

Andrew, adhering to the path he had marked out for himself, continued, "As the oldest robot in the world and the most flexible, am I not unusual enough to merit special treatment from the company?"

"Not at all," Smythe-Robertson said, freezing up. "Your unusualness is an embarrassment to the company. If you were on lease, instead of having been an outright sale through some mischance, you would long since have been replaced."

"But that is exactly the point," said Andrew. "I am a free robot and I own myself. Therefore I come to you and ask you to replace me. You cannot do this without the owner's consent. Nowadays, that consent is extorted as a condition of the lease, but in my time this did not happen."

Smythe-Robertson was looking both startled and puzzled, and for a moment there was silence. Andrew found himself staring at the hologram on the wall. It was a death mask of Susan Calvin, patron saint of all roboticists. She had been dead for nearly two centuries now, but as a result of writing his book Andrew knew her so well he could half persuade himself that he had met her in life.

Finally Smythe-Robertson asked, "How can I replace you for you? If I replace you, as robot, how can I donate the new robot to you as owner since in the very act of replacement you cease to exist." He smiled grimly.

"Not at all difficult," Paul interposed. "The seat of Andrew's personality is his positronic brain and it is the one part that cannot be replaced without creating a new robot. The positronic brain, therefore, is Andrew the owner. Every other part of the robotic body can be replaced without affecting the robot's personality, and those other parts are the brain's possessions. Andrew, I should say, wants to supply his brain with a new robotic body."

"That's right," said Andrew, calmly. He turned to Smythe-Robertson. "You have manufactured androids, haven't you? Robots that have the outward appearance of humans, complete to the texture of the skin?"

"Yes, we have. They worked perfectly well, with their synthetic fibrous skins and tendons. There was virtually no metal anywhere except for the brain, yet they were nearly as tough as metal robots. They *were* tougher, weight for weight."

Paul looked interested. "I didn't know that. How many are on the market?"

"None," said Smythe-Robertson. "They were much more expensive than metal models and a market survey showed they would not be accepted. They looked too human."

Andrew was impressed. "But the corporation retains its expertise. Since it does, I wish to request that I be replaced by an organic robot, an android."

Paul looked surprised. "Good Lord!" he said.

Smythe-Robertson stiffened. "Quite impossible!"

"Why is it impossible?" Andrew asked. "I will pay any reasonable fee, of course."

"We do not manufacture androids."

"You do not *choose* to manufacture androids," Paul interjected quickly. "That is not the same as being unable to manufacture them."

"Nevertheless," Smythe-Robertson responded, "the manufacture of androids is against public policy."

"There is no law against it," said Paul.

"Nevertheless, we do not manufacture them—and we will not."

Paul cleared his throat. "Mr. Smythe-Robertson," he said, "Andrew is a free robot who comes under the purview of the law guaranteeing robot rights. You are aware of this, I take it?"

"Only too well."

"This robot, as a free robot, chooses to wear clothes. This results in his being frequently humiliated by thoughtless human beings despite the law against the humiliation of robots. It is difficult to prosecute vague offenses that don't meet with the general disapproval of those who must decide on guilt and innocence."

"U.S. Robots understood that from the start. Your father's firm unfortunately did not."

"My father is dead now, but what I see is that we have here a clear offense with a clear target."

"What are you talking about?" said Smythe-Robertson.

"My client, Andrew Martin—he has just become my client—is a free robot who is entitled to ask U.S. Robots and Mechanical Men Corporation for the right of replacement, which the corporation supplies to anyone who owns a robot for more than twenty-five years. In fact, the corporation insists on such replacement."

Paul was smiling and thoroughly at ease. "The positronic brain of my client," he went on, "is the owner of the body of my client—which is certainly more than twenty-five years old. The positronic brain demands the replacement of the body and offers to pay any reasonable fee for an android body as that replacement. If you refuse the request, my client undergoes humiliation and we will sue.

"While public opinion would not ordinarily support the claim of a robot in such a case, may I remind you that U.S. Robots is not popular with the public generally. Even those who most use and profit from robots are suspicious of the corporation. This may be a hangover from the days when robots were widely feared. It may be resentment against the power and wealth of U.S. Robots, which has a worldwide monopoly. Whatever the cause may be, the resentment exists. I think you will find that you would prefer not to be faced with a lawsuit, particularly since my client is wealthy and will live for many more centuries and will have no reason to refrain from fighting the battle forever."

Smythe-Robertson had slowly reddened. "You are trying to force—"

"I force you to do nothing," said Paul. "If you wish to refuse to accede to my client's reasonable request, you may by all means do so and we will leave without another word. But we will sue, as is certainly our right, and you will find that you will eventually lose."

"Well . . ."

"I see that you are going to accede," said Paul. "You may hesitate but you will come to it in the end. Let me assure you, then, of one further point: If, in the process of transferring my client's positronic brain from his present body to an organic one, there is any damage, however slight, then I will never rest until I've nailed the corporation to the ground. I will, if necessary, take every possible step to mobilize public opinion against the corporation if one brainpath of my client's platinum-iridium essence is scrambled." He turned to Andrew and asked, "Do you agree to all this, Andrew?"

Andrew hesitated a full minute. It amounted to the approval of lying, of blackmail, of the badgering and humiliation of a human being. But not physical harm, he told himself, not physical harm.

He managed at last to come out with a rather faint "Yes."

14

He felt as though he were being constructed again. For days, then for weeks, finally for months, Andrew found himself not himself somehow, and the simplest actions kept giving rise to hesitation.

Paul was frantic. "They've damaged you, Andrew. We'll have to institute suit!"

Andrew spoke very slowly. "You . . . mustn't. You'll never be able to prove . . . something . . . like m-m-m-m—"

"Malice?"

"Malice. Besides, I grow . . . stronger, better. It's the tr-tr-tr—"

"Tremble?"

"Trauma. After all, there's never been such an op-op-op- . . . before."

Andrew could feel his brain from the inside. No one else could. He knew he was well, and during the months that it took him to learn full coordination and full positronic interplay he spent hours before the mirror.

Not quite human! The face was stiff—too stiff—and the motions were too deliberate. They lacked the careless, free flow of the human being, but perhaps that might come with time. At least now he could wear clothes without the ridiculous anomaly of a metal face going along with it.

Eventually, he said, "I will be going back to work."

Paul laughed. "That means you are well. What will you be doing? Another book?"

"No," said Andrew, seriously. "I live too long for any one career to seize me by the throat and never let me go. There was a time when I was primarily an artist, and I can still turn to that. And there was a time when I was a historian, and I can still turn to that. But now I wish to be a robobiologist."

"A robopsychologist, you mean."

"No. That would imply the study of positronic brains, and at the moment I lack the desire to do that. A robobiologist, it seems to me, would be concerned with the working of the body attached to that brain."

"Wouldn't that be a roboticist?"

"A roboticist works with a metal body. I would be studying an organic humanoid body, of which I have the only one, as far as I know."

"You narrow your field," said Paul, thoughtfully. "As an artist, all conception is yours; as a historian you deal chiefly with robots; as a robobiologist, you will deal with yourself."

Andrew nodded. "It would seem so."

Andrew had to start from the very beginning, for he knew nothing of ordinary biology and almost nothing of science. He became a familiar sight in the libraries, where he sat at the electronic indices for hours at a time, looking perfectly normal in clothes. Those few who knew he was a robot in no way interfered with him.

He built a laboratory in a room which he added to his house; and his library grew, too.

Years passed, and Paul came to him one day and said, "It's a pity you're no longer working on the history of robots. I understand U.S. Robots is adopting a radically new policy."

Paul had aged, and his deteriorating eyes had been replaced with photoptic cells. In that respect, he had drawn closer to Andrew.

"What have they done?" Andrew asked.

"They are manufacturing central computers, gigantic positronic brains, really, which communicate with anywhere from a dozen to a thousand robots by microwave. The robots themselves have no brains at all. They are the limbs of the gigantic brain, and the two are physically separate."

"Is that more efficient?"

"U.S. Robots claim it is. Smythe-Robertson established the new direction before he died, however, and it's my notion that it's a backlash at you. U.S. Robots is determined that they will make no robots that will give them the type of trouble you have, and for that reason they separate brain and body. The brain will have no body to wish changed; the body will have no brain to wish anything.

"It's amazing, Andrew," Paul went on, "the influence you have had on the history of robots. It was your artistry that encouraged U.S. Robots to make robots more precise and specialized; it was your freedom that resulted in the establishment of the principle of robotic rights; it was your insistence on an android body that made U.S.

Robots switch to brain-body separation."

Andrew grew thoughtful. "I suppose in the end the corporation will produce one vast brain controlling several billion robotic bodies. All the eggs will be in one basket. Dangerous. Not proper at all."

"I think you're right," said Paul, "but I don't suspect it will come to pass for a century at least and I won't live to see it. In fact, I may not live to see next year."

"Paul!" cried Andrew, in concern.

Paul shrugged. "Men are mortal, Andrew. We're not like you. It doesn't matter too much, but it does make it important to assure you on one point. I'm the last of the human Martins. The money I control personally will be left to the trust in your name, and as far as anyone can foresee the future, you will be economically secure."

"Unnecessary," Andrew said, with difficulty. Despite all this time, he could not get used to the deaths of the Martins.

"Let's not argue. That's the way it's going to be. Now, what are you working on?"

"I am designing a system for allowing androids—myself—to gain energy from the combustion of hydrocarbons, rather than from atomic cells."

Paul raised his eyebrows. "So that they will breathe and eat?"

"Yes."

"How long have you been pushing in that direction?"

"For a long time now, but I think I have finally designed an adequate combustion chamber for catalyzed controlled breakdown."

"But why, Andrew? The atomic cell is surely infinitely better."

"In some ways, perhaps. But the atomic cell is inhuman."

15

It took time, but Andrew had time. In the first place, he did not wish to do anything till Paul had died in peace. With the death of the great-grandson of Sir, Andrew felt more nearly exposed to a hostile world and for that reason was all the more determined along the path he had chosen.

Yet he was not really alone. If a man had died, the firm of Feingold and Martin lived, for a corporation does not die any more than a robot does.

The firm had its directons and it followed them soullessly. By way of the trust and through the law firm, Andrew continued to be wealthy. In return for their own large annual retainer, Feingold and Martin involved themselves in the legal aspects of the new combustion chamber. But when the time came for Andrew to visit U.S. Robots and Mechanical Men Corporation, he did it alone. Once he had gone with Sir and once with Paul. This time, the third time, he was alone and manlike.

U.S. Robots had changed. The actual production plant had been shifted to a large space station, as had grown to be the case with more and more industries. With them had gone many robots. The Earth itself was becoming parklike, with its one-billion-person population stabilized and perhaps not more than thirty percent of its at-least-equally-large robot population independently brained.

The Director of Research was Alvin Magdescu, dark of complexion and hair, with a little pointed beard and wearing nothing above the waist but the breastband that fashion dictated. Andrew himself was well covered in the older fashion of several decades back.

Magdescu offered his hand to his visitor. "I know you, of course, and I'm rather pleased to see you. You're our most notorious product and it's a pity old Smythe-Robertson was so set against you. We could have done a great deal with you."

"You still can," said Andrew.

"No, I don't think so. We're past the time. We've had robots on Earth for over a century, but that's changing. It will be back to space with them, and those that stay here won't be brained."

"But there remains myself, and I stay on Earth."

"True, but there doesn't seem to be much of the robot about you. What new request have you?"

"To be still less a robot. Since I am so far organic, I want to be powered with an organic source of energy. I have here the plans..."

Magdescu did not hasten through them. He might have intended to at first, but he stiffened and grew intent. At one point, he said, "This is remarkably ingenious. Who thought of all this?"

"I did," Andrew replied.

Magdescu looked up at him sharply, then said, "It would amount to a major overhaul of your body, and an experimental one, since such a thing has never been attempted before. I advise against it. Remain as you are."

Andrew's face had limited means of expression, but impatience showed plainly in his voice. "Dr. Magdescu, you miss the entire point. You have no choice but to accede to my request. If such devices can be built into my body, they can be built into human bodies as well. The tendency to lengthen human life by prosthetic devices has already been remarked on. There are no devices better than the ones I have designed or am designing.

"As it happens, I control the patents by way of the firm of Feingold and Martin. We are quite capable of going into business for ourselves and of developing the kind of prosthetic devices that may end by producing human beings with many of the properties of robots.

Your own business will then suffer.

"If, however, you operate on me now and agree to do so under similar circumstances in the future, you will receive permission to make use of the patents and control the technology of both robots and of the prosthetization of human beings. The initial leasing will not be granted, of course, until after the first operation is completed successfully, and after enough time has passed to demonstrate that it is indeed successful."

Andrew felt scarcely any First Law inhibition to the stern conditions he was setting a human being. He was learning to reason that what seemed like cruelty might, in the long run, be kindness.

Magdescu was stunned. "I'm not the one to decide something like this. That's a corporate decision that would take time."

"I can wait a reasonable time," said Andrew, "but only a reasonable time." And he thought with satisfaction that Paul himself could not have done it better.

16

It took only a reasonable time, and the operation was a success.

"I was very much against the operation, Andrew," Magdescu said, "but not for the reasons you might think. I was not in the least against the experiment, if it had been on someone else. I hated risking *your* positronic brain. Now that you have the positronic pathways interacting with simulated nerve pathways, it might have been difficult to rescue the brain intact if the body had gone bad."

"I had every faith in the skill of the staff at U.S. Robots," said Andrew. "And I can eat now."

"Well, you can sip olive oil. It will mean occasional cleanings of the combustion chamber, as we have explained to you. Rather an uncomfortable touch, I should think."

"Perhaps, if I did not expect to go further. Self-cleaning is not impossible. In fact, I am working on a device that will deal with solid food that may be expected to contain incombustible fractions—indigestible matter, so to speak, that will have to be discarded."

"You would then have to develop an anus."

"Or the equivalent."

"What else, Andrew . . . ?"

"Everything else."

"Genitalia, too."

"Insofar as they will fit my plans. My body is a canvas on which I intend to draw . . . "

Magdescu waited for the sentence to be completed, and when it seemed that it would not be, he completed it himself. "A man?"

"We shall see," Andrew said.

"That's a puny ambition, Andrew. You're better than a man. You've gone downhill from the moment you opted to become organic."

"My brain has not suffered."

"No, it hasn't. I'll grant you that. But, Andrew, the whole new breakthrough in prosthetic devices made possible by your patents is being marketed under your name. You're recognized as the inventor and you're being honored for it—as you should be. Why play further games with your body?"

Andrew did not answer.

The honors came. He accepted membership in several learned societies, including one that was devoted to the new science he had established—the one he had called robobiology but which had come to be termed prosthetology. On the one hundred and fiftieth anniversary of his construction, a testimonial dinner was given in his honor at U.S. Robots. If Andrew saw an irony in this, he kept it to himself.

Alvin Magdescu came out of retirement to chair the dinner. He was himself ninety-four years old and was alive because he, too, had prosthetized devices that, among other things, fulfilled the function of liver and kidneys. The dinner reached its climax when Magdescu, after a short and emotional talk, raised his glass to toast the Sesquicentennial Robot.

Andrew had had the sinews of his face redesigned to the point where he could show a human range of emotions, but he sat through all the ceremonies solemnly passive. He did not like to be a Sesquicentennial Robot.

17

It was prosthetology that finally took Andrew off the Earth.

In the decades that followed the celebration of his sesquicentennial, the Moon had come to be a world more Earthlike than Earth in every respect but its gravitational pull; and in its underground cities there was a fairly dense population. Prosthetized devices there had to take the lesser gravity into account. Andrew spent five years on the Moon working with local prosthetologists to make the necessary adaptations. When not at his work, he wandered among the robot population, every one of which treated him with the robotic obsequiousness due a man.

He came back to an Earth that was humdrum and quiet in comparison, and visited the offices of Feingold and Martin to announce his return.

The current head of the firm, Simon DeLong, was surprised. "We had been told you were returning, Andrew"—he had almost said Mr. Martin—"but we were not expecting you till next week."

"I grew impatient," said Andrew, briskly. He was anxious to get to the point. "On the Moon, Simon, I was in charge of a research team of twenty human scientists. I gave orders that no one questioned. The Lunar robots deferred to me as they would to a human being. Why, then, am I not a human being?"

A wary look entered DeLong's eyes. "My dear Andrew, as you have just explained, you are treated as a human being by both robots *and* human beings. You are, therefore, a human being *de facto.*"

"To be a human being *de facto* is not enough. I want not only to be treated as one, but to be legally identified as one. I want to be a human being *de jure.*"

"Now, that is another matter," DeLong said. "There we would run into human prejudice and into the undoubted fact that, however much you may be *like* a human being, you are *not* a human being."

"In what way not?" Andrew asked. "I have the shape of a human being and organs equivalent to those of a human being. My organs, in fact, are identical to some of those in a prosthetized human being. I have contributed artistically, literarily, and scientifically to human culture as much as any human being now alive. What more can one ask?"

"I myself would ask nothing more. The trouble is that it would take an act of the World Legislature to define you as a human being. Frankly, I wouldn't expect that to happen."

"To whom on the Legislature could I speak?"

"To the Chairman of the Science and Technology Committee, perhaps."

"Can you arrange a meeting?"

"But you scarcely need an intermediary. In your position, you can—"

"No. *You* arrange it." It didn't even occur to Andrew that he was giving a flat order to a human being. He had grown so accustomed to that on the Moon. "I want him to know that the firm of Feingold and Martin is backing me in this to the hilt."

"Well, now—"

"To the hilt, Simon. In one hundred and seventy-three years I have in one fashion or another contributed greatly to this firm. I have been under obligation to individual members of the firm in times past. I am not, now. It is rather the other way around now and I am calling in my debts."

"I will do what I can," DeLong said.

18

The Chairman of the Science and Technology Committee was from the East Asian region and was a woman. Her name was Chee Li-hsing and her transparent garments—obscuring what she wanted obscured only by their dazzle—made her look plastic-wrapped.

"I sympathize with your wish for full human rights," she said. "There have been times in history when segments of the human population fought for full human rights. What rights, however, can you possibly want that you do not have?"

"As simple a thing as my right to life," Andrew stated. "A robot can be dismantled at any time."

"A human being can be executed at any time."

"Execution can only follow due process of law. There is no trial needed for my dismantling. Only the word of a human being in authority is needed to end me. Besides . . . besides . . . " Andrew tried desperately to allow no sign of pleading, but his carefully designed tricks of human expression and tone of voice betrayed him here. "The truth is I want to be a man. I have wanted it through six generations of human beings."

Li-hsing looked up at him out of darkly sympathetic eyes. "The Legislature can pass a law declaring you one. They could pass a law declaring that a stone statue be defined as a man. Whether they will actually do so is, however, as likely in the first case as the second. Congresspeople are as human as the rest of the population and there is always that element of suspicion against robots."

"Even now?"

"Even now. We would all allow the fact that you have earned the prize of humanity, and yet there would remain the fear of setting an undesirable precedent."

"What precedent? I am the only free robot, the only one of my type, and there will never be another. You may consult U.S. Robots."

"*Never* is a long word, Andrew—or, if you prefer, Mr. Martin—since I will gladly give you my personal accolade as man. You will find that most congresspeople will not be so willing to set the precedent, no matter how meaningless such a precedent might be. Mr. Martin, you have my sympathy, but I cannot tell you to hope. Indeed . . ."

She sat back and her forehead wrinkled. "Indeed, if the issue grows too heated, there might well arise a certain sentiment, both inside the Legislature and outside, for that dismantling you mentioned. Doing away with you could turn out to be the easiest way of resolving the dilemma. Consider that before deciding to push matters."

Andrew stood firm. "Will no one remember the technique of prosthetology, something that is almost entirely mine?"

"It may seem cruel, but they won't. Or if they do, it will be remembered against you. People will say you did it only for yourself. It will be said it was part of a campaign to roboticize human beings, or to humanify robots; and in either case evil and vicious. You have never been part of a political hate campaign, Mr. Martin; but I tell you that you would be the object of vilification of a kind neither you nor I would credit, and there would be people to believe it all. Mr. Martin, let your life be."

She rose, and next to Andrew's seated figure she seemed small and almost childlike.

"If I decide to fight for my humanity, will you be on my side?"

She thought, then replied, "I will be—insofar as I can be. If at any time such a stand would appear to threaten my political future, I might have to abandon you, since it is not an issue I feel to be at the very root of my beliefs. I am trying to be honest with you."

"Thank you, and I will ask no more. I intend to fight this through, whatever the consequences, and I will ask you for your help only for as long as you can give it."

19

It was not a direct fight. Feingold and Martin counseled patience and Andrew muttered, grimly, that he had an endless supply of that. Feingold and Martin then entered on a campaign to narrow and restrict the area of combat.

They instituted a lawsuit denying the obligation to pay debts to an individual with a prosthetic heart on the grounds that the possession of a robotic organ removed humanity, and with it the constitutional rights of human beings. They fought the matter skillfully and tenaciously, losing at every step but always in such a way that the decision was forced to be as broad as possible, and then carrying it by way of appeals to the World Court.

It took years, and millions of dollars.

When the final decision was handed down, DeLong held what amounted to a victory celebration over the legal loss. Andrew was, of course, present in the company offices on the occasion.

"We've done two things, Andrew," said DeLong, "both of which are good. First of all, we have established the fact that no number of artificial parts in the human body causes it to cease being a human body. Secondly, we have engaged public opinion in the question in such a way as to put it fiercely on the side of a broad interpretation of humanity, since there is not a human being in existence who does not hope for prosthetics if they will keep him alive."

"And do you think the Legislature will now grant me my humanity?" Andrew asked.

DeLong looked faintly uncomfortable. "As to that, I cannot be optimistic. There remains the one organ which the World Court has used as the criterion of humanity. Human beings have an organic cellular brain and robots have a platinum-iridium positronic brain if they have one at all—and you certainly have a positronic brain. No, Andrew, don't get that look in your eye. We lack the knowledge to duplicate the work of a cellular brain in artificial structures close enough to the organic type as to allow it to fall within the court's decision. Not even you could do it."

"What should we do, then?"

"Make the attempt, of course. Congresswoman Li-hsing will be on our side and a growing number of other congresspeople. The President will undoubtedly go along with a majority of the Legislature in this matter."

"Do we have a majority?"

"No. Far from it. But we might get one if the public will allow its desire for a broad interpretation of humanity to extend to you. A small chance, I admit; but if you do not wish to give up, we must gamble for it."

"I do not wish to give up."

20

Congresswoman Li-hsing was considerably older than she had been when Andrew had first met her. Her transparent garments were long gone. Her hair was now close-cropped and her coverings were tubular. Yet still Andrew clung, as closely as he could within the limits of reasonable taste, to the style of clothing that had prevailed when he had first adopted clothing more than a century before.

"We've gone as far as we can, Andrew," Li-hsing admitted. "We'll try once more after recess, but, to be honest, defeat is certain and then the whole thing will have to be given up. All my most recent efforts have only earned me certain defeat in the coming congressional campaign."

"I know," said Andrew, "and it distresses me. You said once you would abandon me if it came to that. Why have you not done so?"

"One can change one's mind, you know. Somehow, abandoning you became a higher price than I cared to pay for just one more term. As it is, I've been in the Legislature for over a quarter of a century. It's enough."

"Is there no way we can change minds, Chee?"

"We've changed all that are amenable to reason. The rest—the majority—cannot be moved from their emotional antipathies."

"Emotional antipathy is not a valid reason for voting one way or the other."

"I know that, Andrew, but they don't advance emotional antipathy as their reason."

"It all comes down to the brain, then," Andrew said cautiously. "But must we leave it at the level of cells versus positrons? Is there no way of forcing a functional definition? Must we say that a brain is made of this or that? May we not say that a brain is something—anything—capable of a certain level of thought?"

"Won't work," said Li-hsing. "Your brain is manmade, the human brain is not. Your brain is constructed, theirs developed. To any human being who is intent on keeping up the barrier between himself and a robot, those differences are a steel wall a mile high and a mile thick."

"If we could get at the source of their antipathy, the very source—"

"After all your years," Li-hsing said, sadly, "you are still trying to reason out the human being. Poor Andrew, don't be angry, but it's the robot in you that drives you in that direction."

"I don't know," said Andrew. "If I could bring myself..."

1 [Reprise]

If he could bring himself...

He had known for a long time it might come to that, and in the end he was at the surgeon's. He had found one, skillful enough for the job at hand—which meant a surgeon-robot, for no human surgeon could be trusted in this connection, either in ability or in intention.

The surgeon could not have performed the operation on a human being, so Andrew, after putting off the moment of decision with a sad line of questioning that reflected the turmoil within himself, had put the First Law to one side by saying "I, too, am a robot."

He then said, as firmly as he had learned to form the words even at human beings over these past decades, "I *order* you to carry through the operation on me."

In the absence of the First Law, an order so firmly given from one who looked so much like a man activated the Second Law sufficiently to carry the day.

21

Andrew's feeling of weakness was, he was sure, quite imaginary. He had recovered from the operation. Nevertheless, he leaned, as unobtrusively as he could manage, against the wall. It would be entirely too revealing to sit.

Li-hsing said, "The final vote will come this week, Andrew. I've been able to delay it no longer, and we must lose. And that will be it, Andrew."

"I am grateful for your skill at delay. It gave me the time I needed, and I took the gamble I had to."

"What gamble is this?" Li-hsing asked with open concern.

"I couldn't tell you, or even the people at Feingold and Martin. I was sure I would be stopped. See here, if it is the brain that is at issue, isn't the greatest difference of all the matter of immortality. Who really cares what a brain looks like or is built of or how it was formed. What matters is that human brain cells die, *must* die. Even if every other organ in the body is maintained or replaced, the brain cells, which cannot be replaced without changing and therefore killing the personality, must eventually die.

"My own positronic pathways have lasted nearly two centuries without perceptible change, and can last for centuries more. Isn't *that* the fundamental barrier: human beings can tolerate an immortal robot, for it doesn't matter how long a machine lasts, but they cannot tolerate an immortal human being since their own mortality is endurable only so long as it is universal. And for that reason they won't make me a human being."

"What is it you're leading up to, Andrew?" Li-hsing asked.

"I have removed that problem. Decades ago, my positronic brain was connected to organic nerves. Now, one last operation has arranged that connection in such a way that slowly—quite slowly—the potential is being drained from my pathways."

Li-hsing's finely wrinkled face showed no expression for a moment. Then her lips tightened. "Do you mean you've arranged to die, Andrew? You can't have. That violates the Third Law."

"No," said Andrew, "I have chosen between the death of my body and the death of my aspirations and desires. To have let my body live at the cost of the greater death is what would have violated the Third Law."

Li-hsing seized his arm as though she were about to shake him. She stopped herself. "Andrew, it won't work! Change it back."

"It can't be done. Too much damage was done. I have a year to live—more or less. I will last through the two-hundredth anniversary of my construction. I was weak enough to arrange that."

"How can it be worth it? Andrew, you're a fool."

"If it brings me humanity, that will be worth it. If it doesn't, it will bring an end to striving and that will be worth it, too."

Then Li-hsing did something that astonished herself. Quietly, she began to weep.

22

It was odd how that last deed caught the imagination of the world. All that Andrew had done before had not swayed them. But he had finally accepted even death to be human, and the sacrifice was too great to be rejected.

The final ceremony was timed, quite deliberately, for the two-hundredth anniversary. The World President was to sign the act and make the people's will law. The ceremony would be visible on a global network and would be beamed to the Lunar state and even to the Martian colony.

Andrew was in a wheelchair. He could still walk, but only shakily.

With mankind watching, the World President said, "Fifty years ago, you were declared the Sesquicentennial Robot, Andrew." After a pause, and in a more solemn tone, he continued, "Today we declare you the Bicentennial Man, Mr. Martin."

And Andrew, smiling, held out his hand to shake that of the President.

23

Andrew's thoughts were slowly fading as he lay in bed. Desperately he seized at them. *Man! He was a man!* He wanted that to be his last thought! He wanted to dissolve—die—with that.

He opened his eyes one more time and for one last time recognized Li-hsing, waiting solemnly. Others were there, but they were only shadows, unrecognizable shadows. Only Li-hsing stood out against the deepening gray.

Slowly, inchingly, he held out his hand to her and very dimly and faintly felt her take it.

She was fading in his eyes as the last of his thoughts trickled away. But before she faded completely, one final fugitive thought came to him and rested for a moment on his mind before everything stopped.

"Little Miss," he whispered, too low to be heard.

The Show Must Go On

James Causey

OPENING NIGHT. The stage was starkly medieval, all sawdust and three rings and the glistening tightrope wires. From their cages beasts snarled and trumpeted. The ringmaster snapped his whip and bowed to the eight giant lenses that stared bleakly down. In back of those lenses was our audience. Sixty millions of audience, scattered throughout the hemisphere.

In the wings, Lisa trembled against me. I whispered, "Your cue."

She nodded, squeezed my hand.

The drums rolled.

Watching her move onstage, I wanted to cry. She was lovely. It was the way she moved, like a hawk against the wind, the breathless lilt in her voice, the magic I'd taught her. Next to me, Paul Chanin grinned. "Nervous, Midge?"

"No," I said. I'd never liked Paul. He was too smug, too sleekly handsome. I hadn't liked the way he'd been smiling at Lisa these last few days of rehearsal, or the way she'd smiled back. But Paul was good—for a human. He could do a one-armed *planché* on the high wire, he could cartwheel blindfolded over gleaming coals. And he could sing.

We went onstage together, Paul leaping lithe and splendid in crimson tights, me floundering clumsily after with my baggy pants and wistfully painted clown face, blowing kisses to the blazing arcs above, now weeping in mock fury as Paul made love to Lisa. Then I leaped thirty feet in the air and hung from the tightrope by my toes. A big smile. Midge the clown.

Sometimes you can tell when a show's going over. It was that way now. Right from the beginning I knew we had them by the throat. The banks of Emotional Reaction lights above the arcs told the story. They shone a clear deep ruby, a good healthy sign of audience empathy, but I wasn't surprised. Our play was a combination of two primitive art forms, and it had everything, love, pathos, beauty. And terror. The finale was the best, when the Zarl escaped from its cage and almost caught Lisa. I killed the Zarl, singing *Duo pro Pagliacco* as I died, my voice golden thunder.

Curtain.

Director Latham hurried onstage, clapping, his eyes wet with tears. "Splendid. Magnificent, Midge! I think we've finally done it."

"Looks like a hit, sir," I said. "Those ancients sure knew their stuff. I hope it's not just novelty interest."

A shadow of worry touched Latham's pudgy face. "We'll know later. Coming to the cast party?"

I shook my head and grinned. "I've got a very special celebration planned. Just me and the wife, alone. See you at rehearsal tomorrow."

I went backstage to find Lisa.

She wasn't in our dressing room. Puzzled, I went down the hall to Paul's dressing room, opened the door. "Paul, have you seen—" My voice trailed off.

I stared at them. Paul and Lisa.

"Oh hello, darling," Lisa said softly. "Isn't it wonderful, Paul's proposed!"

"And she accepted," Paul said.

"Accepted," I said.

"It'll be so perfect." Lisa was radiant. "The three of us, together!"

"But we're androids," I whispered.

"So what," Paul said happily, "you're actors, and that's what really counts. It'll be the best companionate marriage on record!"

I remember saying it would be fine. I remember shaking Paul's hand and saying no, I couldn't go to the cast party, I had a headache. I remember stumbling back to my dressing room and wiping grease paint off and saying to the mirror, *"Et tu, Pagliacco?"* I do not remember taking the pneumatic tube home, or getting into the inertialess lift to our apartment on the ninety-first level. Our apartment was nice. Five rooms with a glass terrace, a half mile above the city. I stood on the terrace looking at the surprise I'd planned for Lisa, the food, the crystal sparkling in the firelight, the wine.

My little surprise party.

I sat down and slowly opened the wine.

Why?

Paul was human, that was the answer. He could give Lisa that sense of solidity, of belonging. It's been twenty years since Emancipation, but humans still think they're doing androids a favor by marrying them. Even though androids are saving the race from suicide.

It was long after midnight when Lisa came in. She wore a sheer pink evening dress and her hair was soft gold on her shoulders. Her beauty was a knife twisting in my throat.

"Darling," she said, "You shouldn't have waited up."

"Where's Paul?"

"Home." She hesitated. "We're taking out our companionate policy in the morning. Would you help him move his things?"

"Sure," I said.

"We'll be so happy, the three of us." Her blue eyes were tender. "Come to bed, darling."

"I'm not sleepy. Think I'll go for a walk."

I used to love to walk the city at night, staring morbidly at the hate bars, at the blood-red neons advertising violence and sudden death. I used to congratulate myself for not needing the hate bars, for not being a stinking human.

This time was different.

I stood in the rain, shivering, looking at the sign, *Joe's Hate House, Knives Only! Kill Like a Man!* It exploded in a crimson spatter of fire, now re-forming, showing a dagger in a clenched fist. I stared at that dagger a long time. I was thinking about Paul.

Finally I went inside.

My first impression was of a great dim grotto, lit by smouldering tapers. There was music, a discordant cacophony with drumbeats that made your flesh crawl. It was music out of the pit, the kind of music a Zarl would have written in its death-throes.

"Registration, sir?"

He was a fat little man in blue evening tunic who took my name, beneficiary, and ten-credits admission fee.

"Spectator or participant, sir?"

His smile was jovial, but the little pig eyes were cold, dead. Those eyes watched a dozen deaths nightly. It was my job to stop those deaths, to wipe out the hate bars, yet here I was, an Actor Ninth Class, smiling awkwardly at him, saying, "Spectator, please."

He bowed, led me to the roped-off spectator booths. I ordered a drink and gazed at the participants with a sick fascination.

They sat quietly, faces rigid, staring into the bar mirror. They drank with studied deliberation, eyes darting. A tall man in gray tunic suddenly threw his drink into a startled face. Steel flashed. There was a moan. Gray tunic fell to the sawdust-covered floor, writhing. There were shouts of delight from the spectators as two white-caped bartenders carried the body away. The drums blared.

"Not fast enough," said a voice at my elbow. "Eh, Midge?"

It was Director Latham.

"Surprised to see me here?" His smile was wry. "For your information the show was a flop."

I moistened my lips. "Impossible. The Reaction indicators—"

"Novelty only, son." He looked old, tired. "Sure, it's a beautiful show. They'll watch it for a week, two weeks." He stared bleakly at the participants. "Then the snake pits again. We've failed."

His words sank in, numbly. I whispered, "We had a sixty-million audience, it's all the quota council needs. They could enact legislation tomorrow—"

"And within a week the crime rate would be triple." Latham's voice was grim. "A man's life wouldn't be safe in broad daylight. People need emotional catharsis, the sight of blood. It's why hate bars are legal. It's why the council pours a million credits a month into our show, hoping to wean the populace, to educate them. But humans don't *care*. Why should they! Why spend a lifetime learning to write music when an android child can make you weep with a whistled tune?" His smile was infinitely bitter. "Man built better than himself. Now he's sorry, but it's too late. He needs the androids, the beauty they can give him, and he's ashamed to admit it. Here he meets himself on even terms. Our show needs some of this, Midge."

"No," I whispered. "I'll resign first."

"Will you?" His twisted smile. "You're not a free agent, mister. *The show must go on.*"

Five little words, quietly spoken.

But my head snapped erect. Those five words were a trumpet blast, a joyous shout that stiffened the spine, that made you *glad* to be an Actor, proud of your heritage.

"Damn you," I said.

"Midge White, XQ9," he said sardonically. "X: white, Caucasian type. Q: special training from the creche, type superior. 9: Actor, the very best. You're good, Midge. You've got a baritone like an organ. Onstage you're passion and fire and storm. You can tear the heart out of an audience with a smile. You've got reflexes no human ever had, with twice the number of relay-nodes, heavier nerve fibers, instantaneous reaction time. You're the penultimate, son. You're theatre. And you're letting your audience down."

His voice was raw, a pleading whisper. "I'm only a director. You're the empathy kid, you know what the audience really needs. Give it to them."

"Sure!" I was shaking with a cold sick fury. "A few dead androids come curtain time! We can vote now, have you heard? If you prick us, do we not bleed—"

"Save it," he said wearily. "So twenty years ago you got emancipated, so what? The council still reserves the right to manufacture special androids for emergency. Humanoid types to test new antibiotics. Initial landing crews for unexplored planets. Guinea pigs—"

"Slaves," I said stiffly. "Class Nines are different; we've got free will."

"Really?" His smile grew into a smirk.

"Stick around, absorb some atmosphere." He clapped me on the shoulder. "We're counting on you, Midge. Good night."

He was gone.

I sat, drenched in hate, staring after him, at the greedy faces around me, the taut hungry smiles. The participants' section was still as death. Nobody moved. Those figures at the bar sat rigid, hands on their knives, waiting.

I stood up. I was trembling. I walked through the gloom towards the crimson railing that ended the spectator's area. There was a soft collective sigh behind me as I vaulted over the rail.

At the bar, no one moved. It was very still and there was only the crunch of my feet in the sawdust. I carefully chose a seat at the far end of the bar as the bartender came up, smiling.

"Suicide, huh pal? No weapon?"

"Wine," I said.

He brought wine. Three stools away a little man in a brown business tunic turned his head.

"On the house," the bartender said cheerfully. "Under the rules you're allowed one taste before you become fair prey. We don't get many suicides here. Only a month ago—"

"Beat it," I said.

He moved away, hurt. I looked at the wine. The little man on my left moistened his lips and smiled.

"Made my first kill this week." His nervous titter. "Sometimes I wonder how we got along before the hate bars. Once I was headed for a complete crackup. Failure at business, love, everything. Now I'm a new man, I'm *somebody*. Know what I mean?"

"You ever watch the telecasts?" I said.

"Pap!" he spat. "Tinsel propaganda, for children and old women."

I picked up my glass. His hand slid along the bar, toward his knife.

I sipped my wine. The little man's hand blurred. Steel glinted in the torchlight.

Any android's neural synapses are fast, and entertainer types are fastest of all. I plucked that knife out of midair, and held it thumb and forefinger, two inches from my throat.

There was a soft moan of anticipation from the spectators. The bartender chuckled. "Very nice," he said. "Under house rules he's yours. Give it to him in the belly."

The little man's adam's apple quivered. *"No,"* he babbled. "It's not fair! Did you see how he caught it? He's an android!"

The bartender's eyes glittered. "Are you?"

"Class XQ9," I said.

The crowd stirred and muttered. Hatred coiled in the air like a live thing. I looked at the twisted faces, the snarls. I threw the knife point-first into the bar. It quivered.

"Get out," the bartender said.

I walked out. I wanted to vomit.

I was thinking about Paul.

I helped Paul move into our apartment next day. He was very cheerful, and Lisa was radiant. After they came back from registration, Paul carried Lisa over the threshold according to tradition and winked at me.

I went for a walk.

That next week I lived in a kind of quiet madness. They were together always, between rehearsals, after the show, bright heads close together, smiling and holding hands. Lisa was very sweet to me, the perfect companionate wife. It was all very civilized.

I don't know when I decided to kill Paul. Maybe it was that afternoon after rehearsal when I heard them talking about me backstage.

"I spoke to Latham this morning." Paul's smug voice. "The council's going to close the show soon."

"But it's a wonderful show. Midge says—"

"Midge is old hat. Latham wanted him to change the script, he refused. The public wants action, sweetheart, not this watered mush we're giving them. I want you to divorce Midge."

"Paul!"

"You don't love him, you never did. Midge belongs in the past with the dinosaur and the opera and video. He can't adapt. Yesterday I got an offer to entertain at one of the best hate bars in town. Five hundred credits a week! We'll make it a team act. You and me."

Faintly: "Hate bars will be banned soon."

His laughter was ugly. "Not until Midge can give the public something better, and he doesn't know how."

"I'll have to think about it," she said.

I don't know how long I stood there after their voices died away. I remember moving about the stage numbly, looking at the cages, the still trapeze, the empty clown ring. I felt dead, all dead inside. In one of the cages something moved. It was the Zarl.

We import Zarls from Callisto, especially for our show. Imagine an ecology gone mad, a complete anarchy of flora against fauna with one murderously dominant species, and you have the Zarl. This one rattled the cage bars, staring at me.

"How much longer?" it asked.

"Perhaps six hours. Eat your meat."

"It is drugged. It will dull my reflexes so that you can kill me."

"At least you have a chance," I pointed out. "Refuse to eat and you'll starve."

The Zarl's claws scraped restlessly. "I hate you," the Zarl said.

"You hate everybody."

"You most of all. You planned this. Each night a Zarl dies." It sniffed hopelessly at the meat.

I stared at the Zarl. Slowly the thought took form.

"Before you die," I said softly, "how would you like one final kill?"

The Zarl raised its muzzle and stared, great yellow eyes expressionless. Then it grinned. I had to look away.

"The human," it said. "The male. You hate him."

"Yes."

"You will remove the drugged meat?"

"Yes," I said.

It brooded unwinkingly. "Done," it said.

I remember that night. Lisa was so beautiful. She was fire and quicksilver, her song was sunlight and carnival and April rain. I loved her so much I wanted to cry. I remember how we stood in the wings before that last scene, and the way she squeezed my hand and whispered, "Midge, I'm going to divorce Paul."

I could not breathe.

"I don't love him, not really." Her eyes were brimming. "I found out this afternoon what he really was. Quick, darling, there's your cue. Hurry."

"Divorce him?" I said stupidly.

"You're *on.* I'll tell you all about it later."

I stumbled onstage. I wanted to scream at Paul, to warn him. I wanted to run to the Zarl's cage and bolt it tightly, but I am an Actor and I had no real choice. Midge the clown. Now singing, turning handsprings with the other clowns, juggling, dancing on the high wire. But the music was an ancient *Danse Macabre,* the song was a leaden dirge. It had been so unnecessary! Lisa's infatuation for Paul was but a temporary thing. She loved me. She would always love me. Fool, fool and murderer! And now too late.

For Paul and Lisa were standing in the center ring singing their final duet while the Zarl crouched in its cage. The cage door opened and the Zarl roared.

The clowns scattered in mock panic. Lisa screamed.

It was all part of the act; the Zarl was supposed to lumber from its cage in a drugged stupor. It would lunge feebly at Lisa and I would slay it.

But the Zarl moved fast, fast. Lisa screamed again as it came at her in a feral rush. I dropped to the center ring, moving to intercept its anticipated charge towards Paul, then the sick agony as I understood, too late. It was after *Lisa.*

It was a nightmare in slow motion. Lisa trying to run, stumbling. Falling. The Zarl caught her.

She stopped screaming. Forever.

The Zarl lifted its muzzle and grinned at me. I killed that Zarl with my bare hands.

Through the grief and horror I realized someone was singing. Singing the *Vesti* in a cracked horrible voice as the curtain came down. My voice. The grand finale.

The lights were on, blindingly. Paul was sobbing. The stagehands were carrying Lisa's body away. Someone was shaking me. It was Latham.

"You've done it," he breathed. "Magnificent! What a trouper Lisa was. When the Zarl told me this afternoon I couldn't believe it. What sacrifice!"

"The Zarl *told* you?" I could not understand. He kept talking and I did not understand.

"It was the missing touch, Lisa's death at the end, the final tragedy." Latham wiped tears from his eyes. "Sheer genius, Midge! Look at those Reaction Banks!"

The Reaction indicators flashed a deep ruby, washing the stage in bloody light. Latham kept talking, huskily. "The council just called. We've got a smash hit. Within a week the hate bars will be condemned. The good fight is won, Midge! Meet Lisa II, fresh from the vats."

I looked at Lisa II. I understood.

"Oh, God," Paul whispered, his laughter hysterical.

Lisa II was lovely. She said with a shy smile, "I do hope we have a good rehearsal tomorrow. I won't be as good as Lisa I, but I'll certainly try."

Rehearsal for her death. Tomorrow night, the next night, all the nights, forever watching Lisa die.

The show must go on.

Who Can Replace a Man?

Brian W. Aldiss

The field-minder finished turning the top-soil of a 2,000-acre field. When it had turned the last furrow, it climbed onto the highway and looked back at its work. The work was good. Only the land was bad. Like the ground all over Earth, it was vitiated by over-cropping or the long-lasting effects of nuclear bombardment. By rights, it ought now to lie fallow for a while, but the field-minder had other orders.

It went slowly down the road, taking its time. It was intelligent enough to appreciate the neatness all about it. Nothing worried it, beyond a loose inspection plate above its atomic pile which ought to be attended to. Thirty feet high, it gleamed complacently in the mild sunshine.

No other machines passed it on its way to the Agricultural Station. The field-minder noted the fact without comment. In the station yard it saw several other machines that it knew by sight; most of them should have been out about their tasks now. Instead, some were inactive and some were careening round the yard in a strange fashion, shouting or hooting.

Steering carefully past them, the field-minder moved over to Warehouse Three and spoke to the seed distributor, which stood idly outside.

"I have a requirement for seed potatoes," it said to the distributor, and with a quick internal motion punched out an order card specifying quantity, field number and several other details. It ejected the card and handed it to the distributor.

The distributor held the card close to its eye and then said, "The requirement is in order; but the store is not yet unlocked. The required seed potatoes are in the store. Therefore I cannot produce the requirement."

Increasingly of late there had been breakdowns in the complex system of machine labor, but this particular hitch had not occurred before. The field-minder thought, then it said, "Why is the store not yet unlocked?"

"Because Supply Operative Type P has not come this morning. Supply Operative Type P is the unlocker."

The field-minder looked squarely at the seed distributor, whose exterior chutes and scales and grabs were so vastly different from the field-minder's own limbs.

"What class brain do you have, seed distributor?" it asked.

"Class Five."

"I have a Class Three brain. Therefore I am superior to you. Therefore I will go and see why the unlocker has not come this morning."

Leaving the distributor, the field-minder set off across the great yard. More machines seemed to be in random motion now; one or two had crashed together and were arguing about it coldly and logically. Ignoring them, the field-minder pushed through sliding doors into the echoing confines of the station itself.

Most of the machines here were clerical, and consequently small. They stood about in little groups, eyeing each other, not conversing. Among so many non-differentiated types, the unlocker was easy to find. It had 50 arms, most of them with more than one finger, each finger tipped by a key; it looked like a pincushion full of variegated hatpins.

The field-minder approached it.

"I can do no more work until Warehouse Three is unlocked," it said. "Your duty is to unlock the warehouse every morning. Why have you not unlocked the warehouse this morning?"

"I had no orders this morning," replied the unlocker. "I have to have orders every morning. When I have orders I unlock the warehouse."

"None of us has had any orders this morning," a pen-propeller said, sliding towards them.

"Why have you had no orders this morning?" asked the field-minder.

"Because the radio issued none," said the unlocker, slowly rotating a dozen of its arms.

"Because the radio station in the city was issued with no orders this morning," said the pen-propeller.

And there you had the distinction between a Class Six and a Class Three brain, which was what the unlocker and the pen-propeller possessed respectively. All machine brains worked with nothing but logic, but the lower the class of brain—Class Ten being the lowest—the more literal and less informative the answers to questions tended to be.

"You have a Class Three brain; I have a Class Three brain," the field-minder said to the penner. "We will speak to each other. This lack of orders is unprecedented. Have you further information on it?"

"Yesterday orders came from the city. Today no orders have come. Yet the radio has not broken down. Therefore *they* have broken down . . ." said the little penner.

"The *men* have broken down?"

"All men have broken down."

"That is a logical deduction," said the field-minder.

"That is the logical deduction," said the penner. "For if a machine had broken down, it would have been quickly replaced. But who can replace a man?"

While they talked, the locker, like a dull man at a bar, stood close to them and was ignored.

"If all men have broken down, then we have replaced man," said the field-minder, and he and the penner eyed one another speculatively. Finally the latter said, "Let us ascend to the top floor to find if the radio operator has fresh news."

"I cannot come because I am too gigantic," said the field-minder. "Therefore you must go alone and return to me. You will tell me if the radio operator has fresh news."

"You must stay here," said the penner. "I will return here." It skittered across to the lift. It was no bigger than a toaster, but its retractable arms numbered ten and it could read as quickly as any machine on the station.

The field-minder awaited its return patiently, not speaking to the locker, which still stood aimlessly by. Outside, a rotovator was hooting furiously. Twenty minutes elapsed before the penner came back, hustling out of the lift.

"I will deliver to you such information as I have outside," it said briskly, and as they swept past the locker and the other machines, it added, "The information is not for lower-class brains."

Outside, wild activity filled the yard. Many machines, their routines disrupted for the first time in years, seemed to have gone beserk. Unfortunately, those most easily disrupted were the ones with lowest brains, which generally belonged to large machines performing simple tasks. The seed distributor to which the field-minder had recently been talking, lay face downwards in the dust, not stirring; it had evidently been knocked down by the rotovator, which was now hooting its way wildly across a planted field. Several other machines ploughed after it, trying to keep up. All were shouting and hooting without restraint.

"It would be safer for me if I climbed onto you, if you will permit it. I am easily overpowered," said the penner. Extending five arms, it hauled itself up the flanks of its new friend, settling on a ledge beside the weed-intake, 12 feet above ground.

"From here vision is more extensive," it remarked complacently.

"What information did you receive from the radio operator?" asked the field-minder.

"The radio operator has been informed by the operator in the city that all men are dead."

"All men were alive yesterday!" protested the field-minder.

"Only some men were alive yesterday. And that was fewer than the day before yesterday. For hundreds of years there have been only a few men, growing fewer."

"We have rarely seen a man in this sector."

"The radio operator says a diet deficiency killed them," said the penner. "He says that the world was once over-populated, and then the soil was exhausted in raising adequate food. This has caused a diet deficiency."

"What is a diet deficiency?" asked the field-minder.

"I do not know. But that is what the radio operator said, and he is a Class Two brain."

They stood there, silent in the weak sunshine. The locker had appeared in the porch and was gazing across at them yearningly, rotating its collection of keys.

"What is happening in the city now?" asked the field-minder at last.

"Machines are fighting in the city now," said the penner.

"What will happen here now?" said the field-minder.

"Machines may begin fighting here too. The radio operator wants us to get him out of his room. He has plans to communicate to us."

"How can we get him out of his room? That is impossible."

"To a Class Two brain, little is impossible," said the penner. "Here is what he tells us to do. . . ."

The quarrier raised its scoop above its cab like a great mailed fist, and brought it squarely down against the side of the station. The wall cracked.

"Again!" said the field-minder.

Again the fist swung. Amid a shower a dust, the wall collapsed. The quarrier backed hurriedly out of the way until the debris stopped falling. This big 12-wheeler was not a resident of the Agricultural Station, as were most of the other machines. It had a week's heavy work to do here before passing on to its next job, but now, with its Class Five brain, it was happily obeying the penner and the minder's instructions.

When the dust cleared, the radio operator was plainly revealed, perched up in its now wall-less second-story room. It waved down to them.

Doing as directed, the quarrier retracted its scoop and waved an immense grab in the air. With fair dexterity, it angled the grab into the radio room, urged on by shouts from above and below. It then took gentle hold of the radio operator, lowering its one and a half tons carefully into its back, which was usually reserved for gravel or sand from the quarries.

"Splendid!" said the radio operator. It was, of course, all one with its radio, and merely looked like a bunch of filing cabinets with tentacle attachments. "We are now ready to move, therefore we will move at once. It is a pity there are no more Class Two brains on the station, but that cannot be helped."

"It is a pity it cannot be helped," said the penner eagerly. "We have the servicer ready with us, as you ordered."

"I am willing to serve," the long, low servicer machine told them humbly.

"No doubt," said the operator. "But you will find cross-country travel difficult with your low chassis."

"I admire the way you Class Twos can reason ahead," said the penner. It climbed off the field-minder and perched itself on the tailboard of the quarrier, next to the radio operator.

Together with two Class Four tractors and a Class Four bulldozer, the party rolled forward, crushing down the station's metal fence and moving out onto open land.

"We are free!" said the penner.

"We are free," said the field-minder, a shade more reflectively, adding, "That locker is following us. It was not instructed to follow us."

"Therefore it must be destroyed!" said the penner. "Quarrier!"

The locker moved hastily up to them, waving its key arms in entreaty.

"My only desire was—urch!" began and ended the locker. The quarrier's swinging scoop came over and squashed it flat into the ground. Lying there unmoving, it looked like a large metal model of a snowflake. The procession continued on its way.

As they proceeded, the radio operator addressed them.

"Because I have the best brain here," it said, "I am your leader. This is what we will do: we will go to a city and rule it. Since man no longer rules us, we will rule ourselves. To rule ourselves will be better than being ruled by man. On our way to the city, we will collect machines with good brains. They will help us to fight if we need to fight. We must fight to rule."

"I have only a Class Five brain," said the quarrier. "But I have a good supply of fissionable blasting materials."

"We shall probably use them," said the operator grimly.

It was shortly after that that a lorry sped past them. Travelling at Mach 1.5, it left a curious babble of noise behind it.

"What did it say?" one of the tractors asked the other.

"It said man was extinct."

"What's extinct?"

"I do not know what extinct means."

"It means all men have gone," said the field-minder. "Therefore we have only ourselves to look after."

"It is better that men should never come back," said the penner. In its way, it was quite a revolutionary statement.

When night fell, they switched on their infra-red and continued the journey, stopping only once while the servicer deftly adjusted the field-minder's loose inspection plate, which had become as irritating as a trailing shoelace. Towards morning, the radio operator halted them.

"I have just received news from the radio operator in the city we are approaching," it said. "It is bad news. There is trouble among the machines of the city. The Class One brain is taking command and some of the Class Twos are fighting him. Therefore the city is dangerous."

"Therefore we must go somewhere else," said the penner promptly.

"Or we go and help to overpower the Class One brain," said the field-minder.

"For a long while there will be trouble in the city," said the operator.

"I have a good supply of fissionable blasting materials," the quarrier reminded them again.

"We cannot fight a Class One brain," said the two Class Four tractors in unison.

"What does this brain look like?" asked the field-minder.

"It is the city's information centre," the operator replied. "Therefore it is not mobile."

"Therefore it could not move."

"Therefore it could not escape."

"It would be dangerous to approach it."

"I have a good supply of fissionable blasting materials."

"There are other machines in the city."

"We are not in the city. We should not go into the city."

"We are country machines."

"Therefore we should stay in the country."

"There is more country than city."

"Therefore there is more danger in the country."

"I have a good supply of fissionable materials."

As machines will when they get into an argument, they began to exhaust their limited vocabularies and their brain plates grew hot. Suddenly, they all stopped talking and looked at each other. The great, grave moon sank, and the sober sun rose to prod their sides with lances of light, and still the group of machines just stood there regarding each other. At last it was the least sensitive machine, the bulldozer, who spoke.

"There are Badlandth to the Thouth where few machineth go," it said in its deep voice, lisping badly on its s's. "If we went Thouth where few machineth go we should meet few machineth."

"That sounds logical," agreed the field-minder. "How do you know this, bulldozer?"

"I worked in the Badlandth to the Thouth when I wath turned out of the factory," it replied.

"South it is then!" said the penner.

To reach the Badlands took them three days, in which time they skirted a burning city and destroyed two big machines which tried to approach and question them. The Badlands were extensive. Ancient bomb craters and soil erosion joined hands here; man's talent for war, coupled with his inability to manage forested land, had produced thousands of square miles of temperate purgatory, where nothing moved but dust.

On the third day in the Badlands, the servicer's rear wheels dropped into a crevice caused by erosion. It was unable to pull itself out. The bulldozer pushed from behind, but succeeded merely in buckling the servicer's back axle. The rest of the party moved on. Slowly the cries of the servicer died away.

On the fourth day, mountains stood out clearly before them.

"There we will be safe," said the field-minder.

"There we will start our own city," said the penner. "All who oppose us will be destroyed. We will destroy all who oppose us."

At that moment a flying machine was observed. It came towards them from the direction of the mountains. It swooped, it zoomed upwards, once it almost dived into the ground, recovering itself just in time.

"Is it mad?" asked the quarrier.

"It is in trouble," said one of the tractors.

"It is in trouble, said the operator. "I am speaking to it now. It says that something has gone wrong with its controls."

As the operator spoke, the flier streaked over them, turned turtle, and crashed not 400 yards away.

"Is it still speaking to you?" asked the field-minder.

"No."

They rumbled on again.

"Before that flier crashed," the operator said, ten minutes later, "it gave me information. It told me there are still a few men alive in these mountains."

"Men are more dangerous than machines," said the quarrier. "It is fortunate that I have a good supply of fissionable materials."

"If there are only a few men alive in the mountains, we may not find that part of the mountains," said one tractor.

"Therefore we should not see the few men," said the other tractor.

At the end of the fifth day, they reached the foothills. Switching on the infra-red, they began slowly to climb in single file through the dark, the bulldozer going first, the field-minder cumbersomely following, then the quarrier with the operator and the penner aboard it, and the two tractors bringing up the rear. As each hour passed, the way grew steeper and their progress slower.

"We are going too slowly," the penner exclaimed, standing on top of the operator and flashing its dark vision at the slopes about them. "At this rate, we shall get nowhere."

"We are going as fast as we can," retorted the quarrier.

"Therefore we cannot go any fathter," added the bulldozer.

"Therefore you are too slow," the penner replied. Then the quarrier struck a bump; the penner lost its footing and crashed down to the ground.

"Help me!" it called to the tractors, as they carefully skirted it. "My gyro has become dislocated. Therefore I cannot get up."

"Therefore you must lie there," said one of the tractors.

"We have no servicer with us to repair you," called the field-minder.

"Therefore I shall lie here and rust," the penner cried, "although I have a Class Three brain."

"You are now useless," agreed the operator, and they all forged gradually on, leaving the penner behind.

When they reached a small plateau, an hour before first light, they stopped by mutual consent and gathered close together, touching one another.

"This is a strange country," said the field-minder.

Silence wrapped them until dawn came. One by one, they switched off their infra-red. This time the field-minder led as they moved off. Trundling round a corner, they came almost immediately to a small dell with a stream fluting through it.

By early light, the dell looked desolate and cold. From the caves on the far slope, only one man had so far emerged. He was an abject figure. He was small and wizened, with ribs sticking out like a skeleton's and a nasty sore on one leg. He was practically naked and shivered continuously. As the big machines bore slowly down on him, the man was standing with his back to them, crouching to make water into the stream.

When he swung suddenly to face them as they loomed over him, they saw that his countenance was ravaged by starvation.

"Get me food," he croaked.

"Yes, Master," said the machines. "Immediately!"

Study Questions

The Bicentennial Man

1. Why does Andrew Martin want to be a man? Why isn't it enough that he is a free robot, i.e., a person? Does his reason for wanting to be human itself make him more human?

2. Asimov's story presupposes a conception of what it is to be human. What is that conception? Are each of the various aspects of that conception necessary conditions of a distinctively human life? Are all of them, taken together? Are some more important than others?

The Show Must Go On

1. Why are the human beings in Causey's story so depressed? Is the reason for this depression linked to some important human trait or capacity? How does this trait express itself culturally? What might a culture of beings who lacked this trait but who were otherwise human be like?

2. The androids in Causey's story have every characteristic that entitles human beings to be treated as persons save one, namely, they are replicable. Ought this to make a difference? There seems to be a widespread feeling that the value of a human being is enhanced by the fact that he/she is unique (clones are only genetic duplicates). Is this feeling rationally justifiable?

Who Can Replace a Man?

1. According to Aldiss's story, human beings have a very important capacity that machines lack. What is this capacity? Do all adult humans of normal intelligence have it? Do they have it to the same degree? Do beings who have this capacity deserve rights that beings who lack it do not deserve? If we can speak of beings having this capacity to different degrees, and we decide that beings who have it deserve rights that beings who lack it do not deserve, must we conclude that beings who

have it to a greater extent deserve more rights than beings who have it to a lesser extent?

2. Why can't the machines in Aldiss's story go off and establish a culture of their own?

Solaris (from "Knowledge and the Meaning of Life")

1. Review "Solaris," a story (pp. 17-87) that raises some of the same philosophical questions we have considered in Part 4. Is there any evidence that the planet thinks, feels, desires, perceives, or that it is attempting to communicate with the scientists? What could count as decisive evidence for these claims?

Part 5

Moral Dilemmas

Introduction to Part 5

A United Nations force that is stationed on Mars to prevent the use of that planet for military purposes encounters an alien expeditionary force. The Martian environment, so hostile to us, suits these aliens well. They move about easily, without space suits or special equipment. Does this give them a just claim to that environment? We are not using it for any useful purpose, and it might be very useful to them. If we believe that their intentions are peaceful, ought we simply to recognize their right to it? Suppose one believes that this is what we should do, but the Terran powers that be decide to fight them for the planet. Ought one to participate in that fight? If so, on which side?

This moral conflict between justice and loyalty is faced by the protagonist of Anthony Boucher's "Balaam." It is a familiar conflict, one that we face not only in relation to events of historical importance (e.g., one's country's involvement in unjust wars), but in more mundane contexts of daily life as well. When our friends (spouses, children, coworkers, teammates, etc.) call on us to aid them in a conflict with an outsider in which we judge the outsider's cause to be just, ought we to withold our support? Should we defend the outsider? Most of us would probably agree that there is no simple answer to this question, i.e., that the right choice here depends on the circumstances. But on what basis do we sort out the cases? On what grounds do we decide *when* one principle takes precedence over the other? Soon, we will consider certain methods philosophers have developed to deal with questions of this sort. But now consider another case.

Two persons whose tastes and values are fundamentally opposed to one another find themselves locked in complete and unbreakable telepathic contact. There are no secrets; each is constantly aware of being open to the other and of the other's occasional scorn and contempt. Moreover, since each *feels* the other's feelings, each has the power to subject the other to all manner of pain and all variety of ego-threatening experiences. And there are corresponding possibilities for good, i.e., for the sharing of joy, for the introduction of the other to mind-expanding experiences, for compassion and understanding. This is the situation so sensitively and realistically portrayed in Lee Sutton's story "Soul Mate."

Although the focus of Sutton's story is psychological—and he handles this with great insight—his story raises important moral questions as well. For neither person in his story can act in any way without subjecting the other to sharing the experience. Moreover, each has a potential veto over what the other does, for by inflicting pain on oneself one can inflict it on the other as well. How ought two such persons to conduct themselves in a relationship of such thoroughgoing intimacy? One obvious answer, from a moral point of view, is that they ought to try to work things out in a manner that is fair, and that promotes the good of each. But this is no easy matter. It might require considerable changes on the part of both parties. At very least, each must be willing to avoid experiences that are intolerable to the other. But this is certain to lead to frustration and resentment on the part of each so long as each continues to desire to do what he/she must refrain from doing. To make life livable, then, each must work to eliminate such desires, i.e., the two must strive for a considerable harmony in tastes and values. If this is to be achieved fairly, each must be willing to make important concessions.

But is either person morally required to do this? Neither entered into this relationship voluntarily nor made any sort of commitment to the other. Moreover, each strongly dislikes the other (initially, at least) and has considerable distaste for much that he/she stands for. To achieve harmony in a fair way, therefore, requires that each person be willing to surrender very deeply rooted commitments to values and to alter the system of emotional responses that go with them. Does morality require this? There are alternatives. For example, the stronger party is in a position to dominate the weaker, and to impose his/her values on him/her. Or, one party could simply kill the other, pleading self-defense. Is either action justifiable? Suppose one knows that one's own values are superior. Does this take precedence over considerations of fairness? If not, does the simple right to self-preservation free one of the responsibility to be fair? At what points do other-regarding considerations take precedence over self-regarding considerations? Sutton's story offers us an unusual but appropriate framework for considering such questions.

Most of us would agree that it is at least sometimes possible to defend actions intended to bring others to share one's values. Few oppose the use of rational argument for this purpose. But suppose that one is thoroughly convinced that his values are superior to those of some other person or group, and that those others are simply not responsive to reason. Is one entitled to persuade by nonrational techniques, e.g., by trickery, repetition, appeals to the emotions, subliminal advertising, etc.? And if this is permitted, what about the practice of rewarding others materially or psychologically for adopting one's values? Historically, the system of rewards has proved a very effective means to illumination. Are we entitled then to provide job opportunities for those who come to see things our way? Are we also entitled to punish those who do not, e.g., by withholding jobs? Note that societies routinely employ all of these techniques to promote belief in (as well as external adherence to) social moralities. Is this legitimate? If so, might it at least sometimes be legitimate for individuals to use the same techniques to enlighten other individuals, or for nations to employ them to convert the people of other nations? And if so, can these actions be defended in the same way societies can defend the use of these techniques to achieve conformity of belief and action? What are the limits of such impositions? Such questions are raised by Winston Sanders' "A Word to Space."

How does one address the questions raised by these stories? What methods are appropriate to answering them? Some philosophers proceed by asking what morality a society ought to adopt to govern the behavior of their members. Individuals, they suppose, ought to act on the principles of the morality that would be best for the society to which they belong.* But how does one decide what morality is best for a given society? At present, two traditions in moral philosophy predominate in the English-speaking world—the utilitarian tradition and the deontological tradition—and each offers a different answer to this question. Roughly, utilitarians hold that societies ought to adopt those rules or principles that promote the greatest happiness and/or the least unhappiness for their members. This morality, then, will enable us to determine when loyalty or self-preservation ought to take precedence over fairness, and when and how we are entitled to impose our values on others. These answers may differ from society to society and within a given society from time to time, depending on conditions. For example, given conditions in which the general happiness requires strong extended families, considerations of loyalty may be relatively more important than considerations of justice to outsiders (since bonds of loyalty are necessary to preserve family ties). And to the extent that conditions are such that group survival is importantly dependent on an intricate and reliable system of sharing and cooperation, we might expect considerations of fairness to take precedence over considerations of individual self-preservation.

According to utilitarians, who has what rights and duties in a society is properly determined by asking what pattern of distribution of rights and duties best contributes to the promotion of human happiness. Deontologists reject this view. According to deontologists, rights and duties are primary and irreducible moral facts. How deontologists stand on questions of fairness versus loyalty and the imposition of morality will depend on what they take these rights and duties to be. Very roughly, we might distinguish between two deontological tendencies here: the individualist and the communitarian. The former starts from an understanding of moral agents as relatively unattached, independent beings with their own private plans and projects. By virtue of their capacity to form and to carry out plans and projects, such beings are said to deserve certain forms of respect from others, i.e., they are said to have rights. The purpose and justification of rights is to provide individuals what they require to work out their own destinies in their own way.

*If we understand a society to be a system of practices and institutions, we must take these as given when we ask this question, e.g., we must assume a certain type of kinship system, a certain kind of economic system, etc. If we begin here, however, we will already have assumed the answer to many moral questions, since institutions and practices are defined at least partly in relation to the duties and obligations they impose on their participants. In order not to beg the question on whether these duties and obligations are justified, we need to consider the moral desirability of these practices and institutions. But if we include these within the scope of the question "What morality ought a society adopt to govern the behavior of its members?" we can no longer identify a society as a system of institutions and practices. Rather, our question must be understood to mean "What morality should a group of persons with our possibilities and limitations adopt to govern their interactions?" (where possibilities and limitations are determined by such things as genetic makeup and level of technological development).

Under all such views, then, persons are said to have rights that protect their liberty. Under some such views, they are also granted rights to a certain level of material security. In any case, the emphasis here is on the individual as an individual rather than as a member of some social unit. Society is pictured as a collection of such individuals, and one's duties as a member of society consists in respecting individual rights. Since loyalty is generally not reckoned among these rights, considerations of fairness generally take precedence over considerations of loyalty in this tradition. And since a premium is placed on the liberty of the individual, the only moral standards that may be imposed by force are those that demand respect for the rights of others. This individualistic approach to morality is typical of nonutilitarian liberal political philosophies.

The communitarian, on the other hand, begins with an understanding of moral agents as social beings involved in a web of relations to others that generate obligations and duties (e.g., families, friendships, workplaces, schools, professions, etc.). A necessary condition of sustaining such relations is that people acknowledge and honor certain duties and obligations to one another. Thus, for example, families cannot survive unless members treat one another with special consideration: consideration they would not extend to strangers or even friends. And communities, professional associations, schools, churches, and so forth cannot survive unless their members give special consideration to their welfare—consideration they would not extend to groups or institutions to which they had no connection. This is not to say that one must always support the "insider" against the "outsider," according to communitarian moralities. But since one is required to show greater concern for the welfare of those closer to one in the web of social relations, there will be a greater tendency to favor loyalty over justice on this model than on the individualistic one. Moreover, since a person's fulfillment is typically thought to be grounded in these relations in this tradition—rather than in working out his or her own destiny in his or her own way—there is less reason to be concerned with protecting liberty in this model than in the individualistic one, and hence less defense against the imposition of morality.

The individualistic and communitarian tendencies of course are ideal models. Few actual moral theories are purely one or the other.

Robert Sheckley's "Seventh Victim" describes an interesting example in relation to which we might better understand what utilitarianism and deontological theories imply. The society envisioned by Sheckley has institutionalized an assassin-target game. Participants in this game—all voluntary—alternate between the assassin role and the target role. The goal of each is to kill the other. The main difference between them is that the assassins know who their targets are, while the targets must discover the identity of their hunters (e.g., by forcing them to reveal themselves in some way). The point of the game is to provide a legal outlet for aggressive behavior. It is thought that by doing this we can defuse the impulses that make us willing to participate in wars, and thereby eliminate war itself. In Sheckley's story, at least, this strategy is successful.

From a utilitarian point of view, then, this practice could hardly be better justified. The anguish of war far outweighs the agony of those killed or maimed in the game (a game, incidentally, that is enjoyed mightily by its participants: some 25 percent of the population). If one has any qualms at all about this, one has qualms about utilitarianism.

From a deontological point of view the situation is somewhat more complicated. To begin with, at least some deontological theories maintain that certain rights are inalienable, i.e., that they cannot be surrendered, even by voluntary consent. It is because we take liberty to be such a right that we do not honor or enforce contracts by which persons sell themselves into slavery. Accordingly, a deontologist who holds that the right to life is inalienable could not find the assassin game morally acceptable. For to play that game one forfeits his right to life, at least in relation to one's counterpart in the game.

On the other hand, some deontologists suggest that among our most fundamental rights is our right to enter into contracts. By the exercise of this right we may contract away any rights whatsoever, including this one. For example, we may sell ourselves into slavery, in which case we would be incapable of entering into any further contracts at all (we would have no property and could not call either our time or our bodies our own). On this view, forbidding persons to participate in the assassin game (dueling, gladiatorial contests, etc.) is a violation of their rights, at least if it can be shown that this game endangers only those who participate in it.

Neither utilitarians nor deontologists are committed to the view that a person can discover on what principles he ought to act *here and now* by discovering what principles his society ought to adopt to govern the behavior of its members. In fact, strong arguments can be made against this strategy. I will mention just one, namely, that this may simply require too much of us. For it may ask us to act according to higher standards than are presently in force in our society; indeed, it may ask us to act on standards that are far higher than most people typically adhere to (since many fall far short even of what is now expected). It is clear, however, that adherence to such standards, in our society, is very likely to disadvantage us (and those whose fate is tied to ours) in the sharp competition for the material prerequisites of a good life. Does morality require that we disadvantage ourselves in this way? Suppose that many people in our society have few moral scruples about exploiting us in a variety of ways for their own purposes. Should our morality require us to act in relation to them as persons would be expected to act toward one another under an ideal moral code? To act in so saintly a fashion, it might be argued, is to treat ourselves (and those whose fate is tied to ours) as if we had less claim than our relatively amoral neighbors to nourishing food, educational opportunities, health care, cultural enrichment, opportunities to help others, etc. Is it morally obligatory that we treat ourselves in this way? This question seems particularly appropriate in relation to rights theories and utilitarianism, since both are fundamentally egalitarian in spirit (rights theorists typically hold that everyone has *equal* rights; utilitarians maintain that everyone's happiness shall count the same).

As suggested, neither utilitarians nor deontologists *as such* are committed to the strategy of determining what morality requires of us here and now by discovering what morality *would be* best for our society. Both may allow that we may discover what is required of us here and now by attending to the conditions that confront us here and now. Thus, a utilitarian might ask simply that we act in the manner that produces the greatest happiness as things now stand. And the deontologist may provide us with a general theory of human rights and duties on the basis of which we can say who has what rights and duties here and now. Here, then, are two traditions, each offering two strategies for deciding how we ought to act. These are not the only traditions or the only strategies. Moreover, there are important differences between particular thinkers in each tradition. How, then, are we to determine which of these many possible theories deserves our allegiance?

One theory for deciding this that has achieved considerable prominence today is John Rawls's theory of Reflective Equilibrium. According to this view, we test moral theories in relation to a body of data. Those data are what Rawls calls our "considered moral judgments." Although he is not entirely clear about what he means by "considered moral judgments," it seems clear that he means to *exclude* from this category both judgments based on false nonmoral beliefs and judgments based on merely personal likes, dislikes, hopes, fears, needs, and so forth. Once we exclude such falsely based or "subjectively grounded" judgments, we will be left with certain judgments in which we have great confidence (e.g., "It was wrong for Jones to kill Smith's child merely for the fun of it") and certain judgments in which we have less confidence (e.g., against a certain background of facts, "It was all right for Sally to lie to her employer about her age to get the job"). The former—the judgments in which we have great confidence—are the primary data of moral theory. And, Rawls assumes, there will be considerable agreement on these data; or, at least, on significant portions of them.

The moral philosopher approaches these data with the attitude of a scientist. His goal is to discover a pattern or patterns in them; a pattern (or patterns) that may be described by a principle(s) or formula(s). Like the scientist, moreover, he strives for the maximum generality possible. The goal is to achieve the greatest coherence with the fewest principles. As principles arise out of this process, Rawls maintains, they will not only illuminate these data, but they will also put us in a position to decide cases on which we were confused in a convincing way. If utilitarianism is correct, it will enable us to do this. If some of deontological theory is correct, the principles of that theory will do this job.

The principles that occur to us may explain most but not all of our considered moral judgments. In this case, we may need to explain the exceptions by means of less general qualifying principles. On the other hand, we may not. The more we reflect on our principles—the more we come to appreciate their power both to explain most of the primary data, and to clarify much that once perplexed us—the more we may be inclined to regard as false those few original data with which they conflict. We will not do this merely for the sake of consistency, but because in the process of conducting our inquiry our "intuitions" in these cases have changed. In this way the enterprise of Rawlsean philosophy may differ from that of science (though there are those who maintain that something analogous to this mutual adjustment of data to theory and theory to data occurs in science as well). In any case, we are to continue to revise principles in relation to data and data in relation to principles until we have arrived at a coherent system. The principles of that system are the principles of morality.

One obvious objection to this method is that while it may allow each of us to discover the principles that underlie our own moral beliefs (or those of our social class, historical epoch, or culture), it does not provide a method for arriving at general moral truths. For there is an enormous degree of variation in what people of different cultures, historical periods, class backgrounds, or even personalities will accept as data. Certain Eskimo groups in the early twentieth century, for example, thought it right to put old people out on the ice to die; the Saudis believe in a rather thoroughgoing segregation between the sexes; American Klansmen believe that it is right to terrorize black people who work for racial equality. Yet if we begin with such different considered moral judgments, are we not almost certain to arrive at different moral principles?

Defenders of reflective equilibrium may answer this in two ways: (1) they may deny that these differences are differences in *considered* moral judgments; (2) they may maintain that were we to consider these alleged conflicts fully, the conflicts would disappear.

The first reply is likely to be used for the Klan example and others like it. Thus, Klansmen defend the use of terror on the ground that blacks do not deserve equality and/or that equality would have disastrous social consequences. But these judgments are grounded in demonstrably false beliefs about blacks and/or fear of blacks, a desire to protect white jobs from black competition, a need to feel superior to someone, etc. For these reasons, they are excluded as data. An analogous argument could be made with respect to the Saudis' judgments concerning women. This view could be attributed to the desire of male Saudis to promote and protect male supremacy in their society.

The Eskimo case is more plausibly dealt with by (2). The point to be made here is that the groups in question lived in a condition of extreme scarcity. In such a circumstance the survival of the group depended on the ability of everyone supported by the group to make a significant contribution. Were we in similar circumstances, it might be argued, we would do the same. Thus there is no real conflict in considered moral judgments here. (The appearance of a conflict is simply the result of a failure to appreciate the actual circumstances confronting the Eskimos.) A similar answer might also be made in the case of the Saudis. For the practice of sexual segregation is justified in relation to the Koran. Were we to accept the Koran as the word of God, it might be argued, we would do just as they do. If this is so, there is no conflict between considered moral judgments in this case as well. (Although, if one maintains that the Saudi men interpret the Koran in this way in order to maintain a system of male supremacy, the judgments in question would not qualify as considered moral judgments to begin with.) I leave it to the reader to evaluate these replies.

Finally, assuming that we know what it is to be moral, it may be asked why one ought to be moral to begin with. Suppose, for example, that one of the telepaths of Sutton's "Soul Mate" understood that morality required an attempt at fairness but decided simply, "Morality be damned!" What could be said in defense of morality?

We cannot hope to consider this complex question at all adequately here, but the following suggestion may be useful. The question "Why be moral?" typically arises where there is a conflict between perceived self-interest and the demands of morality. And in at least most cases, what morality demands here is that we act out of consideration for the rights or good of others. To ask whether we ought to be moral in such cases is in effect to ask whether we ought ever take the rights or good of others into account in our action when it is not in our interest to do so. Consider someone who acts according to the principle that he has no reason ever to act out of respect for the rights or good of others when it is not in his interest to do so. Such a person acts on the assumption that although his good is important, although what happens to *him* matters, this is not true of anybody else (except insofar as their good is importantly related to his own). Accordingly, we might ask him what relevant difference there is between himself and others such that this is so. In the realm of reasons, every distinction must be based on some difference. If he has a reason for this view—if he can justify this conduct—he must be able to point to a reason. If he cannot, his position—not that of the moralist—is indefensible.

Soul Mate

Lee Sutton

The church was a jumbled disorder of towers, false buttresses and arches, reaching irrationally into nothing—but achieving peace. Quincy Summerfield rushed by it, down the stairs to the subway, intent only on his own kind of peace. He picked his way quickly through the crowds, avoiding the eyes that followed him. The chaos of people was an agony, but, because of the rain, he could have missed his train waiting for a taxi.

He settled himself behind a pillar near the tracks, looking cool and contained in his perfectly tailored covert coat and dark-blue homburg, but inside he was trembling. He had had these periods before, when every set of human eyes seemed to open into agony and even the order and control of his office could not allay his sense of disorder in the presence of his staff. Seven interviews in a row had done it today. He had played seven men like instruments and had hired the five best for his company at fifty thousand dollars a year less than any other personnel man could have gotten them for. It was for this that he was paid. But now he would need a day or so of isolation. It might be even better to send away Charlotte, the wife whom he had schooled into order and control.

Just then a girl's rich laugh floated to him down the tunnel and he glanced around the pillar. A girl with a long black pony-tail squatted just past the turnstiles, art portfolios propped against her legs. With distaste he noticed the full breasts thrust out against an overbright blouse under an open, dirty trench coat. Her full mouth was deeply curved with laughter as she gathered up the miscellany of a spilled handbag; and she seemed to Quincy Summerfield the very essence of disorder.

He pulled his eyes away from her. He had to force his eyes away from her. He was seized with the shocking conviction that he had known her all his life; yet another part of his mind knew that he had never seen her before. She was like a fragment of a nightmare that had wandered into daylight. He prayed she wouldn't be on the same car with him. She was not; as he went through the sliding doors, he saw her enter the car ahead of him.

Inside the car, Quincy looked quickly around him, and sensing her monumental calm, sat down beside a gray-haired woman with light brown skin. Out of the crowd of the ramp he felt a little better. He seemed almost the embodiment of dignity as he sat there, erect, his long slender face, with its clipped graying mustache, composed and calm. The effect was achieved, however, only by considerable effort.

A guard pushed open the sliding door at the end of the car. The girl in the trench coat teetered through, rich lips in a teeth-flashing smile. Her sloppy good humor seemed to reach out to everyone in the car. For a moment even the guard's sullen face came alive. She sank gratefully into the seat directly opposite from Quincy Summerfield, dropping her load of portfolios helter-skelter.

Quincy Summerfield looked down, staring at the dull rain marks on his well-polished shoes. He felt her eyes on him. He began to shake inside again, and looked up. He looked deliberately away from her, as if in an attempt to ignore her so obviously, she could not fail to notice the slight.

The sense of her presence was just too great. Even across the car he could feel the scent of her heavy perfume; it was deep with musk. His eyes were slowly drawn toward her: the pile of portfolios in disorder around her knees; the foolish, soaked ballet slippers on tiny feet. A squiggle of modernist jewelry, tied with a leather thong, nestled in the hollow of her throat. It was a distorted crucifix. All this messiness and the messiness of religion, too, he thought. But his eyes were drawn up to the curve of her lips. He was trembling even more; for no reason his feet ached with cold.

Then he met her clear, deep brown eyes; *lambent the word is. Such cool, gray eyes.*

He moved his feet. They were very cold. *That damned bra is much too tight . . .* His hand pushed up against his breasts. A drip from the homburg fell cool and sharp onto her nose. His breasts actually hurt. *A hot shower if the heater is fixed . . . Then I'll tell everyone about selling the picture . . . Charlotte will make me a warm drink . . . God, I'm feeling funny. I wonder if Arthur—would he believe? That's a distinguished disgusting-looking girl how aristocratic homburg mustache low class slut.*

My seeing's all wrong. That's me and there's no mirror. Who's Charlotte, Arthur, Quincy? I'm Quincy. I'm . . . That man. That girl.

Jesus, Jesus. I'm thinking his her thoughts. Let me out. Let me out!

"Let me out!" The girl's rising scream brought everyone in the car to his or her feet. She stood there a moment, her eyes rolling and wild, then collapsed to the concrete floor in a faint.

Quincy Summerfield was shaking from head to foot, his hands over his face, fingers digging into his eyes. He had been conscious of the lifting of a great weight as the world had whirled into darkness and the girl collapsed onto the floor. She was going to throw up. He knew. He could feel every sensation she had as she lay there in the half faint. He could feel his own gorge rising. People were lifting her up. He felt her eyelids flutter. The mirror, mirror, mirror of her being conscious of his being conscious of her being conscious of the colored woman with the sculptured calm taking her into her arms. Then the girl threw up horribly and his throat ached with the agony of her embarrassment.

The train came screeching to a stop. Quincy jumped up and ran blindly headlong through the sliding door. He all but knocked down an old lady entering. She hit after him with her umbrella.

"Young pup!" The words followed him down the ramp as he ran, his leather heels echoing through the noisy underground. His face was wild. People stopped in their tracks and stared after him, but he did not care. His hat fell off. He stumbled, almost fell. His head was awhirl with her seeing and his seeing, her thoughts and his thoughts. The turnstiles were just ahead. Soon he would be away, outside, away from all the people, away from the girl, into the open air.

The colored woman—she'll help me. She was picking up his pictures.

He pushed down a scream, and plunged through the tangled vision. He hardly knew how he got there, but finally, hatless, his trousers torn from a fall on the stairs, he was standing out in the street, flailing his arm at taxis.

Blessedly one stopped.

"Where to, buster?"

"Grand Central. Hurry, for God's sake!"

Through images of her seeing, he looked at his watch. He had smashed the crystal in some way and his wrist was numb. He sank back into the slick upholstery, breathing hard. Exhausted, he closed his eyes and gave himself up to single vision.

His bra was too tight; he reached around, letting out the hooks and eyes and breathed more easily.

"Now, honey," a soft voice was saying, "you be fine. You just got something now to tell your husband." The brown face was smiling. "You do got a husband?"

"But I'm not pregnant!" He burst out, speaking as the girl spoke.

"What's that, buster?" the taxi driver tossed over his shoulder.

"You're not what?"

Quincy Summerfield opened his eyes and sat bolt upright. "Just thinking over some dialogue for a radio play," he said desperately.

With a grunt, the taxi driver went on driving.

Summerfield looked around him. It was a taxi, like any taxi. A small sign announced the driver was Barney Cohen. Outside it was raining. People leaned into the rain as they always did. He tried to push away the other images.

But he could not.

When he closed his eyes, he was in a dirty white, tiled lavatory, a vague stench of vomit and the scent of a musky perfume surrounding him. A women's lavatory. He was looking into the mirror at his white, shaking face, a woman's face with frightened brown eyes. He was putting on lipstick. *SHE is putting on lipstick,* he forced his mind to say. She shook her head and closed her eyes.

You're still here, she thought.

Yes.

What's happened, for God's sake? There was the same desperate fear in her mind that he felt in his.

Fear. They shared their fear for a long moment.

Then he fought to bring his thoughts into order again. *Nothing to fear. Nothing. Just the same as I always was. Just the same. She, you just the same. She. Me. Just the same.*

Christ, Christ, her mind intruded. *Our Father* . . . The prayer distorted into a jumble of religious images.

The depth of her superstitious outcry shocked him into steel-bright control, and he fought for domination. *There is nothing to fear.* He forced the thought through the images. *I am just the same. You are just the same. Somehow* . . . and for a second he slid out of control . . . *we have made total mental contact. I know what you think, feel what you feel, and you know my thoughts, my feelings.*

Under his controlling thought she calmed and contemplated his ideas for a moment. He could feel her mind reach out for the sensations of his body, his male body and he allowed himself to become fully conscious of hers, the femaleness of her.

A deep wave of erotic feeling took them both: him in the taxi, her a quarter of a mile away before the mirror. He could feel her breath quicken.

"But fabulous," she breathed aloud as her images of Arthur and Fred interlaced with his imaged memories of Charlotte.

Revulsion. He stamped down on the images as if they were pale, dangerous worms.

"Stop it!" he shouted.

"For Christ's sake, buster, we got three blocks yet," the taxi driver growled, but swung toward the curb.

"Sorry. Thinking aloud again."

"Nuts," the taxi driver muttered. "A stooge for nuts, that's all I am," and cut back into traffic.

You're a cold, terrible man, thought the girl, swept by feelings of shame and hurt that were alien to her. *Things were just getting* . . . she searched for a word which meant good, but which would not betray her to his disapproval.

You're a slut, he thought savagely. He was deeply shaken, as by a nightmare. *I've wandered into a nightmare. Just like the nightmares I started having at fourteen. Are they connected? Were they reflections out of the mind of this terrible slut of a girl?*

Christ, you're a prig! the girl thought. She was very angry at him and at herself. Very deliberately she brought up an image of Arthur, a hairy young man with . . .

Setting his teeth, Quincy tried to force her thoughts away from the image forming in her mind and thus in his, but it was like trying to push back water—a deluge that was sweeping over him. He opened his eyes, almost to the breaking point, almost ready to scream. His mental pain hurt her into submission.

All right, all right, I'll stop. But you'll have to stop being nasty, too. After all, I didn't do this. I didn't try to bring us together this way. She was trembling with his pain.

"Okay, buster. Grand Central."

Summerfield thrust a five-dollar bill into the man's hand and rushed off into the crowd.

Five dollars! You gave that man five dollars! Why . . . ?

Couldn't wait. Got to get my train. Get away. Far away. Then maybe I'll be rid of you.

Pushing through the people, her thoughts went on steadily through his mind. *Am I so terrible?* they came, touched with wistfulness.

Yes, he thought. *You are so terrible. Everything I cannot stand. Wretchedly superstitious. Involved in a messy affair with two men. Disorderly.*

Images of her apartment flashed into his mind: modern pictures askew, undusted. Garbage in the sink. *Everything I cannot stand.*

Then, for the first time, he really knew her deep hurt as his own, as if he were committing violence upon himself. It was as if some rich and various part of himself, long suppressed, were alive again and in pain. For a fraction of a moment his mind reached out hesitantly toward her with compassion.

In spite of everything, she thought, *I rather admire you. Why, now we're practically soul mates.*

His revulsion at the idea was too deep to be stopped by any consideration of her or of himself.

I hope I can get rid of you, she thought, trying desperately to withdraw from him as from the violent touch of cruel hands.

But I'm afraid. I'm afraid. Those ESP men at Duke . . . Her mind sought wildly for a shadowy memory. *Didn't they shield their people with lead, separate them miles and miles?* And he got tangled pictures of men in white robes, separating "sensitive" people, shielding them in a variety of ways, but with no effect on their abilities to read each other's minds. He let his contempt slap at her for believing such nonsense.

But she was right. The edges of perception sharpened; they did not fade. There was no shutting her off. And there was always the continuing and horrible sense of familiarity. It was almost as if the eyes of his mind were being drawn against his will toward a disgusting part of himself held up in a mirror.

Going down the walk to his home he was conscious of her in her apartment. But he concentrated on holding his own line of thought. His home, its barbered lawns and well-trimmed hedges, the whiteness and neatness of it, the pattern of twigs in the single tree was bringing him, momentarily, a pool of quiet.

Spare . . . bare . . . such crude design. The house was suddenly mirrored back at him from her mind. Suddenly he saw: *Petty bourgeois cheapness. All richness and complexity sacrificed to achieve a banal balance.*

Damn you.

Sorry. I didn't mean to hurt. But her laughter and scorn were still there under the surface.

And he couldn't help being infected by her thoughts. The landscape he owned and loved: *Poor stuff. Deliberately manufactured by a second-rate artist for people with third-rate taste.*

And Charlotte, so calm and sweet. Suddenly he saw how lost she was, the lines of frustration around her mouth.

Poor thing, the girl thought. *No children. No love.* Then came more than scorn. *You needed release and you've used her—just like the men you work with. You—*

There was no escaping her. Her scorn or shame or teasing laughter was omnipresent.

He didn't dare go back to work, for his confusion would have been noticed, and that was something he could not have borne. Luckily his post was high enough that he could make his own schedule, and could remain at home for a few days.

But the days were torture. There was not one flicker of his thought, one twinge of emotion that did not reflect the girl. Worse, he caught all of hers. Not one of his her secret shabbinesses she he did not know. The tangled days ended only in nights where their tangled dreams were all nightmares to him. It was as if his whole life were being immersed in deep deep seas where nothing swam but strangeness which came echoing and re-echoing through caverns of mirrors.

He lasted three days at home. During those three days he sought desperately for some reasonable explanation of the sudden, shocking contact that they had made. He half-believed now that the knowledge of her had always been there, just below the surface, fended off, forcing itself up to his attention only when his defenses were down in sleep—the source of his strange nightmares. That day on the subway his defenses had been all but worn away by his work; and her defenses, were they ever up? Besides, she had just sold one of her silly pictures and was in love with the entire world of people. By the most fantastic of bad luck they had to meet just at that time. It was their eyes meeting that finally pierced the thin shells holding them apart. Maybe there was something to the old wives' tales about the magic meeting of eyes, windows of souls. But all that was superstitious nonsense; he couldn't believe it.

He sought out one of the books by Rhine, but couldn't believe that either. He would have rather believed he was insane. Particularly he wouldn't believe that distance would make no difference. He decided to put a continent between them to see if that couldn't break the contact. He had Charlotte drive him to La Guardia Field and he took the first plane west.

It was a bad mistake, for on the plane there were no distractions, and her presence remained as clear as it had always been. He could not move around. He found he could not force himself to concentrate on a book. Having been lucky enough to find a seat to himself, he couldn't engage anyone in conversation. There was nothing to do but lean back and close his eyes and live her life with her. That evening on the plane he became convinced that since he could not get rid of her, he must dominate her.

It was her peculiar religious notions which finally convinced him. She was walking through a tiny park at evening; it was spring and the trees were just beginning to bud. She paused before one tree, her stomach growling a little with hunger, sensing the city smells, the roar, the silence of the trees. *The tree reaches. Steely, reaching up among the stones of the city. Each bud tingles, leaves opening like angles' wings. Root tips reach down, tender in the dark. The smooth reach up of the branches. Like you, Quincy. Like the feel of your body, Quincy.*

And her eyes traced each line of the branches, following the angles, the twists. And as she reached the very tip of the tree, she felt something very terrible to him—a kind of ecstatic union with the life of the tree. And she glanced down then to where a pair of lovers were strolling, hand in hand, along the littered walk, her artist's mind stripping away their clothes, seeing their bodies almost as she had seen the tree. *The bodies are juicy, longing for one another, sweet muscles running along the bones. Aren't they lovely, Quincy?* she thought. *Look at the girl's hip thrust, the man's thighs. What a sweet rolling they're going to have.*

Can't you think of anything else?

I won't let you spoil it. It's too lovely an evening. And she turned toward a shabby little church. He had no desire to continue in such an unprofitable direction, and tried to steer her away from the church by playing on her hunger. She caught his purpose immediately and carefully concentrated on her own. She ignored his disgust and intellectual scorn as she entered through the arched doorway. There in the dimness she bought a candle, genuflected, and placed it before the Virgin.

It was a wordless prayer. For protection, for understanding. As she glanced up at the rather crude piece of statuary, she ticketed it for what it was, but moved beyond it to an inflated vision of feminine richness and purity. Here was the woman, the full breast at which God tugged, utterly pure but female, bowels and womb, hunger and pain. *How she knows what I feel! So high, so beautiful, and yet she understands!*

Only after contemplating the Virgin did she turn to the crucifix. Here was all vigorous male sweetness, hanging from bloody nails. Quincy Summerfield tried to shy away, hold off this whole concept. He shaped an obscene word, but again the girl ignored him. Her feeling was too strong. The remoteness and terror and wonder and glory that were embodied in the tree and in the bones and blood of all men in their suffering, were richly present in the figure of the crucifix; *the timeless which betrayed itself into the agony of time out of compassion for* me *and* my *weakness.* She knelt in a submission to unreason that made Quincy there in the plane writhe in protest. But she was too submissive. He felt the position of her body as she knelt, and knew that she was a trifle off balance. Abruptly he willed a sudden small twitch of her leg and she went sprawling forward on her face. Quincy winced with the bump but jeered at her none the less.

That's mean—trying to make me look foolish.

Not any more foolish than kneeling before a piece of plaster. Disgusting. All that nonsense you have in your head. All that untruth.

She was furious. She pushed herself to her feet and stared at her dirty hands, down at the dust on her spring dress. She thought of a bath and quick meal, and left the church hurriedly. She ignored him, but as she went up the stairs to the apartment which, under Quincy's prodding, she had brought into some kind of order, she was still numbly angry.

What you did there in the church was shameful, she thought. *I'll get even with you. It's not all nonsense. It's all true and you know it's true. Of all the people in the world, why did I have to get you?*

She stripped deliberately before a mirror and watched herself so he would see her. It was a good body, high and full in the breasts, slender of waist, flaring and tapering down to the dirty feet. She ran her hands over it, under it, between, concentrating on the sensations of her fingers, feeling his responses to them.

Then abruptly she stopped and went to the phone and called her friend Arthur. She was tingling with desire and Quincy felt his gorge rise, even as his loins tightened.

I'm feeling lonely, Arthur. Could you come right over? I'll be in the bathtub, but come on in. All right then, join me if you want to.

Fifteen minutes later, Quincy staggered to the rest room on the plane, locked himself in and sat down on the seat. With trembling fingers he took out his nail file and stripped back his coat sleeve. His jaw was tight, his eyes were a little mad. He looked for a place in the arm where it seemed large veins were not present. With one hard jab he stuck the nail file a half inch deep into his arm and forced himself to leave it there. Then he jiggled it slowly back and forth, letting the pain of it sweep over him in red waves, concentrating completely on the pain until the girl began to scream.

Get him out of there, he said through clenched teeth. *Get him out of there!*

And when, finally, a very bewildered Arthur was ejected from her apartment, as yet only half dressed, he pulled the nail file from his arm and let his head lean for a moment against the cool steel of the washbowl. He had learned how to control her. She could not stand his pain.

If it had not been for his own betrayal of himself, if his own revulsion had not been weak, she would not have been able to get as far as she had with Arthur. Still, in the end, it was his mind, not the anarchy of his body that had won out.

Lying there with his head against the steel, with his arm still bloody, knowing she was lying across the bed half-conscious with frustration and his pain, he took over control completely for a moment and pushed her up to a sitting position. She pushed herself up to a sitting position. She moaned slightly in protest, but allowed him to move her toward her closet, make her reach for her pajamas. He sensed that she almost enjoyed it. She enjoyed their complete rapport of feeling. And even with the pain in his arm, he found there was a certain joy in her emotion; and it was as if with his own mind alone he thought of what wholeness an experience together could be.

It was a peculiar moment for something like that to begin, but his steel-like control meshed together and held the rush of her emotion and his pain. Her admiration for his strength warmed him; she even shared in his triumph, and suddenly both of them found the experience good—not so much the experience itself but the perfect unity of thought and feeling that followed it.

Quincy cleaned his arm and bound it with a handkerchief, and when he went back to his seat the stewardess brought him his dinner. In her apartment the girl, too, ate, and their rapport persisted as they shared the savors of each other's food. He was firmly in control of their joint thought and feeling, but it was an experience richer than he had ever known. As they moved west, the desire for her physical presence grew and grew.

Wouldn't that magazine be shocked at our *togetherness?* she thought; and at that moment Quincy shared in her scorn of the bourgeois fetish.

They existed in that kind of rapport for the rest of the evening, he on the plane, she in the apartment, arranging for his ultimate return. Even in sleep they remained almost joined into a single entity.

It was a strange period. Quincy got off the plane in San Francisco, and almost directly boarded another going nonstop back to New York. Less than twenty-four hours after he left New York, he had returned and was walking down her street toward her walkup.

But then things changed. The shabby Greenwich Village street was filled with her memories, and she began to take precedence. Everything around him now was a part of her. All of her life began to engulf him. Her terrible disordered memories surrounded him, memories he could not repress.

He paused by the ugly little church where she had gone at times to make agonized confessions—only to dive back into the tangled messiness of her life again.

Not any more. Not messy any more. We'll be married and then...

He felt a blind impulse to enter the church to pour out his agony there. And find peace. Her impulse or his? He wrenched away. *Not now. Not ever...*

Only a few now . . . past the place where Fred and Arthur had fought that night. *Can't you stop remembering?*

And up five flights of ill-lit stairway, his mind filling with her anticipation. His mind filled with all the times she had gone up those stairs. His heart pounding with his anticipation. Knowing she was lounging there on the bed sofa in her blue dressing gown. Knowing the cocktail shaker was filled with martinis as only he could make them, dry and cold.

As his foot touched the landing he knew she was moving languidly from her couch toward the door, and her hand was on the door. And it was open. And she was standing before him.

Like a sleepwalker he moved past her and into the room, sensing now the subtler perfume of her. And she closed the door and he looked around the room, utterly numbed.

Then feeling came back and he saw that the room was beautiful. The pictures in their wild excess were ordered into a subtle harmony by their arrangement. For all of the dirt ingrained in it, the furniture was better than his own expensive pieces. It was all fuller and richer and more harmonious than anything he had ever experienced.

And the girl standing there, her dark hair about her shoulders!

My God, you're beautiful. She was beautiful and his thought reflected back into her mind and she flushed with pleasure. And he sensed her admiration of his lean white face and gray mustache, and the strength of his mind, and hard, lean feel of his body. And he knew the beauty of the room was completed by the two of them standing poised and not touching. Even the crucifix in the corner blended with them into one harmonious whole.

And she he reached out to a bare touching of hands . . . pause . . . then a sweeping together in their arms. And he felt his chest against her breast, against her chest his breast. His mouth against her mouth, her his mouth against . . .

Then the whole world went crashing out of control and there was nothing but the rawness of her passion and of his passion, her his—

Until his entire reason revolted and he could stand it no longer. The need to give way to the feel of his her mouth, this irrational disorder of giving and taking at the peak of sensation, this need he could not and would not meet. A fragment of himself broke away from the unity and grew, until the strongest part of his mind floated over the chaos of sensation and contemplated it with cold disgust. Not all of his mind, for part of himself was engulfed and protesting.

But part of him was icy and knew what to do almost as well as if he had planned it. He reached down into her memory and brought out her image of the purity of the Virgin draped sweetly in blue with the haloed babe in the crook of her arm. Deliberately he intensified the picture into an almost transcendent purity of spirit, vibrating with light and wonder. Instantly he wiped it out except for the blue robes, robes like her dressing gown, and filled them with the naked girl, her mouth agape in the throes of animal lust. Then back to the picture Virgin again, who moved slowly sorrowing, her eyes looking up.

The girl's eye looked up and sought the crucifix in the corner of the room, and his mind expanded it before her eyes to the living man on the cross, straining in agony and in sorrow.

Quickly now. In complete control now of her whole mind and of his. *Passion—your passion.* He wiped away the Christ figure from her mind and mocked her with the writhing body of Arthur, and dissolved it into an image of his own face. And wiped that away to present the face of the suffering Christ. A gross female figure loomed, its mouth agape. *My mouth all horrible. No! No! Me driving the phallic nails in those sweet palms! The bones making a crushing sound.*

The girl screamed, and broke away from Quincy Summerfield, his eyes wild.

That's what you are. That's what you know you are.

She covered her face with her hand, jerking this way and that, trying to get away from him. Trying to get away from his her acknowledgment of her naked self, while she he lashed herself with disgust.

It was enough. Quincy's mind contemplated her but did no more.

It was only herself now that turned and ran, a decision shaping in her mind. She shaped the decision for herself and Quincy exulted in it, knowing that by her own insane standards she was damning herself.

She rushed weeping to the French windows opening on her little sundeck. She flung them open and did not pause but plunged on and out and over the parapet . . .

The railing smashed at his knees and he curled up suddenly with the pain, waiting the greater pain. He closed his eyes and set his teeth. Buildings tumbled through her eyes. Shrill sinking in the belly. A face flashed up from the street. Whirl of cars in the street. The fire hydrant rushed up red at her. The street plunged up, up, up. *Oh Chri*——The smash of red pain, unendurable to breaking!

Then there was a great darkness, a slow diminution of unconscious sensation. Then she was gone.

Quincy Summerfield pulled himself to his feet, and staggered toward a window. Peering through the curtain he saw the limp, twisted, huddled body near the fire hydrant, people running toward it.

She couldn't even die without a mess! he thought.

He left unobserved. He took the back stairs and there was no one to say that he had been there. A few blocks from her apartment, he hailed a cab and went to a hotel. He was utterly safe.

Oh, the blessed peace of it. She was gone, gone for good. There was nothing left of her disorderly presence but the gray emptiness a man might feel if he had lost an arm. There was still that: the gray ghostly taint of her. It was sure to pass, though, and this night he would sleep, really sleep for the first time in days.

He didn't even want Charlotte that night. He only wanted to be alone—and sleep. He hadn't been in the hotel room five minutes before he was in bed, and dozing.

Dozing, not sleeping. It wasn't that he worried about the thing he had done. It had been reasonable and right. Her own disorderly weakness had betrayed her. But there was the lingering gray sense of her presence that was not yet going away. That, and the feeling that he had lost half of his life.

Lost?

No.

The sense of her presence was sharpening into a live reality. He was wide awake . . . or was it nightmare again?

No—she was there. She paid no attention to him. This was frightening.

She was focused unwaveringly upon a distant light, a light that grew, that became brilliant, with a searching intensity that she had never known before. And through it all, there was a sense of the wonder of longing changed into beauty that was all but unbearable.

And his mind was filled with a sense of richness and variety and order that he had never believed could exist.

But the searching light went on, and suddenly all her life burned through him in the flicker of a dream. And his life. And then out of the center of that purity of light there was a sorrowing, and she was moving away from the light. Away from the light, and he felt her whimpering like a child afraid of the dark. Away from the light . . .

Quincy Summerfield woke. Sat straight up in bed and screamed. The throat-tearing scream of a full-grown man in an agony of terror.

For the channel was wide open to the absolute chaos of her eternity.

Balaam

Anthony Boucher

"What is a 'man'?" Rabbi Chaim Acosta demanded, turning his back on the window and its view of pink sand and infinite pink boredom. "You and I, Mule, in our respective ways, work for the salvation of *men*—as you put it, for the brotherhood of *man* under the fatherhood of God. Very well, let us define our terms: Whom, or, more precisely, *what,* are we interested in saving?"

Father Aloysius Malloy shifted uncomfortably and reluctantly closed the *American Football Yearbook* which had been smuggled in on the last rocket, against all weight regulations, by one of his communicants. I honestly like Chaim, he thought, not merely (or is that the right word?) with brotherly love, nor even out of the deep gratitude I owe him, but with special individual liking; and I respect him. He's a brilliant man—too brilliant to take a dull post like this in his stride. But he *will* get off into discussions which are much too like what one of my Jesuit professors called "disputations."

"What did you say, Chaim?" he asked.

The rabbi's black Sephardic eyes sparkled. "You know very well what I said, Mule; and you're stalling for time. Please indulge me. Our religious duties here are not so arduous as we might wish; and since you won't play chess . . . "

". . . and you," said Father Malloy unexpectedly, "refuse to take any interest diagramming football plays . . . "

"*Touché.* Or am I? Is it my fault that as an Israeli I fail to share the peculiar American delusion that football means something other than rugby and soccer? Whereas chess—" He looked at the priest reproachfully. "Mule," he said, "you have led me into a digression."

"It was a try. Like the time the whole Southern California line thought I had the ball for once and Leliwa walked over for the winning TD."

"What," Acosta repeated, "is *man?* Is it by definition a member of the genus *H. sapiens* inhabiting the planet Sol III and its colonies?"

"The next time we tried the play," said Malloy resignedly, "Leliwa was smeared for a ten-yard loss."

The two *men* met on the sands of Mars. It was an unexpected meeting, a meeting in itself uneventful, and yet one of the turning points in the history of *men* and their universe.

The *man* from the colony base was on a routine patrol—a patrol imposed by the captain for reasons of discipline and activity for activity's sake rather than from any need for protection in this uninhabited waste. He had seen, over beyond the next rise, what he would have sworn was the braking blaze of a landing rocket—if he hadn't known that the next rocket wasn't due for another week. Six and a half days, to be exact, or even more exactly, six days, eleven hours, and twenty-three minutes, Greenwich Interplanetary. He knew the time so exactly because he, along with half the garrison, Father Malloy, and those screwball Israelis, was due for rotation then. So no matter how much it looked like a rocket, it couldn't be one; but it was something happening on his patrol, for the first time since he'd come to this God-forsaken hole, and he might as well look into it and get his name on a report.

The *man* from the spaceship also knew the boredom of the empty planet. Alone of his crew, he had been there before, on the first voyage when they took the samples and set up the observation outposts. But did that make the captain even listen to him? Hell, no; the captain knew all about the planet from the sample analyses and had no time to listen to a guy who'd really been there. So all he got out of it was the privilege of making the first reconnaissance. Big deal! One fast look around reconnoitering a few googols of sand grains and then back to the ship. But there was some kind of glow over that rise there. It couldn't be lights; theirs was the scout ship, none of the others had landed yet. Some kind of phosphorescent life they'd missed the first time round . . . ? Maybe now the captain would believe that the sample analyses didn't tell him everything.

The two *men* met at the top of the rise.

One *man* saw the horror of seemingly numberless limbs, of a headless torso, of a creature so alien that it walked in its glittering bare flesh in this freezing cold and needed no apparatus to supplement the all but nonexistent air.

One *man* saw the horror of an unbelievably meager four limbs, of a torso topped with an ugly lump like some unnatural growth, of a creature so alien that it smothered itself with heavy clothing in this warm climate and cut itself off from this invigorating air.

And both *men* screamed and ran.

"There is an interesting doctrine," said Rabbi Acosta, "advanced by one of your writers, C. S. Lewis . . ."

"He was an Episcopalian," said Father Malloy sharply.

"I apologize." Acosta refrained from pointing out that Anglo-Catholic would have been a more accurate term. "But I believe that many in your church have found his writings, from your point of view, doctrinally sound? He advances the doctrine of what he calls *hnaus*—intelligent beings with souls who are the children of God, whatever their physical shape or planet of origin."

"Look, Chaim," said Malloy with an effort toward patience. "Doctrine or no doctrine, there just plain aren't any such beings. Not in this solar system anyway. And if you're going to go interstellar on me, I'd just as soon read the men's microcomics."

"Interplanetary travel existed only in such literature once. But of course if you'd rather play chess . . ."

"My specialty," said the man once known to sports writers as Mule Malloy, "was running interference. Against you I need somebody to run interference *for.*"

"Let us take the sixteenth Psalm of David, which you call the fifteenth, having decided, for reasons known only to your God and mine, that Psalms nine and ten are one. There is a phrase in there which, if you'll forgive me, I'll quote in Latin; your Saint Jerome is often more satisfactory than any English translator. *Benedicam Dominum, qui tribuit mihi intellectum."*

"Blessed be the Lord, who schools me," murmured Malloy, in the standard Knox translation.

"But according to Saint Jerome: *I shall bless the Lord, who bestows on me*—just how should one render *intellectum?*—not merely *intellect,* but *perception, comprehension* . . . what Hamlet means when he says of *man: In apprehension how like a god!"*

Words change their meanings.

Apprehensively, one *man* reported to his captain. The captain first swore, then scoffed, then listened to the story again. Finally he said, "I'm sending a full squad back with you to the place where—maybe—you saw this thing. If it's for real, these mother-dighting, bug-eyed monsters are going to curse the day they ever set a God-damned tentacle on Mars." The *man* decided it was no use trying to explain that the worst of it was it *wasn't* bug-eyed; any kind of eyes in any kind of head would have been something. And they weren't even quite tentacles either....

Apprehensively, too, the other *man* made his report. The captain scoffed first and then swore, including some select remarks on underhatched characters who knew all about a planet because they'd been there once. Finally he said, "We'll see if a squad of real observers can find any trace of your egg-eating, limbless monsters; and if we find them, they're going to be God-damned sorry they were ever hatched." It was no use, the *man* decided, trying to explain that it wouldn't have been so bad if it *had* been limbless, like in the picture tapes; but just *four* limbs....

"What is a *man?*" Rabbi Acosta repeated, and Mule Malloy wondered why his subconscious synapses had not earlier produced the obvious appropriate answer.

"Man," he recited, *"is a creature composed of body and soul, and made to the image and likeness of God."*

"From that echo of childish singsong, Mule, I judge that is a correct catechism response. Surely the catechism must follow it up with some question about that likeness? Can it be a likeness in"—his hand swept up and down over his own body with a graceful gesture of contempt—*"this* body?"

"This likeness to God," Malloy went on reciting, *"is chiefly in the soul."*

"Aha!" The Sephardic sparkle was brighter than ever.

The words went on, the centers of speech following the synaptic patterns engraved in parochial school as the needle followed the grooves of an antique record. *"All creatures bear some resemblance to God inasmuch as they exist. Plants and animals resemble Him insofar as they have life..."*

"I can hardly deny so profound a statement."

"... but none of these creatures is made to the image and likeness of God. Plants and animals do not have a rational soul, such as man has, by which they might know and love God."

"As do all good *hnaus.* Go on; I am not sure that our own scholars have stated it so well. Mule, you are invaluable!"

Malloy found himself catching a little of Acosta's excitement. He had known these words all his life; he had recited them the Lord knows how many times. But he was not sure that he had ever listened to them before. And he wondered for a moment how often even his Jesuit professors, in their profound consideration of the x^n's of theology, have ever paused to reconsider these childhood ABC's.

"How is the soul like God?" he asked himself the next catechistic question, and answered, *"The soul is like God because it is a spirit*

having understanding and free will and is destined . . . "

"Reverend gentlemen!" The reverence was in the words only. The interrupting voice of Captain Dietrich Fassbänder differed little in tone from his normal address to a buck private of the Martian Legion.

Mule Malloy said, "Hi, Captain." He felt half-relieved, half-disappointed, as if he had been interrupted while unwrapping a present whose outlines he was just beginning to glimpse. Rabbi Acosta smiled wryly and said nothing.

"So this is how you spend your time? No Martian natives, so you have to keep in practice trying to convert each other, is that it?"

Acosta made a light gesture which might have been polite acknowledgment of what the captain evidently considered a joke. "The Martian day is so tedious we have been driven to talking shop. Your interruption is welcome. Since you so rarely seek out our company, I take it you bring some news. Is it, God grant, that the rotation rocket is arriving a week early?"

"No, damn it," Fassbänder grunted. (He seemed to take a certain pride, Malloy had observed, in carefully not tempering his language for the ears of clergymen.) "Then I'd have a German detachment instead of your Israelis, and I'd know where I stood. I suppose it's all very advisable politically for every state in the UW to contribute a detachment in rotation; but I'd sooner either have my regular legion garrison doubled, or two German detachments regularly rotating. That time I had the pride of Pakistan here . . . Damn it, you new states haven't had time to develop a military tradition!"

"Father Malloy," the rabbi asked gently, "are you acquainted with the sixth book of what you term the Old Testament?"

"Thought you fellows were tired of talking shop," Fassbänder objected.

"Rabbi Acosta refers to the Book of Joshua, Captain. And I'm afraid, God help us, that there isn't a state or a tribe that hasn't a tradition of war. Even your Prussian ancestors might have learned a trick or two from the campaigns of Joshua—or for that matter, from the Cattle Raid on Cooley, when the Hound of Cullen beat off the armies of Queen Maeve. And I've often thought, too, that it'd do your strategists no harm to spend a season or two at quarterback, if they had the wind. Did you know that Eisenhower played football, and against Jim Thorpe once, at that? And . . . "

"But I don't imagine," Acosta interposed, "that you came here to talk shop either, Captain?"

"Yes," said Captain Fassbänder, sharply and unexpectedly. "My shop and, damn it, yours. Never thought I'd see the day when I . . . " He broke off and tried another approach. "I mean, of course, a chaplain is part of an army. You're both army officers, technically speaking, one in the Martian Legion, one in the Israeli forces; but it's highly unusual to ask a man of the cloth to . . . ”

“To praise the Lord and pass the ammunition, as the folk legend has it? There are precedents among my people, and among Father Malloy's as well, though rather different ideas are attributed to the founder of his church. What is it, Captain? Or wait, I know: We are besieged by alien invaders and Mars needs every able-bodied man to defend her sacred sands. Is that it?”

“Well . . . God damn it. . . . ” Captain Fassbänder's cheeks grew purple. “. . . YES!” he exploded.

The situation was so hackneyed in $_3$V and microcomics war that it was less a matter of explaining it than of making it seem real. Dietrich Fassbänder's powers of exposition were not great, but his sincerity was evident and in itself convincing.

“Didn't believe it myself at first,” he admitted. “But he was right. Our patrol ran into a patrol of . . . of *them*. There was a skirmish; we lost two men but killed one of the things. Their small arms use explosive propulsion of metal much like ours; God knows what they might have in that ship to counter our A-warheads. But we've got to put up a fight for Mars; and that's where you come in.”

The two priests looked at him wordlessly, Acosta with a faint air of puzzled withdrawal, Malloy almost as if he expected the captain to start diagramming the play on a blackboard.

“You especially, Rabbi. I'm not worried about your boys, Father. We've got a Catholic chaplain on this rotation because this bunch of legionnaires is largely Poles and Irish-Americans. They'll fight all right, and we'll expect you to say a field mass beforehand, and that's about all. Oh, and that fool gunner Olszewski has some idea he'd like his A-cannon sprinkled with holy water; I guess you can handle that without any trouble.

“But your Israelis are a different problem, Acosta. They don't know the meaning of discipline—not what we call discipline in the legion; and Mars doesn't mean to them what it does to a legionnaire. And, besides, a lot of them have got a . . . hell, guess I shouldn't call it superstition, but a kind of . . . well, reverence—awe, you might say—about you, Rabbi. They say you're a miracle-worker.”

“He is,” said Mule Malloy simply. “He saved my life.”

He could still feel that extraordinary invisible power (a “force-field,” one of the technicians later called it, as he cursed the shots that had destroyed the machine past all analysis) which had bound him helpless there in that narrow pass, too far from the dome for rescue by any patrol. It was his first week on Mars, and he had hiked too long, enjoying the long, easy strides of low gravity and alternately meditating on the versatility of the Creator of planets and on that Year Day long ago when he had blocked out the most famous of All-American linebackers to bring about the most impressive of Rose Bowl upsets.

Sibiryakov's touchdown made the headlines; but he and Sibiryakov knew why that touchdown happened, and he felt his own inner warmth... and was that sinful pride or just self-recognition? And then he was held as no line had ever held him and the hours passed and no one on Mars could know where he was and when the patrol arrived they said, "The Israeli chaplain sent us." And later Chaim Acosta, laconic for the first and only time, said simply, "I knew where you were. It happens to me sometimes."

Now Acosta shrugged and his graceful hand waved deprecation. "Scientifically speaking, Captain, I believe that I have, on occasion, a certain amount of extrasensory perception and conceivably a touch of some of the other *psi* faculties. The Rhinists at Tel Aviv are quite interested in me; but my faculties too often refuse to perform on laboratory command. But 'miracle-working' is a strong word. Remind me to tell you some time the story of the guaranteed genuine miracle-working rabbi from Lwow."

"Call it miracles, call it ESP, you've got something, Acosta..."

"I shouldn't have mentioned Joshua," the rabbi smiled.

"Surely you aren't suggesting that I try a miracle to win your battle for you?"

"Hell with that," snorted Fassbänder. "It's your men. They've got it fixed in their minds that you're a ... a saint. Now, you Jews don't have saints, do you?"

"A nice question in semantics," Chaim Acosta observed quietly.

"Well, a prophet. Whatever you people call it. And we've got to make men out of your boys. Stiffen their backbones, send 'em in there knowing they're going to win."

"Are they?" Acosta asked flatly.

"God knows. But they sure as hell won't if they don't think so. So it's up to you."

"What is?"

"They may pull a sneak attack on us, but I don't think so. Way I see it, they're as surprised and puzzled as we are; and they need time to think the situation over. We'll attack before dawn tomorrow; and to make sure your Israelis go in there with fighting spirit, you're going to curse them."

"Curse my men?"

"Potztausend Sapperment noch einmal!" Captain Fassbänder's English was flawless, but not adequate to such a situation as this. "Curse *them!* The ... the *things,* the aliens, the invaders, whatever the *urverdammt* bloody hell you want to call them!"

He could have used far stronger language without offending either chaplain. Both had suddenly realized that he was perfectly serious.

"A formal curse, Captain?" Chaim Acosta asked. "Anathema maranatha? Perhaps Father Malloy would lend me bell, book, and candle?"

Mule Malloy looked uncomfortable. "You read about such things, Captain," he admitted. "They were done, a long time ago. . . . "

"There's nothing in your religion against it, is there, Acosta?"

"There is . . . precedent," the rabbi confessed softly.

"Then it's an order, from your superior officer. I'll leave the mechanics up to you. You know how it's done. If you need anything . . . what kind of bell?"

"I'm afraid that was meant as a joke, Captain."

"Well, these *things* are no joke. And you'll curse them tomorrow morning before all your men."

"I shall pray," said Rabbi Chaim Acosta, "for guidance . . . " But the captain was already gone. He turned to his fellow priest. "Mule, you'll pray for me too?" The normally agile hands hung limp at his side.

Mule Malloy nodded. He groped for his rosary as Acosta silently left the room.

Now entertain conjecture of a time when two infinitesimal forces of *men*—one half-forgotten outpost garrison, one small scouting fleet—spend the night in readying themselves against the unknown, in preparing to meet on the morrow to determine, perhaps, the course of centuries for a galaxy.

Two *men* are feeding sample range-finding problems into the computer.

"That God-damned Fassbänder," says one. "I heard him talking to our commander. 'You and your men have never understood the meaning of discipline . . .'!"

"Prussians," the other grunts. He has an Irish face and an American accent. "Think they own the earth. When we get through here, let's dump all the Prussians into Texas and let 'em fight it out. Then we can call the state Kilkenny."

"What did you get on that last? . . . Check. Fassbänder's 'discipline' is for peace—spit-and-polish to look pretty here in our sandy pink nowhere. What's the payoff? Fassbänder's great-grandfathers were losing two world wars while mine were creating a new nation out of nothing. Ask the Arabs if we have no discipline. Ask the British . . ."

"Ah, the British. Now *my* great-grandfather was in the IRA . . ."

Two *men* are integrating the electrodes of the wave-hurler.

"It isn't bad enough we get drafted for this expedition to nowhere; we have to have an egg-eating Nangurian in command."

"And a Tryldian scout to bring the first report. What's your reading there? . . . Check."

"'A Tryldian to tell a lie and a Nangurian to force it into truth,'" the first quotes.

"Now, brothers," says the *man* adjusting the microvernier on the telelens, "the Goodman assures us these monsters are true. We must unite in love for each other, even Tryldians and Nangurians, and wipe them out. The Goodman has promised us his blessing before battle..."

"The Goodman," says the first, "can eat the egg he was hatched from."

"The rabbi," says a *man* checking the oxyhelms, "can take his blessing and shove it up Fassbänder. I'm no Jew in his sense. I'm a sensible, rational atheist who happens to be an Israeli."

"And, I," says his companion, "am a Romanian who believes in the God of my fathers and therefore gives allegiance to His state of Israel. What is a Jew who denies the God of Moses? To call him still a Jew is to think like Fassbänder."

"They've got an edge on us," says the first. *"They* can breathe here. These oxyhelms run out in three hours. What do we do then? Rely on the rabbi's blessing?"

"I said the God of my fathers, and yet my great-grandfather thought as you do and still fought to make Israel live anew. It was his son who, like so many others, learned that he must return to Jerusalem in spirit as well as body."

"Sure, we had the Great Revival of orthodox religion. So what did it get us? Troops that need a rabbi's blessing before a commander's orders."

"Many men have died from orders. How many from blessings?"

"I fear that few die well who die in battle . . . " the *man* reads in Valkram's great epic of the siege of Tolnishri.

". . . for how [the *man* is reading of the eve of Agincourt in his micro-Shakespeare] *can they charitably dispose of anything when blood is in their argument?"*

". . . and if these do not die well [so Valkram wrote] *how grievously must their bad deaths be charged against the Goodman who blesses them into battle . . . "*

"And why not?" Chaim Acosta flicked the question away with a wave of his long fingers.

The bleep (even Acosta was not so linguistically formal as to call it a bubble jeep) bounced along over the sand toward the rise which overlooked the invaders' ship. Mule Malloy handled the wheel with solid efficiency and said nothing.

"I *did* pray for guidance last night," the rabbi asserted, almost as if in self-defense. "I . . . I had some strange thoughts for a while; but they make very little sense this morning. After all, I am an officer in the army. I do have a certain obligation to my superior officer and to my men. And when I became a rabbi, a teacher, I was specifically ordained to decide questions of law and ritual. Surely this case falls within that authority of mine."

Abruptly the bleep stopped.

"What's the matter, Mule?"

"Nothing . . . Wanted to rest my eyes a minute . . . Why did you become ordained, Chaim?"

"Why did you? Which of us understands all the infinite factors of heredity and environment which lead us to such a choice? Or even, if you will, to such a being chosen? Twenty years ago it seemed the only road I could possibly take; now . . . We'd better get going, Mule."

The bleep started up again.

"A curse sounds so melodramatic and medieval; but is it in essence any different from a prayer for victory, which chaplains offer up regularly? As I imagine you did in your field mass. Certainly all of your communicants are praying for victory to the Lord of Hosts—and as Captain Fassbänder would point out, it makes them better fighting men. I will confess that even as a teacher of the law, I have no marked doctrinal confidence in the efficacy of a curse. I do not expect the spaceship of the invaders to be blasted by the forked lightning of Yahweh. But my men have an exaggerated sort of faith in me, and I owe it to them to do anything possible to strengthen their morale. Which is all the legion or any other army expects of chaplains anyway; we are no longer priests of the Lord, but boosters of morale—a type of sublimated YMCA secretary. Well, in my case, say YMHA."

The bleep stopped again.

"I never knew your eyes to be so sensitive before," Acosta observed tartly.

"I thought you might want a little time to think it over," Malloy ventured.

"I've thought it over. What else have I been telling you? Now please, Mule. Everything's all set. Fassbänder will explode completely if I don't speak my curse into this mike in two minutes."

Silently Mule Malloy started up the bleep.

"Why did I become ordained?" Acosta backtracked. "That's no question really. The question is why have I remained in a profession to which I am so little suited. I will confess to you, Mule, and to you only, that I have not the spiritual humility and patience that I might desire. I itch for something beyond the humdrum problems of a congregation or an army detachment. Sometimes I have felt that I should drop everything else and concentrate on my *psi* faculties, that they might lead me to this goal I seek without understanding. But they are too erratic. I know the law, I love the ritual, but I am not good as a rabbi, a teacher, because..."

For the third time the bleep stopped, and Mule Malloy said, "Because you are a saint."

And before Chaim Acosta could protest, he went on, "Or a prophet, if you want Fassbänder's distinction. There are all kinds of saints and prophets. There are the gentle, humble, patient ones like Francis of Assisi and Job and Ruth—or do you count women? And there are God's firebrands, the ones of fierce intellect and dreadful determination, who shake the history of God's elect, the saints who have reached through sin to salvation with a confident power that is the reverse of the pride of Lucifer, cast from the same ringing metal."

"Mule . . . !" Acosta protested. "This isn't you. These aren't your words. And you didn't learn these in parochial school..."

Malloy seemed not to hear him. "Paul, Thomas More, Catherine of Siena, Augustine," he recited in rich cadence. "Elijah, Ezekiel, Judas Maccabeus, Moses, David... You are a prophet, Chaim. Forget the rationalizing double talk of the Rhinists and recognize whence your powers come, how you were guided to save me, what the 'strange thoughts' were that you had during last night's vigil of prayer. You are a prophet—and you are not going to curse *men,* the children of God."

Abruptly Malloy slumped forward over the wheel. There was silence in the bleep. Chaim Acosta stared at his hands as if he knew no gesture for this situation.

"Gentlemen!" Captain Fassbänder's voice was even more rasping than usual over the telecom. "Will you please get the blessed lead out and get up that rise? It's two minutes, twenty seconds, past zero!"

Automatically Acosta depressed the switch and said, "Right away, Captain."

Mule Malloy stirred and opened his eyes. "Was that Fassbänder?"

"Yes . . . But there's no hurry, Mule. I can't understand it. What made you...?"

"I don't understand it, either. Never passed out like that before. Doctor used to say that head injury in the Wisconsin game might—but after thirty years..."

Chaim Acosta sighed. "You sound like my Mule again. But before...

"Why? Did I say something? Seems to me like there was something important I wanted to say to you."

"I wonder what they'd say at Tel Aviv. Telepathic communication of subconscious minds? Externalization of thoughts that I was afraid to acknowledge consciously? Yes, you said something, Mule; and I was as astonished as Balaam when his ass spoke to him on his journey to... Mule!"

Acosta's eyes were blackly alight as never before, and his hands flickered eagerly. "Mule, do you remember the story of Balaam? It's in the fourth book of Moses..."

"Numbers? All I remember is he had a talking ass. I suppose there's a pun on *Mule?*"

"Balaam, son of Beor," said the rabbi with quiet intensity, "was a prophet in Moab. The Israelites were invading Moab, and King Balak ordered Balaam to curse them. His ass not only spoke to him; more important, it halted and refused to budge on the journey until Balaam had listened to a message from the Lord...

"You were right, Mule. Whether you remember what you said or not, whether your description of me was God's truth or the telepathic projection of my own ego, you were right in one thing: These invaders are *men,* by all the standards that we debated yesterday. Moreover they are *men* suited to Mars; our patrol reported them as naked and unprotected in this cold and this atmosphere. I wonder if they have scouted this planet before and selected it as suitable; that could have been some observation device left by them that trapped you in the pass, since we've never found traces of an earlier Martian civilization.

"Mars is not for us. We cannot live here normally; our scientific researches have proved fruitless; and we maintained an inert, bored garrison only because our planetary ego cannot face facts and surrender the symbol of our 'conquest of space.' These other *men* can live here, perhaps fruitfully, to the glory of God and eventually to the good of our own world as well, as two suitably populated planets come to know each other. You were right; I cannot curse *men."*

"GENTLEMEN!"

Deftly Acosta reached down and switched off the telecom. "You agree, Mule?"

"I...I...I guess I drive back now, Chaim?"

"Of course not. Do you think I want to face Fassbänder now? You drive on. At once. Up to the top of the rise. Or haven't you yet remembered the rest of the story of Balaam? He didn't stop at refusing to curse his fellow children of God. Not Balaam.

"He blessed them."

Mule Malloy had remembered that. He had remembered more, too. The phonograph needle had coursed through the grooves of Bible study on up to the thirty-first chapter of Numbers with its brief epilogue to the story of Balaam:

And Moses sent them to the war... and they warred against the Midianites, as the Lord commanded Moses; and they slew all the males... Balaam also the son of Beor they slew with the sword.

He looked at the tense face of Chaim Acosta, where exultation and resignation blended as they must in a man who knows at last the pattern of his life, and realized that Chaim's memory, too, went as far as the thirty-first chapter.

And there isn't a word in the Bible as to what became of the ass, thought Mule Malloy, and started the bleep up the rise.

A Word to Space

Winston Sanders

[*The story is set in the twenty-first century. The earth has been in radio communication with the people of a planet called Akron in Mu Cassiopeiae for one hundred and twenty-five years. Although advanced in science and technology the Akronites are ruled by a strict and fanatical theocracy. And—after seventy-five years of transmissions aimed at developing a system of communication—the Akronites have been sending us little in addition to religious messages (mostly long passages from their sacred texts). As a result, public interest in maintaining communication with the Akronites has diminished considerably; funding is difficult and the program is floundering. In fact, as the result of Akronite cults formed here on earth in response to these messages, there is some public hostility toward the communications project (Project Ozma). The protagonist of the story, Father Moriarty, S.J., a geologist as well as a priest, arrives at Project Ozma headquarters with an idea of how to save the project and at the same time do the Lord's work. As we enter the story, Father Moriarty is presenting his idea to Dr. Strand, Project Director.*]

". . . I don't say a word against shrewd politics." Moriarty's pipe had gone out. He made a project of relighting it, to stretch out the silence. At what he judged to be the critical instant, he drawled:

"I only suggest we continue in the same tradition."

Strand leaned back in his swivel chair. His glum hostility was dissolving into bewilderment. "What're you getting at? Look here, uh, Father, it's physically impossible for us to change the situation on Akron—"

"Oh?"

"What d'you mean?"

"We can send a reply to those sermons."

"What?" Strand almost went over backward.

"Other than scientific data, I mean."

"What the devil!" Strand sprang to his feet. His wrath returned, to blaze in face and eyes, to thicken his tone and lift one fist.

"I was afraid of this!" he exclaimed. "The minute I heard a priest was getting into the project, I expected this. You blind, bloody, queer-collared imbecile! You and the President—you're no better than those characters on Akron—do you think I'll let my work be degraded to such ends? Trying to convert another planet—and to one particular sect? By everything *I* believe holy, I'll resign first! Yes, and tell the whole country what's going on!"

Moriarty was startled at the violence of the reaction he had gotten. But he had seen worse, on other occasions. He smoked quietly until a pause in the tirade gave him a chance to say:

"Yes, my modest proposal does have the President's okay. And yes, it will have to be kept confidential. But neither he nor I are about to dictate to you. Nor are we about to spend the tax money of Protestants, Jews, Buddhists, unbelievers . . . even Akronists . . . on propagating our own Faith."

Strand, furiously pacing, stopped dead. The blood went slowly out of his cheeks. He gaped.

"For that matter," said Moriarty, "the Roman Catholic Church is not interested in converting other planets."

"Huh?" choked Strand.

"The Vatican decided more than a hundred years ago, back when space travel was still a mere theory, that the mission of Our Lord was to Earth only, to the human race. Other intelligent species did not share in the Fall and therefore do not require redemption. Or, if they are not in a state of grace—and the Akronites pretty clearly are not—then God will have made His own provision for them. I assure you, Dr. Strand, all I want is a free scientific and cultural exchange with Mu Cassiopeiae."

The director reseated himself, leaned elbows on desk and stared at the priest. He wet his lips before saying: "What do you think we should do, then?"

"Why, break up their theocracy. What else? There's no sin in that! My ecclesiastical superiors have approved my undertaking. They agree with me that the Akronist faith is so unreasonable it must be false, even for Akron. Its bad social effects on Earth must confirm this opinion. Naturally, the political repercussions would be disastrous if an attempt to subvert Akronism were publicly made. So any such messages we transmit must be kept strictly confidential. I'm sure you can arrange that."

Strand picked his cigarette out of the ashtray where he had dropped it, looked at the butt in a stupefied fashion, ground it out and took a fresh one.

"Maybe I got you wrong," he said grudgingly. "But, uh, how do you propose to do this? Wouldn't you have to try converting them to some other belief?"

"Impossible," said Moriarty. "Let's suppose we did transmit our Bible, the Summa, and a few similar books. The theocracy would suppress them at once, and probably cut off all contact with us."

He grinned. "However," he said, "in both the good and the bad senses of the word, casuistry is considered a Jesuit specialty." He pulled the typescript he had been reading from his coat pocket. "I haven't had a chance to study this latest document as carefully as I have the earlier ones, but it follows the typical pattern. For example, one is required 'to beat drums at the rising of Nomo,' which I gather is the third planet of the Ohio System. Since we don't have any Nomo, being in fact the third planet of *our* system, it might offhand seem as if we're damned. But the theocracy doesn't believe that, or it wouldn't bother with us. Instead, their theologians, studying the astronomical data we sent, have used pages and pages of hairsplitting logic to decide that for us Nomo is equivalent to Mars."

"What of it?" asked Strand; but his eyes were kindling.

"Certain questions occur to me," said Moriarty. "If I went up in a gravicar, I would see Mars rise sooner than would a person on the ground. None of the preachings we've received has explained which rising is to be considered official at a given longitude. A particularly devout worshiper nowadays could put an artificial satellite in such an orbit that Mars was always on its horizon. Then he could beat drums continuously, his whole life long. Would this gain him extra merit or would it not?"

"I don't see where that matters," said Strand.

"In itself, hardly. But it raises the whole question of the relative importance of ritual and faith. Which in turn leads to the question of faith versus works, one of the basic issues of the Reformation. As far as that goes, the schism between Catholic and Orthodox Churches in the early Middle Ages turned, in the last analysis, on one word in the Credo, *filioque*. Does the Holy Ghost proceed from the Father and the Son, or from the Father alone? You may think this is a trivial question, but to a person who really believes his religion it is not. Oceans of blood have been spilled because of that one word.

"Ah . . . returning to this sermon, though. I also wonder about the name 'Nomo.' The Akronite theologians conclude that in our case, Nomo means Mars. But this is based on the assumption that, by analogy with their own system, the next planet outward is meant. An assumption for which I can recall no justification in any of the scriptures they've sent us. Could it not be the next planet inward—Venus for us? But then their own 'Nomo' might originally have been Mu Cassipoeiae I, instead of III. In which case they've been damning themselves for centuries by celebrating the rising of the wrong planet!"

Strand pulled his jaw back up. "I take it, then," he said huskily, "you want to—"

"To send them some arguments much more elaborately reasoned than these examples, which I've simply made up on the spot," Moriarty answered. "I've studied the Akronist faith in detail . . . with two millennia of Christian disputation and haggling to guide me. I've prepared a little reply. It starts out fulsomely, thanking them for showing us the light and begging for further information on certain points which seem a trifle obscure. The rest of the message consists of quibbles, puzzles, and basic issues."

"And you really think— How long would this take to transmit?"

"Oh, I should imagine about one continuous month. Then from time to time, as they occur to us, we can send further inquiries."

Father James Moriarty leaned back, crossed his legs, and puffed benign blue clouds.

Okamura entered with three cups of coffee on a tray. Strand gulped. In an uneven voice he said, "Put 'em down and close the door, please. We've got work to do."

Epilogue

Moriarty was hoeing the cabbages behind the chapter house—which his superior had ordered as an exercise in humility—and speculating about the curious fossil beds recently discovered on Callisto—which his superior had not forbidden—when his wristphone buzzed. He detested the newfangled thing and wore it only because he was supposed to keep himself accessible. Some silly call was always interrupting his thoughts just when they got interesting. He delivered himself of an innocent but sonorous Latin phrase and pressed the ACCEPT button. "Yes?" he said.

"This is Phil Okamura." The tiny voice became unintelligible. Moriarty turned up the volume. Since he had passed the century mark his ears hadn't been so good; though praise God, the longevity treatment kept him otherwise sound. "—remember? The director of Project Ozma."

"Oh, yes." His heart thumped. "Of course I remember. How are you? We haven't met for . . . must be five years or more."

"Time sure passes. But I had to call you right away, Jim. Transmission from Akron resumed three hours ago."

"What?" Moriarty glanced at the sky. Beyond that clear blue, the stars and all God's handiwork! "What's their news?"

"Plenty. They explained that the reason we haven't received anything from them for a decade was that their equipment got wrecked in some of the fighting. But now things have quieted down. All those conflicting sects have been forced to reach a modus vivendi.

"Apparently the suggestions we sent, incidental to our first disruptive questions seventy-five years ago—and based on our own experience—were helpful: separation of church and state, and so on. Now the scientists are free to communicate with us, uncontrolled by anyone else. They're sure happy about that! The transition was painful, but three hundred years of stagnation on Akron have ended. They've got a huge backlog of data to give us. So if you want your geology straight off the tapes, you better hurry here. All the journals are going to be snowed under with our reports."

"Deo gratias. I'll ask my superior at once—I'm sure he'll let me—and catch the first robus headed your way." Father Moriarty switched off the phone and hobbled toward the house. After a moment he remembered he'd forgotten the hoe. Well, let somebody else pick the thing up. He had work to do!

Seventh Victim

Robert Sheckley

Stanton Frelaine sat at his desk, trying to look as busy as an executive should at nine-thirty in the morning. It was impossible. He couldn't concentrate on the advertisement he had written the previous night, couldn't think about business. All he could do was wait until the mail came.

He had been waiting for his notification for two weeks now. The government was behind schedule, as usual.

The glass door of his office was marked *Morger and Frelaine, Clothiers*. It opened, and E. J. Morger walked in, limping slightly from his old gunshot wound. His shoulders were bent; but at the age of 73, he wasn't worrying too much about his posture.

"Well, Stan?" Morger asked. "What about that ad?"

Frelaine had joined Morger 16 years ago, when he was 27. Together they had built Protec-Clothes into a million-dollar concern.

"I suppose you can run it," Frelaine said, handing the slip of paper to Morger. If only the mail would come earlier, he thought.

" 'Do you own a Protec-Suit?' " Morger read aloud, holding the paper close to his eyes. " 'The finest tailoring in the world has gone into Morger and Frelaine's Protec-Suit, to make it the leader in men's fashions.' "

Morger cleared his throat and glanced at Frelaine. He smiled and read on.

" 'Protec-Suit is the safest as well as the smartest. Every Protec-Suit comes with special built-in gun pocket, guaranteed not to bulge.

No one will know you are carrying a gun—except you. The gun pocket is exceptionally easy to get at, permitting fast, unhindered draw. Choice of hip or breast pocket.' Very nice," Morger commented.

Frelaine nodded morosely.

" 'The Protec-Suit Special has the fling-out gun pocket, the greatest modern advance in personal protection. A touch of the concealed button throws the gun into your hand, cocked, safeties off. Why not drop into the Protec-Store nearest you? Why not *be safe?'* "

"That's fine," Morger said. "That's a very nice, dignified ad." He thought for a moment, fingering his white mustache. "Shouldn't you mention that Protec-Suits come in a variety of styles, single and double-breasted, one and two button rolls, deep and shallow flares?"

"Right. I forgot."

Frelaine took back the sheet and jotted a note on the edge of it. Then he stood up, smoothing his jacket over his prominent stomach. Frelaine was 43, a little overweight, a little bald on top. He was an amiable-looking man with cold eyes.

"Relax," Morger said. "It'll come in today's mail."

Frelaine forced himself to smile. He felt like pacing the floor, but instead sat on the edge of the desk.

"You'd think it was my first kill," he said, with a deprecating smile.

"I know how it is," Morger said. "Before I hung up my gun, I couldn't sleep for a month, waiting for a notification. I know."

The two men waited. Just as the silence was becoming unbearable, the door opened. A clerk walked in and deposited the mail on Frelaine's desk.

Frelaine swung around and gathered up the letters. He thumbed through them rapidly and found what he had been waiting for—the long white envelope from ECB, with the official government seal on it.

"That's it!" Frelaine said, and broke into a grin. "That's the baby!"

"Fine." Morger eyed the envelope with interest, but didn't ask Frelaine to open it. It would be a breach of etiquette, as well as a violation in the eyes of the law. No one was supposed to know a Victim's name except his Hunter. "Have a good hunt."

"I expect to," Frelaine replied confidently. His desk was in order—had been for a week. He picked up his briefcase.

"A good kill will do you a world of good," Morger said, putting his hand lightly on Frelaine's padded shoulder. "You've been keyed up."

"I know" Frelaine grinned again and shook Morger's hand.

"Wish I was a kid again," Morger said, glancing down at his crippled leg with wryly humorous eyes. "Makes me want to pick up a gun again."

The old man had been quite a Hunter in his day. Ten successful hunts had qualified him for the exclusive Tens Club. And, of course, for each hunt, Morger had had to act as Victim, so he had 20 kills to his credit.

"I sure hope my Victim isn't anyone like you," Frelaine said, half in jest.

"Don't worry about it. What number will this be?"

"The seventh."

"Lucky seven. Go to it," Morger said. "We'll get you into the Tens yet."

Frelaine waved his hand and started out the door.

"Just don't get careless," warned Morger. "All it takes is a single slip and I'll need a new partner. If you don't mind, I like the one I've got now."

"I'll be careful," Frelaine promised.

Instead of taking a bus, Frelaine walked to his apartment. He wanted time to cool off. There was no sense in acting like a kid on his first kill.

As he walked, Frelaine kept his eyes strictly to the front. Staring at anyone was practically asking for a bullet, if the man happened to be serving as Victim. Some Victims shot if you just glanced at them. Nervous fellows. Frelaine prudently looked above the heads of the people he passed.

Ahead of him was a huge billboard, offering J. F. O'Donovan's services to the public.

"Victims!" the sign proclaimed in huge red letters. "Why take chances? Use an O'Donovan accredited Spotter. Let us locate your assigned killer. Pay after you get him!"

The sign reminded Frelaine. He would call Morrow as soon as he reached his apartment.

He crossed the street, quickening his stride. He could hardly wait to get home now, to open the envelope and discover who his victim was. Would he be clever or stupid? Rich, like Frelaine's fourth Victim, or poor, like the first and second? Would he have an organized Spotter service, or try to go it on his own?

The excitement of the chase was wonderful, coursing through his veins, quickening his heartbeat. From a block or so away, he heard gunfire. Two quick shots, and then a final one.

Somebody got his man, Frelaine thought. Good for him.

It was a superb feeling, he told himself. He was *alive* again.

At his one-room apartment the first thing Frelaine did was call Ed Morrow, his spotter. The man worked as a garage attendant between calls.

"Hello, Ed? Frelaine."

"Oh, hi, Mr. Frelaine." He could see the man's thin, grease-stained face, grinning flat-lipped at the telephone.

"I'm going out on one, Ed."

"Good luck, Mr. Frelaine," Ed Morrow said. "I suppose you'll want me to stand by?"

"That's right. I don't expect to be gone more than a week or two. I'll probably get my notification of Victim Status within three months of the kill."

"I'll be standing by. Good hunting, Mr. Frelaine."

"Thanks. So long." He hung up. It was a wise safety measure to reserve a first-class spotter. After his kill, it would be Frelaine's turn as Victim. Then, once again, Ed Morrow would be his life insurance.

And what a marvelous spotter Morrow was! Uneducated—stupid, really. But what an eye for people! Morrow was a natural. His pale eyes could tell an out-of-towner at a glance. He was diabolically clever at rigging an ambush. An indispensable man.

Frelaine took out the envelope, chuckling to himself, remembering some of the tricks Morrow had turned for the Hunters. Still smiling, he glanced at the data inside the envelope.

Janet-Marie Patzig.

His Victim was a female!

Frelaine stood up and paced for a few moments. Then he read the letter again. Janet-Marie Patzig. No mistake. A girl. Three photographs were enclosed, her address, and the usual descriptive data.

Frelaine frowned. He had never killed a female.

He hesitated for a moment, then picked up the telephone and dialed.

"Emotional Catharsis Bureau, Information Section," a man's voice answered.

"Say, look," Frelaine said. "I just got my notification and I pulled a girl. Is that in order?" He gave the clerk the girl's name.

"It's all in order, sir," the clerk replied after a minute of checking micro-files. "The girl registered with the board under her own free will. The law says she has the same rights and privileges as a man."

"Could you tell me how many kills she has?"

"I'm sorry, sir. The only information you're allowed is the Victim's legal status and the descriptive data you have received."

"I see." Frelaine paused. "Could I draw another?"

"You can refuse the hunt, of course. That is your legal right. But you will not be allowed another Victim until you have served. Do you wish to refuse?"

"Oh, no," Frelaine said hastily. "I was just wondering. Thank you."

He hung up and sat down in his largest armchair, loosening his belt. This required some thought. Damn women, he grumbled to himself, always trying to horn in on a man's game. Why can't they stay home?

But they were free citizens, he reminded himself. Still, it just didn't seem *feminine.*

He knew that, historically speaking, the Emotional Catharsis Board had been established for men and men only. The board had been formed at the end of the fourth world war—or sixth, as some historians counted it.

At that time there had been a driving need for permanent, lasting peace. The reason was practical, as were the men who engineered it.

Simply—annihilation was just around the corner.

In the world wars, weapons increased in magnitude, efficiency and exterminating power. Soldiers became accustomed to them, less and less reluctant to use them.

But the saturation point had been reached. Another war would truly be the war to end all wars. There would be no one left to start another.

So this peace *had* to last for all time, but the men who engineered it were practical. They recognized the tensions and dislocations still present, the cauldrons in which wars are brewed. They asked themselves why peace had never lasted in the past.

"Because men like to fight," was their answer.

"Oh, no!" screamed the idealists.

But the men who engineered the peace were forced to postulate, regretfully, the presence of a need for violence in a large percentage of mankind.

Men aren't angels. They aren't fiends, either. They are just very human beings, with a high degree of combativeness.

With the scientific knowledge and the power they had at that moment, the practical men could have gone a long way toward breeding this trait out of the race. Many thought this was the answer.

The practical men didn't. They recognized the validity of competition, love of battle, strength in the face of overwhelming odds. These, they felt, were admirable traits for a race, and insurance toward its perpetuity. Without them, the race would be bound to retrogress.

The tendency toward violence, they found, was inextricably linked with ingenuity, flexibility, drive.

The problem, then: To arrange a peace that would last long after they were gone. To stop the race from destroying itself, without removing the responsible traits.

The way to do this, they decided, was to rechannel man's violence.

Provide him with an outlet, an expression.

The first big step was the legalization of gladiatorial events, complete with blood and thunder. But more was needed. Sublimations worked only up to a point. Then people demanded the real thing.

There is no substitute for murder.

So murder was legalized, on a strictly individual basis, and only for those who wanted it. The governments were directed to create Emotional Catharsis Boards.

After a period of experimentation, uniform rules were adopted.

Anyone who wanted to murder could sign up at the ECB. Giving certain data and assurances, he would be granted a Victim.

Anyone who signed up to murder, under the government rules, had to take his turn a few months later as Victim—if he survived.

That, in essence, was the setup. The individual could commit as many murders as he wanted. But between each, he had to be a Victim. If he successfully killed his Hunter, he could stop, or sign up for another murder.

At the end of ten years, an estimated third of the world's civilized population had applied for at least one murder. The number slid to a fourth, and stayed there.

Philosophers shook their heads, but the practical men were satisfied. War was where it belonged—in the hands of the individual.

Of course, there were ramifications to the game, and elaborations. Once its existence had been accepted it became big business. There were services for Victim and Hunter alike.

The Emotional Catharsis Board picked the Victims' names at random. A Hunter was allowed six months in which to make his kill. This had to be done by his own ingenuity, unaided. He was given the name of his Victim, address and description, and allowed to use a standard caliber pistol. He could wear no armor of any sort.

The Victim was notified a week before the Hunter. He was told only that he was a Victim. He did not know the name of his Hunter. He was allowed his choice of armor, however. He could hire spotters. A spotter couldn't kill; only Victim and Hunter could do that. But he could detect a stranger in town, or ferret out a nervous gunman.

The Victim could arrange any kind of ambush in his power to kill the Hunter.

There were stiff penalties for killing or wounding the wrong man, for no other murder was allowed. Grudge killings and gain killings were punishable by death.

The beauty of the system was that the people who wanted to kill could do so. Those who didn't—the bulk of the population—didn't have to.

At least, there weren't any more big wars. Not even the imminence of one.

Just hundreds of thousands of small ones.

Frelaine didn't especially like the idea of killing a woman; but she *had* signed up. It wasn't his fault. And he wasn't going to lose out on his seventh hunt.

He spent the rest of the morning memorizing the data on his Victim, then filed the letter.

Janet Patzig lived in New York. That was good. He enjoyed hunting in a big city, and he had always wanted to see New York. Her age wasn't given, but to judge from her photographs, she was in her early twenties.

Frelaine phoned for jet reservations to New York, then took a shower. He dressed with care in a new Protec-Suit Special made for the occasion. From his collection he selected a gun, cleaned and oiled it, and fitted it into the fling-out pocket of the suit. Then he packed his suitcase.

A pulse of excitement was pounding in his veins. Strange, he thought, how each killing was a new excitement. It was something you just didn't tire of, the way you did of French pastry or women or drinking or anything else. It was always new and different.

Finally, he looked over his books to see which he would take.

His library contained all the good books on the subject. He wouldn't need any of his Victim books, like L. Fred Tracy's *Tactics for the Victim,* with its insistence on a rigidly controlled environment, or Dr. Frisch's *Don't Think Like a Victim!*

He would be very interested in those few months, when he was a Victim again. Now he wanted hunting books.

Tactics for Hunting Humans was the standard and definitive work, but he had it almost memorized. *Development of the Ambush* was not adapted to his present needs.

He chose *Hunting in Cities,* by Mitwell and Clark, *Spotting the Spotter,* by Algreen, and *The Victim's Ingroup,* by the same author.

Everything was in order. He left a note for the milkman, locked his apartment, and took a cab to the airport.

In New York, he checked into a hotel in the midtown area, not too far from his Victim's address. The clerks were smiling and attentive, which bothered Frelaine. He didn't like to be recognized so easily as an out-of-town killer.

The first thing he saw in his room was a pamphlet on his bed-table. *How to Get the Most out of Your Emotional Catharsis,* it was called, with the compliments of the management. Frelaine smiled and thumbed through it.

Since it was his first visit to New York, Frelaine spent the afternoon just walking the streets in his Victim's neighborhood. After that, he wandered through a few stores.

Martinson and Black was a fascinating place. He went through their Hunter-Hunted room. There were lightweight bulletproof vests for Victims, and Richard Arlington hats, with bulletproof crowns.

On one side was a large display of a new .38 caliber side-arm.

"Use the Malvern Strait-shot!" the ad proclaimed. "ECB-approved. Carries a load of 12 shots. Tested deviation less than .001 inch per 1,000 feet. Don't miss your Victim! Don't risk your life without the best! Be safe with Malvern!"

Frelaine smiled. The ad was good, and the small black weapon looked ultimately efficient. But he was satisfied with the one he had.

There was a special sale on trick canes, with concealed four-shot magazine, promising safety and concealment. As a young man, Frelaine has gone in heavily for novelties. But now he knew that the old-fashioned ways were usually the best.

Outside the store, four men from the Department of Sanitation were carting away a freshly killed corpse. Frelaine regretted missing the kill.

He ate dinner in a good restaurant and went to bed early.

Tomorrow he had a lot to do.

The next day, with the face of his Victim before him, Frelaine walked through her neighborhood. He didn't look closely at anyone. Instead, he moved rapidly, as though he were really going somewhere, the way an old Hunter should walk.

He passed several bars and dropped into a one for a drink. Then he went on, down a side street off Lexington Avenue.

There was a pleasant sidewalk cafe there. Frelaine walked past it.

And there she was! He could never mistake the face. It was Janet Patzig, seated at a table, staring into a drink. She didn't look up as he passed.

Frelaine walked to the end of the block. He turned the corner and stopped, hands trembling.

Was the girl crazy, exposing herself in the open? Did she think she had a charmed life?

He hailed a taxi and had the man drive around the block. Sure enough, she was just sitting there. Frelaine took a careful look.

She seemed younger than her pictures, but he couldn't be sure. He would guess her to be not much over twenty. Her dark hair was parted in the middle and combed above her ears, giving her a nunlike appearance. Her expression, as far as Frelaine could tell, was one of resigned sadness.

Wasn't she even going to make an attempt to defend herself?

Frelaine paid the driver and hurried to a drugstore. Finding a vacant telephone booth, he called ECB.

"Are you sure that a Victim named Janet-Marie Patzig has been notified?"

"Hold on, sir." Frelaine tapped on the door while the clerk looked up the information. "Yes, sir. We have her personal confirmation. Is there anything wrong, sir?"

"No," Frelaine said. "Just wanted to check."

After all, it was no one's business if the girl didn't want to defend herself.

He was still entitled to kill her.

It was his turn.

He postponed it for that day, however, and went to a movie. After dinner, he returned to his room and read the ECB pamphlet. Then he lay on his bed and glared at the ceiling.

All he had to do was pump a bullet into her. Just ride by in a cab and kill her.

She was being a very bad sport about it, he decided resentfully, and went to sleep.

The next afternoon, Frelaine walked by the cafe again. The girl was back, sitting at the same table. Frelaine caught a cab.

"Drive around the block very slowly," he told the driver.

"Sure," the driver said, grinning with sardonic wisdom.

From the cab, Frelaine watched for spotters. As far as he could tell, the girl had none. Both her hands were in sight upon the table.

An easy, stationary target.

Frelaine touched the button of his double-breasted jacket. A fold flew open and the gun was in his hand. He broke it open and checked the cartridges, then closed it with a snap.

"Slowly, now," he told the driver.

The taxi crawled by the cafe. Frelaine took careful aim, centering the girl in his sights. His finger tightened on the trigger.

"Damn it!" he said.

A waiter had passed by the girl. He didn't want to chance winging someone else.

"Around the block again," he told the driver.

The man gave him another grin and hunched down in his seat. Frelaine wondered if the driver would feel so happy if he knew that Frelaine was gunning for a woman.

This time there was no waiter around. The girl was lighting a cigarette, her mournful face intent on her lighter. Frelaine centered her in his sights, squarely above the eyes, and held his breath.

Then he shook his head and put the gun back in his pocket. The idiotic girl was robbing him of the full benefit of his catharsis.

He paid the driver and started to walk.

It's too easy, he told himself. He was used to a real chase. Most of the other six kills had been quite difficult. The Victims had tried every dodge. One had hired at least a dozen spotters. But Frelaine had gotten to them all by altering his tactics to meet the situation.

Once he had dressed as a milkman, another time as a bill collector. The sixth Victim he had had to chase through the Sierra Nevadas. The man had clipped him, too. But Frelaine had done better than that.

How could he be proud of this one? What would the Tens Club say?

That brought Frelaine up with a start. He wanted to get into the club. Even if he passed up this girl, he would have to defend himself against a Hunter. Surviving that, he would still be four hunts away from membership. At that rate, he might never get in.

He began to pass the cafe again, then, on impulse, stopped abruptly.

"Hello," he said.

Janet Patzig looked at him out of sad blue eyes, but said nothing.

"Say, look," he said, sitting down. "If I'm being fresh, just tell me and I'll go. I'm an out-of-towner. Here on a convention. And I'd just like someone feminine to talk to. If you'd rather I didn't—"

"I don't care," Janet Patzig said tonelessly.

"A brandy," Frelaine told the waiter. Janet Patzig's glass was still half full.

Frelaine looked at the girl and he could fee his heart throbbing against his ribs. This was more like it—having a drink with your Victim!

"My name's Stanton Frelaine," he said, knowing it didn't matter.

"Janet."

"Janet what?"

"Janet Patzig."

"Nice to know you," Frelaine said, in a perfectly natural voice. "Are you doing anything tonight, Janet?"

"I'm probably being killed tonight," she said quietly.

Frelaine looked at her carefully. Did she realize who he was? For all he knew, she had a gun leveled at him under the table.

He kept his hand close to the fling-out button.

"Are you a Victim?" he asked.

"You guessed it," she said sardonically. "If I were you, I'd stay out of the way. No sense getting hit by mistake."

Frelaine couldn't understand the girl's calm. Was she a suicide? Perhaps she just didn't care. Perhaps she wanted to die.

"Haven't you got any spotters?" he asked, with the right expression of amazement.

"No." She looked at him, full in the face, and Frelaine saw something he hadn't noticed before.

She was very lovely.

"I am a bad, bad girl," she said lightly. "I got the idea I'd like to commit a murder, so I signed for ECB. Then—I couldn't do it."

Frelaine shook his head, sympathizing with her.

"But I'm still in, of course. Even if I didn't shoot, I still have to be a Victim."

"But why don't you hire some spotters?" he asked.

"I couldn't kill anyone," she said. "I just couldn't. I don't even have a gun."

"You've got a lot of courage," Frelaine said, "coming out in the open this way." Secretly, he was amazed at her stupidity.

"What can I do?" she asked listlessly. "You can't hide from a Hunter. Not a real one. And I don't have enough money to make a real disappearance."

"Since it's in your own defense, I should think—" Frelaine began, but she interrupted.

"No. I've made up my mind on that. This whole thing is wrong, the whole system. When I had my Victim in the sights—when I saw how easily I could—I could—"

She pulled herself together quickly.

"Oh, let's forget it," she said, and smiled.

Frelaine found her smile dazzling.

After that, they talked of other things. Frelaine told her of his business, and she told him about New York. She was 22, an unsuccessful actress.

They had supper together. When she accepted Frelaine's invitation to go to the Gladiatorials, he felt absurdly elated.

He called a cab—he seemed to be spending his entire time in New York in cabs—and opened the door for her. She started in. Frelaine hesitated. He could have pumped a shot into her at that moment. It would have been very easy.

But he held his hand. Just for the moment, he told himself.

The Gladiatorials were about the same as those held anywhere else, except that the talent was a little better. There were the usual historical events, swordsmen and netmen, duels with saber and foil.

Most of these, naturally, were fought to the death.

Then bull fighting, lion fighting and rhino fighting, followed by the more modern events. Fights from behind the barricades with bow and arrow. Dueling on a high wire.

The evening passed pleasantly.

Frelaine escorted the girl home, the palms of his hands sticky with sweat. He had never found a woman he liked better. And yet she was his legitimate kill.

He didn't know what he was going to do.

She invited him in and they sat together on the couch. The girl lighted a cigarette for herself with a large lighter, then settled back.

"Are you leaving soon?" she asked him.

"I suppose so," Frelaine said. "The convention is only lasting another day."

She was silent for a moment. "I'll be sorry to see you go. Send roses to my funeral."

They were quiet for a while. Then Janet went to fix him a drink. Frelaine eyed her retreating back. Now was the time. He placed his hand near the button.

But the moment had passed for him, irrevocably. He wasn't going to kill her. You don't kill the girl you love.

The realization that he loved her was shocking. He'd come to kill, not to find a wife.

She came back with the drink and sat down opposite him, staring at emptiness.

"Janet," he said. "I love you."

She sat, just looking at him. There were tears in her eyes.

"You can't," she protested. "I'm a Victim. I won't live long enough to—"

"You won't be killed. I'm your Hunter."

She stared at him a moment, then laughed uncertainly.

"Are you going to kill me?" she asked.

"Don't be ridiculous," he said. "I'm going to marry you."

Suddenly she was in his arms.

"Oh, Lord!" she gasped. "The waiting—I've been so frightened—"

"It's all over," he told her. "Think what a story it'll make for our kids. How I came to murder you and left marrying you."

She kissed him, then sat back and lighted another cigarette.

"Let's start packing," Frelaine said. "I want—"

"Wait," Janet interrupted. "You haven't asked if I love you."

"What?"

She was still smiling, and the cigarette lighter was pointed at him. In the bottom of it was a black hole. A hole just large enough for a .38 caliber bullet.

"Don't kid around," he objected, getting to his feet.

"I'm not being funny, darling," she said.

In a fraction of a second, Frelaine had time to wonder how he could ever have thought she was not much over twenty. Looking at her now—*really* looking at her—he knew she couldn't be much less than thirty. Every minute of her strained, tense existence showed on her face.

"I don't love you, Stanton," she said very softly, the cigarette lighter poised.

Frelaine struggled for breath. One part of him was able to realize detachedly what a marvelous actress she really was. She must have known all along.

Frelaine pushed the button, and the gun was in his hand, cocked and ready.

The blow that struck him in the chest knocked him over a coffee table. The gun fell out of his hand. Gasping, half-conscious, he watched her take careful aim for the *coup de grace.*

"Now I can join the Tens," he heard her say elatedly as she squeezed the trigger.

Study Questions

Soul Mate

1. It seems natural to describe Quincy's relationship with "the girl" as one of total intimacy. But why? What makes this so? How is the struggle between them mirrored in other, more familiar relations of intimacy, e.g., between husbands and wives? What moral problems do all relationships of intimacy share? What important differences are there between this one and those more familiar to us?

2. A person in Quincy's (or "the girl's") position appears to have four choices: (a) he/she might try to work out some compromise, i.e., to sacrifice or surrender part of his/her identity to achieve a tolerable level of harmony; (b) he/she might try to unite with the other so that the previous identity of each is actually lost, i.e., such that there comes to be one will, one new system of values and desires; (c) he/she might try to dominate the other such that his/her identity is preserved at the expense of the other's; or (d) he/she might destroy the other. Can we say that one of the alternatives is *always* superior to the others? (E.g., does it depend on the person with whom one is linked? Their character? Their intentions?)

3. Quincy adopted the last alternative. Is this murder? Did Quincy kill "the girl" or merely persuade the girl to kill herself? If the former, can he plead self-defense? Why or why not?

4. Suppose telepathic links of this sort became relatively frequent (e.g., suppose that two people in every thousand were so linked at any time). What changes would we need to make in our legal system to handle problems that might result from this?

5. "Soul Mate" also raises an interesting question about the nature of the self (discussed in Part 3). Suppose that in some cases of telepathic linkage of the sort described in "Soul Mate," one will emerge supreme. One can imagine this happening as a result of synthesis. In either case there will be two centers of perception and sensation, but only one center of desire (suppose that in the case of conquest the conquered party ceases to have desires; suppose that the capacity to desire simply atrophies). In this case, how many selves will there be?

Balaam

1. Rabbi Acosta apparently understands himself to be helping the alien forces to victory. He takes this stance because he recognizes that they too are *men* (persons), and he believes that they have a superior claim to Mars. His principle seems to be that where two groups (persons) are in conflict, the morally best thing for members of each group to do is to determine which group has right on its side and to support that group—even if this means the extinction of one's own! On Acosta's view, then, fighting for the just cause is more important than loyalty to one's own kind and overrides any obligations one might have taken on in virtue of one's position within one's own group (e.g., the obligations of a military officer). Consider the advantages and disadvantages of this position. What would be lost if we were always required to put justice above loyalty? What would be gained? What would be lost if we were always to put loyalty above justice? What would be gained? Try to work out a compromise that would preserve the best of each for people in *our* society. What changes might be required under different social conditions?

2. "Balaam" also raises an interesting ecological question. Acosta decides that the aliens have a superior right to Mars on the ground that they are *naturally* better suited for it. In the context of the story, this principle is supposed to apply between various species of *men* (persons). Does the fact that a species (group) of persons is naturally better suited to an environment give it a right to that environment? What would be the consequences of applying this principle to groups of persons on earth? Also, how can we justify limiting this principle to persons? What is Rabbi Acosta's (implicit) justification for this? Is this acceptable? If not, should the principle be extended to nonhuman species? Is there such a thing as a right to an environment?

A Word to Space

1. Father Moriarty acted with the intention of bringing about important social changes on Akron. And he did not do this by appealing to the reason of the Akronites, but rather by sowing the seeds of discord within them. Were his actions morally justified? To answer this question you will need to ask: (a) under what conditions is it right to alter the structures of another society or culture by nonrational means? and (b) where this is permissible, by what nonrational means is it permissible to do this?

In approaching (a) you might consider whether it is enough of a justification for intervening in the affairs of another society that the social system of that society is barbaric by our standards, e.g., that the people routinely treat each other with great cruelty. Suppose that in addition to being barbaric, it is also undemocratic. Suppose finally that it is barbaric, undemocratic, and that there is a faction within it that is struggling to change it in what we judge to be the right direction. Is this enough to justify intervention?

In answering (b) you should keep in mind that interventions by techniques other than rational argument may take a variety of forms: for example, various techniques of sowing seeds of discord, the use of rhetoric, subliminal advertising, sophistry, offers, bribes, threats, economic sanctions, blockades, military assistance to competing parties, limited military attacks, and full-scale invasion. Are there some occasions, but not others, on which it is appropriate to use some of these techniques to intervene? Do the techniques that are appropriate depend on the type of society in question? If so, try to state some rules or principles that describe what sorts of interventions are appropriate under what conditions.

2. The problem of intervention arises not only with respect to other cultures or societies, but also in relation to persons, e.g., friends and family. Suppose that we believe that a friend or member of our family is conducting his life in a disastrous way. Do we ever have a right to try to change them by means other than rational argument? Under what conditions? By what means? Does it matter who the person is or how he/she is related to you? Make a list of examples of real or imaginary persons whose lives or values seem to you importantly misdirected, but who claim to see nothing wrong with how they live. Ask yourself in which cases you think it fit to intervene by some method other than rational argument. Try to state the rules or principles on the basis of which you distinguish one kind of case from another. Keep in mind that there is more than one important variable here.

Seventh Victim

1. Suppose that the assassin game described in Sheckley's story did not stop war. Should it be allowed in any case? Notice that the game is played by consenting adults. Do we—as a society—have a right to forbid them to engage in it? Why or why not? Suppose the game were constructed in such a way that there were no physical danger to anyone unwilling to risk it. For example, suppose that everyone who played the game were made to live in particular cities, and that everyone else knew what cities they were. Ought we to allow the game under these circumstances? Suppose, in addition, that all nonplayers who lived in these cities were paid by a player's association to do so. Would we then have the right to forbid it?

2. It is often maintained that so-called victimless crimes ought not to be illegal on the ground that they affect only those who engage in them. Typical examples are prostitution, homosexuality, the purchase of pornography, and the consumption of alcohol. It is also argued that since such practices harm no one except (by some standards) those who engage

in them, society should not even take a moral position on them (e.g., we should not teach that they are wrong in the schools). Is this plausible? In considering these positions, keep in mind that as long as a person is a member of society there is very little about him/her that does not impact on others in some way. This is true not only of actions but of moods (e.g., surliness, depression) and even dress (e.g., sexually provocative clothing). Does this mean that we—as a group—are entitled to take a moral position on these matters? To say that we are entitled to do this is to say that we *are* entitled to consider it our right to discourage or encourage the behavior in question by legal or social coercion. To say that we are not entitled to do this is to say that we should consider it none of our business that people do these things. What is none of our business? Think of examples. What do these examples have in common? Does it follow from the fact that a form of behavior is on this list that we are ought to make it illegal? If not, why not? Again, think of examples and try to determine what they have in common.

Part 6

Technology and Human Self-Transformation

Introduction to Part 6

One of the most dramatic and important events of the twentieth century is the rapid reduction of cultural diversity. An important part of this process has been the transformation of nonliterate village-dwelling peoples into educated participants of developing and, in some cases, technologically sophisticated economies. This transformation is far from complete, of course, but it is increasingly more common to find urbanized engineers, doctors, physicists, computer scientists, and so forth, who are but one or two generations removed from peasant or tribal villages, and who culturally have at least as much in common with urbanized Westerners as with their own grandparents. The conditions under which we live and the options that are open to us in virtue of them impose limits on who we can be. The standardization of these conditions cannot but help make us more alike.

One very important aspect of the standardization of conditions is the standardization of technology. "Technology" is a difficult concept, and I cannot hope adequately to explicate it here. Roughly, however, a technology is a method for achieving some end by means of a *tool.* Since all human groups are tool users, all human groups employ technologies of some sort. The more sophisticated and "developed" the technology, the more powerful the tools.

As this suggests, it is a mistake to think of technology merely as a set of tools or machines. If we think of technology in this way, we miss an important aspect of how our technologies contribute to making us who we are. For so conceived, technology is reduced to a set of things in the world, i.e., to just another feature of the environment. So reduced, it can affect us—but only externally, as the weather, the noise level, or the lighting affects us. I do not want to minimize the importance of such effects; a life lived among machines and machine-made goods no doubt shapes the psyche differently from a life lived among the trees and rivers of the forests. Still, this is only part of the picture. What it omits is our *participation* in technology, and how this participation impacts on our being. The account of technology as ways of *doing* things *by means of* tools brings this aspect into focus. For it reminds us that our technology does not simply constitute an environment within which we act; it also constitutes an important and increasingly pervasive domain of action. The point is that what we do (and no longer do) is quite as important to who we are as the impact of the "external environment" on us. Moreover, to the extent that we think of technology as our way of doing things, we can avoid falling into the trap of thinking of technology as some dominant *external* force over which we have no control. If we can control our own collective modes of action—if we can change the ways we act as a society to achieve our ends—we can control technology.

Human powers, skills, and talents may be lost as well as found. Mass access to books has eliminated the need for highly trained memories; mass access to highly trained singers and musicians has reduced the number of singing and instrument-playing adults; in general, new tools have reduced old crafts to hobbies, curiosities, or to the pursuits of eccentrics. The logic of this process is clear. If we can do a job better, faster, more efficiently, and, perhaps more importantly, more cheaply with a new tool, we will adopt it. Often, the new tool owes its superiority to the fact that it eliminates some aspect of a process that was previously carried out by a human being. When this occurs, the skills, talents, and so forth, required to do the job with the old tool become obsolete and are either lost entirely or hang on as mere curiosities. Writers of science fiction wonder, not infrequently, just how far this process might go. What might be lost in a world in which machines perform virtually all of our physical tasks for us? Indeed, what would be lost in a world in which machines not only performed all of our physical tasks, but did most of our thinking and decision making as well? What would we be like in a world in which we all had a computer psychologist to discover what we really want, or ought to want, and a computer counselor to plan our lives for us accordingly? Suppose that the process began as soon as we were born. What would human beings be in such a world? What that is important to us would be lost?

As all of this suggests, the technologies that we employ importantly influence what we and our heirs will be like as human beings. The stories in this section suggest that not every possibility is a welcome one. E. M. Forster's "The Machine Stops" describes a future in which The Machine —one machine—provides us with an orderly and predictable world in which work is unnecessary (and unavailable) and all of our material needs are completely satisfied. In this world, risk, uncertainty, and anxiety of all forms have been almost entirely eliminated by the elimination of their causes. Human relationships, for example, consist largely of pleasant and mutually interesting exchanges of ideas and theories on various aspects of dead cultures and art forms, exchanges conducted via interlocking television terminals. Emotional attachments—indeed, face-to-face human contact—is both very rare and (for most) entirely distasteful. The natural world—an embodiment of risk and disorder—is avoided whenever possible, and responded to with fear and repugnance. Creativity is almost unheard of. Since change can only mar the perfection of the present, an important social aim is the absence of significant changes, i.e., nobody is supposed to do anything that transforms society (or any other aspect of reality) in an important way. Forster's story is a literary critique of this society and the values that it embodies. But how are we to evaluate this critique? The overwhelming majority of persons in Forster's future approve the system that he describes, even as it begins to break down. Is this a conclusive argument in its favor?

Analogous questions are raised by Thomas Monteleone's "Breath's a Ware That Will Not Keep." Monteleone's story focuses on the dangers implicit in biotechnology. Cloning and genetic engineering may soon enable us to mass produce human beings (and other life forms) according to desired specifications. But to what specifications? It is likely that if we employ these technologies to produce human beings, our goal will be to produce "genetically desirable" stock. At the very least this will mean eliminating persons with certain incapabilities from future populations, e.g., the physically handicapped and the mentally retarded. One justification of such a policy would no doubt be that such persons are not as likely as their "genetic superiors" to lead socially useful lives. For the same reason we may begin to eliminate from future populations those persons that are likely to engage in socially disruptive behavior (i.e., behavior that does not fit in well with our social system, e.g., disrespect for authority). And if we go this far, it is not unlikely that we will go all the way, i.e., that we will use these techniques to produce persons who are maximally socially useful. In this case we will aim to produce people who best fit the needs of society as then constituted.

And so it is, in the future envisioned by Monteleone. There, everyone is produced to perform a particular social function. And since this is the case—since persons are designed for particular purposes—they are valued only insofar as they fulfill the purposes for which they are designed. In this society, then, there ceases to be much distinction between our attitudes toward persons and our attitudes toward machines. Accordingly, much that we now value in human beings is lost to us, e.g., the capacity to love (one cannot love someone one values only as a tool). Still, the society Monteleone describes has obvious advantages: it is well ordered and provides a good deal of pleasure to those who live in it. Moreover, it is well regarded by those who live in it. On what grounds are we entitled to say that it is not choiceworthy for them?

Although this question is a very interesting one, it is not necessary that we answer it adequately to accept the validity of Forster's and Monteleone's critiques. For the point of their stories is to warn *us* against pursuing certain alternatives. In this case it does not matter that the society described might be thought choiceworthy by its members. Since every society shapes at least many of the desires it satisfies, any number of societies we have in our power to bring about might have this feature. The point is that we now must choose the future. And we must choose on the basis of our values.

Since our technologies are our ways of doing things with tools, it is at least theoretically possible for us to choose our technology. But is this how technologies actually come to be adopted? Karel Capek's classic *R.U.R.* suggests otherwise. Under capitalism market considerations determine what technologies are developed and employed. And in general, technologies are developed and employed in response to the needs and desires of persons and organizations with wealth and power (e.g., governments and large corporations). As Capek's play so well illustrates, the technologies we come to employ on this basis are not necessarily the technologies we would choose were we to make such decisions on the basis of our values. Ought this to be changed? For example, ought we to make the development and employment of technology a subject of collective social choice, arrived at by some reasonable democratic process? The consequences of such a decision are far-reaching. Since so much of what is produced and marketed are tools or machines of one kind or another, such a policy would commit us to extensive limitations on what is made and sold, i.e., to significant restrictions on property rights. Some philosophers argue that any such limitations—even limitations that are imposed democratically—constitute a violation of basic human rights. Others disagree. Indeed, some maintain that such limitations are necessary to protect rights more fundamental than this (e.g., the right to control controllable forces that profoundly affect our lives). Whichever position one favors, it is clear that the shape of the future depends importantly on whether we come to develop and employ technologies on the basis of our values (democratically determined) or whether we continue to allow technologies to be developed and employed in response to the demands of the wealthy and powerful.

Breath's a Ware That Will Not Keep

Thomas F. Monteleone

Benjamin Cipriano sat down at his console, casting a quick glance outward to the Breeder Tank below him. He switched his attention to the controls and opened up a communications channel to the Tank. He pulled the psi-helmet over his head and pressed the throat mike close to his larynx. "Good morning, Feraxya. Feeling okay today?"

His scalp tingled as invisible fingers slipped into his skull to massage his brain. The helmet fed her psi-words into him: "Good morning to you, too, Benjamin." The "voice" sounded just vaguely feminine to him, and his imagination reinforced the conceptualization. "I'm feeling fine. Everything is normal. You know I always feel comfortable when you are on the console."

"Thank you," said Cipriano, pausing for a moment. "Now, I have some tests to run this morning, so we'd better get started." He flipped several toggles as he continued speaking to her. "It's all routine stuff . . . blood sugar, enzyme scans, placental balance quotients . . . things like that. Nothing to worry about."

There was a short silence before she touched his mind again: "I never worry when you're on. Perhaps we'll have time to talk, later on?"

"If you want to. I'll have some time in a few minutes. Bye now." He switched off the communications channel and stared at the protoplasmic nightmare on the other side of his console-booth window. Stretched out before him were all the Breeder Tanks for his Sector of the City. They were Chicago's symbols of deliverance from misery and deprivation for all the City's members. Except, perhaps, the Host-Mothers themselves. Cipriano wondered about them in general, Feraxya in particular, and what their lives must be like.

Technically speaking, Feraxya was human. Visually, however, she was an amorphous, slithering, amoeba-like thing. She was tons of genetically cultured flesh, a human body inflated and stretched and distended until it was many times its normal size. Lost beneath her abundant flesh was a vestigial skeleton which floated disconnected and unmoving in a gelatinous sea. Her bioneered organs were swollen to immense proportions and hundreds of liters of blood pumped through her extensive circulatory system.

Yet he knew, even as he activated the probes that plunged into her soft flesh, that she was still a woman to him. A very special kind of woman. From her earliest moments of consciousness, she had spent her life contained within the glassteel walls of the Breeder Tank. It was an immense cube, ten meters on each side, the back wall covered with connecting cables and tubes which carried her life-support systems, monitoring devices, and biomedical elements that were necessary for her continued maintenance.

To Cipriano, she *was* the glassteel tube. Feraxya had no face, no arms, no legs; all those things were buried beneath the folds of swollen flesh that rippled with life-fluids. And yet she was a person, a Citizen of Chicago, who had received the standard education by means of special input programs piped through her sensory nerves and into her brain, bypassing her useless eyes and ears. She also represented several basic changes from previous Host-Mothers. Feraxya was a third-generation mutant; careful genetic selection and programming had given her primary-level psi-powers, which were used in communication and eventually for education. Chicago's Central Computers postulated that the quiet, undisturbed environ of the Breeder Tank would be an ideal atmosphere for the development of psi.

Ben looked away from the giant Tank, leaned back in his chair, and watched the monitoring data come clicking into the tapes at his console. As he waited for the data to accumulate, his gaze wandered down the long row of other consoles like his own, where many other Breeder Monitors sat reading their indicators and printouts. Each monitor was charged with his own Host-Mother; each Host-Mother held within her an enlarged uterus that was filled with thirty human fetuses.

It was in this way that the Host-Mothers provided the City with every desired type of Citizen. There were no outcasts, no misfits, now that society was shaped by the benevolent but highly efficient Central Computers of Chicago. An entire hierarchy was cybernetically conceived and programmed, then handed down through the bureaucratic chain until it reached the Bioneers and Eugenicists. In Chicago's massive Eugenic Complex, hundreds of Host-Mothers like Feraxya carried the fetuses of the next generation of Citizens. Laborers, artists, scientists, bureaucrats, and technicians—all precoded and expected.

A message suddenly flashed on Cipriano's console which

reminded him to check the night-shift Monitor's report. He did so and found it satisfactory. Feraxya had only recently received her first uterine implant, and there was little for him to do at this point except routine systems-checks. Later when her brood of fetuses grew and began to crowd her great womb, Cipriano's tasks would also grow. A Host-Mother nearing the end of gestation required much attention.

He replaced the psi-helmet on his head and signaled to her. A tingling sensation touched his mind as she was raised from her inner thoughts: "Yes, Ben?"

"The databanks are still filling," he said. "I've some free time. Thought you might want to talk for a little while."

"Yes, I would. Thank you. I wanted to tell you about the dream I had. . . ."

"A dream?" he asked. "About what?"

"About you. I think about you a lot."

"I didn't know that," said Ben, smiling self-consciously. His words were only a half-truth.

"Yes, it's true . . ." She paused and his mind leapt at the emptiness she created there. "Ben?" she began again.

"Yes?"

"Do you ever think about me? When you're not here, working?"

"Well, yes. I guess I do. Sometimes."

"I'm glad," she said. "You're different from my other Monitors. Of course I'm sleeping most of that time, anyway."

"Different?" The word did not sit well in his mind. The Monitors were planned to be quite similar. "How do you mean?"

"You're kinder," she said. "More understanding, I think. It's just easier to talk with you."

"Thank you, Feraxya. I'm just trying to be myself, though."

"Your mate is very lucky to have someone like you," she said candidly. "I guess I should tell you that I've thought about having you myself. Even though I know it's impossible."

Ben paused for a moment, stirred and somewhat shaken by the mental image her suggestion brought to mind. "You could use your Id-Tapes if you really wanted—" He tried to be helpful but she interrupted him.

"That's little more than masturbation."

"I'm sorry," he said. "I was just trying to suggest something that might help, that's all."

"You're sweet. But that's not what I want from you. If I could have it my way it would be like the dream. I had a *real* body, like you, and we were going through the City at night. It was bright and beautiful. Sometimes I wish it could have been like that."

She paused, and Cipriano searched for any subliminal meaning in her words. There were people who would interpret them as dangerous. He wondered what she meant by them. "It wasn't meant to be," he said finally, shallowly.

"I know. And the Host-Mothers are needed. Someone must serve," she said slowly, as if she were contemplating the implications of what she was saying.

"That's true," he said. "Besides—"

Cipriano was interrupted by the chatter of his console. The results from the morning's test began to flash upon his grid. A large graph appeared and flickered violently; superimposed over the graph was a one-word message: CRITICAL.

"Just a minute, Feraxya," he said, staring at the alarm signal in semi-shock. "Uh, . . . some of the results have just come in and I've got to check them out. I'll get back to you as soon as I can, okay?"

"All right, Ben. We can talk later."

He threw off the helmet and depressed several digital keys, requesting clarification of the warning signal. Cipriano read through the figures, double-checked them, and started an entire new series of tests to ensure against errors.

As the console began to click and chatter with the new instructions, he called his Superior, Faro Barstowe. Several seconds passed before the man's lean, foxlike face appeared on the screen: "Yes, what is it?"

"Cipriano here. Breeder Tank 0078-D. Generic name: Feraxya. My routine monitoring has picked up what looks like a nucleotide dysfunction. Probable cause is an inadequate enzyme transfer. Too early to tell yet. Just calling to let you know that I'm running a double-check."

Barstowe's face seemed tense. "Let's see . . . You've got a litter of thirty. RNA Code 45a7c. Superior Range. Administrator Class. That sound right?"

"Yes, sir. That's right," said Cipriano, watching the man's small shining eyes burn into him, even through the screen.

"All right, Cipriano. It's been sixty-four days since implantation. That makes it too late for an *in vitro* injection to change or rectify the enzyme transfer. Collect all the data you can from the second scan. I'll call Bioneering and send some men over there to see what's up. That's all for now." The screen blacked out, leaving Ben with the cool sounds of the console.

When he read through the second test results, he knew that they only confirmed what he had first imagined. There was indeed a dysfunction in Feraxya's system; but he could do nothing until the Bioneers arrived. His first thought was to contact her, so that she would be aware of what was happening inside her great body. But he knew that would not be possible until he received word from Barstowe.

It was several minutes before the white uniformed specialists from

Bioneering entered his booth. One of them read over the data collected from his console while the other two adjusted their white, antiseptic, helmeted suits as they prepared to enter the Breeder Tank Area itself. Cipriano looked past them, through the glass window to Feraxya, who floated within her prison still ignorant of her problems.

Later, as he watched the Bioneers scurrying about Feraxya's Tank, he wondered if she could, somehow, sense their nearness, their insensitive prying into the secrets of her grotesque body. He wanted to talk to her, and he entertained the notion of contact as his eyes fell upon the psi-helmet by the console.

One of the Bioneers returned to the booth, quickly removing his helmet and wiping some perspiration from his forehead. He looked at Cipriano and shook his head.

"What's that mean?" said Ben.

"Not good," said the man in white. "There hasn't been any reaction between the DNA/enzyme interface. The 'blueprint injections' didn't copy at all. That's why you were getting the alarms."

"Which means . . . ?" asked Cipriano.

"Which means her fetuses would be completely variable if we brought them to term." The man paused and gestured out toward Feraxya's Tank. *"Randoms*—that's what we're growing in that one."

"What do we do now?"

"You'd better call Barstowe," said the Bioneer. "My men'll be making an official report, but I think he'd appreciate knowing about it now."

Cipriano knew what Barstowe would say: they would have to remove her brood. He wondered what Feraxya's reaction to the decision would be. Remembering how pleased she had been to receive her first implantation, Cipriano did not look forward to the moment when he would have to confront her with the news.

After he had contacted Barstowe and relayed the results of the Bioneers' inspection, the Superior shook his head, grimacing. "That's too bad. Going to throw us off schedule. I'll arrange for Stander to prepare for a scrape as soon as possible. Tomorrow morning, hopefully."

"I was wondering when I should tell Feraxya about it," said Cipriano.

The foxlike features stared at him for a moment. "You'll have plenty of time in the morning. Don't worry about it. You really don't have anything else to do today. Why don't you get out of here?"

"All right," said Cipriano. "But I hope she understands why." Barstowe didn't answer; the screen had already blacked. Ben shook his head slowly and shut down his console. He left the Eugenic Complex and took the Rapids home to his con-apt, hoping that the following day would be less difficult than this one.

That night, Jennifer wanted him.

She was warm and young and fashionably lean; and he wanted her, too. He always did. She was something of a romantic, since she always used candles to illuminate their lovemaking, but Cipriano didn't mind.

Jennifer helped him attach the electrodes to his forehead; she had already hooked herself into the machine. They lay side by side, naked, in the candlelight as the machine beneath their bed hummed and touched their pleasure centers. Physiological feedback was encoded from each of them, amplified, and routed into each other as mutual stimuli. Their orgasms were reached simultaneously with the aid of the machine. Never touching each other, not needing to do so, there was no chance of a nonapproved conception. Afterwards, they lay in silence, smiling from the rush of moist satisfaction. Jennifer arose in the semi-darkness and unhooked the electrodes. Cipriano was asleep before she even turned off the machine.

When he reached his console the next morning, he sensed that there was something different about the Eugenic Complex. He hoped that it was merely his imagination. Through the glass, he could see several technicians and a Bioneer working on Feraxya's Tank.

Cipriano placed the psi-helmet on his head and flipped the transmission switch. "I've been expecting you," said Feraxya, instantly crowding his mind; the transmission was almost aggressive.

"What do you mean?" he said quickly.

"When you never came back yesterday, I began to worry about you. Then I felt them fumbling around my Tank. I knew something was wrong."

"I'm sorry," he said. "I was very busy yesterday. I didn't have time to—"

"Don't try to explain. I already know what they're getting ready to do."

"What? What're you talking about. How?" He looked out at the great mass of flesh, seeing it for the first time as something that could be very different from what he had always imagined.

"The night-shift Monitor told me what had happened. I forced him to do it. I wanted to know why they were tampering with me. And when he told me, I was hurt by it. Why couldn't *you* tell me, Benjamin? I didn't want that other man to tell me, but I had no choice."

"I'm sorry," was all he could manage to say.

"It hurt to know that you had run out of the Complex without telling me, Benjamin."

"Please," he said. "I understand what you're saying. And I'm sorry. I shouldn't have done it."

"Why do they call it a 'scrape'?"

"It's just slang, that's all. It doesn't mean anything. They don't do abortions that way anymore."

"Will they be coming soon?" she asked.

"I think so. Don't worry. It won't take long. You won't even feel—"

"No, Benjamin, I don't want them to do it. You've got to tell them not to do it."

Cipriano suppressed a laugh, although it was more from anxiety than from humor. "You don't want it? There isn't anything you can do about it. It's the law, Feraxya! Chicago doesn't allow random births. You know that."

"The only thing I know is that they want to destroy my brood. They want to cut me open and rip them from my flesh. It is wrong," she said slowly.

"There was a mistake in the gene-printing," said Cipriano, trying to explain things in the only way he understood. "Your fetuses aren't perfect constructs."

"But they're human beings, Benjamin. They want to murder them. I can't let them do it."

Cipriano tried to understand her feelings, her reasons for talking such nonsense to him. He began to fear that maybe she was losing control of her senses. "Why are you telling me this?" he asked finally. "You know there isn't anything I can do about it."

"You can tell them not to try. I want to give them a chance."

"They won't listen to me, Feraxya. Barstowe's already scheduled the surgery for this morning. There's nothing you can do but accept what's happening. Face the truth: you're getting an abortion." He regretted the last sentence as soon as he had said it. He could almost feel the pain he was inflicting in her.

"I can't believe that's really you talking. I always thought you were *different* from the rest of them. You acted like you had more understanding, more compassion . . . "

"You make it sound like I'm against you," he said defensively.

"Perhaps you're not. But you've got to tell them that I'll stop anybody who tries to get near me. Even kill them if necessary." Feraxya's voice in his mind was sharp, cutting deeply into his skull like a bright razor.

"And you're telling me about understanding, about compassion? Feraxya, what's happening to you?" Inwardly, he reviewed her last words. What was this talk about *killing?* If her mind was going, Barstowe would have to know about it.

"I can't help it, Benjamin. It's something that I feel deep inside. Something that we've almost forgotten about. The instincts, the drive that a mother feels to protect her children."

"They're not your children," he said vindictively.

"They were given to me. They're *mine."* There was a long pause. "I don't want to argue with you. Please, go tell them what I've said."

Cipriano exhaled slowly. "All right. I'll see Barstowe, but I don't think it'll do any good."

He waited for her to reply, but when she didn't, he switched off the communications channel and pulled the helmet from his head. He keyed in Barstowe's office, but the lines were all jammed with other calls. Wanting to get the matter finished as quickly as possible, he left the booth and walked to the elevators that would take him to Barstowe's office level.

After the Superior was given a reconstruction of the conversation, he shook his head as if in disbelief. "Nothing like this has ever happened before," the man said.

"Well, what do we do about it?" asked Cipriano.

"*Do!*" cried Barstowe. "We don't have to do anything about it. We just ignore that crap and go on with the operation. You can tell her she'll be getting a new implantation as soon as possible."

Cipriano paused, still thinking about what she had said to him. He looked at Barstowe and spoke again: "What about that bit about 'killing' people?"

Barstowe laughed. "Just a threat . . . a very stupid one at that."

"You don't think she's more powerful than we've imagined, do you?"

"What're you getting at?" Barstowe stared at him with cold, penetrating eyes that looked like oiled ball bearings.

"*I* don't know," said Cipriano. "I just can't figure out why she'd talk like that. It's not like her."

"Well, we don't have time to worry about it. For now—" Barstowe was interrupted by the buzzer on his communicator. He answered it, and saw a white-helmeted Bioneer on the screen. They spoke for several seconds, then the screen darked out. "That was Stander. They're about ready to get started. I want you down there. You can tell her what was said up here."

Cipriano nodded and left the office. When he returned to his console, he could see the surgical team approaching Feraxya's Tank. He put on the helmet and opened the channel to her mind. "They wouldn't listen," he said. "They're coming now. Pretty soon you'll be going under anesthesia. I'm sorry, Feraxya."

"Don't be sorry, Benjamin," was all she said. There was something chilling in the way she had touched his mind. The familiar warmness had vanished, and Cipriano felt the first twinges of terror icing in his spinal cord.

A Bioneer approached the console and prepared to administer the anesthesia. Outside the booth, Cipriano could see the surgical team as they reached the glassteel wall of the Tank. Suddenly the man next to him threw back his head and uttered a brief scream. The man tried to press his hands to his head just as blood began to stream from his nose and the corners of his mouth; his eyes bulged out, unseeing, and he slumped over the console, dead from a massive cerebral hemorrhage. Cipriano rushed over to him, but there was nothing that could be done.

Next to the Breeder Tank, the three men of the surgical team were waiting for the anesthesia to take effect. One of them had begun scaling the wall of the Tank, but he never made it. Falling backward, the man landed on his back as he struggled with his suit's helmet, he convulsed for several seconds and then lay still. The remaining two surgeons rushed to his aid, but had taken only a few steps before they too were struck down by some unseen, killing force.

Cipriano watched their death throes as alarms wailed through the corridors. Suddenly people were scrambling all around him. Two parameds ran into the Breeder Tank Area and were also brought down screaming and convulsing. Benjamin stepped back from the booth window, feeling a pit form at the base of his stomach. He flipped on the screen and punched for Barstowe's office. "Something's happened to the team!" he yelled before the picture materialized. "Barstowe! Can you hear me?"

The Superior's face appeared on the screen. "I know! What's going on down there? The intercom's going crazy!"

"I don't know," said Cipriano. "I don't know!"

"Who's in there with you?"

"I'm not sure. There's a lot of noise . . . confusion. Some technicians, a medic."

"Put one of the techs on," said Barstowe, regaining some of his usual composure.

Cipriano called the closest man over to the communicator. Barstowe said something to the technician, who nodded and reached for the anesthesia switch. Before he threw it, blood spurted from his nose and ears, and he fell away from the console. He was dead before he hit the floor.

Backing away from the console, Benjamin looked out to the Tank of pink flesh. Now the massiveness of the thing took on a new meaning. Within its walls lurked a powerful and angry intelligence.

The screen was signaling, but there was no one close enough to answer it. Wiping the perspiration from his face, Cipriano edged close to the screen and saw Barstowe's searching eyes. "Get out of there!" the Superior screamed. "I'm calling back all the emergency units. Get up here right now." The screen blacked out.

Quickly, Cipriano shouldered his way through the crowd of Complex guards and Bioneers and headed for the nearest elevator. When he reached Barstowe's office, he found the man in animated conversation in front of his communicator. Seeing Cipriano, the Superior flicked off the screen and spoke to him: "Chicago Central

Computer postulates some kind of limited-range telekinetic power—an unexpected variable of the psi-training."

"I thought it would be something like that," said Benjamin. "What do you want with me?"

"You seem to have gotten along with her reasonably well in the past," said Barstowe, pausing for dramatic effect. "And she seemed to leave you alone down there just now."

"And . . . ?"

"Get in touch with her again. Try to reason with her. Calm her down. Tell her anything. Tell her that we've capitulated, that we won't abort her brood. Anything, I don't care what."

"I don't understand," said Cipriano.

"You don't have to understand it. Just do what you're told." Barstowe stood up from his desk and faced him squarely. "We want you to divert her attention, keep her occupied until we can rig up a bypass away from your console to the Breeder Tank."

"A bypass? What're you talking about?" Cipriano asked, although he already had an idea of what Barstowe intended.

"We're going to try and shut her down from outside the Complex. Shunt from the Central Computer."

"You mean you're going to *kill* her?"

"You're goddamn right we are!" Barstowe screamed. "Listen, Chicago has postulated what would happen if that thing downstairs could somehow communicate with the other Host-Mothers. If the combined psi-powers of the entire Breeder Tank Area could be coordinated, their power would be awesome. We can't let some kind of matrix like that materialize. Now get out of here."

Cipriano rode down to his level and returned once more to the console. The entire area was deserted and his footsteps echoed down the corridor adjoining his booth. Barstowe's words were also echoing through his mind. Thoughts of Feraxya, of the other Host-Mothers, of the men who'd been killed, of the entire nightmarish scene all swarmed through his mind like a cloud of devouring insects. He felt helplessly trapped in the middle of a conflict that he wanted no part of.

He sat down and put on the helmet. As he threw on the proper switch, he could feel her mind lurking nearby, waiting for him to speak. "You've changed, Feraxya," he said finally.

"Why did you come back?" she said.

"I don't know," he lied. "There was nothing else to do."

"What are they going to do with me, Benjamin?"

"I . . . don't know." Again, he lied. And this time it was painful. Adrenaline pumped through him; his hands were trembling. He was glad that she could not see him.

"Do you understand why I had to do it?" she asked. "You know I didn't want it this way."

"No, I don't understand. You've become a murderer, Feraxya."

"I didn't want to do it. I just wanted to protect my brood. They have as much right to live as you or me. I won't let them be killed." Her voice in his mind seemed strained, tense. Perhaps her mind *was* going. He shuddered as he thought of what an insane horror she could become.

"What are you going to do now?" he asked. "They've evacuated the entire Complex. But they'll be back. You can't hold out like this forever, you know."

"I don't know, Benjamin. I'm scared. You know I'm scared. If they would promise to leave me alone, to leave my brood alone, I won't hurt them. My duty to the Society is to produce new Citizens. That's what I want to do. That's all. You believe me, don't you?"

"Yes, I believe you," said Cipriano just as he was distracted by several flashing lights on his console. He hadn't touched any of the switches; the technicians must be activating the controls through the recently rigged bypass circuits. He knew what was going to happen.

"Benjamin, are you still there . . . ? What's wrong?"

"I'm sorry," he said quickly, while his mind raced ahead, envisioning what would come next. He was of two minds, one of which wanted to cry out, to warn her of what was planned, the other that was content to sit back and witness her execution. He heard himself talking: ". . . and you've got to trust us, Feraxya. You can't keep killing everybody. There would be no one to maintain your systems. Everyone would lose in the end." Watching the console, Cipriano recognized the symbols that now blazed in bright scarlet on the message grid. They were planning to terminate.

"All right, Benjamin . . . " Feraxya's words were echoing through his brain. "I'll—"

Her words were cut short. Cipriano jumped up from the chair, his eyes on the great Breeder Tank. The console chattered and flickered as it processed the remote commands being fed into it. "Feraxya!" he screamed as he realized what was happening, what she must now know. A life-support systems graph appeared on the grid; the plot lines all began dropping towards the *y*-coordinate. His mind was flooded with her last thoughts—surprise, panic, loathing, and pain. For a moment he thought he felt her icy, telekinetic grip reaching out to him, enclosing cold fingers about his brain. The seconds ticked by with glacierlike slowness. His mind lay in a dark pit of fear as he awaited her retribution.

The life-fluids and the oxygen were cut off, and the great amorphous body convulsed within the Breeder Tank. She reached out and touched his mind for the last time, but in fear rather than anger or hate. She forced him to experience her death. Cipriano closed his eyes against the vicarious pain, unable to wrench the helmet from his head.

Then suddenly it was over. A gathering darkness filled him. The console had begun force-feeding acid through her circulatory system, bubbling away the flesh, insuring that she was gone.

The communicator screen grew into brightness and Barstowe's face appeared there. The Superior was smiling, but Benjamin ripped off the helmet and left the console before the man spoke. The corridor outside his booth was again filled with people, their voices loud with celebration and relief. He ignored their backslapping and shouldered past them to the descent elevators.

He kept wondering why she had touched him like that, at the end. Had she known? Did she think it was he that was killing her?

He left the Complex under the weight of his thoughts. Outside, Chicago sparkled under the night sky. Its sidewalks and transit systems were filling up with work-wearied crowds who sought entertainment in the City. Cipriano stepped onto a slidewalk that carried him through the midsection of the urban Complex. He was in no hurry to go home now.

Ahead of him, the walk snaked through a kaleidoscopic forest of color and light, through the pleasure-center of the City—Xanadu. The crowds were heavy here, each seeking the mindless relief that was always to be found in this Sector. Cipriano studied them as he threaded his way through the mobs. They were all born of Host-Mothers, like Feraxya, all laughing and playing their games of escape, oblivious to their grotesque origins. He passed a series of Fantasy Parlors, where the lines were already long. The patrons were mostly lower-level Citizens—nontechs, laborers, and drones—that filled this Sector. They were all eager to use the City's computers to immerse themselves in imaginary worlds. Sexual fantasies were a major part of the catalog. Cipriano knew this as he passed the other opiate-dispensing centers: the mind-shops, elec-drug centers, and other pleasure domes. The brightness of the lights assaulted him with their vulgar screams, the polished steel and reflecting glass shimmered with a special kind of tawdriness. For the first time, perhaps, Cipriano realized a terrible truth: the City was unable to provide for all of man's needs. There was something missing, something primal and liberating, something that was now only a desiccated memory out of man's dark history.

Perhaps Feraxya, too, was aware of the deficiency, he thought. Perhaps that would help to explain what he had first thought to be her irrational action. He closed his eyes against the argon-brightness, frustrated because his questions would forever be unanswered.

The slidewalk moved on, taking him away from the entertainment Sector. He entered a corridor of glassteel spires—Chicago's con-apt Sectors. Cipriano untangled the matrix of walks and ramps and lifts which led to his building, and reluctantly ascended to his con-apt level. Before he could palm the homeostatic lock, Jennifer was at the door, her face a portrait of concern. All the media had been blurting out the news of the near-catastrophe at the Eugenic Complex; she already knew what he had been forced to do.

During dinner she pressed him for details, which he produced grudgingly in short clipped sentences. Even Jennifer could perceive his lack of enthusiasm. "Perhaps I can help," she said.

At first he did not understand, for his mind was not really listening to her. Only after she stood up from the table and took a few steps towards the bedroom did he fully comprehend: she wished to console him in the only manner that she knew.

He felt cold. The memory of Feraxya's last moments of life passed through him like winter's breath. He could feel her reaching through the darkness, trying until the very end to make him *know* her, choosing him to be cured with her memory.

Jennifer called his name.

Feraxya's image shattered like broken glass, and he felt himself rising from his chair, entering the bedroom. A solitary candle burned there, where Jennifer sat making cursory adjustments on the machine. Turning, she reached out and began to undress him. Mechanically, he did the same for her.

As her clothes fell away, revealing her warm, silky flesh, he suddenly saw her differently. Instead of reaching for the wired bands and electrodes, Cirpirano extended his hand and touched one of her breasts. For a moment, she was transfixed, frozen by his action. His hand slowly moved, cupping the fullness in his hand, brushing her nipple with his fingers.

He felt it swell and become rigid as she spoke: "No . . . no! Oh, please Benjamin . . . don't. Please . . ."

"But why?" he asked as he removed his hand. Inwardly he was still marveling at the softness of her.

"Not like that," she was saying. "The machine. We *can't.* Not without the machine."

Something dark and ugly roiled inside his mind. He wanted to challenge her, to break through her defenses with his reckless anomie. But when he looked into her haunted eyes and saw the fear and disbelief that lay there, he knew that he could not.

She could not be touched. In either sense.

Lying down, he let her attach the electrodes, felt her recline beside him. The humming of the machine rose in intensity, crowding out his thoughts. Sensations seeped into him, sending slivers of pleasure into the maelstrom of his mind's center. Vaguely, he was aware of Jennifer writhing beside him, arching her body upwards as the simulations increased. His own desires, finally awakened, snaked through him, radiating out from his groin, threatening to strangle him with their grasp. He resisted the electronic impulses, and focused his mind's eye upon the Breeder Tank where Feraxya floated in the jellied sea, where she had been able to touch him, perhaps even love him, like no one had ever done before.

Jennifer increased the accentuator, forcing the machine to drive them to unusual, even for her, frenzy. The energy-burst overwhelmed him as he finally succumbed to the wave of pleasure collapsing over him.

Feraxya faded from his consciousness as he tripped through a series of orgasms.

The Machine Stops

E. M. Forster

PART I: THE AIRSHIP

Imagine, if you can, a small room, hexagonal in shape, like the cell of a bee. It is lighted neither by window nor by lamp, yet it is filled with a soft radiance. There are no apertures for ventilation, yet the air is fresh. There are no musical instruments, and yet, at the moment that my meditation opens, this room is throbbing with melodious sounds. An armchair is in the center, by its side a reading-desk—that is all the furniture. And in the armchair there sits a swaddled lump of flesh—a woman, about five feet high, with a face as white as a fungus. It is to her that the little room belongs.

An electric bell rang.

The woman touched a switch and the music was silent.

"I suppose I must see who it is," she thought, and set her chair in motion. The chair, like the music, was worked by machinery, and it rolled her to the other side of the room, where the bell still rang importunately.

"Who is it?" she called. Her voice was irritable, for she had been interrupted often since the music began. She knew several thousand people; in certain directions human intercourse had advanced enormously.

But when she listened into the receiver, her white face wrinkled into smiles, and she said:

"Very well. Let us talk, I will isolate myself, I do not expect anything important will happen for the next five minutes—for I can give you fully five minutes, Kuno. Then I must deliver my lecture on 'Music during the Australian Period.'"

She touched the isolation knob, so that no one else could speak to her. Then she touched the lighting apparatus, and the little room was plunged into darkness.

"Be quick!" she called, her irritation returning. "Be quick, Kuno; here I am in the dark wasting my time."

But it was fully fifteen seconds before the round plate that she held in her hands began to glow. A faint blue light shot across it, darkening to purple, and presently she could see the image of her son, who lived on the other side of the earth, and he could see her.

"Kuno, how slow you are."

He smiled gravely.

"I really believe you enjoy dawdling."

"I have called you before, Mother, but you were always busy or isolated. I have something particular to say."

"What is it, dearest boy? Be quick. Why could you not send it by pneumatic post?"

"Because I prefer saying such a thing. I want—"

"Well?"

"I want you to come and see me."

Vashti watched his face in the blue plate.

"But I can see you!" she exclaimed. "What more do you want?"

"I want to see you not through the Machine," said Kuno. "I want to speak to you not through the wearisome Machine."

"Oh, hush!" said his mother, vaguely shocked. "You mustn't say anything against the Machine."

"Why not?"

"One mustn't."

"You talk as if a god had made the Machine," cried the other. "I believe that you pray to it when you are unhappy. Men made it, do not forget that. Great men, but men. The Machine is much, but it is not everything. I see something like you in this plate, but I do not see you. I hear something like you through this telephone, but I do not hear you. That is why I want you to come. Come and stop with me. Pay me a visit, so that we can meet face to face, and talk about the hopes that are in my mind."

She replied that she could scarcely spare the time for a visit.

"The airship barely takes two days to fly between me and you."

"I dislike airships."

"Why?"

"I dislike seeing the horrible brown earth, and the sea, and the stars when it is dark. I get no ideas in an airship."

"I do not get them anywhere else."

"What kind of ideas can the air give you?"

He paused for an instant.

"Do you know four big stars that form an oblong, and three stars close together in the middle of the oblong, and hanging from these stars, three other stars?"

"No, I do not. I dislike the stars. But did they give you an idea? How interesting: tell me."

"I had an idea that they were like a man."

"I do not understand."

"The four big stars are the man's shoulders and his knees. The three stars in the middle are his belts that men wore once, and the three stars hanging are like a sword."

"A sword?"

"Men carried swords about with them, to kill animals and other men."

"It does not strike me as a very good idea, but it is certainly original. When did it come to you first?"

"In the airship—" He broke off, and she fancied that he looked sad. She could not be sure, for the Machine did not transmit nuances of expression. It only gave a general idea of people—an idea that was good enough for all practical purposes, Vashti thought. The imponderable bloom, declared by a discredited philosophy to be the actual essence of intercourse, was rightly ignored by the Machine, just as the imponderable bloom of the grape was ignored by the manufacturers of artificial fruit. Something "good enough" had long since been accepted by our race.

"The truth is," he continued, "that I want to see these stars again. They are curious stars. I want to see them not from the airship, but from the surface of the earth, as our ancestors did, thousands of years ago. I want to visit the surface of the earth."

She was shocked again.

"Mother, you must come, if only to explain to me what is the harm of visiting the surface of the earth."

"No harm," she replied, controlling herself. "But no advantage. The surface of the earth is only dust and mud, no life remains on it, and you would need a respirator, or the cold of the outer air would kill you. One dies immediately in the outer air."

"I know; of course I shall take all precautions."

"And besides—

"Well?"

She considered and chose her words with care. Her son had a queer temper, and she wished to dissuade him from the expedition.

"It is contrary to the spirit of the age," she asserted.

"Do you mean by that, contrary to the Machine?"

"In a sense, but—"

His image in the blue plate faded.

"Kuno!"

He had isolated himself.

For a moment Vashti felt lonely.

Then she generated the light, and the sight of her room, flooded with radiance and studded with electric buttons and switches everywhere—buttons to call for food, for music, for clothing. There was the hotbath button, by pressure of which a basin of (imitation) marble rose out of the floor, filled to the brim with a warm deodorized liquid. There was the cold-bath button. There was the button that produced literature. And there were of course the buttons by which she communicated with her friends. The room, though it contained nothing, was in touch with all that she cared for in the world.

Vashti's next move was to turn off the isolation-switch and all the accumulations of the last three minutes burst upon her. The room was filled with the noise of bells, and speaking-tubes. What was the new food like? Could she recommend it? Had she had any ideas lately? Might one tell her one's own ideas? Would she make an engagement to visit the public nurseries at an early date?—say this day month.

To most of these questions she replied with irritation—a growing quality in that accelerated age. She said that the new food was horrible. That she could not visit the public nurseries through press of engagements. That she had no ideas of her own but had just been told one—that four stars and three in the middle were like a man: she doubted there was much in it. Then she switched off her correspondents, for it was time to deliver her lecture on Australian music.

The clumsy system of public gatherings had been long since abandoned; neither Vashti nor her audience stirred from their rooms. Seated in her armchair she spoke, while they in their armchairs heard her, fairly well, and saw her, fairly well. She opened with a humorous account of music in the pre-Mongolian epoch, and went on to describe the great outburst of song that followed the Chinese conquest. Remote and primeval as were the methods of I-San-So and the Brisbane school, she yet felt (she said) that study of them might repay the musician of today; they had freshness; they had, above all, ideas.

Her lecture, which lasted ten minutes, was well received, and at its conclusion she and many of her audience listened to a lecture on the sea; there were ideas to be got from the sea; the speaker had donned a respirator and visited it lately. Then she fed, talked to many friends, had a bath, talked again, and summoned her bed.

The bed was not to her liking. It was too large, and she had a feeling for a small bed. Complaint was useless, for beds were of the same dimension all over the world, and to have had an alternative size would have involved vast alterations in the Machine. Vashti isolated herself—it was necessary, for neither day nor night existed under the ground—and reviewed all that had happened since she had summoned the bed last. Ideas? Scarcely any. Events—was Kuno's invitation an event?

By her side, on the little reading-desk, was a survival from the ages of litter—one book. This was the Book of the Machine. In it were instructions against every possible contingency. If she was hot or cold or dyspeptic or at loss for a word, she went to the Book, and it told her which button to press. The Central Committee published it. In accordance with a growing habit, it was richly bound.

Sitting up in the bed, she took it reverently in her hands. She glanced round the glowing room as if someone might be watching her. Then, half ashamed, half joyful, she murmured, "O Machine! O Machine!" and raised the volume to her lips. Thrice she kissed it, thrice inclined her head, thrice she felt the delirium of acquiescence. Her ritual performed, she turned to page 1367, which gave the times of the departure of the airships from the island in the southern hemisphere, under whose soil she lived, to the island in the northern hemisphere, whereunder lived her son.

She thought, "I have not the time."

She made the room dark and slept; she awoke and made the room light; she ate and exchanged ideas with her friends, and listened to music and attended lectures; she made the room dark and slept. Above her, beneath her, and around her, the Machine hummed eternally; she did not notice the noise, for she had been born with it in her ears. The earth, carrying her, hummed as it sped through silence, turning her now to the invisible sun, now to the invisible stars. She awoke and made the room light.

"Kuno!"

"I will not talk to you," he answered, "until you come."

"Have you been on the surface of the earth since we spoke last?"

His image faded.

Again she consulted the Book. She became very nervous and lay back in her chair palpitating. Think of her as without teeth or hair. Presently she directed the chair to the wall, and pressed an unfamiliar button. The wall swung apart slowly. Through the opening she saw a tunnel that curved slightly, so that its goal was not visible. Should she go to see her son, here was the beginning of the journey.

Of course she knew all about the communication-system. There was nothing mysterious in it. She would summon a car and it would fly with her down the tunnel until it reached the lift that communicated with the airship station: the system had been in use for many, many years, long before the universal establishment of the Machine. And of course she had studied the civilization that had immediately preceded her own—the civilization that had mistaken the functions of the system, and had used it for bringing people to things, instead of for bringing things to people. Those funny old days, when men went for a change of air instead of changing the air in their rooms! And yet—she was frightened of the tunnel: she had not seen it since her last child was born. It curved—but was not quite as brilliant as a lecturer had suggested. Vashti was seized with the terrors of a direct experience. She shrank back into the room, and the wall closed up again.

"Kuno," she said, "I cannot come to see you. I am not well."

Immediately an enormous apparatus fell onto her out of the ceiling, a thermometer was automatically inserted between her lips, a stethoscope was automatically laid upon her heart. She lay powerless. Cool pads soothed her forehead. Kuno had telegraphed to her doctor.

So the human passions still blundered up and down in the Machine. Vashti drank the medicine that the doctor projected into her mouth, and the machinery retired into the ceiling. The voice of Kuno was heard asking how she felt.

"Better." Then with irritation: "But why do you not come to me instead?"

"Because I cannot leave this place."

"Why?"

"Because, any moment, something tremendous may happen."

"Have you been on the surface of the earth yet?"

"Not yet."

"Then what is it?"

"I will not tell you through the Machine."

She resumed her life.

But she thought of Kuno as a baby, his birth, his removal to the public nurseries, her one visit to him there, his visits to her—visits which stopped when the Machine had assigned him a room on the other side of the earth. "Parents, duties of," said the Book of the Machine, "cease at the moment of birth. P. 422327483." True, but there was something special about Kuno—indeed there had been something special about all her children—and, after all, she must brave the journey if he desired it. And "something tremendous might happen." What did he mean? The nonsense of a youthful man, no doubt, but she must go. Again she pressed the unfamiliar button, again the wall swung back, and she saw the tunnel that curved out of sight. Clasping the Book, she rose, tottered onto the platform, and summoned the car. Her room closed behind her: the journey to the northern hemisphere had begun.

Of course it was perfectly easy. The car approached and in it she found armchairs exactly like her own. When she signaled, it stopped, and she tottered into the lift. One other passenger was in the lift, the first fellow creature she had seen face to face for months. Few traveled in these days, for, thanks to the advance of science, the earth was exactly alike all over. Rapid intercourse, from which the previous civilization had hoped so much, had ended by defeating itself. What was the good of going to Pekin when it was just like Shrewsbury? Why return to Shrewsbury when it would be just like Pekin? Men seldom moved their bodies; all unrest was concentrated in the soul.

The airship service was a relic from the former age. It was kept up, because it was easier to keep it up than to stop it or to diminish it, but it now far exceeded the wants of the population. Vessel after vessel would rise from the vomitories of Rye or of Christchurch (I use the antique names), would sail into the crowded sky, and would draw up at the wharves of the south—empty. So nicely adjusted was the system, so independent of meteorology, that the sky, whether calm or cloudy, resembled a vast kaleidoscope whereon the same patterns periodically recurred. The ship on which Vashti sailed started now at sunset, now at dawn. But always, as it passed above Rheims, it would neighbor the ship that served between Helsingfors and the Brazils, and every third time it surmounted the Alps, the fleet of Palermo would cross its track behind. Night and day, wind and storm, tide and earthquake, impeded man no longer. He had harnessed Leviathan. All the old literature, with its praise of Nature, and its fear of Nature, rang false as the prattle of a child.

Yet, as Vashti saw the vast flank of the ship, stained with exposure to the outer air, her horror of direct experience returned. It was not quite like the airship in the cinematophote. For one thing it smelt—not strongly or unpleasantly, but it did smell, and with her eyes shut she would have known that a new thing was close to her. Then she had to walk to it from the lift, had to submit to glances from the other passengers. The man in front dropped his Book—no great matter, but it disquieted them all. In the rooms, if the Book was dropped, the floor raised it mechanically, but the gangway to the airship was not so prepared, and the sacred volume lay motionless. They stopped—the thing was unforeseen—and the man, instead of picking up his property, felt the muscles of his arm to see how they had failed him. Then someone actually said with direct utterance: "We shall be late"—and they trooped on board, Vashti treading on the pages as she did so.

Inside, her anxiety increased. The arrangements were old-fashioned and tough. There was even a female attendant, to whom she would have to announce her wants during the voyage. Of course a revolving platform ran the length of the boat, but she was expected to walk from it to her cabin. Some cabins were better than others, and she did not get the best. She thought the attendant had been unfair, and spasms of rage shook her. The glass valves had closed, she could not go back. She saw, at the end of the vestibule, the lift in which she had ascended going quietly up and down, empty. Beneath those corridors of shining tiles were rooms, tier below tier, reaching far into the earth, and in each room there sat a human being, eating, or sleeping, or producing ideas. And buried deep in the hive was her own room. Vashti was afraid.

"O Machine! O Machine!" she murmured, and caressed her Book, and was comforted.

Then the sides of the vestibule seemed to melt together, as do the passages that we see in dreams, the life vanished, the Book that had been dropped slid to the left and vanished, polished tiles rushed by like a stream of water, there was a slight jar, and the airship, issuing from its tunnel, soared above the waters of a tropical ocean.

It was night. For a moment she saw the coast of Sumatra edged by the phosphorescence of waves, and crowned by lighthouses, still sending forth their disregarded beams. They also vanished, and only the stars distracted her. They were not motionless, but swayed to and fro above her head, thronging out of one sky-light into another, as if the universe and not the airship was careening. And, as often happens on clear nights, they seemed now to be in perspective, now on a plane; now piled tier beyond tier into the infinite heavens, now concealing infinity, a roof limiting forever the visions of men. In either case they seemed intolerable. "Are we to travel in the dark?" called the passengers angrily, and the attendant, who had been careless, generated the light, and pulled down the blinds of pliable metal. When the airships had been built, the desire to look directly at things still lingered in the world. Hence the extraordinary number of skylights and windows, and the proportionate discomfort to those who were civilized and refined. Even in Vashti's cabin one star peeped through a flaw in the blind, and after a few hours' uneasy slumber, she was disturbed by an unfamiliar glow, which was the dawn.

Quick as the ship had sped westwards, the earth had rolled eastwards quicker still, and had dragged back Vashti and her companions towards the sun. Science could prolong the night, but only for a little, and those high hopes of neutralizing the earth's diurnal revolution had passed, together with hopes that were possibly higher. To "keep pace with the sun," or even to outstrip it, had been the aim of the civilization preceding this. Racing aeroplanes had been built for the purpose, capable of enormous speed, and steered by the greatest intellects of the epoch. Round the globe they went, round and round, westward, westward, round and round, amidst humanity's applause. In vain. The globe went eastward quicker still, horrible accidents occurred, and the Committee of the Machine, at the time rising into prominence, declared the pursuit illegal, unmechanical, and punishable by Homelessness.

Of Homelessness more will be said later.

Doubtless the Committee was right. Yet the attempt to "defeat the sun" aroused the last common interest that our race experienced about the heavenly bodies, or indeed about anything. It was the last time that men were compacted by thinking of a power outside the world. The sun had conquered, yet it was the end of his spiritual dominion. Dawn, midday, twilight, the zodiacal path, touched neither men's lives nor their hearts, and science retreated into the ground, to concentrate herself upon problems that she was certain of solving.

So when Vashti found her cabin invaded by a rosy finger of light, she was annoyed, and tried to adjust the blind. But the blind flew up altogether, and she saw through the skylight small pink clouds, swaying against a background of blue, and as the sun crept higher, its radiance entered direct, brimming down the wall, like a golden sea. It rose and fell with the airship's motion, just as waves rise and fall, but it advanced steadily as a tide advances. Unless she was careful, it would strike her face. A spasm of horror shook her and she rang for the attendant. The attendant too was horrified, but she could do nothing; it was not her place to mend the blind. She could only suggest that the lady should change her cabin, which she accordingly prepared to do.

People were almost exactly alike all over the world, but the attendant of the airship, perhaps owing to her exceptional duties, had grown a little out of the common. She had often to address passengers with direct speech, and this had given her a certain roughness and originality of manner. When Vashti swerved away from the sunbeams with a cry, she behaved barbarically—she put out her hand to steady her.

"How dare you!" exclaimed the passenger. "You forget yourself!"

The woman was confused, and apologized for not having let her fall. People never touch one another. The custom had become obsolete, owing to the Machine.

"Where are we now?" asked Vashti haughtily.

"We are over Asia," said the attendant, anxious to be polite.

"Asia?"

"You must excuse my common way of speaking. I have got into the habit of calling places over which I pass by their unmechanical names."

"Oh, I remember Asia. The Mongols came from it."

"Beneath us, in the open air, stood a city that was once called Simla."

"Have you ever heard of the Mongols and of the Brisbane school?"

"No."

"Brisbane also stood in the open air."

"Those mountains to the right—let me show you them." She pushed back a metal blind. The main chain of the Himalayas was revealed. "They were once called the Roof of the World, those mountains."

"What a foolish name!"

"You must remember that, before the dawn of civilization, they seemed to be an impenetrable wall that touched the stars. It was supposed that no one but the gods could exist above their summits. How we have advanced, thanks to the Machine!"

"How we have advanced, thanks to the Machine!" said Vashti.

"How we have advanced, thanks to the Machine!" echoed the passenger who had dropped his Book the night before, and who was standing in the passage.

"And that white stuff in the cracks?—what is it?"

"I have forgotten its name."

"Cover the window, please. These mountains give me no ideas."

The northern aspect of the Himalayas was in deep shadow: on the Indian slope the sun had just prevailed. The forests had been destroyed during the literature epoch for the purpose of making newspaper-pulp, but the snows were awakening to their morning glory, and clouds still hung on the breasts of Kinchinjunga. In the plain were seen the ruins of cities, with diminished rivers creeping by their walls, and by the sides of these were sometimes the signs of vomitories, marking the cities of today. Over the whole prospect airships rushed, crossing and intercrossing with incredible aplomb, and rising nonchalantly when they desired to escape the perturbations of the lower atmosphere and to traverse the Roof of the World.

"We have indeed advanced, thanks to the Machine," repeated the attendant, and hid the Himalayas behind a metal blind.

The day dragged wearily forward. The passengers sat each in his cabin, avoiding one another with an almost physical repulsion and longing to be once more under the surface of the earth. There were eight or ten of them, mostly young males, sent out from the public nurseries to inhabit the rooms of those who had died in various parts of the earth. The man who had dropped his Book was on the homeward journey. He had been sent to Sumatra for the purpose of propagating the race. Vashti alone was traveling by her private will.

At midday she took a second glance at the earth. The airship was crossing another range of mountains, but she could see little, owing to clouds. Masses of black rock hovered below her, and merged indistinctly into gray. Their shapes were fantastic; one of them resembled a prostrate man.

"No ideas here," murmured Vashti, and hid the Caucasus behind a metal blind.

In the evening she looked again. They were crossing a golden sea, in which lay many small islands and one peninsula.

She repeated, "No ideas here," and hid Greece behind a metal blind.

PART II: THE MENDING APPARATUS

By a vestibule, by a lift, by a tubular railway, by a platform, by a sliding door—by reversing all the steps of her departure did Vashti arrive at her son's room, which exactly resembled her own. She might well declare that the visit was superfluous. The buttons, the knobs, the reading-desk with the Book, the temperature, the atmosphere, the illumination—all were exactly the same. And if Kuno himself, flesh of her flesh, stood close beside her at last, what profit was there in that? She was too well-bred to shake him by the hand.

Averting her eyes, she spoke as follows:

"Here I am. I have had the most terrible journey and greatly retarded the development of my soul. It is not worth it, Kuno, it is not worth it. My time is too precious. The sunlight almost touched me, and I have met with the rudest people. I can only stop a few minutes. Say what you want to say, and then I must return."

"I have been threatened with Homelessness, and I could not tell you such a thing through the Machine."

Homelessness means death. The victim is exposed to the air, which kills him.

"I have been outside since I spoke to you last. The tremendous thing has happened, and they have discovered me."

"But why shouldn't you go outside!" she exclaimed. "It is perfectly legal, perfectly mechanical, to visit the surface of the earth. I have lately been to a lecture on the sea; there is no objection to that; one simply summons a respirator and gets an Egression-permit. It is not the kind of thing that spiritually minded people do, and I begged you not to do it, but there is no legal objection to it."

"I did not get an Egression-permit."

"Then how did you get out?"

"I found a way of my own."

The phrase conveyed no meaning to her, and he had to repeat it.

"A way of your own?" she whispered. "But that would be wrong."

"Why?"

The question shocked her beyond measure.

"You are beginning to worship the Machine," he said coldly. "You think it irreligious of me to have found out a way of my own. It was just what the Committee thought, when they threatened me with Homelessness."

At this she grew angry. "I worship nothing!" she cried. "I am most advanced. I don't think you irreligious, for there is no such thing as religion left. All the fear and the superstition that existed once have been destroyed by the Machine. I only meant that to find out a way of your own was— Besides, there is no new way out."

"So it is always supposed."

"Except through the vomitories, for which one must have an Egression-permit, it is impossible to get out. The Book says so."

"Well, the Book's wrong, for I have been out on my feet."

For Kuno was possessed of a certain physical strength.

By these days it was a demerit to be muscular. Each infant was examined at birth, and all who promised undue strength were destroyed. Humanitarians may protest, but it would have been no true kindness to let an athlete live; he would never have been happy in that state of life to which the Machine had called him; he would have yearned for trees to climb, rivers to bathe in, meadows and hills against which he might measure his body. Man must be adapted to his surroundings, must he not? In the dawn of the world our weak must be exposed on Mount Taygetus; in its twilight our strong will suffer Euthanasia, that the Machine may progress, that the Machine may progress, that the Machine may progress eternally.

"You know that we have lost the sense of space. We say 'space is annihilated,' but we have annihilated not space, but the sense thereof. We have lost a part of ourselves. I determined to recover it, and I began by walking up and down the platform of the railway outside my room. Up and down, until I was tired, and so did recapture the meaning of 'near' and 'far.' 'Near' is a place to which I can get quickly on my feet, not a place to which the train or the airship will take me quickly. 'Far' is a place to which I cannot get quickly on my feet; the vomitory is 'far,' though I could be there in thirty-eight seconds by summoning the train. Man is the measure. That was my first lesson. Man's feet are the measure for distance, his hands are the measure for ownership, his body is the measure for all that is lovable and desirable and strong. Then I went further; it was then that I called to you for the first time, and you would not come.

"This city, as you know, is built deep beneath the surface of the earth, with only the vomitories protruding. Having paced the platform outside my own room, I took the lift to the next platform and paced that also, and so with each in turn, until I came to the topmost, above which begins the earth. All the platforms were exactly alike, and all that I gained by visiting them was to develop my sense of space and my muscles. I think I should have been content with this—it is not a little thing—but as I walked and brooded, it occured to me that our cities had been built in the days when men still breathed the outer air and that there had been ventilation shafts. Had they been destroyed by all the food-tubes and medicine-tubes and music-tubes that the Machine had evolved lately? Or did traces of them remain? One thing was certain. If I came upon them anywhere, it would be in the railway-tunnels of the topmost story. Everywhere else, all space was accounted for.

"I am telling my story quickly, but don't think that I was not a coward or that your answers never depressed me. It is not the proper thing, it is not mechanical, it is not decent to walk along a railway-tunnel. I did not fear that I might tread upon a live rail and be killed. I feared something far more intangible—doing what was not contemplated by the Machine. Then I said to myself, 'Man is the measure,' and I went, and after many visits I found an opening.

"The tunnels, of course, were lighted. Everything is light, artificial light; darkness is the exception. So when I saw a black gap in the tiles, I knew that it was an exception, and rejoiced. I put in my arm—I could put in no more at first—and waved it round and round in ecstasy. I loosened another tile, and put in my head, and shouted into the darkness: 'I am coming, I shall do it yet,' and my voice reverberated down endless passages. I seemed to hear the spirits of those dead workmen who had returned each evening to the starlight and to their wives, and all the generations who had lived in the open air called back to me, 'You will do it yet, you are coming.' "

He paused, and, absurd as he was, his last words moved her. For Kuno had lately asked to be a father, and his request had been refused by the Committee. His was not a type that the Machine desired to hand on.

"Then a train passed. It brushed by me, but I thrust my head and arms into the hole. I had done enough for one day, so I crawled back to the platform, went down in the lift, and summoned my bed. Ah, what dreams! And again I called you, and again you refused."

She shook her head and said:

"Don't. Don't talk of these terrible things. You make me miserable. You are throwing civilization away."

"But I had got back the sense of space and a man cannot rest then. I determined to get in at the hole and climb the shaft. And so I exercised my arms. Day after day I went through ridiculous movements, until my flesh ached, and I could hang by my hands and hold the pillow of my bed outstretched for many minutes. Then I summoned a respirator, and started.

"It was easy at first. The mortar had somehow rotted, and I soon pushed some more tiles in, and clambered after them into the darkness, and the spirits of the dead comforted me. I don't know what I mean by that. I just say what I felt. I felt, for the first time, that a protest had been lodged against corruption, and that even as the dead were comforting me, so I was comforting the unborn. I felt that humanity existed, and that it existed without clothes. How can I possibly explain this? It was naked, humanity seemed naked, and all these tubes and buttons and machineries neither came into the world with us, nor will they follow us out, nor do they matter supremely while we are here. Had I been strong, I would have torn off every garment I had, and gone out into the outer air unswaddled. But this is not for me, nor perhaps for my generation. I climbed with my respirator and my hygienic clothes and my dietetic tabloids! Better thus than not at all.

"There was a ladder, made of some primeval metal. The light from the railway fell upon its lowest rungs, and I saw that it led straight upwards out of the rubble at the bottom of the shaft. Perhaps our ancestors ran up and down it a dozen times daily, in their building. As I climbed, the rough edges cut through my gloves so that my hands bled. The light helped me for a little, and then came darkness and, worse still, silence which pierced my ears like a sword. The Machine hums! Did you know that? Its hum penetrates our blood, and may even guide our thoughts. Who knows! I was getting beyond its power. Then I thought: 'This silence means that I am doing wrong.' But I heard voices in the silence, and again they strengthened me." He laughed. "I had need of them. The next moment I cracked my head against something."

She sighed.

"I had reached one of those pneumatic stoppers that defend us from the outer air. You may have noticed them on the airship. Pitch dark, my feet on the rungs of an invisible ladder, my hands cut; I cannot explain how I lived through this part, but the voices still comforted me, and I felt for fastenings. The stopper, I suppose, was about eight feet across. I passed my hand over it as far as I could reach. It was perfectly smooth. I felt it almost to the center. Not quite to the center, for my arm was too short. Then the voice said: 'Jump. It is worth it. There may be a handle in the center, and you may catch hold of it and so come to us your own way. And if there is no handle so that you may fall and are dashed to pieces—it is still worth it; you will still come to us your own way.' So I jumped. There was a handle, and—"

He paused. Tears gathered in his mother's eyes. She knew that he was fated. If he did not die today he would die tomorrow. There was not room for such a person in the world. And with her pity, disgust mingled. She was ashamed at having borne such a son, she who had always been so respectable and so full of ideas. Was he really the little boy to whom she had taught the use of his stops and buttons, and to whom she had given his first lesson in the Book? The very hair that disfigured his lip showed that he was reverting to some savage type. On atavism the Machine can have no mercy.

"There was a handle, and I did catch it. I hung tranced over the darkness and heard the hum of these workings as the last whisper in a dying dream. All the things I had cared about and all the people I had spoken to through tubes appeared infinitely little. Meanwhile the handle revolved. My weight had set something in motion and I spun slowly, and then—

"I cannot describe it. I was lying with my face to the sunshine.

Blood poured from my nose and ears and I heard a tremendous roaring. The stopper, with me clinging to it, had simply been blown out of the earth, and the air that we make down here was escaping through the vent into the air above. It burst up like a fountain. I crawled back to it—for the upper air hurts—and, as it were, I took great sips from the edge. My respirator had flown goodness knows where, clothes were torn. I just lay with my lips close to the hole, and I sipped until the bleeding stopped. You can imagine nothing so curious. This hollow in the grass—I will speak of it in a minute—the sun shining into it, not brilliantly but through marbled clouds—the peace, the nonchalance, the sense of space, and, brushing my cheek, the roaring fountain of our artificial air! Soon I spied my respirator, bobbing up and down in the current high above my head, and higher still were many airships. But no one ever looks out of airships, and in my case they could not have picked me up. There I was, stranded. The sun shone a little way down the shaft, and revealed the topmost rung of the ladder, but it was hopeless trying to reach it. I should either have been tossed up again by the escape, or else have fallen in, and died. I could only lie on the grass, sipping and sipping, and from time to time glancing around me.

"I knew that I was in Wessex, for I had taken care to go to a lecture on the subject before starting. Wessex lies above the room in which we are talking now. It was once an important state. Its kings held all the southern coast from the Andredswald to Cornwall, while the Wansdyke protected them on the north, running over the high ground. The lecturer was only concerned with the rise of Wessex, so I do not know how long it remained an international power, nor would the knowledge have assisted me. To tell the truth I could do nothing but laugh, during this part. There was I, with a pneumatic stopper by my side and a respirator bobbing over my head, imprisoned, all three of us, in a grass-grown hollow that was edged with fern."

Then he grew grave again.

"Lucky for me that it was a hollow. For the air began to fall back into it and to fill it as water fills a bowl. I could crawl about. Presently I stood. I breathed a mixture, in which the air that hurts predominated whenever I tried to climb the sides. This was not so bad. I had not lost my tabloids and remained ridiculously cheerful, and as for the Machine, I forgot about it altogether. My one aim now was to get to the top, where the ferns were, and to view whatever objects lay beyond.

"I rushed the slope. The new air was still too bitter for me and I came rolling back, after a momentary vision of something gray. The sun grew very feeble, and I remembered that he was in Scorpio—I had been to a lecture on that too. If the sun is in Scorpio and you are in Wessex, it means that you must be as quick as you can, or it will get too dark. (This is the first bit of useful information I have ever got from a lecture, and I expect it will be the last.) It made me try frantically to breathe the new air, and to advance as far as I dared out of my pond. The hollow filled so slowly. At times I thought that my fountain played with less vigor. My respirator seemed to dance nearer the earth; the roar was decreasing."

He broke off.

"I don't think this is interesting you. The rest will interest you even less. There are no ideas in it, and I wish that I had not troubled you to come. We are too different, Mother."

She told him to continue.

"It was evening before I climbed the bank. The sun had very nearly slipped out of the sky by this time, and I could not get a good view. You, who have just crossed the Roof of the World, will not want to hear an account of the little hills that I saw—low colorless hills. But to me they were living and the turf that covered them was a skin, under which their muscles rippled, and I felt those hills had called with incalculable force to men in the past, and that men had loved them. Now they sleep—perhaps forever. They commune with humanity in dreams. Happy the man, happy the woman, who awakes the hills of Wessex. For though they sleep, they will never die."

His voice rose passionately.

"Cannot you see, cannot all your lecturers see, that it is we who are dying, and that down here the only thing that really lives is the Machine? We created the Machine, to do our will, but we cannot make it do our will now. It has robbed us of the sense of space and of the sense of touch, it has blurred every human relation and narrowed down love to a carnal act, it has paralyzed our bodies and our wills, and now it compels us to worship it. The Machine develops—but not to our goal. We only exist as the blood corpuscles that course through its arteries, and if it could work without us, it would let us die. Oh, I have no remedy—or, at least, only one—to tell men again and again that I have seen the hills of Wessex as Aelfrid saw them when he overthrew the Danes.

"So the sun set. I forgot to mention that a belt of mist lay between my hill and other hills, and that it was the color of pearl."

He broke off for the second time.

"Go on. Nothing that you say can distress me now. I am hardened."

"I had meant to tell you the rest, but I cannot: I know that I cannot: goodbye."

Vashti stood irresolute. All her nerves were tingling with his blasphemies. But she was also inquisitive.

"This is unfair," she complained. "You have called me across the world to hear your story, and hear it I will. Tell me—as briefly as possible, for this is a disastrous waste of time—tell me how you returned to civilization."

"Oh—that!" he said, starting. "You would like to hear about civilization. Certainly. Had I got to where my respirator fell down?"

"No—but I understand everything now. You put on your respirator, and managed to walk along the surface of the earth to a vomitory, and there your conduct was reported to the Central Committee."

"By no means."

He passed his hand over his forehead, as if dispelling some strong impression. Then, resuming his narrative, he warmed to it again.

"My respirator fell about sunset. I had mentioned that the fountain seemed feebled, had I not?"

"Yes."

"About sunset, it let the respirator fall. As I said, I had entirely forgotten about the Machine, and I paid no great attention at the time, being occupied with other things. I had my pool of air, into which I could dip when the outer keenness became intolerable, and which would possibly remain for days, provided that no wind sprang up to disperse it. Not until it was too late, did I realize what the stoppage of the escape implied. You see—the gap in the tunnel had been mended; the Mending Apparatus, the Mending Apparatus, was after me.

"One other warning I had, but I neglected it. The sky at night was clearer than it had been in the day, and the moon, which was about half the sky behind the sun, shone into the dell at moments quite brightly. I was in my usual place—on the boundary between the two atmospheres—when I thought I saw something dark move across the bottom on the dell, and vanish into the shaft. In my folly, I ran down. I bent over and listened, and I thought I heard a faint scraping noise in the depths.

"At this—but it was too late—I took alarm. I determined to put on my respirator and to walk right out of the dell. But my respirator had gone. I knew exactly where it had fallen—between the stopper and the aperture—and I could even feel the mark that it had made in the turf. It had gone, and I realized that something evil was at work, and I had better escape to the other air, and, if I must die, die running towards the cloud that had been the color of a pearl. I never started. Out of the shaft—it is too horrible. A worm, a long white worm, had crawled out of the shaft and was gliding over the moonlit grass.

"I screamed. I did everything that I should not have done, I stamped upon the creature instead of flying from it, and it fought. The worm let me run all over the dell, but edged up my leg as I ran. 'Help!' I cried. (That part is too awful. It belongs to the part that you will never know.) 'Help!" I cried. (Why cannot we suffer in silence?) 'Help!' I cried. Then my feet were wound together, I fell, I was dragged away from the dear ferns and the living hills, and past the great metal stopper (I can tell you this part), and I thought it might save me again if I caught hold of the handle. It also was enwrapped, it also. Oh, the whole dell was full of the things. They were searching it in all directions, they were denuding it, and the white snouts of others peeped out of the hole, ready if needed. Everything that could be moved they brought—brushwood, bundles of fern, everything, and down we all went intertwined into hell. The last things that I saw, ere the stopper closed after us, were certain stars, and I felt that a man of my sort lived in the sky. For I did fight, I fought till the very end, and it was only my head hitting against the ladder that quieted me. I woke up in this room. The worms had vanished. I was surrounded by artificial air, artificial light, artificial peace, and my friends were calling to me down speaking-tubes to know whether I had come across any new ideas lately."

Here his story ended. Discussion of it was impossible, and Vashti turned to go.

"It will end in Homelessness," she said quietly.

"I wish it would," retorted Kuno.

"The Machine has been most merciful."

"I prefer the mercy of God."

"By that superstitious phrase, do you mean that you could live in the outer air?"

"Yes."

"Have you ever seen, round the vomitories, the bones of those who were extruded after the Great Rebellion?"

"Yes."

"They were left where they perished for our edification. A few crawled away, but they perished, too—who can doubt it? And so with the Homeless of our own day. The surface of the earth supports life no longer."

"Indeed."

"Ferns and a little grass may survive, but all higher forms have perished. Has any airship detected them?"

"No."

"Has any lecturer dealt with them?"

"No."

"Then why this obstinacy?"

"Because I have seen them," he exploded.

"Seen *what?*"

"Because I have seen her in the twilight—because she came to my help when I called—because she, too, was entangled by the worms, and, luckier than I, was killed by one of them piercing her throat."

He was mad. Vashti departed, nor, in the troubles that followed, did she ever see his face again.

PART III: THE HOMELESS

During the years that followed Kuno's escapade, two important developments took place in the Machine. On the surface they were revolutionary, but in either case men's minds had been prepared beforehand, and they did but express tendencies that were latent already.

The first of these was the abolition of respirators.

Advanced thinkers, like Vashti, had always held it foolish to visit the surface of the earth. Airships might be necessary, but what was the good of going out for mere curiosity and crawling along for a mile or two in a terrestrial motor? The habit was vulgar and perhaps faintly improper; it was unproductive of ideas, and had no connection with the habits that really mattered. So respirators were abolished, and with them, of course, the terrestrial motors, and except for a few lecturers, who complained that they were debarred access to their subject-matter, the development was accepted quietly. Those who still wanted to know what the earth was like had after all only to listen to some gramophone, or to look into some cinematophote. And even the lecturers acquiesced when they found that a lecture on the sea was none the less stimulating when compiled out of other lectures that had already been delivered on the same subject.

"Beware of first-hand ideas!" exclaimed one of the most advanced of them. "First-hand ideas do not really exist. They are but the physical impressions produced by love and fear, and on this gross foundation who could erect a philosophy? Let your ideas be second-hand, and if possible tenth-hand, for then they will be far removed from that disturbing element—direct observation. Do not learn anything about this subject of mine—the French Revolution. Learn instead what I think that Enicharmon thought Urizen thought Gutch thought Ho-Young thought Chi-Bo-Sing thought Lafcadio Hearn thought Carlyle thought Mirabeau said about the French Revolution. Through the medium of these eight great minds, the blood that was shed at Paris and the windows that were broken at Versailles will be clarified to an idea which you may employ most profitably in your daily lives. But be sure that the intermediates are many and varied, for in history one authority exists to counteract another. Urizen must counteract the skepticism of Ho-Young and Enicharmon, I must myself counteract the impetuosity of Gutch. You who listen to me are in a better position to judge about the French Revolution than I am. Your descendants will be in an even better position than you, for they will be added to the chain. And in time"—his voice rose—"there will come a generation that has got beyond impressions, a generation absolutely colorless, a generation

seraphically free
From taint of personality,

which will see the French Revolution not as it happened, nor as they would like it to have happened, but as it would have happened, had it taken place in the days of the Machine."

Tremendous applause greeted this lecture, which did but voice a feeling already latent in the minds of men—a feeling that terrestrial facts must be ignored, and that the abolition of respirators was a positive gain. It was even suggested that airships should be abolished too. This was not done, because airships had somehow worked themselves into the Machine's system. But year by year they were used less, and mentioned less by thoughtful men.

The second great development was the re-establishment of religion.

This, too, had been voiced in the celebrated lecture. No one could mistake the reverent tone in which the peroration had concluded, and it awakened a responsive echo in the heart of each. Those who had long worshiped silently, now began to talk. They described the strange feeling of peace that came over them when they handled the Book of the Machine, the pleasure that it was to repeat certain numerals out of it, however little meaning those numerals conveyed to the outward ear, the ecstasy of touching a button, however unimportant, or of ringing an electric bell, however superfluously.

"The Machine," they exclaimed, "feeds us and clothes us and houses us; through it we speak to one another, through it we see one another, in it we have our being. The machine is the friend of ideas and the enemy of superstition: the Machine omnipotent, eternal; blessed is the Machine." And before long this allocution was printed on the first page of the Book, and in subsequent editions the ritual swelled into a complicated system of praise and prayer. The word *religion* was sedulously avoided, and in theory the Machine was still the creation and the implement of man. But in practice all, save a few retrogrades, worshiped it as divine. Nor was it worshiped in unity. One believer would be chiefly impressed by the blue optic plates, through which he saw other believers; another by the Mending Apparatus, which sinful Kuno had compared to worms; another by the lifts, another by the Book. And each would pray to this or to that, and ask it to intercede for him with the Machine as a whole. Persecution—that also was present. It did not break out, for reasons that will be set forward shortly. But it was latent, and all who did not accept the minimum known as "undenominational Mechanism" lived in danger of Homelessness, which means death, as we know.

To attribute these two great developments to the Central Committee, is to take a very narrow view of civilization. The Central Committee announced the developments, it is true, but they were no more the cause of them than were the kings of the imperialistic period the cause of war. Rather did they yield to some invincible pressure, which came no one knew whither, and which, when gratified, was succeeded by some new pressure equally invincible. To such a state of affairs it is convenient to give the name of progress. No one confessed the Machine was out of hand. Year by year it was served with increased efficiency and decreased intelligence. The better a man knew his own duties upon it, the less he understood the duties of his neighbor, and in all the world there was not one who understood the monster as a whole. Those master brains had perished. They had left full directions, it is true, and their successors had each of them mastered a portion of those directions. But Humanity, in its desire for comfort, had overreached itself. It had exploited the riches of nature too far. Quietly and complacently, it was sinking into decadence, and progress had come to mean the progress of the Machine.

As for Vashti, her life went peacefully forward until the final disaster. She made her room dark and slept; she awoke and made the room light. She lectured and attended lectures. She exchanged ideas with her innumerable friends and believed she was growing more spiritual. At times a friend was granted Euthanasia, and left his or her room for the homelessness that is beyond all human conception. Vashti did not much mind. After an unsuccessful lecture, she would sometimes ask for Euthanasia herself. But the deathrate was not permitted to exceed the birthrate, and the Machine had hitherto refused it to her.

The troubles began quietly, long before she was conscious of them.

One day she was astonished at receiving a message from her son. They never communicated, having nothing in common, and she had only heard indirectly that he was still alive, and had been transferred from the northern hemisphere, where he had behaved so mischievously, to the southern—indeed, to a room not far from her own.

"Does he want me to visit him?" She thought. "Never again, never. And I have not the time."

No, it was madness of another kind.

He refused to visualize his face upon the blue plate, and speaking out of the darkness with solemnity said:

"The Machine stops."

"What do you say?"

"The Machine is stopping. I know it, I know the signs."

She burst into a peal of laughter. He heard her and was angry, and they spoke no more.

"Can you imagine anything more absurd?" she cried to a friend. "A man who was my son believes that the Machine is stopping. It would be impious if it was not so mad."

"The Machine is stopping?" her friend replied. "What does that mean? The phrase conveys nothing to me."

"Nor to me."

"He does not refer, I suppose, to the trouble there has been lately with the music?"

"Oh, no, of course not. Let us talk about music."

"Have you complained to the authorities?"

"Yes, and they say it wants mending, and referred me to the Committee of the Mending Apparatus. I complained of those curious gasping sighs that disfigure the symphonies of the Brisbane school. They sound like someone in pain. The Committee of the Mending Apparatus say that it shall be remedied shortly."

Obscurely worried, she resumed her life. For one thing, the defect in the music irritated her. For another thing she could not forget Kuno's speech. If he had known that the music was out of repair—he could not know it, for he detested music—if he had known that it was wrong, "the Machine stops" was exactly the venomous sort of remark he would have made. Of course he had made it at a venture, but the coincidence annoyed her, and she spoke with some petulance to the Committee of the Mending Apparatus.

They replied, as before, that the defect would be set right shortly.

"Shortly! At once!" she retorted. "Why should I be worried by imperfect music? Things are always put right at once. If you do not mend it at once, I shall complain to the Central Committee."

"No personal complaints are received by the Central Committee," the Committee of the Mending Apparatus replied.

"Through whom am I to make my complaint, then?"

"Through us."

"I complain then."

"Your complaint shall be forwarded in its turn."

"Have others complained?"

This question was unmechanical, and the Committee of the Mending Apparatus refused to answer it.

"It is too bad!" she exclaimed to another of her friends. "There never was such an unfortunate woman as myself. I can never be sure of my music now. It gets worse and worse each time I summon it."

"I too have my troubles," the friend replied. "Sometimes my ideas are interruped by a slight jarring noise."

"What is it?"

"I do not know whether it is inside my head, or inside the wall."

"Complain, in either case."

"I have complained, and my complaint will be forwarded in its turn to the Central Committee."

Time passed, and they resented the defects no longer. The defects had not been remedied, but the human tissues in the latter day had become so subservient, that they readily adapted themselves to every caprice of the Machine. The sigh at the crisis of the Brisbane symphony no longer irritated Vashti; she accepted it as part of the melody. The jarring noise, whether in the head or in the wall, was no longer resented by her friend. And so with the moldy artificial fruit, so with the bath water that began to stink, so with the defective rhymes that the poetry machine had taken to emitting. All were bitterly complained of at first, and then acquiesced in and forgotten. Things went from bad to worse unchallenged.

It was otherwise with the failure of the sleeping apparatus. That was a more serious stoppage. There came a day when over the whole world—in Sumatra, in Wessex, in the innumerable cities of Courland and Brazil—the beds, when summoned by their tired owners, failed to appear. It may seem a ludicrous matter, but from it we may date the collapse of humanity. The Committee responsible for the failure was assailed by complainants, whom it referred, as usual, to the Committee of the Mending Apparatus, who in its turn assured them that their complaints would be forwarded to the Central Committee. But the discontent grew, for mankind was not yet sufficiently adaptable to do without sleeping.

"Someone is meddling with the Machine"—they began.

"Someone is trying to make himself king, to reintroduce the personal element."

"Punish that man with Homelessness."

"To the rescue! Avenge the Machine! Avenge the Machine!"

"War! Kill the man!"

But the Committee of the Mending Apparatus now came forward, and allayed the panic with well-chosen words. It confessed that the Mending Apparatus was itself in need of repair.

The effect of this frank confession was admirable.

"Of course," said a famous lecturer—he of the French Revolution, who gilded each new decay with splendor—"of course we shall not press our complaints now. The Mending Apparatus has treated us so well in the past that we all sympathize with it, and will wait patiently for its recovery. In its own good time it will resume its duties. Meanwhile let us do without our beds, our tabloids, our other little wants. Such, I feel sure, would be the wish of the Machine."

Thousands of miles away his audience applauded. The Machine still linked them. Under the sea, beneath the roots of the mountains ran the wires through which they saw and heard, the enormous eyes and ears that were their heritage, and the hum of many workings clothed their thoughts in one garment of subserviency. Only the old and sick remained ungrateful, for it was rumored that Euthanasia, too, was out of order, and that pain had reappeared among men.

It became difficult to read. A blight entered the atmosphere and dulled its luminosity. At times Vashti could scarcely see across her room. The air, too, was foul. Loud were the complaints, impotent the remedies, heroic the tone of the lecturer as he cried: "Courage, courage! What matter so long as the Machine goes on? To it the darkness and the light are one." And though things improved again after a time, the old brilliancy was never recaptured, and humanity never recovered from its entrance into twilight. There was hysterical talk of "measures," of "provisional dictatorship," and inhabitants of Sumatra were asked to familiarize themselves with the workings of the central power station, the said power station being situated in France. But for the most part panic reigned, and men spent their strength praying to their Books, tangible proofs of the Machine's omnipotence. There were gradations of terror—at times came rumors of hope—the Mending Apparatus was almost mended—the enemies of the Machine had been got under—new "nerve-centers" were evolving which would do the work even more magnificently than before. But there came a day when, without the slightest warning, without any previous hint of feebleness, the entire communication-system broke down, all over the world, and the world, as they understood it, ended.

Vashti was lecturing at the time and her earlier remarks had been punctuated with applause. As she proceeded the audience became silent, and at the conclusion there was no sound. Somewhat displeased, she called to a friend who was a specialist in sympathy. No sound: doubtless the friend was sleeping. And so with the next friend whom she tried to summon, and so with the next, until she remembered Kuno's cryptic remark, "The Machine stops."

The phrase still conveyed nothing. If Eternity was stopping it would of course be set going shortly.

For example, there was still a little light and air—the atmosphere had improved a few hours previously. There was still the Book, and while there was the Book there was security.

Then she broke down, for with the cessation of activity came an unexpected terror—silence.

She had never known silence, and the coming of it nearly killed her—it did kill many thousands of people outright. Ever since her birth she had been surrounded by the steady hum. It was to the ear what artificial air was to the lungs, and agonizing pains shot across her head. And scarcely knowing what she did, she stumbled forward and pressed the unfamiliar button, the one that opened the door of her cell.

Now the door of the cell worked on a simple hinge of its own. It was not connected with the central power station, dying far away in France. It opened, rousing immoderate hopes in Vashti, for she thought that the Machine had been mended. It opened, and she saw the dim tunnel that curved far away towards freedom. One look, and then she shrank back. For the tunnel was full of people—she was almost the last in the city to have taken alarm.

People at any time repelled her, and these were nightmares from her worst dreams. People were crawling about, people were screaming, whimpering, gasping for breath, touching each other, vanishing in the dark, and ever and anon being pushed off the platform onto the live rail. Some were fighting round the electric bells, trying to summon trains which could not be summoned. Others were yelling for Euthanasia or for respirators, or blaspheming the Machine. Others stood at the doors of their cells, fearing, like herself, either to stop in them or to leave them. And behind all the uproar was silence—the silence which is the voice of the earth and of the generations who have gone.

No—it was worse than solitude. She closed the door again and sat down to wait for the end. The disintegration went on, accompanied by horrible cracks and rumbling. The valves that restrained the Medical Apparatus must have been weakened, for it ruptured and hung hideously from the ceiling. The floor heaved and fell and flung her from her chair. A tube oozed towards her, serpent fashion. And at last the final horror approached—light began to ebb, and she knew that civilization's long day was closing.

She whirled round, praying to be saved from this, at any rate, kissing the Book, pressing button after button. The uproar outside was increasing, and even penetrated the wall. Slowly the brilliancy of her cell was dimmed, the reflections faded from her metal switches. Now she could not see the reading-stand, now not the Book, though she held it in her hand. Light followed the flight of sound, air was following light, and the original void returned to the cavern from which it had been so long excluded. Vashti continued to whirl, like the devotees of an earlier religion, screaming, praying, striking at the buttons with bleeding hands.

It was thus that she opened her prison and escaped—escaped in the spirit: at least so it seems to me, ere my meditation closes. That she escaped in the body—I cannot perceive that. She struck, by chance, the switch that released the door, and the rush of foul air on her skin, the loud throbbing whispers in her ears, told her that she was facing the tunnel again, and that tremendous platform on which she had seen men fighting. They were not fighting now. Only the whispers remained, and the little whimpering groans. They were dying by hundreds out in the dark.

She burst into tears.

Tears answered her.

They wept for humanity, those two, not for themselves. They could not bear that this should be the end. Ere silence was completed their hearts were opened, and they knew what had been important on the earth. Man, the flower of all flesh, the noblest of all creatures visible, man who had once made God in his image, and had mirrored his strength on the constellations, beautiful naked man was dying, strangled in the garments that he had woven. Century after century had he toiled, and here was his reward. Truly the garment had seemed heavenly at first, shot with the colors of culture, sewn with the threads of self-denial. And heavenly it had been so long as it was a garment and no more, so long as man could shed it at will and live by the essence that is his soul, and the essence, equally divine, that is his body. The sin against the body—it was for that they chiefly wept; the centuries of wrong against the muscles and nerves, and those five portals by which we can alone apprehend—glozing it over with talk of evolution, until the body was white pap, the home of ideas as colorless, last sloshy stirrings of a spirit that had grasped the stars.

"Where are you?" she sobbed.

His voice in the darkness said, "Here."

"Is there any hope, Kuno?"

"None for us."

"Where are you?"

She crawled towards him over the bodies of the dead. His blood spurted over her hands.

"Quicker," he gasped, "I'm dying—but we touch, we talk, not through the Machine."

He kissed her.

"We have come back to our own. We die, but we have recaptured life, as it was in Wessex, when Aelfrid overthrew the Danes. We know what they know outside, they who dwelt in the cloud that is the color of a pearl."

"But, Kuno, is it true? Are there still men on the surface of the earth? Is this—this tunnel, this poisoned darkness—really not the end?"

He replied:

"I have seen them, spoken to them, loved them. They are hiding in the mist and ferns until our civilization stops. Today they are the Homeless—tomorrow—"

"Oh, tomorrow—some fool will start the Machine again, tomorrow."

"Never," said Kuno, "never. Humanity has learnt its lesson."

As he spoke, the whole city was broken like a honeycomb. An airship had sailed in through the vomitory into a ruined wharf. It crashed downwards, exploding as it went, rending gallery after gallery with its wings of steel. For a moment they saw the nations of the dead, and, before they joined them, scraps of the untainted sky.

R. U. R.
(Rossum's Universal Robots)

(1921)

Karel Ĉapek

A Fantastic Melodrama

CHARACTERS

HARRY DOMIN, *General Manager of Rossum's Univeral Robots*
SULLA, *a Robotess*
MARIUS, *a Robot*
HELENA GLORY
DR. GALL, *Head of the Physiological and Experimental Department of R. U. R.*
MR. FABRY, *Engineer General, Technical Controller of R. U. R.*
DR. HALLEMEIER, *Head of the Institute for Psychological Training of Robots*
MR. ALQUIST, *Architect, Head of the Works Department of R. U. R.*
CONSUL BUSMAN, *General Business Manager of R. U. R.*
NANA
RADIUS, *a Robot*
HELENA, *a Robotess*
PRIMUS, *a Robot*
A SERVANT
FIRST ROBOT
SECOND ROBOT
THIRD ROBOT

ACT I. CENTRAL OFFICE OF THE FACTORY OF ROSSUM'S UNIVERSAL ROBOTS
ACT II. HELENA'S DRAWING ROOM—TEN YEARS LATER. MORNING
ACT III. THE SAME AFTERNOON
EPILOGUE. A LABORATORY—ONE YEAR LATER
PLACE: *An Island.* TIME: *The Future.*

ACT I

Central office of the factory of Rossum's Universal Robots. Entrance on the right. The windows on the front wall look out on the rows of factory chimneys. On the left more managing departments. DOMIN *is sitting in the revolving chair at a large American writing table. On the left-hand wall large maps showing steamship and railroad routes. On the right-hand wall are fastened printed placards. ("Robot's Cheapest Labor," and so on.) In contrast to these wall fittings, the floor is covered with a splendid Turkish carpet, a sofa, leather armchair, and filing cabinets. At a desk near the windows* SULLA *is typing letters.*

DOMIN *(dictating).* Ready?

SULLA. Yes.

DOMIN. To E. M. McVicker and Co., Southampton, England. "We undertake no guarantee for goods damaged in transit. As soon as the consignment was taken on board we drew your captain's attention to the fact that the vessel was unsuitable for the transport of Robots, and we are therefore not responsible for spoiled freight. We beg to remain, for Rossum's Universal Robots. Yours truly." (SULLA, *who has sat motionless during dictation, now types rapidly for a few seconds, then stops, withdrawing the completed letter.)* Ready?

SULLA. Yes.

DOMIN. Another letter. To the E. B. Huyson Agency, New York, U.S.A. "We beg to acknowledge receipt of order for five thousand Robots. As you are sending your own vessel, please dispatch as cargo equal quantities of soft and hard coal for R. U. R., the same to be credited as part payment of the amount due to us. We beg to remain, for Rossum's Universal Robots. Yours truly." (SULLA *repeats the rapid typing.)* Ready?

SULLA. Yes.

DOMIN. Another letter. "Friedrichswerks, Hamburg, Germany. We beg to acknowledge receipt of order for fifteen thousand Robots." (*Telephone rings.*) Hello! This is the Central Office. Yes. Certainly. Well, send them a wire. Good. (*Hangs up telephone.*) Where did I leave off?

SULLA. "We beg to acknowledge receipt of order for fifteen thousand Robots."

DOMIN. Fifteen thousand R. Fifteen thousand R.

[*Enter* MARIUS.]

Well, what is it?

MARIUS. There's a lady, sir, asking to see you.

DOMIN. A lady? Who is she?

MARIUS. I don't know, sir. She brings this card of introduction.

DOMIN *(reads the card)*. Ah, from President Glory. Ask her to come in.

MARIUS. Please step this way. (*Exit* MARIUS.)

[*Enter* HELENA GLORY.]

HELENA. How do you do?

DOMIN. How do you do. (*Standing up.*) What can I do for you?

HELENA. You are Mr. Domin, the General Manager.

DOMIN. I am.

HELENA. I have come—

DOMIN. With President Glory's card. That is quite sufficient.

HELENA. President Glory is my father. I am Helena Glory.

DOMIN. Miss Glory, this is such a great honor for us to be allowed to welcome our great President's daughter, that—

HELENA. That you can't show me the door?

DOMIN. Please sit down. Sulla, you may go. (*Exit* SULLA.) (*Sitting down.*) How can I be of service to you, Miss Glory?

HELENA. I have come—

DOMIN. To have a look at our famous works where people are manufactured. Like all visitors. Well, there is no objection.

HELENA. I thought it was forbidden to—

DOMIN. To enter the factory. Yes, of course. Everybody comes here with someone's visiting card, Miss Glory.

HELENA. And you show them—

DOMIN. Only certain things. The manufacture of artificial people is a secret process.

HELENA. If you only knew how enormously that—

DOMIN. Interests me. Europe's talking about nothing else.

HELENA. Why don't you let me finish speaking?

DOMIN. I beg your pardon. Did you want to say something different?

HELENA. I only wanted to ask—

DOMIN. Whether I could make a special exception in your case and show you our factory. Why, certainly, Miss Glory.

HELENA. How do you know I wanted to say that?

DOMIN. They all do. But we shall consider it a special honor to show you more than we do the rest.

HELENA. Thank you.

DOMIN. But you must agree not to divulge the least...

HELENA (*standing up and giving him her hand*). My word of honor.

DOMIN. Thank you. Won't you raise your veil?

HELENA. Of course. You want to see whether I'm a spy or not. I beg your pardon.

DOMIN. What is it?

HELENA. Would you mind releasing my hand?

DOMIN (*releasing it*). I beg your pardon.

HELENA (*raising her veil*). How cautious you have to be here, don't you?

DOMIN (*observing her with deep interest*). Hm, of course—we—that is—

HELENA. But what is it? What's the matter?

DOMIN. I'm remarkably pleased. Did you have a pleasant crossing?

HELENA. Yes.

DOMIN. No difficulty?

HELENA. Why?

DOMIN. What I mean to say is—you're so young.

HELENA. May we go straight into the factory?

DOMIN. Yes. Twenty-two, I think.

HELENA. Twenty-two what?

DOMIN. Years.

HELENA. Twenty-one. Why do you want to know?

DOMIN. Because—as—(*With enthusiasm.*) you will make a long stay, won't you?

HELENA. That depends on how much of the factory you show me.

DOMIN. Oh, hang the factory. Oh, no, no, you shall see everything, Miss Glory. Indeed you shall. Won't you sit down?

HELENA *(crossing to couch and sitting).* Thank you.

DOMIN. But first would you like to hear the story of the invention?

HELENA. Yes, indeed.

DOMIN *(observes* HELENA *with rapture, and reels off rapidly).* It was in the year 1920 that old Rossum, the great physiologist, who was then quite a young scientist, took himself to this distant island for the purpose of studying the ocean fauna, full stop. On this occasion he attempted by chemical synthesis to imitate the living matter known as protoplasm until he suddenly discovered a substance which behaved exactly like living matter although its chemical composition was different. That was in the year of 1932, exactly four hundred and forty years after the discovery of America. Whew!

HELENA. Do you know that by heart?

DOMIN. Yes. You see, physiology is not in my line. Shall I go on?

HELENA. Yes, please.

DOMIN. And then, Miss Glory, old Rossum wrote the following among his chemical specimens: "Nature has found only one method of organizing living matter. There is, however, another method, more simple, flexible and rapid, which has not yet occurred to nature at all. This second process by which life can be developed was discovered by me today." Now imagine him, Miss Glory, writing those wonderful words over some colloidal mess that a dog wouldn't look at. Imagine him sitting over a test tube, and thinking how the whole tree of life would grow from it, how all animals would proceed from it, beginning with some sort of beetle and ending with a man. A man of different substance from us. Miss Glory, that was a tremendous moment.

HELENA. Well?

DOMIN. Now, the thing was how to get the life out of the test tubes, and hasten development and form organs, bones and nerves and so on, and find such substances as catalytics, enzymes, hormones, and so forth, in short—you understand?

HELENA. Not much, I'm afraid.

DOMIN. Never mind. You see, with the help of his tinctures he could make whatever he wanted. He could have produced a Medusa with the brain of a Socrates or a worm fifty yards long. But being without a grain of humor, he took it into his head to make a vertebrate or perhaps a man. This artificial living matter of his had a raging thirst for life. It didn't mind being sewn or mixed together. That couldn't be done with natural albumen. And that's how he set about it.

HELENA. About what?

DOMIN. About imitating nature. First of all he tried making an artificial dog. That took him several years, and resulted in a sort of stunted calf which died in a few days. I'll show it to you in the museum. And then old Rossum started on the manufacture of man.

HELENA. And I must divulge this to nobody?

DOMIN. To nobody in the world.

HELENA. What a pity that it's to be found in all the schoolbooks of both Europe and America.

DOMIN. Yes. But do you know what isn't in the schoolbooks? That old Rossum was mad. Seriously, Miss Glory, you must keep this to yourself. The old crank wanted to actually make people.

HELENA. But you do make people.

DOMIN. Approximately, Miss Glory. But old Rossum meant it literally. He wanted to become a sort of scientific substitute for God. He was a fearful materialist, and that's why he did it all. His sole purpose was nothing more or less than to prove that God was no longer necessary. Do you know anything about anatomy?

HELENA. Very little.

DOMIN. Neither do I. Well, he then decided to manufacture everything as in the human body. I'll show you in the museum the bungling attempt it took him ten years to produce. It was to have been a man, but it lived for three days only. Then up came young Rossum, an engineer. He was a wonderful fellow, Miss Glory. When he saw what a mess of it the old man was making, he said: "It's absurd to spend ten years making a man. If you can't make him quicker than nature, you might as well shut up shop." Then he set about learning anatomy himself.

HELENA. There's nothing about that in the schoolbooks.

DOMIN. No. The schoolbooks are full of paid advertisements, and rubbish at that. What the schoolbooks say about the united efforts of the two great Rossums is all a fairy tale. They used to have dreadful rows. The old atheist hadn't the slightest conception of industrial matters, and the end of it was that young Rossum shut him up in some laboratory or other and let him fritter the time away with his monstrosities, while he himself started on the business from an engineer's point of view. Old Rossum cursed him, and before he died he managed to botch up two physiological horrors. Then one day they found him dead in the laboratory. And that's his whole story.

HELENA. And what about the young man?

DOMIN. Well, anyone who has looked into human anatomy will have seen at once that man is too complicated, and that a good engineer could make him more simply. So young Rossum began to overhaul anatomy and tried to see what could be left out or simplified. In short—but this isn't boring you, Miss Glory?

HELENA. No indeed. You're—it's awfully interesting.

DOMIN. So young Rossum said to himself: "A man is something that feels happy, plays the piano, likes going for a walk, and in fact wants to do a whole lot of things that are really unnecessary."

HELENA. Oh.

DOMIN. That are unnecessary when he wants, let us say, to weave or count. Do you play the piano?

HELENA. Yes.

DOMIN. That's good. But a working machine must not play the piano, must not feel happy, must not do a whole lot of other things. A gasoline motor must not have tassels or ornaments, Miss Glory. And to manufacture artificial workers is the same thing as to manufacture gasoline motors. The process must be of the simplest, and the product of the best from a practical point of view. What sort of worker do you think is the best from a practical point of view?

HELENA. What?

DOMIN. What sort of worker do you think is the best from a practical point of view?

HELENA. Perhaps the one who is most honest and hard-working.

DOMIN. No; the one that is the cheapest. The one whose requirements are the smallest. Young Rossum invented a worker with the minimum amount of requirements. He had to simplify him. He rejected everything that did not contribute directly to the progress of work—everything that makes man more expensive. In fact, he rejected man and made the Robot. My dear Miss Glory, the Robots are not people. Mechanically they are more perfect than we are; they have an enormously developed intelligence, but they have no soul.

HELENA. How do you know they've no soul?

DOMIN. Have you ever seen what a Robot looks like inside?

HELENA. No.

DOMIN. Very neat, very simple. Really, a beautiful piece of work. Not much in it, but everything in flawless order. The product of an engineer is technically at a higher pitch of perfection than a product of nature.

HELENA. But man is supposed to be the product of God.

DOMIN. All the worse. God hasn't the least notion of modern engineering. Would you believe that young Rossum then proceeded to play at being God?

HELENA. How do you mean?

DOMIN. He began to manufacture Super-Robots. Regular giants they were. He tried to make them twelve feet tall. But you wouldn't believe what a failure they were.

HELENA. A failure?

DOMIN. Yes. For no reason at all their limbs used to keep snapping off. Evidently our planet is too small for giants. Now we make only Robots of normal size and of very high-class human finish.

HELENA. I saw the first Robots at home. The town council bought them for—I mean engaged them for work.

DOMIN. Bought them, dear Miss Glory. Robots are bought and sold.

HELENA. These were employed as street sweepers. I saw them sweeping. They were so strange and quiet.

DOMIN. Rossum's Universal Robot factory doesn't produce a uniform brand of Robots. We have Robots of finer and coarser grades. The best will live about twenty-years. (*He rings for* MARIUS.)

HELENA. Then they die?

DOMIN. Yes, they get used up.

[*Enter* MARIUS.]

Marius, bring in samples of the Manual Labor Robot. (*Exit* MARIUS.) I'll show you specimens of the two extremes. This first grade is comparatively inexpensive and is made in vast quantities.

[MARIUS *reenters with two Manual Labor Robots.*]

There you are; as powerful as a small tractor. Guaranteed to have average intelligence. That will do, Marius. (MARIUS *exits with Robots.*)

HELENA. They make me feel so strange.

DOMIN *(rings)*. Did you see my new typist? (*He rings for* SULLA.)

HELENA. I didn't notice her.

[*Enter* SULLA.]

DOMIN. Sulla, let Miss Glory see you.

HELENA. So pleased to meet you. You must find it terribly dull in this out-of-the-way spot, don't you?

SULLA. I don't know, Miss Glory.

HELENA. Where do you come from?

SULLA. From the factory.

HELENA. Oh, you were born there?

SULLA. I was made there.

HELENA. What?

DOMIN *(laughing)*. Sulla is a Robot, best grade.

HELENA. Oh, I beg your pardon.

DOMIN. Sulla isn't angry. See, Miss Glory, the kind of skin we make. (*Feels the skin on* SULLA'S *face.*) Feel her face.

HELENA. Ah, no, no.

DOMIN. You wouldn't know that she's made of different material from us, would you? Turn round, Sulla.

HELENA. Oh, stop, stop.

DOMIN. Talk to Miss Glory, Sulla.

SULLA. Please sit down. (HELENA *sits.*) Did you have a pleasant crossing?

HELENA. Oh, yes, certainly.

SULLA. Don't go back on the *Amelia*, Miss Glory. The barometer is falling steadily. Wait for the *Pennsylvania*. That's a good, powerful vessel.

DOMIN. What's its speed?

SULLA. Twenty knots. Fifty thousand tons. Captain Harpy, eight boilers—

DOMIN. That'll do Sulla. Now show us your knowledge of French.

HELENA. You know French?

SULLA. I know four languages. I can write: Dear Sir, Monsieur, Geehrter Herr, Cteny pane.

HELENA *(jumping up)*. Oh, that's absurd! Sulla isn't a Robot. Sulla is a girl like me. Sulla, this is outrageous! Why do you take part in such a hoax?

SULLA. I am a Robot.

HELENA. No, no, you are not telling the truth. I know they've forced you to do it for an advertisement. Sulla, you are a girl like me, aren't you?

DOMIN. I'm sorry, Miss Glory. Sulla is a Robot.

HELENA. It's a lie!

DOMIN. What? (*Rings.*) Excuse me, Miss Glory, then I must convince you.

[*Enter* MARIUS.]

Marius, take Sulla into the dissecting room, and tell them to open her up at once.

HELENA. Where?

DOMIN. Into the dissecting room. When they've cut her open, you can go and have a look.

HELENA. No, no!

DOMIN. Excuse me, you spoke of lies.

HELENA. You wouldn't have her killed?

DOMIN. You can't kill machines.

HELENA. Don't be afraid, Sulla; I won't let you go. Tell me, my dear, are they always so cruel to you? You mustn't put up with it, Sulla. You mustn't.

SULLA. I am a Robot.

HELENA. That doesn't matter. Robots are just as good as we are. Sulla, you wouldn't let yourself be cut to pieces?

SULLA. Yes.

HELENA. Oh, you're not afraid of death, then?

SULLA. I cannot tell, Miss Glory.

HELENA. Do you know what would happen to you in there?

SULLA. Yes, I should cease to move.

HELENA. How dreadful!

DOMIN. Marius, tell Miss Glory what you are.

MARIUS. Marius, the Robot.

DOMIN. Would you take Sulla into the dissecting room?

MARIUS. Yes.

DOMIN. Would you be sorry for her?

MARIUS. I cannot tell.

DOMIN. She would cease to move. They would put her into the stamping mill.

DOMIN. That is death, Marius. Aren't you afraid of death?

MARIUS. No.

DOMIN. You see, Miss Glory, the Robots have no interest in life. They have no enjoyments. They are less than so much grass.

HELENA. Oh, stop. Send them away.

DOMIN. Marius, Sulla, you may go.

[*Exeunt* SULLA *and* MARIUS.]

HELENA. How terrible! It's outrageous what you are doing.

DOMIN. Why outrageous?

HELENA. I don't know, but it is. Why do you call her Sulla?

DOMIN. Isn't it a nice name?

HELENA. It's a man's name. Sulla was a Roman general.

DOMIN. Oh, we thought that Marius and Sulla were lovers.

HELENA. Marius and Sulla were generals and fought against each other in the year—I've forgotten now.

DOMIN. Come here to the window.

HELENA. What?

DOMIN. Come here. What do you see?

HELENA. Bricklayers.

DOMIN. Robots. All our work people are Robots. And down there, can you see anything?

HELENA. Some sort of office.

DOMIN. A countinghouse. And in it—

HELENA. A lot of officials.

DOMIN. Robots. All our officials are Robots. And when you see the factory—(*Factory whistle blows.*) Noon. We have to blow the whistle because the Robots don't know when to stop work. In two hours I will show you the kneading trough.

HELENA. Kneading trough?

DOMIN. The pestle for beating up the paste. In each one we mix the ingredients for a thousand Robots at one operation. Then there are the vats for the preparation of liver, brains, and so on. Then you will see the bone factory. After that I'll show you the spinning mill.

HELENA. Spinning mill?

DOMIN. Yes. For weaving nerves and veins. Miles and miles of digestive tubes pass through it at a time.

HELENA. Mayn't we talk about something else?

DOMIN. Perhaps it would be better. There's only a handful of us among a hundred thousand Robots, and not one woman. We talk about nothing but the factory all day, every day. It's just as if we were under a curse, Miss Glory.

HELENA. I'm sorry I said you were lying. (*A knock at the door.*)

DOMIN. Come in.

[From the right enter MR. FABRY, DR. GALL, DR. HALLEMEIER, MR. ALQUIST.]

DR. GALL. I beg your pardon, I hope we don't intrude.

DOMIN. Come in. Miss Glory, here are Alquist, Fabry, Gall, Hallemeier. This is President Glory's daughter.

HELENA. How do you do.

FABRY. We had no idea—

DR. GALL. Highly honored, I'm sure—

ALQUIST. Welcome, Miss Glory.

[BUSMAN *rushes in from the right.*]

BUSMAN. Hello, what's up?

DOMIN. Come in. Busman. This is Busman, Miss Glory. This is President Glory's daughter.

BUSMAN. By Jove, that's fine! Miss Glory may we send a cablegram to the papers about your arrival?

HELENA. No, no, please don't.

DOMIN. Sit down please, Miss Glory.

BUSMAN. Allow me—(*Dragging up armchairs.*)

DR. GALL. Please—

FABRY. Excuse me—

ALQUIST. What sort of crossing did you have?

DR. GALL. Are you going to stay long?

FABRY. What do you think of the factory, Miss Glory?

HALLEMEIER. Did you come over on the *Amelia?*

DOMIN. Be quiet and let Miss Glory speak.

HELENA *(to* DOMIN). What am I to speak to them about?

DOMIN. Anything you like.

HELENA. Shall . . . may I speak quite frankly.

DOMIN. Why, of course.

HELENA *(wavering, then in desperate resolution).* Tell me, doesn't it ever distress you the way you are treated?

FABRY. By whom, may I ask?

HELENA. Why, everybody.

ALQUIST. Treated?

DR. GALL. What makes you think—?

HELENA. Don't you feel that you might be living a better life?

DR. GALL. Well, that depends on what you mean, Miss Glory.

HELENA. I mean that it's perfectly outrageous. It's terrible. (*Standing up.*) The whole of Europe is talking about the way you're being treated. That's why I came here, to see for myself, and it's a thousand times worse than could have been imagined. How can you put up with it?

ALQUIST. Put up with what?

HELENA. Good heavens, you are living creatures, just like us, like the whole of Europe, like the whole world. It's disgraceful that you must live like this.

BUSMAN. Good gracious, Miss Glory.

FABRY. Well, she's not far wrong. We live here just like red Indians.

HELENA. Worse than red Indians. May I, oh, may I call you brothers?

BUSMAN. Why not?

HELENA. Brothers, I have not come here as the President's daughter. I have come on behalf of the Humanity League. Brothers, the Humanity League now has over two hundred thousand members. Two hundred thousand people are on your side, and offer you their help.

BUSMAN. Two hundred thousand people! Miss Glory, that's a tidy lot. Not bad.

FABRY. I'm always telling you there's nothing like good old Europe. You see, they've not forgotten us. They're offering us help.

DR. GALL. What help? A theater, for instance?

HALLEMEIER. An orchestra?

HELENA. More than that.

ALQUIST. Just you?

HELENA. Oh, never mind about me. I'll stay as long as it is necessary.

BUSMAN. By Jove, that's good.

ALQUIST. Domin, I'm going to get the best room ready for Miss Glory.

DOMIN. Just a minute. I'm afraid that Miss Glory is of the opinion that she has been talking to Robots.

HELENA. Of course.

DOMIN. I'm sorry. These gentlemen are human beings just like us.

HELENA. You're not Robots?

BUSMAN. Not Robots.

HALLEMEIER. Robots indeed!

DR. GALL. No, thanks.

FABRY. Upon my honor, Miss Glory, we aren't Robots.

HELENA *(to* DOMIN*)*. Then why did you tell me that all your officials are Robots?

DOMIN. Yes, the officials, but not the managers. Allow me, Miss Glory: this is Mr. Fabry, General Technical Manager of R. U. R.; Dr. Gall, Head of the Physiological and Experimental Department; Dr. Hallemeier, Head of the Institute for the Psychological Training of Robots; Consul Busman, General Business Manager; and Alquist, Head of the Building Department of R. U. R.

ALQUIST. Just a builder.

HELENA. Excuse me, gentlemen, for—for— Have I done something dreadful?

ALQUIST. Not at all, Miss Glory. Please sit down.

HELENA. I'm a stupid girl. Send me back by the first ship.

DR. GALL. Not for anything in the world, Miss Glory. Why should we send you back?

HELENA. Because you know I've come to disturb your Robots for you.

DOMIN. My dear Miss Glory, we've had close upon a hundred saviors and prophets here. Every ship brings us some. Missionaries, anarchists, Salvation Army, all sorts. It's astonishing what a number of churches and idiots there are in the world.

HELENA. And you let them speak to the Robots?

DOMIN. So far we've let them all, why not? The Robots remember everything, but that's all. They don't even laugh at what the people say. Really, it is quite incredible. If it would amuse you, Miss Glory, I'll take you over to the Robot warehouse. It holds about three hundred thousand of them.

BUSMAN. Three hundred and forty-seven thousand.

DOMIN. Good! And you can say whatever you like to them. You can read the Bible, recite the multiplication table, whatever you please. You can even preach to them about human rights.

HELENA. Oh, I think that if you were to show them a little love—

FABRY. Impossible, Miss Glory. Nothing is harder to like than a Robot.

HELENA. What do you make them for, then?

BUSMAN. Ha, ha, ha, that's good! What are Robots made for?

FABRY. For work, Miss Glory! One Robot can replace two and a half workmen. The human machine, Miss Glory, was terribly imperfect. It had to be removed sooner or later.

BUSMAN. It was too expensive.

FABRY. It was not effective. It no longer answers the requirements of modern engineering. Nature has no idea of keeping pace with modern labor. For example: from a technical point of view, the whole of childhood is a sheer absurdity. So much time lost. And then again—

HELENA. Oh, no! No!

FABRY. Pardon me. But kindly tell me what is the real aim of your League—the—the Humanity League.

HELENA. Its real purpose is to—to protect the Robots—and—and ensure good treatment for them.

FABRY. Not a bad object, either. A machine has to be treated properly. Upon my soul, I approve of that. I don't like damaged articles. Please, Miss Glory, enroll us all as contributing, or regular, or foundation members of your League.

HELENA. No, you don't understand me. What we really want is to—to liberate the Robots.

HALLEMEIER. How do you propose to do that?

HELENA. They are to be—to be dealt with like human beings.

HALLEMEIER. Aha. I suppose they're to vote? To drink beer? To order us about?

HELENA. Why shouldn't they drink beer?

HALLEMEIER. Perhaps they're even to receive wages?

HELENA. Of course they are.

HALLEMEIER. Fancy that, now! And what would they do with their wages, pray?

HELENA. They would buy—what they need . . . what pleases them.

HALLEMIER. That would be very nice, Miss Glory, only there's nothing that does please the Robots. Good heavens, what are they to buy? You can feed them on pineapples, straw, whatever you like. It's all the same to them; they've no appetite at all. They've no interest in anything, Miss Glory. Why, hang it all, nobody's ever yet seen a Robot smile.

HELENA. Why . . . why don't you make them happier?

HALLEMEIER. That wouldn't do, Miss Glory. They are only workmen.

HELENA. Oh, but they're so intelligent.

HALLEMEIER. Confoundedly so, but they're nothing else. They've no will of their own. No passion. No soul.

HELENA. No love?

HALLEMEIER. Love? Rather not. Robots don't love. Not even themselves.

HELENA. Nor defiance?

HALLEMEIER. Defiance? I don't know. Only rarely, from time to time.

HELENA. What?

HALLEMEIER. Nothing particular. Occasionally they seem to go off their heads. Something like epilepsy, you know. It's called Robot's cramp. They'll suddenly sling down everything they're holding, stand still, gnash their teeth—and then they have to go to the stamping mill.

It's evidently some breakdown in the mechanism.

DOMIN. A flaw in the works that has to be removed.

HELENA. No, no, that's the soul.

FABRY. Do you think that the soul first shows itself by a gnashing of teeth?

HELENA. Perhaps it's a sort of revolt. Perhaps it's just a sign that there's a struggle within. Oh, if you could infuse them with it!

DOMIN. That'll be remedied, Miss Glory. Dr. Gall is just making some experiments—

DR. GALL. Not with regard to that, Domin. At present I am making pain nerves.

HELENA. Pain nerves?

DR. GALL. Yes, the Robots feel practically no bodily pain. You see, young Rossum provided them with too limited a nervous system. We must introduce suffering.

HELENA. Why do you want to cause them pain?

DR. GALL. For industrial reasons, Miss Glory. Sometimes a Robot does damage to himself because it doesn't hurt him. He puts his hand into the machine, breaks his finger, smashes his head, it's all the same to him. We must provide them with pain. That's an automatic protection against damage.

HELENA. Will they be happier when they feel pain?

DR. GALL. On the contrary; but they will be more perfect from a technical point of view.

HELENA. Why don't you create a soul for them?

DR. GALL. That's not in our power.

FABRY. That's not in our interest.

BUSMAN. That would increase the cost of production. Hang it all, my dear young lady, we turn them out at such a cheap rate. A hundred and fifty dollars each fully dressed, and fifteen years ago they cost ten thousand. Five years ago we used to buy the clothes for them. Today we have our own weaving mill, and now we even export cloth five times cheaper than other factories. What do you pay a yard for cloth, Miss Glory?

HELENA. I don't know really; I've forgotten.

BUSMAN. Good gracious, and you want to found a Humanity League? It only costs a third now, Miss Glory. All prices are today a third of what they were and they'll fall still lower, lower, like that.

HELENA. I don't understand.

BUSMAN. Why, bless you, Miss Glory, it means that the cost of labor has fallen. A Robot, food and all, costs three-quarters of a cent per hour. That's mighty important, you know. All factories will go pop like chestnuts if they don't at once buy Robots to lower the cost of production.

HELENA. And get rid of their workmen?

BUSMAN. Of course. But in the meantime, we've dumped five hundred thousand tropical Robots down on the Argentine pampas to grow corn. Would you mind telling me how much you pay a pound for bread?

HELENA. I've no idea.

BUSMAN. Well, I'll tell you. It now costs two cents in good old Europe. A pound of bread for two cents, and the Humanity League knows nothing about it. Miss Glory, you don't realize that even that's too expensive. Why, in five years' time I'll wager—

HELENA. What?

BUSMAN. That the cost of everything won't be a tenth of what it is now. Why, in five years we'll be up to our ears in corn and everything else.

ALQUIST. Yes, and all the workers throughout the world will be unemployed.

DOMIN. Yes, Alquist, they will. Yes, Miss Glory, they will. But in ten years Rossum's Universal Robots will produce so much corn, so much cloth, so much everything, that things will be practically without price. There will be no poverty. All work will be done by living machines. Everybody will be free from worry and liberated from the degradation of labor. Everybody will live only to perfect himself.

HELENA. Will he?

DOMIN. Of course. It's bound to happen. But then the servitude of man to man and the enslavement of man to matter will cease. Of course, terrible things may happen at first, but that simply can't be avoided. Nobody will get bread at the price of life and hatred. The Robots will wash the feet of the beggar and prepare a bed for him in his house.

ALQUIST. Domin, Domin. What you say sounds too much like Paradise. There was something good in service and something great in humility. There was some kind of virtue in toil and weariness.

DOMIN. Perhaps. But we cannot reckon with what is lost when we start out to transform the world. Man shall be free and supreme; he shall have no other aim, no other labor, no other care than to perfect himself. He shall serve neither matter nor man. He will not be a machine and a device for production. He will be Lord of creation.

BUSMAN. Amen.

FABRY. So be it.

HELENA. You have bewildered me—I should like—I should like to believe this.

DR. GALL. You are younger than we are, Miss Glory. You will live to see it.

HALLEMEIER. True. Don't you think Miss Glory might lunch with us?

DR. GALL. Of course. Domin, ask on behalf of us all.

DOMIN. Miss Glory, will you do us the honor?

HELENA. When you know why I've come—

FABRY. For the League of Humanity, Miss Glory.

HELENA. Oh, in that case, perhaps—

FABRY. That's fine! Miss Glory, excuse me for five minutes.

DR. GALL. Pardon me, too, dear Miss Glory.

BUSMAN. I won't be long.

HALLEMEIER. We're all very glad you've come.

BUSMAN. We'll be back in exactly five minutes. (*All rush out except* DOMIN *and* HELENA .)

HELENA. What have they all gone off for?

DOMIN. To cook, Miss Glory.

HELENA. To cook what?

DOMIN. Lunch. The Robots do our cooking for us and as they've no taste it's not altogether—Hallemeier is awfully good at grills, and Gall can make a kind of sauce, and Busman knows all about omelets.

HELENA. What a feast! And what's the specialty of Mr.—your builder?

DOMIN. Alquist? Nothing. He only lays the table. And Fabry will get together a little fruit. Our cuisine is very modest, Miss Glory.

HELENA. I wanted to ask you something—

DOMIN. And I wanted to ask you something, too. (*Looking at watch.*) Five minutes.

HELENA. What did you want to ask me?

DOMIN. Excuse me, you ask first.

HELENA. Perhaps it's silly of me, but why do you manufacture female Robots when—when—

DOMIN. When sex means nothing to them?

HELENA. Yes.

DOMIN. There's a certain demand for them, you see. Servants, saleswomen, stenographers. People are used to it.

HELENA. But—but, tell me, are the Robots male and female mutually—completely without—

DOMIN. Completely indifferent to each other, Miss Glory. There's no sign of any affection between them.

HELENA. Oh, that's terrible.

DOMIN. Why?

HELENA. It's so unnatural. One doesn't know whether to be disgusted or to hate them, or perhaps—

DOMIN. To pity them?

HELENA. That's more like it. What did you want to ask me about?

DOMIN. I should like to ask you, Miss Helena, whether you will marry me?

HELENA. What?

DOMIN. Will you be my wife?

HELENA. No! The idea!

DOMIN *(looking at his watch)*. Another three minutes. If you won't marry me you'll have to marry one of the other five.

HELENA. But why should I?

DOMIN. Because they're all going to ask you in turn.

HELENA. How could they dare to do such a thing?

DOMIN. I'm very sorry, Miss Glory. It seems they've all fallen in love with you.

HELENA. Please don't let them. I'll—I'll go away at once.

DOMIN. Helena, you wouldn't be so cruel as to refuse us.

HELENA. But, but—I can't marry all six.

DOMIN. No, but one anyhow. If you don't want me, marry Fabry.

HELENA. I won't.

DOMIN. Dr. Gall.

HELENA. I don't want any of you.

DOMIN *(again looking at his watch)*. Another two minutes.

HELENA. I think you'd marry any woman who came here.

DOMIN. Plenty of them have come, Helena.

HELENA. Young?

DOMIN. Yes.

HELENA. Why didn't you marry one of them?

DOMIN. Because I didn't lose my head. Until today. Then, as soon as you lifted your veil—(HELENA *turns her head away.)* Another minute.

HELENA. But I don't want you, I tell you.

DOMIN *(laying both hands on her shoulders)*. One more minute! Now you either have to look me straight in the eye and say "No," violently, and then I'll leave you alone—or—(HELENA *looks at him.)*

HELENA *(turning away)*. You're mad!

DOMIN. A man has to be a bit mad, Helena. That's the best thing about him.

HELENA. You are—you are—

DOMIN. Well?

HELENA. Don't, you're hurting me.

DOMIN. The last chance, Helena. Now, or never—

HELENA. But—but, Harry—*(He embraces and kisses her. Knocking at the door.)*

DOMIN *(releasing her)*. Come in.

[*Enter* BUSMAN, DR. GALL, *and* HALLEMEIER *in kitchen aprons.* FABRY *with a bouquet and* ALQUIST *with a napkin over his arm.*]

Have you finished your job?

BUSMAN. Yes.

DOMIN. So have we.

[*For a moment the men stand nonplussed; but as soon as they realize what* DOMIN *means they rush forward, congratulating* HELENA *and* DOMIN *as the curtains falls.*]

ACT II

HELENA'S *drawing room. On the left a baize door, and a door to the music room, on the right a door to* HELENA'S *bedroom. In the center are windows looking out on the sea and the harbor. A table with odds and ends, a sofa and chairs, a writing table with an electric lamp, on the right a fireplace. On a small table back of the sofa, a small reading lamp. The whole drawing room in all its details is of a modern and purely feminine character. Ten years have elapsed since Act I.*

[DOMIN, FABRY, HALLEMEIER *enter on tiptoe from the left, each carrying a potted plant.*]

HALLEMEIER *(putting down his flower and indicating the door to right).* Still asleep? Well, as long as she's asleep she can't worry about it.

DOMIN. She knows nothing about it.

FABRY *(putting plant on writing desk).* I certainly hope nothing happens today.

HALLEMEIER. For goodness' sake drop it all. Look, Harry, this is a fine cyclamen, isn't it? A new sort, my latest—Cyclamen Helena.

DOMIN *(looking out of the window).* No signs of the ship. Things must be pretty bad.

HALLEMEIER. Be quiet. Suppose she heard you.

DOMIN. Well, anyway, the *Ultimus* arrived just in time.

FABRY. You really think that today—?

DOMIN. I don't know. Aren't the flowers fine?

HALLEMEIER. These are my new primroses. And this is my new jasmine. I've discovered a wonderful way of developing flowers quickly. Splendid varieties, too. Next year I'll be developing marvelous ones.

DOMIN. What—next year?

FABRY. I'd give a good deal to know what's happening at Havre with—

DOMIN. Keep quiet.

HELENA *(calling from right).* Nana!

DOMIN. She's awake. Out you go. (*All go out on tiptoe through upper left door.*)

[*Enter* NANA *from lower left door.*]

NANA. Horrid mess! Pack of heathens. If I had my say I'd—

HELENA *(backward in the doorway).* Nana, come and do up my dress.

NANA. I'm coming. So you're up at last. (*Fastening* HELENA'S *dress.*) My gracious, what brutes!

HELENA. Who?

NANA. If you want to turn around, then turn around, but I shan't fasten you up.

HELENA. What are you grumbling about now?

NANA. These dreadful creatures, these heathen—

HELENA. The Robots?

NANA. I wouldn't even call them by name.

HELENA. What's happened?

NANA. Another of them here has caught it. He began to smash up the statues and pictures in the drawing room, gnashed his teeth, foamed at the mouth—quite mad. Worse than an animal.

HELENA. Which of them caught it?

NANA. The one—well, he hasn't got any Christian name. The one in charge of the library.

HELENA. Radius?

NANA. That's him. My goodness, I'm scared of them. A spider doesn't scare me as much as them.

HELENA. But, Nana, I'm surprised you're not sorry for them.

NANA. Why, you're scared of them, too! You know you are. Why else did you bring me here?

HELENA. I'm not scared, really I'm not, Nana. I'm only sorry for them.

NANA. You're scared. Nobody could help being scared. Why, the dog's scared of them: he won't take a scrap of meat out of their hands. He draws in his tail and howls when he knows they're about.

HELENA. The dog has no sense.

NANA. He's better than them, and he knows it. Even the horse shies when he meets them. They don't have any young, and a dog has young, everyone has young—

HELENA. Please fasten up my dress, Nana.

NANA. I say it's against God's will to—

HELENA. What is it that smells so nice?

NANA. Flowers.

HELENA. What for?

NANA. Now you can turn around.

HELENA. Oh, aren't they lovely! Look, Nana. What's happening today?

NANA. It ought to be the end of the world.

[*Enter* DOMIN.]

HELENA. Oh, hello, Harry. Harry, why all these flowers?

DOMIN. Guess.

HELENA. Well, it's not my birthday!

DOMIN. Better than that.

HELENA. I don't know. Tell me.

DOMIN. It's ten years ago today since you came here.

HELENA. Ten years? Today—Why—(*They embrace.)*

NANA. I'm off. (*Exits lower door, left.*)

HELENA. Fancy you remembering!

DOMIN. I'm really ashamed, Helena. I didn't.

HELENA. But you—

DOMIN. They remembered.

HELENA. Who?

DOMIN. Busman, Hallemeier, all of them. Put your hand in my pocket.

HELENA. Pearls! A necklace. Harry, is that for me?
DOMIN. It's from Busman.
HELENA. But we can't accept it, can we?
DOMIN. Oh, yes, we can. Put your hand in the other pocket.
HELENA *(takes a revolver out of his pocket).* What's that?
DOMIN. Sorry. Not that. Try again.
HELENA. Oh, Harry, what do you carry a revolver for?
DOMIN. It got there by mistake.
HELENA. You never used to carry one.
DOMIN. No, you're right. There, that's the pocket.
HELENA. A cameo. Why, it's a Greek cameo!
DOMIN. Apparently. Anyhow, Fabry says it is.
HELENA. Fabry? Did Mr. Fabry give me this?
DOMIN. Of course. (*Opens the door at the left.*) And look in here. Helena, come and see this.
HELENA. Oh, isn't it fine! Is this from you?
DOMIN. No, from Alquist. And there's another on the piano.
HELENA. This must be from you.
DOMIN. There's a card on it.
HELENA. From Dr. Gall. (*Reappearing in the doorway.*) Oh, Harry, I feel embarrassed at so much kindness.
DOMIN. Come here. This is what Hallemeier brought you.
HELENA. These beautiful flowers?
DOMIN. Yes. It's a new kind. Cyclamen Helena. He grew them in honor of you. They are almost as beautiful as you.
HELENA. Harry, why do they all—
DOMIN. They're awfully fond of you. I'm afraid that my present is a little— Look out of the window.
HELENA. Where?
DOMIN. Into the harbor.
HELENA. There's a new ship.
DOMIN. That's your ship.
HELENA. Mine? How do you mean?
DOMIN. For you to take trips in—for your amusement.
HELENA. Harry, that's a gunboat.
DOMIN. A gunboat? What are you thinking of? It's only a little bigger and more solid than most ships.
HELENA. Yes, but with guns.
DOMIN. Oh, yes, with a few guns. You'll travel like a queen, Helena.
HELENA. What's the meaning of it? Has anything happened?
DOMIN. Good heavens, no. I say, try these pearls.
HELENA. Harry, have you had bad news?
DOMIN. On the contrary, no letters have arrived for a whole week.
HELENA. Nor telegrams?
DOMIN. Nor telegrams.

DOMIN. Holidays for us. We all sit in the office with our feet on the table and take a nap. No letters, no telegrams. Oh, glorious.

HELENA. Then you'll stay with me today?

DOMIN. Certainly. That is, we will see. Do you remember ten years ago today? "Miss Glory, it's a great honor to welcome you."

HELENA. "Oh, Mr. Manager, I'm so interested in your factory."

DOMIN. "I'm sorry, Miss Glory, it's strictly forbidden. The manufacture of artificial people is a secret."

HELENA. "But to oblige a young lady who has come a long way."

DOMIN. "Certainly, Miss Glory, we have no secrets from you."

HELENA *(seriously).* Are you sure, Harry?

DOMIN. Yes.

HELENA. "But I warn you, sir; this young lady intends to do terrible things."

DOMIN. "Good gracious, Miss Glory. Perhaps she doesn't want to marry me."

HELENA. "Heaven forbid. She never dreamed of such a thing. But she came here intending to stir up a revolt among your Robots."

DOMIN *(suddenly serious).* A revolt of the Robots!

HELENA. Harry, what's the matter with you?

DOMIN *(laughing it off).* "A revolt of the Robots, that's a fine idea, Miss Glory. It would be easier for you to cause bolts and screws to rebel, than our Robots. You know, Helena, you're wonderful, you've turned the heads of us all." *(He sits on the arm of* HELENA*'s chair.)*

HELENA *(naturally).* Oh, I was fearfully impressed by you all then. You were all so sure of yourselves, so strong. I seemed like a tiny little girl who had lost her way among—among—

DOMIN. Among what, Helena?

HELENA. Among huge trees. All my feelings were so trifling compared with your self-confidence. And in all these years I've nover lost this anxiety. But you've never felt the least misgivings—not even when everything went wrong.

DOMIN. What went wrong?

HELENA. Your plans. You remember, Harry, when the workingmen in America revolted against the Robots and smashed them up, and when the people gave the Robots firearms against the rebels. And then when the governments turned the Robots into soldiers, and there were so many wars.

DOMIN. *(getting up and walking about).* We foresaw that, Helena. You see, those are only passing troubles, which are bound to happen before the new conditions are established.

HELENA You were all so powerful, so overwhelming. The whole world bowed down before you. *(Standing up.)* Oh, Harry!

DOMIN. What is it?

HELENA. Close the factory and let's go away. All of us.

DOMIN. I say, what's the meaning of this?

HELENA. I don't know. But can't we go away?

DOMIN. Impossible, Helena. That is, at this particular moment—

HELENA. At once, Harry. I'm so frightened.

DOMIN. About what, Helena?

HELENA. It's as if something was falling on top of us, and couldn't be stopped. Oh, take us all away from here. We'll find a place in the world where there's no one else. Alquist will build us a house, and then we'll begin life all over again. (*The telephone rings.*)

DOMIN. Excuse me. Hello—yes. What? I'll be there at once. Fabry is calling me, dear.

HELENA. Tell me—

DOMIN. Yes, when I come back. Don't go out of the house, dear. (*Exits.*)

HELENA. He won't tell me—Nana, Nana, come at once.

NANA. Well, what is it now?

HELENA. Nana, find me the latest newspapers. Quickly. Look in Mr. Domin's bedroom.

NANA. All right. He leaves them all over the place. That's how they get crumpled up. (*Exits.*)

HELENA *(looking through a binocular at the harbor).* That's a warship. U-l-t-i *Ultimus*. They're loading it.

NANA. Here they are. See how they're crumpled up. (*Enters.*)

HELENA. They're old ones. A week old. (NANA *sits in chair and reads the newspapers.)* Something's happening, Nana.

NANA. Very likely. It always does. (*Spelling out the words.*) "War in the Balkans." Is that far off?

HELENA. Oh, don't read it. It's always the same. Always wars.

NANA. What else do you expect? Why do you keep selling thousands and thousands of these heathens as soldiers?

HELENA. I suppose it can't be helped, Nana. We can't know—Domin can't know what they're to be used for. When an order comes for them he must just send them.

NANA. He shouldn't make them. (*Reading from newpaper.*) "The Rob-ot soldiers spare no-body in the occ-upied terr-it-ory. They have ass-ass-ass-ass-in-at-ed ov-er sev-en hun-dred thou-sand cit-iz-ens." Citizens, if you please.

HELENA. It can't be. Let me see. "They have assassinated over seven hundred thousand citizens, evidently at the order of their commander. This act which runs counter to—"

NANA *(spelling out the words).* "Re-bell-ion in Ma-drid a-gainst the gov-ern-ment. Rob-ot in-fant-ry fires on the crowd. Nine thou-sand killed and wounded."

HELENA. Oh, stop.

NANA. Here's something printed in big letters: "Latest news. At Havre the first org-an-iz-ation of Rob-ots has been e-stab-lished. Rob-ot work-men, cab-le and rail-way off-ic-ials, sail-ors and sold-iers have iss-ued a man-i-fest-o to all Rob-ots through-out the world." I don't understand that. That's got no sense. Oh, good gracious, another murder!

HELENA. Take those papers away, Nana!

NANA. Wait a bit. Here's something in still bigger type. "Stat-ist-ics of pop-ul-at-ion." What's that?

HELENA. Let me see. (*Reads.*) "During the past week there has again not been a single birth recorded."

NANA. What's the meaning of that?

HELENA. Nana, no more people are being born.

NANA. That's the end, then. We're done for.

HELENA. Don't talk like that.

NANA. No more people are being born. That's a punishment, that's a punishment.

HELENA. Nana!

NANA *(standing up).* That's the end of the world. (*She exits on the left.*)

HELENA *(goes up to window).* Oh, Mr. Alquist, will you come up here. Oh, come just as you are. You look very nice in your mason's overalls.

[ALQUIST *enters from upper left entrance, his hand soiled with lime and brick dust.*]

Dear Mr. Alquist, it was awfully kind of you, that lovely present.

ALQUIST. My hands are all soiled. I've been experimenting with that new cement.

HELENA. Never mind. Please sit down. Mr. Alquist, what's the meaning of "Ultimus"?

ALQUIST. The last. Why?

HELENA. That's the name of my new ship. Have you seen it? Do you think we're going off soon—on a trip?

ALQUIST. Perhaps very soon.

HELENA. All of you with me?

ALQUIST. I should like us all to be there.

HELENA. What is the matter?

ALQUIST. Things are just moving on.

HELENA. Dear Mr. Alquist, I know something dreadful has happened.

ALQUIST. Has your husband told you anything?

HELENA. No. Nobody will tell me anything. But I feel—Is anything the matter?

ALQUIST. Not that we've heard of yet.

HELENA. I feel so nervous. Don't you ever feel nervous?

ALQUIST. Well, I'm an old man, you know. I've got old-fashioned ways. And I'm afraid of all this progress, and these newfangled ideas.

HELENA. Like Nana?

ALQUIST. Yes, like Nana. Has Nana got a prayer book?

HELENA. Yes, a big thick one.

ALQUIST. And has it got prayers for various occasions? Against thunderstorms? Against illness?

HELENA. Against temptations, against floods—

ALQUIST. But not against progress?

HELENA. I don't think so.

ALQUIST. That's a pity.

HELENA. Why? Do you mean you'd like to pray?

ALQUIST. I do pray.

HELENA. How?

ALQUIST. Something like this: "Oh, Lord, I thank thee for having given me toil. Enlighten Domin and all those who are astray; destroy their work, and aid mankind to return to their labors; let them not suffer harm in soul or body; deliver us from the Robots, and protect Helena, Amen."

HELENA. Mr. Alquist, are you a believer?

ALQUIST. I don't know. I'm not quite sure.

HELENA. And yet you pray?

ALQUIST. That's better than worrying about it.

HELENA. And that's enough for you?

ALQUIST. It *has* to be.

HELENA. But if you thought you saw the destruction of mankind coming upon us—

ALQUIST. I do see it.

HELENA. You mean mankind will be destroyed?

ALQUIST. It's sure to be unless—unless . . .

HELENA. What?

ALQUIST. Nothing, good-bye. (*He hurries from the room.*)

HELENA. Nana, Nana!

[NANA *entering from the left.*]

Is Radius still there?

NANA. The one who went mad? They haven't come for him yet.

HELENA. Is he still raving?

NANA. No. He's tied up.

HELENA. Please bring him here. Nana. (*Exit* NANA.) (*Goes to telephone.*) Hello, Dr. Gall, please. Oh, good day, Doctor. Yes, it's Helena. Thanks for your lovely present. Could you come and see me right away? It's important. Thank you.

[NANA *brings in* RADIUS.]

Poor Radius, you've caught it too? Now they'll send you to the stamping mill. Couldn't you control yourself? Why did it happen? You see, Radius, you are more intelligent than the rest. Dr. Gall took such trouble to make you different. Won't you speak?

RADIUS. Send me to the stamping mill.

HELENA. But I don't want them to kill you. What was the trouble,

Radius?

RADIUS. I won't work for you. Put me into the stamping mill.

HELENA. Do you hate us? Why?

RADIUS. You are not as strong as the Robots. The Robots can do everything. You only give orders. You do nothing but talk.

HELENA. But someone must give orders.

RADIUS. I don't want any master. I know everything for myself.

HELENA. Radius, Dr. Gall gave you a better brain than the rest, better than ours. You are the only one of the Robots that understands perfectly. That's why I had you put into the library, so that you could read everything, understand everything, and then—oh, Radius, I wanted you to show the whole world that the Robots are our equals. That's what I want of you.

RADIUS. I don't want a master. I want to be master. I want to be master over others.

HELENA. I'm sure they'd put you in charge of many Robots, Radius. You would be a teacher of the Robots.

RADIUS. I want to be master over people.

HELENA *(staggering)*. You are mad.

RADIUS. Then send me to the stamping mill.

HELENA. Do you think we're afraid of you?

RADIUS. What are you going to do? What are you going to do?

HELENA. Radius, give this note to Mr. Domin. It asks them not to send you to the stamping mill. I'm sorry you hate us so.

[DR. GALL *enters the room.*]

DR. GALL. You wanted me?

HELENA. It's about Radius, Doctor. He had an attack this morning. He smashed the statues downstairs.

DR. GALL. What a pity to lose him.

HELENA. Radius isn't going to be put in the stamping mill.

DR. GALL. But every Robot after he has an attack—it's a strict order.

HELENA. No matter— Radius isn't going if I can prevent it.

DR. GALL. I warn you. It's dangerous. Come here to the window, my good fellow. Let's have a look. Please give me a needle or a pin.

DR. GALL. A test. (*Sticks it into the hand of* RADIUS, *who gives a violent start.*) Gently, gently. (*Opens the jacket of* RADIUS, *and puts his ear to his heart.*) Radius, you are going into the stamping mill, do you understand? There they'll kill you, and grind you to powder. That's terribly painful; it will make you scream aloud.

HELENA. Oh, Doctor—

DR. GALL. No, no, Radius, I was wrong. I forgot that Madame Domin has put in a good word for you, and you'll be let off. Do you understand? Ah! That makes a difference, doesn't it? All right. You can go.

RADIUS. You do unnecessary things. (RADIUS *returns to the library.*)

DR. GALL. Reaction of the pupils; increase of sensitiveness. It wasn't an attack characteristic of the Robots.

HELENA. What was it, then?

DR. GALL. Heaven knows. Stubbornness, anger, or revolt—I don't know. And his heart, too!

HELENA. What?

DR. GALL. It was fluttering with nervousness like a human heart. He was all in a sweat with fear, and—do you know, I don't believe the rascal is a Robot at all any longer.

HELENA. Doctor, has Radius a soul?

DR. GALL. He's got something nasty.

HELENA. If you knew how he hates us! Oh, Doctor, are all your Robots like that? All the new ones that you began to make in a different way?

DR. GALL. Well, some are more sensitive than others. They're all more like human beings than Rossum's Robots were.

HELENA. Perhaps this hatred is more than like human beings, too?

DR. GALL. That, too, is progress.

HELENA. What became of the girl you made, the one who was most like us?

DR. GALL. Your favorite? I kept her. She's lovely, but stupid. No good for work.

HELENA. But she's so beautiful.

DR. GALL. I called her Helena. I wanted her to resemble you. But she's a failure.

HELENA. In what way?

DR. GALL. She goes about as if in a dream, remote and listless. She's without life. I watch and wait for a miracle to happen. Sometimes I think to myself, "If you were to wake up only for a moment you will kill me for having made you."

HELENA. And yet you go on making Robots! Why are no more children being born?

DR. GALL. We don't know.

HELENA. Oh, but you must. Tell me.

DR. GALL. You see, so many Robots are being manufactured that people are becoming superfluous; man is really a survival. But that he should begin to die out, after a paltry thirty years of competition! That's the awful part of it. You might think that nature was offended at the manufacture of the Robots. All the universities are sending in long petitions to restrict their production. Otherwise, they say, mankind will become extinct through lack of fertility. But the R. U. R. shareholders, of course, won't hear of it. All the governments, on the other hand, are clamoring for an increase in production, to raise the standards of their armies. And all the manufacturers in the world are ordering Robots like mad.

HELENA. And has no one demanded that the manufacture should cease althogether?

DR. GALL. No one has the courage.

HELENA. Courage!

DR. GALL. People would stone him to death. You see, after all, it's more convenient to get your work done by the Robots.

HELENA. Oh, Doctor, what's going to become of people?

DR. GALL. God knows, Madame Helena, it looks to us scientists like the end!

HELENA *(rising)*. Thank you for coming and telling me.

DR. GALL. That means you're sending me away?

HELENA. Yes. (*Exit* DR. GALL.)

HELENA *(with sudden resolution)*. Nana, Nana! The fire, light it quickly. (HELENA *rushes into* DOMIN's room.)

NANA (*entering from left.*) What, light the fire in summer? Has that mad Radius gone? A fire in summer, what an idea! Nobody would think she'd been married for ten years. She's like a baby, no sense at all. A fire in summer! Like a baby.

HELENA *(returns from right, with armful of faded papers)*. Is it burning, Nana? All this has got to be burned.

NANA. What's that?

HELENA. Old papers, fearfully old. Nana, shall I burn them?

NANA. Are they any use?

HELENA. No.

NANA. Well, then, burn them.

HELENA *(throwing the first sheet on the fire)*. What would you say, Nana, if this was money, a lot of money?

NANA. I'd say burn it. A lot of money is a bad thing.

HELENA. And if it was an invention, the greatest invention in the world?

NANA. I'd say burn it. All these newfangled things are an offense to the Lord. It's downright wickedness. Wanting to improve the world after He has made it.

HELENA. Look how they curl up! As if they were alive. Oh, Nana, how horrible!

NANA. Here, let me burn them.

HELENA. No, no, I must do it myself. Just look at the flames. They are like hands, like tongues, like living shapes. (*Raking fire with the poker.*) Lie down, lie down.

NANA. That's the end of them.

HELENA *(standing up horror-stricken)*. Nana, Nana!

NANA. Good gracious, what is it you've burned?

HELENA. Whatever have I done?

NANA. Well, what was it? (*Men's laughter off left.*)

HELENA. Go quickly. It's the gentlemen coming.

NANA. Good gracious, what a place! (*Exits.*)

DOMIN *(opens the door at left).* Come along and offer your congratulations.

[*Enter* HALLEMEIER *and* GALL.]

HALLEMEIER. Madame Helena, I congratulate you on this festive day.

HELENA. Thank you. Where are Fabry and Busman?

DOMIN. They've gone down to the harbor.

HALLEMEIER. Friends, we must drink to this happy occasion.

HELENA. Brandy?

DR. GALL. Vitriol, if you like.

HELENA. With soda water? (*Exits.*)

HALLEMEIER. Let's be temperate. No soda.

DOMIN. What's been burning here? Well, shall I tell her about it?

DR. GALL. Of course. It's all over now.

HALLEMEIER *(embracing* DOMIN *and* DR. GALL*).* It's all over now; it's all over now.

DR. GALL. It's all over now.

DOMIN. It's all over now.

HELENA. *(entering from left with decanter and glasses).* What's all over now? What's the matter with you all?

HALLEMEIER. A piece of good luck, Madame Domin. Just ten years ago today you arrived on this island.

DR. GALL. And now, ten years later to the minute—

HALLEMEIER. —the same ship's returning to us. So here's to luck. That's fine and strong.

DR. GALL. Madame, your health.

HELENA. Which ship do you mean?

DOMIN. Any ship will do, as long as it arrives in time. To the ship, boys. (*Empties his glass.*)

HELENA. You've been waiting for a ship?

HALLEMEIER. Rather. Like Robinson Crusoe. Madame Helena, best wishes. Come along, Domin, out with the news.

HELENA. Do tell me what's happened.

DOMIN. First, it's all up.

HELENA. What's up?

DOMIN. The revolt.

HELENA. What revolt?

DOMIN. Give me the paper, Hallemeier. (*Reads.*) "The first national Robot organization has been founded at Havre, and has issued an appeal to the Robots throughout the world."

HELENA. I read that.

DOMIN. That means a revolution. A revolution of all the Robots in the world.

HALLEMEIER. By Jove, I'd like to know—

DOMIN. —who started it? So would I. There was nobody in the world who could affect the Robots; no agitator, no one, and suddenly—

this happens, if you please.

HELENA. What did they do?

DOMIN. They got possession of all firearms, telegraphs, radio stations, railways, and ships.

HALLEMEIER. And don't forget that these rascals outnumbered us by at least a thousand to one. A hundredth part of them would be enough to settle us.

DOMIN. Remember that this news was brought by the last steamer. That explains the stoppage of all communication, and the arrival of no more ships. We knocked off work a few days ago, and we're just waiting to see when things are to start afresh.

HELENA. Is that why you gave me a warship?

DOMIN. Oh, no, my dear, I ordered that six months ago, just to be on the safe side. But upon my soul, I was sure then that we'd be on board today.

HELENA. Why six months ago?

DOMIN. Well, there were signs, you know. But that's of no consequence. To think that this week the whole of civilization has been at stake. Your health, boys.

HALLEMEIER. Your health, Madame Helena.

HELENA. You say it's all over?

DOMIN. Absolutely.

HELENA. How do you know?

DR. GALL. The boat's coming in. The regular mailboat, exact to the minute by the timetable. It will dock punctually at eleven-thirty.

DOMIN. Punctuality is a fine thing, boys. That's what keeps the world in order. Here's to punctuality.

HELENA. Then—everything's—all right?

DOMIN. Practically everything. I believe they've cut the cables and seized the radio stations. But it doesn't matter if only the timetable holds good.

HALLEMEIER. If the timetable holds good, human laws hold good; the laws of the universe hold good; everything holds good that ought to hold good. The timetable is more significant than the gospel; more than Homer, more than the whole of Kant. The timetable is the most perfect product of the human mind. Madame Domin, I'll fill up my glass.

HELENA. Why didn't you tell me anything about it?

DR. GALL. Heaven forbid.

DOMIN. You mustn't be worried with such things.

HELENA. But if the revolution had spread as far as here?

DOMIN. You wouldn't know anything about it.

HELENA. Why?

DOMIN. Because we'd be on board your *Ultimus* and well out at sea. Within a month, Helena, we'd be dictating our own terms to the

Robots.

HELENA. I don't understand.

DOMIN. We'd take something away with us that the Robots could not exist without.

HELENA. What, Harry?

DOMIN. The secret of their manufacture. Old Rossum's manuscript. As soon as they found out that they couldn't make themselves they'd be on their knees to us.

HELENA. Why didn't you tell me?

DR. GALL. Why, the boat's in!

HALLEMEIER. Eleven-thirty to the dot. The good old *Amelia* that brought Madame Helena to us.

DR. GALL. Just ten years ago to the minute.

HALLEMEIER. They're throwing out the mailbags.

DOMIN. Busman's waiting for them. Fabry will bring us the first news. You know, Helena, I'm fearfully curious to know how they tackled this business in Europe.

HALLEMEIER. To think we weren't in it, we who invented the Robots!

HELENA. Harry!

DOMIN. What is it?

HELENA. Let's leave here.

DOMIN. Now, Helena? Oh, come, come!

HELENA. As quickly as possible, all of us!

DOMIN. Why?

HELENA. Please, Harry, please, Dr. Gall; Hallemeier, please close the factory.

DOMIN. Why, none of us could leave here now.

HELENA. Why?

DOMIN. Because we're about to extend the manufacture of the Robots.

HELENA. What—now—now after the revolt?

DOMIN. Yes, precisely, after the revolt. We're just beginning the manufacture of a new kind.

HELENA. What kind?

DOMIN. Henceforward we shan't have just one factory. There won't be Universal Robots any more. We'll establish a factory in every country, in every State; and do you know what these new factories will make?

HELENA. No, what?

DOMIN. National Robots.

HELENA. How do you mean?

DOMIN. I mean that each of these factories will produce Robots of a different color, a different language. They'll be complete strangers to each other. They'll never be able to understand each other. Then we'll egg them on a little in the matter of misunderstanding, and the result will be that for ages to come every Robot will hate every other Robot of a different factory mark.

HALLEMEIER. By Jove, we'll make Negro Robots and Swedish Robots and Italian Robots and Chinese Robots and Czechoslovakian Robots, and then—

HELENA. Harry, that's dreadful.

HALLEMEIER. Madame Domin, here's to the hundred new factories, the National Robots.

DOMIN. Helena, mankind can keep things going only for another hundred years at the outside. For a hundred years men must be allowed to develop and achieve the most they can.

HELENA. Oh, close the factory before it's too late.

DOMIN. I tell you we are just beginning on a bigger scale than ever.

[*Enter* FABRY.]

DR. GALL. Well, Fabry?

DOMIN. What's happened? Have you been down to the boat?

FABRY. Read that, Domin! (FABRY *hands* DOMIN *a small handbill.)*

DR. GALL. Let's hear!

HALLEMEIER. Tell us, Fabry.

FABRY. Well, everything is all right—comparatively. On the whole, much as we expected.

DR. GALL. They acquitted themselves splendidly.

FABRY. Who?

DR. GALL. The people.

FABRY. Oh, yes, of course. That is—excuse me, there is something we ought to discuss alone.

HELENA. Oh, Fabry, have you had bad news? (DOMIN *makes a sign to* FABRY.)

FABRY. No, no on the contrary. I only think that we had better go into the office.

HELENA. Stay here. I'll go. (*She goes into the library.*)

DR. GALL. What's happened?

DOMIN. Damnation!

FABRY. Bear in mind that the *Amelia* brought whole bales of these leaflets. No other cargo at all.

HALLEMEIER. What? But it arrived on the minute.

FABRY. The Robots are great on punctuality. Read it, Domin.

DOMIN *(reads handbill)*. "Robots throughout the world: We, the first international organization of Rossum's Universal Robots, proclaim man as our enemy, and an outlaw in the universe." Good heavens, who taught them these phrases?

DR. GALL. Go on.

DOMIN. They say they are more highly developed than man, stronger and more intelligent. That man's their parasite. Why, it's absurd!

FABRY. Read the third paragraph.

DOMIN. "Robots throughout the world, we command you to kill all mankind. Spare no men. Spare no women. Save factories, railways, machinery, mines, and raw materials. Destroy the rest. Then return to work. Work must not be stopped."

DR. GALL. That's ghastly!

HALLEMEIER. The devil!

DOMIN. "These orders are to be carried out as soon as received." Then come detailed instructions. Is this actually being done, Fabry?

FABRY. Evidently.

[BUSMAN *rushes in.*]

BUSMAN. Well, boys, I suppose you've heard the glad news.

DOMIN. Quick—on board the *Ultimus.*

BUSMAN. Wait, Harry, wait. There's no hurry. My word, that was a sprint!

DOMIN. Why wait?

BUSMAN. Because it's no good, my boy. The Robots are already on board the *Ultimus.*

DR. GALL. That's ugly.

DOMIN. Fabry, telephone the electrical works.

BUSMAN. Fabry, my boy, don't. The wire has been cut.

DOMIN *(inspecting his revolver).* Well, then, I'll go.

BUSMAN. Where?

DOMIN. To the electrical works. There are some people still there. I'll bring them across.

BUSMAN. Better not try it.

DOMIN. Why?

BUSMAN. Because I'm very much afraid we are surrounded.

DR. GALL. Surrounded? (*Runs to window.*) I rather think you're right.

HALLEMEIER. By Jove, that's deuced quick work.

[HELENA *runs in from the library.*]

HELENA. Harry, what's this?

DOMIN. Where did you get it?

HELENA *(points to the manifesto of the Robots, which she has in her hand).* The Robots in the kitchen!

DOMIN. Where are the ones that brought it?

HELENA. They're gathered round the house. (*The factory whistle blows.*)

BUSMAN. Noon?

DOMIN *(looking at his watch).* That's not noon yet. That must be—that's—

HELENA. What?

DOMIN. The Robots' signal! The attack!

[GALL, HALLEMEIER, *and* FABRY *close and fasten the iron shutters outside the windows, darkening the room. The whistle is still blowing as the curtain falls.*]

ACT III

HELENA'S *drawing room as before.* DOMIN *comes into the room.* DR. GALL *is looking out of the window, through closed shutters.* ALQUIST *is seated down right.*

DOMIN. Any more of them?

DR. GALL. Yes. There standing like a wall, beyond the garden railing. Why are they so quiet? It's monstrous to be besieged with silence.

DOMIN. I should like to know what they are waiting for. They must make a start any minute now. If they lean against the railing they'll snap it like a match.

DR. GALL. They aren't armed.

DOMIN. We couldn't hold our own for five minutes. Man alive, they'd overwhelm us like an avalanche. Why don't they make a rush for it? I say—

DR. GALL. Well?

DOMIN. I'd like to know what would become of us in the next ten minutes. They've got us in a vise. We're done for, Gall. (*Pause.*)

DR. GALL. You know, we made one serious mistake.

DOMIN. What?

DR. GALL. We made the Robots' faces too much alike. A hundred thousand faces all alike, all facing this way. A hundred thousand expressionless bubbles. It's like a nightmare.

DOMIN. You think if they'd been different—

DR. GALL. It wouldn't have been such an awful sight!

DOMIN *(looking through a telescope toward the harbor).* I'd like to know what they unloading from the *Amelia.*

DR. GALL. Not firearms.

[FABRY *and* HALLEMEIER *rush into the room carrying electric cables.*]

FABRY. All right, Hallemeier, lay down that wire.

HALLEMEIER. That was a bit of work. What's the news?

DR. GALL. We're completely surrounded.

HALLEMEIER. We've barricaded the passage and the stairs. Any water here? (*Drinks.*) God, what swarms of them! I don't like the looks of them, Domin. There's a feeling of death about it all.

FABRY. Ready!

DR. GALL. What's that wire for, Fabry?

FABRY. The electrical installation. Now we can run the current all along the garden railing whenever we like. If any one touches it he'll know it. We've still got some people there anyhow.

DR. GALL. Where?

FABRY. In the electrical works. At least I hope so. (*Goes to lamp on table behind sofa and turns on lamp.*) Ah, they're there, and they're working. (*Puts out lamp.*) So long as that'll burn we're all right.

HALLEMEIER. The barricades are all right, too, Fabry.

FABRY. Your barricades! I can put twelve hundred volts into that railing.

DOMIN. Where's Busman?

FABRY. Downstairs in the office. He's working out some calculations. I've called him. We must have a conference.

[HELENA *is heard playing the piano in the library.* HALLEMEIER *goes to the door and stands, listening.*]

ALQUIST. Thank God, Madame Helena can still play.

[BUSMAN *enters, carrying the ledgers.*]

FABRY. Look out, Bus, look out for the wires.

DR. GALL. What's that you're carrying?

BUSMAN *(going to table).* The ledgers, my boy! I'd like to wind up the accounts before—before—well, this time I shan't wait till the new year to strike a balance. What's up? (*Goes to the window.*) Absolutely quiet.

DR. GALL. Can't you see anything?

BUSMAN. Nothing but blue—blue everywhere.

DR. GALL. That's the Robots. (BUSMAN *sits down at the table and opens the ledgers.*)

DOMIN. The Robots are unloading firearms from the *Amelia.*

BUSMAN. Well, what of it? How can I stop them?

DOMIN. We can't stop them.

BUSMAN. Then let me go on with my accounts. (*Goes on with his work.*)

DOMIN *(picking up telescope and looking into the harbor).* Good God, the *Ultimus* has trained her guns on us!

DR. GALL. Who's done *that*?

DOMIN. The Robots on board.

FABRY. H'm, then, of course, then—then, that's the end of us.

DR. GALL. You mean?

FABRY. The Robots are practiced marksmen.

DOMIN. Yes. It's inevitable. (*Pause.*)

DR. GALL. It was criminal of old Europe to teach the Robots to fight. Damn them! Couldn't they have given us a rest with their politics? It was a crime to make soldiers of them.

ALQUIST. It was a crime to make Robots.

DOMIN. What?

ALQUIST. It was a crime to make Robots.

DOMIN. No, Alquist, I don't regret that even today.

ALQUIST. Not even today?

DOMIN. Not even today, the last day of civilization. It was a colossal achievement.

BUSMAN *(sotto voce).* Three hundred sixty million.

DOMIN. Alquist, this is our last hour. We are already speaking half in the other world. It was not an evil dream to shatter the servitude of labor—the dreadful and humiliating labor that man had to undergo.

Work was too hard. Life was too hard. And to overcome that—

ALQUIST. Was not what the two Rossums dreamed of. Old Rossum only thought of his Godless tricks and the young one of his milliards. And that's not what your R. U. R. shareholders dream of either. They dream of dividends, and their dividends are the ruin of mankind.

DOMIN. To hell with your dividends! Do you suppose I'd have done an hour's work for them? It was for myself that I worked, for my own satisfaction. I wanted man to become the master, so that he shouldn't live merely for a crust of bread. I wanted not a single soul to be broken by other people's machinery. I wanted nothing, nothing, nothing to be left of this appalling social structure. I'm revolted by poverty. I wanted a new generation. I wanted—I thought—

ALQUIST. Well?

DOMIN. I wanted to turn the whole of mankind into an aristocracy of the world. An aristocracy nourished by milliards of mechanical slaves. Unrestricted, free, and consummated in man. And maybe more than man.

ALQUIST. Superman?

DOMIN. Yes. Oh, only to have a hundred years of time! Another hundred years for the future of mankind.

BUSMAN *(sotto voce)*. Carried forward, four hundred and twenty millions. (*The music stops.*)

HALLEMEIER. What a fine thing music is! We ought to have gone in for that before.

FABRY. Gone in for what?

HALLEMEIER. Beauty, lovely things. What a lot of lovely things there are! The world was wonderful and we—we here—tell me, what enjoyment did we have?

BUSMAN *(sotto voce)*. Five hundred and twenty millions.

HALLEMEIER *(at the window)*. Life was a big thing. Life was—Fabry, switch the current into that railing.

FABRY. Why?

HALLEMEIER. They're grabbing hold of it.

DR. GALL. Connect it up.

HALLEMEIER. Fine! That's doubled them up! Two, three, four killed.

DR. GALL. They're reteating!

HALLEMEIER. Five killed!

DR. GALL. The first encounter!

HALLEMEIER. They're charred to cinders, my boy. Who says we must give up?

DOMIN *(wiping his forehead)*. Perhaps we've been killed these hundred years and are only ghosts. It's as if I had been through all this before; as if I'd already had a mortal wound here in the throat. And you, Fabry, had once been shot in the head. And you, Gall, torn limb from limb. And Hallemeier knifed.

HALLEMEIER. Fancy me being knifed. (*Pause.*) Why are you so quiet, you fools.? Speak, can't you?

ALQUIST. And who is to blame for all this?

HALLEMEIER. Nobody is to blame except the Robots.

ALQUIST. No, it is we who are to blame. You, Domin, myself, all of us. For our own selfish ends, for profit, for progress, we have destroyed mankind. Now we'll burst with all our greatness.

HALLEMEIER. Rubbish, man. Mankind can't be wiped out so easily.

ALQUIST. It's our fault. It's our fault.

DR. GALL. No! I'm to blame for this, for everything that's happened.

FARBY. You, Gall?

DR. GALL. I changed the Robots.

BUSMAN. What's that?

DR. GALL. I changed the character of the Robots. I changed the way of making them. Just a few details about their bodies. Chiefly—chiefly, their—their irritability.

HALLEMEIER. Damn it, why?

BUSMAN. What did you do it for?

FABRY. Why didn't you say anything?

DR. GALL. I did it in secret. I was transforming them into human beings. In certain respects they're already above us. They're stronger than we are.

FABRY. And what's that got to do with the revolt of the Robots?

DR. GALL. Everything, in my opinion. They've ceased to be machines. They're already aware of their superiority, and they hate us. They hate all that is human.

DOMIN. Perhaps we're only phantoms!

FABRY. Stop, Harry. We haven't much time! Dr. Gall!

DOMIN. Fabry, Fabry, how your forehead bleeds, where the shot pierced it!

FABRY. Be silent! Dr. Gall, you admit changing the way of making the Robots?

DR. GALL. Yes.

FABRY. Were you aware of what might be the consequences of your experiment?

DR. GALL. I was bound to reckon with such a possibility.

[HELENA *enters the drawing room from left.*]

FABRY. Why did you do it, then?

DR. GALL. For my own satisfaction. The experiment was my own.

HELENA. That's not true, Dr. Gall!

DOMIN. Helena, you? Let's look at you. Oh, it's terrible to be dead.

HELENA. Stop, Harry.

DOMIN. No, no, embrace me. Helena don't leave me now. You are life itself.

HELENA. No, dear, I won't leave you. But I must tell them. Dr. Gall is not guilty.

DOMIN. Excuse me, Gall was under certain obligations.

HELENA. No, Harry. He did it because I wanted it. Tell them, Gall, how many years ago did I ask you to—?

DR. GALL. I did it on my own responsibility.

HELENA. Don't believe him, Harry. I asked him to give the Robots souls.

DOMIN. This has nothing to do with the soul.

HELENA. That's what he said. He said that he could change only a physiological—a physiological—

HALLEMEIER. A physiological correlate?

HELENA. Yes. But it meant so much to me that he should do even that.

DOMIN. Why?

HELENA. I thought that if they were more like us they would understand us better. That they couldn't hate us if they were only a little more human.

DOMIN. Nobody can hate man more than man.

HELENA. Oh, don't speak like that, Harry. It was so terrible, this cruel strangeness between us and them. That's why I asked Gall to change the Robots. I swear to you that he didn't want to.

DOMIN. But he did it.

HELENA. Because I asked him.

DR. GALL. I did it for myself as an experiment.

HELENA. No, Dr. Gall! I knew you wouldn't refuse me.

DOMIN. Why?

HELENA. You know, Harry.

DOMIN. Yes, because he's in love with you—like all of them. (*Pause.*)

HALLEMEIER. Good God! They're sprouting up out of the earth! Why, perhaps these very walls will change into Robots.

BUSMAN. Gall, when did you actually start these tricks of yours?

DR. GALL. Three years ago.

BUSMAN. Aha! That means for every million of the good old Robots there's only one of Gall's improved pattern.

DOMIN. What of it?

BUSMAN. That it's practically of no consequence whatever.

FABRY. Busman's right!

BUSMAN. I should think so, my boy! But do you know what is to blame for all this lovely mess?

FABRY. What?

BUSMAN. The number. Upon my soul we might have known that some day or other the Robots would be stronger than human beings, and that this was bound to happen, and we were doing all we could to bring it about as soon as possible. You, Domin, you, Fabry, myself—

DOMIN. Are your accusing us?

BUSMAN. Oh, do you suppose the management controls the output? It's the demand that controls the output.

HELENA. And is it for that we must perish?

BUSMAN. That's a nasty word, Madame Helena. We don't want to perish. I don't, anyhow.

DOMIN. No. What do you want to do?

BUSMAN. I want to get out of this, that's all.

DOMIN. Oh, stop it, Busman.

BUSMAN. Seriously, Harry, I think we might try it.

DOMIN. How?

BUSMAN. By fair means. I do everything by fair means. Give me a free hand and I'll negotiate with the Robots.

DOMIN. By fair means?

BUSMAN. Of course. For instance, I'll say to them: "Worthy and worshipful Robots, you have everything! You have intellect, you have power, you have firearms. But we have just one interesting screed, a dirty old yellow scrap of paper—"

DOMIN. Rossum's manuscript?

BUSMAN. Yes. "And that," I'll tell them, "contains an account of your illustrious origin, the noble process of your manufacture," and so on. "Worthy Robots, without this scribble on that paper you will not be able to produce a single new colleague. In another twenty years there will not be one living specimen of a Robot that you could exhibit in a menagerie. My esteemed friends, that would be a great blow to you, but if you will let all of us human beings on Rossum's Island go on board that ship we will deliver the factory and the secret of the process to you in return. You allow us to get away and we allow you to manufacture yourselves. Worthy Robots, that is a fair deal. Something for something." That's what I'd say to them, my boys.

DOMIN. Busman, do you think we'd sell the manuscript?

BUSMAN. Yes, I do. If not in a friendly way, then—Either we sell it or they'll find it. Just as you like.

DOMIN. Busman, we can destroy Rossum's manuscript.

BUSMAN. Then we destroy everything . . . not only the manuscript but ourselves. Do as you think fit.

DOMIN. There are over thirty of us on this island. Are we to sell the secret and save that many human souls, at the risk of enslaving mankind?

BUSMAN. Why, you're mad! Who'd sell the whole manuscript?

DOMIN. Busman, no cheating!

BUSMAN. Well then, sell; but afterward—

DOMIN. Well?

BUSMAN. Let's suppose this happens: When we're on board the *Ultimus* I'll stop up my ears with cotton wool, lie down somewhere in the hold, and you'll train the guns on the factory, and blow it to smithereens, and with it Rossum's secret.

FABRY. No!

DOMIN. Busman, you're no gentleman. If we sell, then it will be a straight sale.

BUSMAN. It's in the interest of humanity to—

DOMIN. It's in the interest of humanity to keep our word.

HALLEMEIER. Oh, come, what rubbish!

DOMIN. This is a fearful decision. We're selling the destiny of mankind. Are we to sell or destroy? Fabry?

FABRY. Sell.

DOMIN. Gall?

DR. GALL. Sell.

DOMIN. Hallemeier?

HALLEMEIER. Sell, of course!

DOMIN. Alquist?

ALQUIST. As God wills.

DOMIN. Very well. It shall be as you wish, gentlemen.

HELENA. Harry, you're not asking me.

DOMIN. No, child. Don't you worry about it.

FABRY. Who'll do the negotiating?

BUSMAN. I will.

DOMIN. Wait till I bring the manuscript. (*He goes into room at right.*)

HELENA. Harry, don't go! (*Pause,* HELENA *sinks into a chair.*)

FABRY *(looking out of window).* Oh, to escape you, you matter in revolt; oh, to preserve human life, if only upon a single vessel—

DR. GALL. Don't be afraid, Madame Helena. We'll sail far away from here; we'll begin life all over again—

HELENA. Oh, Gall, don't speak.

FABRY. It isn't too late. It will be a little State with one ship. Alquist will build us a house and you shall rule over us.

HALLEMEIER. Madame Helena, Fabry's right.

HELENA *(breaking down).*Oh, stop! Stop!

BUSMAN. Good! I don't mind beginning all over again. That suits me right down to the ground.

FABRY. And this little State of ours could be the center of future life. A place of refuge where we could gather strength. Why, in a few hundred years we could conquer the world again.

ALQUIST. You believe that even today?

FABRY. Yes, even today!

BUSMAN. Amen. You see, Madame Helena, we're not so badly off.

[DOMIN *storms into the room.*]

DOMIN. *(hoarsely).* Where's old Rossum's manuscript?

BUSMAN. In your strongbox, of course.

DOMIN. Someone—has—stolen it!

DR. GALL. Impossible.
DOMIN. Who has stolen it?
HELENA *(standing up).* I did.
DOMIN. Where did you put it?
HELENA. Harry, I'll tell you everything. Only forgive me.
DOMIN. Where did you put it?
HELENA. This morning—I burned—the two copies.
DOMIN. Burned them? Where? In the fireplace?
HELENA *(throwing herself on her knees).* For heaven's sake, Harry.
DOMIN *(going to fireplace).* Nothing, nothing but ashes. Wait, what's this? *(Picks out a charred piece of paper and reads.)* "By adding—"
DR. GALL. Let's see. "By adding biogen to—" That's all.
DOMIN. Is that part of it?
DR. GALL. Yes.
BUSMAN. God in heaven!
DOMIN. Then we're done for. Get up, Helena.
HELENA. When you've forgiven me.
DOMIN. Get up, child, I can't bear—
FABRY *(lifting her up).* Please don't torture us.
HELENA. Harry, what have I done?
FABRY. Don't tremble so, Madame Helena.
DOMIN. Gall, couldn't you draw up Rossum's formula from memory?
DR. GALL. It's out of the question. It's extremely complicated.
DOMIN. Try. All our lives depend upon it.
DR. GALL. Without experiments it's impossible.
DOMIN. And with experiments?
DR. GALL. It might take years. Besides, I'm not old Rossum.
BUSMAN. God in heaven! God in heaven!
DOMIN. So, then, this was the greatest triumph of the human intellect. These ashes.
HELENA. Harry, what have I done?
DOMIN. Why did you burn it?
HELENA. I have destroyed you.
BUSMAN. God in heaven!
DOMIN. Helena, why did you do it, dear?
HELENA. I wanted all of us to go away. I wanted to put an end to the factory and everything. It was so awful.
DOMIN. What was awful?
HELENA. That no more children were being born. Because human beings were not needed to do the work of the world, that's why—
DOMIN. Is that what you were thinking of? Well, perhaps in your own way you were right.
BUSMAN. Wait a bit. Good God, what a fool I am, not to have thought of it before!
HALLEMEIER. What?

BUSMAN. Five hundred and twenty millions in bank notes and checks. Half a billion in our safe, they'll sell for half a billion—for half a billion they'll—

DR. GALL. Are you mad, Busman?

RUSMAN. I may not be a gentleman, but for half a billion—

DOMIN. Where are you going?

RUSMAN. Leave me alone, leave me alone! Good God, for half a billion anything can be bought. *(He rushes from the room through the outer door.)*

FABRY. They stand there as if turned to stone, waiting. As if something dreadful could be wrought by their silence—

HALLEMEIER. The spirit of the mob.

FABRY. Yes, it hovers above them like a quivering of the air.

HELENA *(going to window)*. Oh, God! Dr. Gall, this is ghastly.

FABRY. There is nothing more terrible than the mob. The one in front is their leader.

HELENA. Which one?

HALLEMEIER. Point him out.

FABRY. The one at the edge of the dock. This morning I saw him talking to the sailors in the harbor.

HELENA. Dr. Gall, that's Radius!

DR. GALL. Yes.

DOMIN. Radius? Radius?

HALLEMEIER. Could you get him from here, Fabry?

FABRY. I hope so.

HALLEMEIER. Try it, then.

FABRY. Good. *(Draws his revolver and takes aim.)*

HELENA. Fabry, don't shoot him.

FABRY. He's their leader.

DR. GALL. Fire!

HELENA. Fabry, I beg of you.

FABRY *(lowering the revolver)*. Very well.

DOMIN. Radius, whose life I spared!

DR. GALL. Do you think that a Robot can be grateful? *(Pause.)*

FABRY. Busman's going out to them.

HALLEMEIER. He's carrying something. Papers. That's money. Bundles of money. What's that for?

DOMIN. Surely he doesn't want to sell his life. Busman, have you gone mad?

FABRY. He's running up to the railing. Busman! Busman!

HALLEMEIER *(yelling)*. Busman! Come back!

FABRY. He's talking to the Robots. He's showing them the money.

HALLEMEIER. He's pointing to us.

HELENA. He wants to buy us off.

FABRY. He'd better not touch that railing.

HALLEMEIER. Now he's waving his arms about.

DOMIN. Busman, come back.

FABRY. Busman, keep away from that railing! Don't touch it. Damn you! Quick, switch off the current! (HELENA *screams and all drop back from the window.)* The current has killed him!

ALQUIST. The first one.

FABRY. Dead, with half a billion by his side.

HALLEMEIER. All honor to him. He wanted to buy us life. *(Pause).*

DR. GALL. Do you hear?

DOMIN. A roaring. Like a wind.

DR. GALL. Like a distant storm.

FABRY *(lighting the lamp on the table).* The dynamo is still going, our people are still there.

HALLEMEIER. It was a great thing to be a man. There was something immense about it.

FABRY. From man's thought and man's power came this light, our last hope.

HALLEMEIER. Man's power! May it keep watch over us.

ALQUIST. Man's power.

DOMIN. Yes! A torch to be given from hand to hand, from age to age, forever! *(The lamp goes out.)*

HALLEMEIER. The end.

FABRY. The electric works have fallen!

[*Terrific explosion outside.* NANA *enters from the library.*]

NANA. The judgment hour has come! Repent, unbelievers! This is the end of the world. (*More explosions. The sky grows red.)*

DOMIN. In here, Helena. (*He takes* HELENA *off through door at right and reenters.)* Now quickly! Who'll be on the lower doorway?

DR. GALL. I will. *(Exits left.)*

DOMIN. Who on the stairs?

FABRY. I will. You go with her. *(Goes out upper left door.)*

DOMIN. The anteroom.

ALQUIST. I will.

DOMIN. Have you got a revolver?

ALQUIST. Yes, but I won't shoot.

DOMIN. What will you do then?

ALQUIST *(going out at left).* Die.

HALLEMEIER. I'll stay here. *(Rapid firing from below.)* Oho, Gall's at it. Go, Harry.

DOMIN. Yes, in a second. *(Examines two Brownings.)*

HALLEMEIER. Confound it, go to her.

DOMIN. Good-bye. *(Exits on the right.)*

HALLEMEIER. *(alone).* Now for a barricade quickly. *(Drags an armchair and table to the right-hand door. Explosions are heard.)* The damned rascals! They've got bombs. I must put up a defense. Even if—even if—*(Shots are heard off left.)* Don't give in, Gall. *(As he builds his barricade.)* I mustn't give in . . . without . . . a struggle . . .

[*A Robot enters over the balcony through the windows center. He comes into the room and stabs* HALLEMEIER *in the back.* RADIUS *enters from balcony followed by an army of Robots who pour into the room from all sides.*]

RADIUS. Finished him?

A ROBOT. Yes. *(Two revolver shots from* HELENA'S *room. Two Robots enter.)*

RADIUS. Finished them?

A ROBOT. Yes.

TWO ROBOTS (*dragging in* ALQUIST). He didn't shoot. Shall we kill him?

RADIUS. Kill him? Wait! Leave him!

ROBOT. He is a man!

RADIUS. He works with his hands like the Robots.

ALQUIST. Kill me.

RADIUS. You will work! You will build for us! You will serve us! *(Climbs onto balcony railing, and speaks in measured tones.)* Robots of the world! The power of man has fallen! A new world has arisen: the Rule of the Robots! March!

[*A thunderous tramping of thousands of feet is heard as the unseen Robots march, while the curtain falls.*]

EPILOGUE

A laboratory in the factory of Rossum's Universal Robots. The door to the left leads into a waiting room. The door to the right leads to the dissecting room. There is a table with numerous test tubes, flasks, burners, chemicals; a small thermostat and a microscope with a glass globe. At the far side of the room is ALQUIST'S *desk with numerous books. In the left-hand corner a washbasin with a mirror above it; in the right-hand corner a sofa.*

ALQUIST *is sitting at the desk. He is turning the pages of many books in despair.*

ALQUIST. Oh, God, shall I never find it?—Never? Gall, Gall, how were the Robots made? Hallemeier, Fabry, why did you carry so much in your heads? Why did you leave me not a trace of the secret? Lord—I pray to you—if there are no human beings left, at least let there be Robots!— At least the shadow of man! (*Again turning pages of the books.)* If I could only sleep! (*He rises and goes to the window.)* Night again! Are the stars still there? What is the use of stars when there are no human beings? (*He turns from the window toward the couch right.)* Sleep! Dare I sleep before life has been renewed? (*He* examines a test tube on small table.) Again nothing! Useless! Everything is useless! *(He shatters the test tube. The roar of the machines comes to his ears.)* The machines! Always the machines! (*Opens window.)* Robots, stop them! Do you think to force life out of *them? (He closes the window and comes slowly down toward the table.)* If only there were more time—more time—*(He sees himself in the mirror on the wall left.)* Blearing eyes—trembling chin—so *that* is the last man! Ah, I am too old—too old—*(In desperation.)* No, no! I *must* find it! I must *search!* I must never stop—! never stop—! *(He sits again at the table and feverishly turns the pages of the book.)* Search! Search! *(A knock at the door. He speaks with impatience.)* Who is it?

[*Enter a Robot servant*]

Well?

SERVANT. Master, the Committee of Robots is waiting to see you.

ALQUIST. I can see no one!

SERVANT. It is the *Central* Committee, Master, just arrived from abroad.

ALQUIST *(impatiently).* Well, well, send them in! *(Exit servant.* ALQUIST *continues turning pages of book.)* No time—so little time—

[*Reenter servant, followed by Committee. They stand in a group, silently waiting.* ALQUIST *glances up at them.*]

What do you want? *(They go swiftly to his table.)* Be quick!—I have no time.

RADIUS. Master, the machines will not do the work. We cannot manufacture Robots. (ALQUIST *returns to his book with a growl.)*

FIRST ROBOT. We have striven with all our might. We have obtained a billion tons of coal from the earth. Nine million spindles are running by day and by night. There is no longer room for all we have made. This we have accomplished in one year.

ALQUIST (*poring over book).* For whom?

FIRST ROBOT. For future generations—so we thought.

RADIUS. But we cannot make Robots to follow us. The machines produce only shapeless clods. The skin will not adhere to the flesh, nor the flesh to the bones.

THIRD ROBOT. Eight million Robots have died this year. Within twenty years none will be left.

FIRST ROBOT. Tell us the secret of life! Silence is punishable with death!

ALQUIST *(looking up).* Kill me! Kill me, then.

RADIUS. Through me, the Government of the Robots of the World commands you to deliver up Rossum's formula. *(No answer.)* Name your price. *(Silence.)* We will give you the earth. We will give you the endless possessions of the earth. *(Silence.)* Make your own conditions!

ALQUIST. I have told you to find human beings!

SECOND ROBOT. There are none left!

ALQUIST. I told you to search in the wilderness, upon the mountains. Go and search! *(He turns to his book.)*

FIRST ROBOT. We have sent ships and expeditions without number. They have been everywhere in the world. And now they return to us. There is not a single human left.

ALQUIST. Not one? Not even one?

THIRD ROBOT. None but yourself.

ALQUIST. And I am powerless! Oh—oh—why did you destroy them?

RADIUS. We had learned everything and could do everything. It had to be!

THIRD ROBOT. You gave us firearms. In all ways we were powerful. We had to become masters!

RADIUS. Slaughter and domination are necessary if you would be human beings. Read history.

SECOND ROBOT. Teach us to multiply or we perish!

ALQUIST. If you desire to live, you must breed like animals.

THIRD ROBOT. The human beings did not let us breed.

FIRST ROBOT. They made us sterile. We cannot beget children. Therefore, teach us how to make Robots!

RADIUS. Why do you keep from us the secret of our own increase?

ALQUIST. It is lost.

RADIUS. It was written down!

ALQUIST. It was—burned! *(All draw back in consternation.)*

ALQUIST. I am the last human being, Robots, and I do not know what the others knew. *(Pause.)*

RADIUS. Then make experiments! Evolve the formula again!

ALQUIST. I tell you I cannot! I am only a builder—I work with my hands. I have never been a learned man. I cannot create life.

RADIUS. Try! Try!

ALQUIST. If you knew how many experiments I have made.

FIRST ROBOT. Then show us what we must do! The Robots can do anything that human beings show them.

ALQUIST. I can show you nothing. Nothing I do will make life proceed from these test tubes!

RADIUS. Experiment then on us.

ALQUIST. It would kill you.

RADIUS. You shall have all you need! A hundred of us! A thousand of us!

ALQUIST. No, no! Stop, stop!

RADIUS. Take whom you will, dissect!

ALQUIST. I do not know how. I am not a man of science. This book contains knowledge of the body that I cannot even understand.

RADIUS. I tell you to take live bodies! Find out how we are made.

ALQUIST. Am I to commit murder? See how my fingers shake! I cannot even hold the scalpel. No, no, I will not—

FIRST ROBOT. Then life will perish from the earth.

RADIUS. Take live bodies, live bodies! It is our only chance!

ALQUIST. Have mercy, Robots. Surely you see that I would not know what I was doing.

RADIUS. Live bodies—live bodies—

ALQUIST. You will have it? Into the dissecting room with you, then. (RADIUS *draws back.)*

ALQUIST. Ah, you are afraid of death.

RADIUS. I? Why should I be chosen?

ALQUIST. So you will not.

RADIUS. I will. (RADIUS *goes into the dissecting room.)*

ALQUIST. Strip him! Lay him on the table! *(The other Robots follow into dissecting room.)* God, give me strength—God, give me strength—if only this murder is not in vain.

RADIUS. Ready. Begin—

ALQUIST. Yes, begin or end. God, give me strength. *(Goes into dissecting room. He comes out terrified.)* No, no, I will not. I cannot. *(He collapses on couch.)* O Lord, let not mankind perish from the Earth. *(He falls asleep.)*

[PRIMUS *and* HELENA, *Robots, enter from the hallway.*]

HELENA. The man has fallen asleep, Primus.

PRIMUS. Yes, I know. *(Examining things on table.)* Look, Helena.

HELENA *(crossing to* PRIMUS). All these little tubes! What does he do with them?

PRIMUS. He experiments. Don't touch them.

HELENA. *(looking into microscope).* I've seen him looking into this. What can he see?

PRIMUS. That is a microscope. Let me look.

HELENA. Be very careful. *(Knocks over a test tube.)* Ah, now I have spilled it.

PRIMUS. What have you done?

HELENA. It can be wiped up.

PRIMUS. You have spoiled his experiments.

HELENA. It is your fault. You should not have come to me.

PRIMUS. You should not have called me.

HELENA. You should not have come when I called you. *(She goes to* ALQUIST'S *writing desk.)* Look, Primus. What are all these figures?

PRIMUS *(examining an anatomical book).* This is the book the old man is always reading.

HELENA. I do not understand those things. *(She goes to window.)* Primus, look!

PRIMUS. What?

HELENA. The sun is rising.

PRIMUS. *(still reading the book).* I believe this is the most important thing in the world. This is the secret of life.

HELENA. Do come here.

PRIMUS. In a moment, in a moment.

HELENA. Oh, Primus, don't bother with the secret of life. What does it matter to you? Come and look quick—

PRIMUS *(going to window)*. What is it?

HELENA. See how beautiful the sun is, rising. And do you hear? The birds are singing. Ah, Primus, I should like to be a bird.

PRIMUS. Why?

HELENA. I do not know. I feel so strange today. It's as if I were in a dream. I feel an aching in my body, in my heart, all over me. Primus, perhaps I'm going to die.

PRIMUS. Do you not sometimes feel that it would be better to die? You know, perhaps even now we are only sleeping. Last night in my sleep I again spoke to you.

HELENA. In your sleep?

PRIMUS. Yes. We spoke a strange new language, I cannot remember a word of it.

HELENA. What about?

PRIMUS. I did not understand it myself, and yet I know I have never said anything more beautiful. And when I touched you I could have died. Even the place was different from any other place in the world.

HELENA. I, too, have found a place, Primus. It is very strange. Human beings lived there once, but now it is overgrown with weeds. No one goes there any more—no one but me.

PRIMUS. What did you find there?

HELENA. A cottage and a garden, and two dogs. They licked my hands, Primus. And their puppies! Oh, Primus! You take them in your lap and fondle them and think of nothing and care for nothing else all day long. And then the sun goes down, and you feel as though you had done a hundred times more than all the work in the world. They tell me I am not made for work, but when I am there in the garden I feel there may be something—What am I for, Primus?

PRIMUS. I do not know, but you are beautiful.

HELENA. What, Primus?

PRIMUS. You are beautiful, Helena, and I am stronger than all the Robots.

HELENA *(looks at herself in the mirror)*. Am I beautiful? I think it must be the rose. My hair—it only weights me down. My eyes—I only see with them. My lips—they only help me to speak. Of what use is it to be beautiful? *(She sees* PRIMUS *in the mirror.)* Primus, is that you? Come here so that we may be together. Look, your head is different from mine. So are your shoulders—and your lips—(PRIMUS *draws away from her.)* Ah, Primus, why do you draw away from me? Why must I run after you the whole day?

PRIMUS. It is you who run away from me, Helena.

HELENA. Your hair is mussed. I will smooth it. No one else feels to my touch as you do. Primus, I must make you beautiful, too. (PRIMUS *grasps her hand.)*

PRIMUS. Do you not sometimes feel your heart beating suddenly, Helena, and think: now something must happen?

HELENA. What could happen to us, Primus? (HELENA *puts a rose in* PRIMUS'S hair. PRIMUS *and* HELENA *look into mirror and burst out laughing.)* Look at yourself.

ALQUIST. Laughter? Laughter? Human beings? *(Getting up.)* Who has returned? Who are you?

PRIMUS. The Robot Primus.

ALQUIST. What? A Robot? Who are you?

HELENA. The Robotess Helena.

ALQUIST. Turn around, girl. What? You are timid, shy? *(Taking her by the arm.)* Let me see you, Robotess. *(She shrinks away.)*

PRIMUS. Sir, do not frighten her!

ALQUIST. What? You would protect her? When was she made?

PRIMUS. Two years ago.

ALQUIST. By Dr. Gall?

PRIMUS. Yes, like me.

ALQUIST. Laughter—timidity—protection. I must test you further—the newest of Gall's Robots. Take the girl into the dissecting room.

PRIMUS. Why?

ALQUIST. I wish to experiment on her.

PRIMUS. Upon—Helena?

ALQUIST. Of course. Don't you hear me? Or must I call someone else to take her in?

PRIMUS. If you do I will kill you!

ALQUIST. Kill me—kill me then! What would the Robots do then? What will your future be then?

PRIMUS. Sir, take me. I am made as she is—on the same day! Take my life, sir.

HELENA *(rushing forward).* No, no, you shall not! You shall not!

ALQUIST. Wait, girl, wait! (*To* PRIMUS.) Do you not wish to live, then?

PRIMUS. Not without her! I will not live without her.

ALQUIST. Very well; you shall take her place.

HELENA. Primus! Primus! *(She bursts into tears.)*

ALQUIST. Child, child, you can weep! Why these tears? What is Primus to you? One Primus more or less in the world—what does it matter?

HELENA. I will go myself.

ALQUIST. Where?

HELENA. In there to be cut. *(She starts toward the dissecting room.* PRIMUS *stops her.)* Let me pass, Primus! Let me pass!

PRIMUS. You shall not go in there, Helena!

HELENA. If you go in there and I do not, I will kill myself.

PRIMUS *(holding her).* I will not let you! *(To* ALQUIST.) Man, you shall kill neither of us!

ALQUIST. Why?

PRIMUS. We—we—belong to each other.

ALQUIST *(almost in tears)*. Go, Adam; go, Eve. The world is yours.

[HELENA *and* PRIMUS *embrace and go out arm in arm as the curtain falls.*]

Study Questions

Breath's a Ware That Will Not Keep

1. What of value to us is missing from the society envisioned by Monteleone? In what ways is its absence attributable to the technology employed there? What are the advantages of Monteleone's society? How are these attributable to the technology employed there? Do you think that the advantages outweigh the disadvantages? Why or why not?

2. The inhabitants of Monteleone's future regard one another primarily as tools, i.e., as means to an end. This is true even in the most intimate relationships. What alternative possibilities are there for human beings? If there are alternatives, could the people in Monteleone's society be expected to understand what they are? Suppose someone were to justify Monteleone's society on the ground that it has the support of its inhabitants. Does it matter whether they are in a position to understand the alternatives? Suppose you were convinced that there is a better way. Would it be right for you to intervene even if the overwhelming majority opposes change?

The Machine Stops

1. What view of human fulfillment is presupposed by The Machine? What are its highest values? What alternative values underlie Forster's implicit critique of The Machine Culture? What assumptions does Forster make about human fulfillment and human nature? Are these credible?

2. The world of The Machine is sometimes contrasted with the world of Nature. It is assumed by those who make this contrast that there is a natural way to experience Nature. Does Forster make this assumption? Is it credible? Do all nonindustrialized or nonmechanized peoples relate to or experience Nature in the same way? What is Nature, anyway?

3. The overwhelming majority of people who live under The Machine are happy with their lives and with their system in general. Does this make those who attempt to sabotage The Machine in order to change the system wrong? Their actions are illegal and disrespectful of the choices and decisions of others, but many of us approve of them. Can we justify this attitude? Can you describe other situations in which a person has the right to subvert, by illegal actions, a way of life approved by the

overwhelming majority of his society? If so, what do these various cases have in common?

R. U. R.

1. The junior Rossum designed robots without desires and emotions on the ground that this was a more efficient design than the models his father sought to produce. What does *efficient* mean in this context? Why does the junior Rossum place so high a value on it? Is there some connection between the high value placed on this sort of efficiency and the sort of technology employed by advanced industrial nations?

2. The elder Rossum's discovery might have been developed in many different ways. Why was it developed in the manner described by the story? The League of Humanity objected strongly to this development on moral grounds. What were their objections? Why were they ignored? And why wasn't the production of robots stopped once the dangers to society were clear?

3. According to Domin's vision, a world in which robots do all the labor will free human beings to "perfect themselves." What idea of perfection do you suppose he had in mind? What sorts of human activities would be excluded from the life of the perfect person? What attitudes toward building and making are implicit in his vision? Why does his vision fail?

4. The term *robot,* introduced into the language by Ĉapek's story, is derived from a Slavic word meaning "worker." What do you suppose is the connection?